"What is it about you?"
Marcus asked softly.

He'd barely taken his eyes off her all evening. He knew he was drawn to her. He admired her, respected her. She appealed to the chivalrous side of his nature. But here, in the intimacy of the closed carriage, with her flowery perfume filling his nostrils, something moved in him, something dark and primitive that made him want to reach out and take. Only one woman had ever held him enthralled like this. Catalina.

"I must be going out of my mind," he muttered, and reached for her. "No, don't fight me, Catherine. I'm not going to hurt you. Just be still and let me . . . let me . . ." He drew her to his side of the banquette and lowered his mouth to hers.

Her eyes had been drawn to him all evening, and she'd tried not to be taken in by his careless charm. She'd tried to remain immune, really tried, but now, in the warm cocoon of the darkened coach, she found herself softening. Her lips yielded beneath the pressure of his, then parted to the gentle persuasion of his tongue. His fingers brushed through her hair, dislodging pins and flowers, and he wrapped thick strands of silk around his hands, binding her to him.

She couldn't think, couldn't breathe. Nothing in her experience had prepared her for this quickening of the senses. There was a roaring in her ears, her heart was thundering against her ribs. With a helpless moan, she wound her arms around his neck and clung to him. . . .

DANGEROUS TO HOLD

Also by Elizabeth Thornton

Dangerous to Kiss
Dangerous to Love

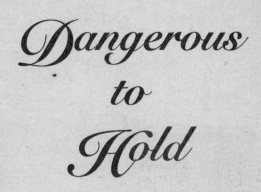

Dangerous
to
Hold

Elizabeth Thornton

BANTAM BOOKS
New York Toronto London
Sdyney Auckland

DANGEROUS TO HOLD
A Bantam Book / May 1996

ISBN 0-553-57479-5

Published simultaneously in the United States and Canada

Bantam Books are published by Bantam Books, a division of Bantam
Doubleday Dell Publishing Group, Inc. Its trademark, consisting of the
words "Bantam Books" and the portrayal of a rooster, is Registered in
U.S. Patent and Trademark Office and in other countries. Marca Reg-
istrada. Bantam Books, 1540 Broadway, New York, New York 10036.

PRINTED IN THE UNITED STATES OF AMERICA
RAD   0 9 8 7 6 5 4 3 2 1

*This one is for my daughter-in-law
Anita George—
my tireless ex-officio promoter, researcher,
and market analyst.
With love and gratitude.*

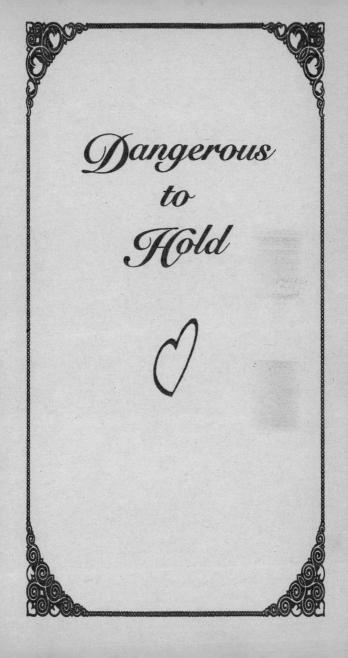

Dangerous
to
Hold

Prologue

She made an arresting picture, seated at the small table in front of the fire, completely absorbed in her
task. Marcus lay unmoving on his pallet and feigned
sleep while he watched her dip pen into ink and begin to
write. If he blocked out the drip of rainwater that fell
through gaps in the roof and ignored the scorched walls,
he could almost imagine that he was in England. It was a
reverie Marcus had evoked many times when the pain
from his wounds had made sleep impossible.

The small priest's cell would be a lady's parlor, and
the woman at the table would be at her escritoire, catching up on her correspondence, or answering invitations to
various functions. They would be at Wrotham at this time
of year, to celebrate Christmas. There would be dinner
parties and balls and beautiful women in pale, transparent gauzes, with fragrant hair and soft skin. But as lovely
as these fair English girls undoubtedly were, none could
compare to the woman at her escritoire.

The steady stream of rain on the tiled roof became a
torrent, and the pleasant reverie faded. This was not
home. This was not England. This was a burned-out,
godforsaken monastery in the hills overlooking the border
between Portugal and Spain. He was behind enemy lines,
and fortunate to be alive, rescued from a French patrol by
El Grande and his band of guerrillas. And the lady who
was so intently writing at the table was, in all probability,
keeping a tally of the ammunition her group of partisans
had expended in their pitiless war against the French.

She was a guerrilla, and was as dangerous as she was

beautiful. The pistol lying on the table by her right hand was no empty threat, nor was the sharp dagger that was thrust into the leather belt at her waist. These women fought side by side with their men, and their savagery to their enemies knew no equal. Fortunately for him, the British were her allies.

Catalina. He liked the sound of her name. He liked the sound of her voice. He didn't know how long he had been cooped up in this place, slipping in and out of consciousness, but he knew that he had her to thank for nursing him back to health. *Catalina.* When her hands touched his body, he couldn't think of her as a soldier. She was soft and womanly, and he wanted to get closer to her warmth.

Still feigning sleep, he moaned, not because the wounds in his shoulder and thigh were giving him more pain than usual, but because he wanted her to come to him. She wouldn't approach him when he was fully awake. If he called for her by name, she would leave the room, and a few moments later, her place would be taken by Juan.

He felt her cool hand on his brow and he allowed his lashes to lift a little so that he could get a better look at her. This woman was worth looking at. She had long dark hair and strong, regular features in an oval face. Her eyes were deep-set and shadowed by long black lashes. She wore a man's shirt and divided skirts, something Marcus had seen only on partisan women. Her masculine attire did not detract from her femininity, but only emphasized it. He had known many beautiful women in his time, but none with this woman's allure. When he looked at her, something moved in him, something entirely masculine and primitive that made him want to reach out and take.

The thought amused him. If he as much as laid a finger on her, she would make short shrift of him in his present weakened condition. She would think nothing of slipping that sharp dagger between his ribs. And even if he could prevent it, one cry from her would bring Juan storming through the door, and he would finish the job for her. In Spain, a man risked life and limb if he dared take liberties with a virtuous girl.

Hell! When had that ever stopped him?

She was examining the wound on his shoulder, checking the bandages for blood and pus. He groaned softly. "Isabella?" He knew perfectly well that the woman's name was Catalina.

She stilled for a moment, then sensing he posed no threat to her, she made soothing sounds and drew back the sheet, draping it to preserve her modesty before she checked the dressing on his thigh. Marcus almost smiled.

He moved his hands as casually as he could manage and rested them on her waist. His eyes remained closed. "Isabella, *querida*. Kiss me."

Evidently assuming that he was half delirious, she reached for the tin cup of water that lay on the floor beside his pallet. With one arm supporting his head, she brought the cup to his lips. Marcus sipped slowly, very slowly. The soft contours of her breasts brushed against his chest, and beneath his hands her waist felt slim and supple. When he finished the water in the cup, and she made to leave him, he tightened his hold and raised his head. Surprise held her immobile, and he quickly kissed her. It wasn't the way he wanted to kiss her. It was no more than a chaste peck. Even so, he braced for the slap that was sure to follow. When she didn't slap him, he drew back and gauged her expression. Her eyes were heavy lidded and uncertain. Blue eyes, and that surprised him.

"Catalina?" he said hoarsely, forgetting the part he was playing.

Then, she slapped him. When he groaned, this time in earnest, she pushed out of his loosened hold and quickly put the distance of the room between them.

He grinned, and raised carefully on one elbow. "My apologies, señorita. I mistook you for someone else. ¿*Comprende*? I thought you were Isabella."

Hands on hips, she let fly at him with a spate of Spanish. When he shrugged, showing his confusion, she took several long breaths and started over in broken English. "*Madre de Dios!* This is *España. Spain,* señor. If my brother . . . if *El Grande* . . . you must never touch me, never kiss me. *¡Jamás!* If you do, you will be punished. *¿Comprende?*"

Marcus was well aware that *El Grande* was a man to fear. Though he was hardly more than a boy, he'd become a legend in his own time. Some said he was the son of a Spanish nobleman, others that he had been a poor student at the university in Madrid when the French invaded Spain. His exploits were a source of pride to the Spanish peasants. In Marcus's opinion, however, the stories that circulated about the young man became exaggerated in the telling. No man could be that barbaric. What he knew for a certainty was that *El Grande* was tireless in his war against the French, and sometimes extreme. One French commander had tried to clip his wings by ordering Spanish hostages shot whenever *El Grande* attacked his soldiers. The guerrilla leader retaliated by executing four Frenchmen for every Spaniard shot. It was the French commander who eventually backed down.

He eased himself to a sitting position and gave her his infectious grin, but it did not soften her. "*El Grande* will kill me. Is that it?"

He wasn't taking her seriously, and that made her temper boil over. "He will do a lot worse than that."

"Torture? I hardly think so. It was an honest mistake."

She was silent for a moment, then said, "Worse than torture."

He detected the mockery in her tone and decided to take the bait. "What could be worse than torture?"

"Marriage, señor. Does that not frighten you?"

"One needs a priest for that, señorita."

She smiled a slow smile. "*Sí.* A priest. Our *padre* is playing cards with Juan. Shall I fetch him for you?"

Marcus did not return her smile. "Point taken, señorita."

Her eyes searched his face and after a moment, she began to gather her writing materials together.

"No, don't leave me," Marcus protested. "*Por favor.* Stay. Talk to me." He searched his mind for the few Spanish words he knew, but most of those he'd picked up from the whores who followed the army and those words were of no use to him with a virtuous girl. What was the Spanish for "talk"? *"Parler,"* he said. It was a French word, but he hoped it would do.

She hesitated, then slowly seated herself. "What do you wish to talk about?"

"Well, your brother for a start."

"*¿Sí?*"

"I wish to thank him for rescuing me."

"*El Grande* is not here. He is . . . how do you say? . . . making war on our enemies."

"When will he return?"

"Soon, very soon, when the rains stop. The rivers . . ." She shrugged helplessly. "It's too dangerous to cross."

"Then who is in charge here?"

She frowned at him. "Who . . . ?"

"Who is your captain?"

"Ah. Juan."

He said incredulously, "Juan? My nursemaid? Is he the only man here?" Juan was seventy if he was a day.

Her eyes were downcast and he had the strangest impression that she was laughing at him, but when she lifted her head, she was unsmiling and her eyes were clear. "There are the women soldiers, señor, and the *padre,* and the other English."

"What English?"

"Soldiers, like you. *El Grande* rescued them too."

"How many?"

She held up six fingers.

"So many? Who are they? Where are they?"

"I cannot say. I do not talk with the English. My brother forbids it. I shall send Juan to you. He will answer your questions."

She rose gracefully and thrust the pistol into her belt, gathered her writing materials and locked them in a carved commode that flanked the hearth.

She was almost at the door when Marcus called out, "Wait!"

"Señor?"

She had stiffened at his peremptory tone, and

Marcus immediately moderated it. "You visit me, don't you, and I'm English?"

"I come to be alone, señor, and for the candle and the fire. And yes, to nurse you when Juan cannot come. But now that you are well, you see how it is. My brother would be very angry if he knew I was here."

Marcus was staring at the carved commode. "This is your room, isn't it?" Another thought struck him. "You come here to write?"

She inclined her head gravely.

"What is it you write?"

"How do you say . . . my *jornal, diario.*"

"You keep a journal?"

"*Sí.*"

"And what do you write in it?"

"Things that are dear to a woman's heart."

"And what is dear to your heart, Catalina? Do you dream of love?"

Her smile was hard to read. "Doesn't every woman?"

"No. Some women dream of fine clothes and precious jewels and a soft life." His lips parted slightly and he inhaled a slow breath. "Could a woman like you dream about a man like me, a poor soldier with nothing to offer but a hard life?"

"She might. You are very handsome, I suppose, in your English way." She studied his dark hair, and deeply tanned face.

"Some people," said Marcus, "say I could pass myself off as a Spaniard."

"*¡Jamás!* You are too big. Juan cannot find clothes to fit you."

"I presume my uniform was ruined by those French lancers?"

"And the blood you lost. *El Grande* said you were very brave."

"And you are very beautiful."

For a long, silent interval, she gazed at him, but when she spoke, all she said was, "Remember, señor, no more Isabella. *¡Jamás! ¿Comprende?*" She was unsmiling.

"*Jamás*," promised Marcus. "Will you come to me tomorrow? I'm quite harmless. No, really, I mean it."

"We shall see." She closed the door softly as she exited.

Over the next three weeks, Marcus gradually regained his strength, and the more his strength returned, the more he strained at the bit to be up and doing. These were critical times. Wellington and his armies were falling back toward Lisbon while the French regained lost ground. When they finally made a stand, the British would be vastly outnumbered. And here he was, an experienced cavalry officer, stranded in the middle of nowhere, going nowhere. He might as well be marooned on a desert island.

The other English soldiers, who had all been rescued by *El Grande* at one time or another, were not as impatient as he was. Their injuries were superficial, and the senior officer, Major Sheppard, kept them busy, helping the women guerrillas who had been left to guard the monastery. Marcus could sometimes catch glimpses of them from the small turret window that overlooked the courtyard. There were six Englishmen in all, three cavalry officers whom Marcus knew slightly, a young ensign, and two enlisted men, Riflemen of the 95th. Had Marcus not been gravely wounded when the guerrillas brought him to their hideout, he would have been billeted with the other English soldiers in the monastery's crypt. He was still not well enough to be moved and his fellow officers took turns visiting him. The enlisted men, as was the way of all enlisted men, kept pretty much to themselves.

Catalina kept away during these visits. Except for Marcus, she avoided the English. She came to him every evening and stayed until the candle burned low. Sometimes, she wrote in her journal, but more often than not they talked. She was curious about him, as he was about her. She told him about the Spanish peasants, and their terrible sufferings at the hands of the French soldiers, and he told her about England and the life he would return to if he survived the war.

There was one thing, however, that he kept to himself. He was not the ordinary soldier he pretended to be. She knew him as Captain Marcus Lytton of the 3rd Dragoons. In fact, he was a wealthy English lord, the Earl of Wrotham, and the possessor of vast holdings in England. Though his title was no secret in army circles, he never permitted anyone to address him by it. He despised it when people played up to him because of his title, or conversely, how it distanced him in the minds of men he liked and respected.

With women it was a different matter. Sometimes, Marcus used his wealth and title quite unscrupulously to lure them to his bed. He had discovered that a woman's head was easily turned by the attentions of a man of property, however worthless that man might be in himself. As a consequence, his opinion of women in general was not very high. He saw them as grasping opportunists who would sell their bodies for a few worthless trinkets.

This was not how he thought of Catalina. He admired her courage and dignity. Her life was hard, but it was the life she had chosen. With her face and form, she could easily have found a rich protector or have become a rich man's wife. Instead, she had thrown in her lot with the partisans. Marcus wasn't sure how she would feel if she knew who he really was. He didn't want to change anything between them. She saw him as a man and what she saw she liked. Marcus was very sure about that. When they were together, the air between them was charged with a sexual energy. Sometimes, when he forgot to guard his expression, she would stop in mid-sentence and, ignoring his protests, quietly leave the room. But she always came back, and he knew that she wanted him almost as much as he wanted her.

Three days after the torrential rains had stopped, *El Grande* and his band of guerrillas returned to the monastery. Marcus watched their arrival from the turret window. They were a motley lot, some dressed in peasant homespun and others in the jackets of various French regiments, booty they'd stripped from soldiers they'd killed. Their black horses were in better condition than the men who rode them, and Marcus's respect for the partisans rose.

He turned slightly when the door opened. Catalina came to stand beside him at the window. She was wearing a long white dress, and her dark hair streamed over her shoulders. Her eyes were misted with unshed tears. Marcus forgot about the men in the courtyard.

"The fords are passable," she said. "You will leave tonight. All the English are going."

He didn't want to frighten her, so he did no more than clasp her hands and bring them to his chest. "Listen to me, Catalina." He spoke earnestly, trying to convince her of his sincerity, though she might not understand all his words. "This isn't the end for us. I'll find a way to come to you. Do you understand? Even if we have to wait until the war is over, I'll find you. I give you my word."

Her voice trembled. "Once, just once, I want to feel your lips on mine."

He kissed her chastely, no more than a gentle pressure of mouth on mouth. He was drawing away when her teeth bit savagely into his lower lip. His head jerked, and in the next moment, she struck him across the face with her open palm.

He wasn't angry, he was frozen in shock. Then he remembered that she was an innocent, and he blamed himself for frightening her. "Catalina," he said, "don't be afraid. I would never hurt you."

She backed away from him, and he saw the blood, his blood, smeared on her lips. He heard the tread of boots on the stairs, and laughter, and a man's voice above the din, calling her by name. And even when she tore her dress from hem to waist, exposing bare thigh, Marcus still stood there stupidly, not understanding what was going on.

She called out in rapid-fire Spanish, and there was a sudden silence on the other side of the door. Then she whipped out her dagger as if to threaten him, and she said in a deadly tone, "*El Grande* will kill you when he sees how you have tried to rape me."

Comprehension ripped through him like a bolt of lightning. It wasn't the first time a woman had tried to compromise him, but it was the first time a woman had succeeded. His bloodied lip, her torn dress, and the mark of her blow that still stung his cheek—the evidence against him must seem incontrovertible.

He went for her just as the door crashed back on its hinges. She discarded the dagger and flung herself into the arms of the man who crossed the threshold. Marcus had an impression of a young man, younger than Catalina, with dark ascetic looks, then several armed partisans pushed into the room and hauled Marcus back, shoving him against the wall. He was so incensed, felt so betrayed, that he fought them like a madman. His injuries were forgotten. He felt no pain. Every muscle bunched and strained as he tried to throw off his attackers so that he could get to the girl. It took three of them to subdue him, but it was not until the knife at his throat drew blood that he finally quieted.

He could not follow her outburst, but one word jumped out at him—"Wrotham." Now he understood everything. Somehow, she had discovered who he was and she had made her plans in meticulous detail, down to the moment her brother would return to the monastery. He could not contain his bile. She had duped him as though he were a green boy. Everything was a sham. She wasn't attracted to Marcus Lytton the man. She wanted what every woman wanted, position and money.

When she had run out of words, *El Grande* set her aside and crossed to Marcus. Not a flicker of emotion showed in his dark eyes. His accent was flawless. "Is this how the English repay a friend's hospitality?"

Marcus did not answer. His eyes blazed with hatred as they fastened on Catalina. "You lying bitch! I should have taken what you were offering while I had the chance. *¡Puta!*"

El Grande's blow sent him to his knees. Marcus swallowed a mouthful of blood and gritted through clenched teeth, "I will never marry her. *¡Jamás!*"

Another blow followed, and Catalina cried out. When *El Grande* lifted his fist again, she threw herself in front of him. Her voice was low and pleading, and she went on at some length. Her brother heard her out in silence.

He barked out an order and Marcus was yanked to his feet. *El Grande* moved back and smiled deprecatingly, a boyish smile that made him seem harmless. Marcus had trouble believing that this was the legendary guerrilla leader whose very name struck terror in the hearts of his enemies.

El Grande said, "You are fortunate that my sister loves you. You will marry her, señor, or your English comrades will pay for your sins."

Marcus looked into those pitiless black eyes and he knew that he was beaten.

The wedding took place that very night under the stars in the monastery's burned-out nave. The mass was short, for *El Grande* had arranged to conduct Marcus and his comrades to British lines under cover of darkness and he was impatient to get under way. Though the bride and groom held themselves stiffly, there was an air of jubilation among the partisans. It was known that Catalina had snared an English lord, and though the marriage was in haste, Juan had seen to it that everyone, including Marcus's comrades, believed that the young people were in love. When the groom kissed the bride, only Catalina saw the violence in his eyes, only Marcus saw the loathing in hers.

As cheers erupted around them, he grasped her by the wrist and hauled her off to one side. He bared his teeth in a sneer. "You belong to me now, Catalina, not your brother. Think on that while I am gone. One day, there will be a reckoning, then, you scheming bitch, you will know your victory is hollow."

He kissed her then, not as he had done before, reverencing her innocence, but as savagely and as insultingly as he could make it. Her head was forced back over his arm, and he plunged his tongue into her mouth. She jerked once, then went limp in his arms. His hands moved down her back, over her waist, and he dragged her against him, grinding his groin into the lower part of her body. The partisans saw only two lovers locked in a passionate embrace and they roared their approval.

When Marcus let her go, she stumbled back, one hand covering her bruised lips. Her eyes were wide in her pale face, and he nodded, satisfied with what he read there.

His voice was low and chilling. "You've made a bad bargain, Lady Wrotham. Remember that when you sit dreaming of my wealth and title."

He turned on his heel and did not look at her again as he shouldered his way past beaming partisans to the men who were eager to be off.

Chapter 1

England, August 1815

Catherine heaved a sigh, straightened in her chair, and rubbed the small of her back with the knuckles of one hand. Long tendrils of vivid red hair had escaped their pins, and she took a moment to secure them to the loose knot at her nape. A dozen balled papers littered the floor at her feet; ink stained her fingers. She had been writing for hours and she still wasn't satisfied. Though she wanted to stop, she had to continue. Her employer, Melrose Gunn, who was proprietor of *The Journal,* would expect to have her article on his desk by tomorrow afternoon at the latest. There was another reason for her determination to finish the piece. She really needed the money. She wasn't a pauper by any means. There was this small house and an annuity from her father's estate, but it was barely enough to meet her expenses. Doctors, especially army doctors, did not make a fortune from practicing their profession.

Another long sigh, then she picked up the pages she had completed and quickly scanned them. This was to be the first in a series of essays describing the atrocious living conditions of soldiers and their families and demanding that the government make radical changes. Now that the war was over, and with Napoleon exiled on Saint Helena, there would never be a better time to implement the changes she was suggesting. And she knew what she was writing about. She should. She'd observed everything with her own eyes when she'd followed her father to Spain, when he'd served in the medical corps.

Accuracy. That was the hallmark of A. W. Euman,

the name she'd chosen to write under. If she wrote about Newgate, her readers could be sure that she'd investigated the prison in person. He, not she, she amended. Women were only taken seriously if they wrote tracts on domestic trivia. If they tried to step out of the domestic sphere and use their God-given talents, they were held up to ridicule. It was an iniquitous state of affairs, but that was the way things were. If it became generally known that A. W. Euman was a woman, no one would take her seriously or read her articles, and she would be out of a job.

Frowning, she brought her mind round to the matter at hand. There was something about this article that missed the mark. Then she had it. The tone was wrong. It was too serious, too censorious. This wasn't the voice of A. W. Euman. Humor and irony were the tools he used to make his point. She would have to do it over.

She groaned and looked at the clock on the mantel. It would have to wait until later. Soon it would be dark, and she had an important appointment to keep. Appointment? She supposed that was the right word for it, though her sister would not be expecting her, not at this time of night. She'd made two attempts to gain admittance to the house during the daylight hours, and footmen had turned her away both times. She'd written letters which had never been answered. This time around, nothing was going to stop her from seeing Amy.

Rising, she opened the top drawer of her desk and carefully slipped the pages of her article inside. From another drawer, she withdrew a pistol, a sleek piece of French design that her father had found at the siege of Badajoz. She'd always suspected that it had once belonged to a French officer's mistress, something that had been especially made for her in Paris, though really, Catherine had no way of knowing. As pistols went it was light, much lighter than her father's pistol. It wasn't loaded. From the back of the same drawer, she extracted everything that was necessary to arm the pistol. Her movements were quick and practiced. She'd armed this dainty piece more times than she cared to remember. Her father had taught her how.

She shook her head at the incongruity of what she

was doing. How had it come to this? Who could have foretold that this was the way things would have turned out? Once, a century ago it seemed now, they had been happy in this little house on the edge of Hampstead Heath. It was in the country, yet it was only four miles from the center of London. They weren't rich, but they had never wanted for anything. As the local doctor, their father had good standing in the village. He was an educated man. Their mother was educated too. She'd been a governess at one time and had undertaken the education of her own two daughters. This happy world had shattered the day their mother had come down with a fever. One day later, she was dead.

Catherine was twelve years old when their father's sister had come to look after them. Aunt Bea was much stricter than their mother. Catherine had adapted quite well, but Amy had rebelled. Amy was so much older than Catherine, so much prettier. At eighteen, she'd wanted to go to parties and meet other young people. She'd wanted pretty frocks and dancing lessons and all the things she thought she was entitled to. There had been ferocious quarrels. Amy had taken to slipping away to be with friends whom she never brought home to meet her family. Aunt Bea appealed to their father, but she got no help there. Martin Courtnay was either sunk in despair or off drinking somewhere. It would be a long, long time before he came to accept his wife's death, and by that time, it was too late.

Catherine's fingers tightened on the pistol in her palm, and she asked herself the same question. How had it come to this? She and Amy were the only ones left. She had a sister, yet she might as well be alone in the world.

The back door slammed, and she heard the soft murmur of voices in the kitchen. It took a moment, but the tightness in her throat eased. She wasn't alone in the world. She had the McNallys with her now. McNally had been her father's batman during the Spanish campaign. Mrs. McNally had been there too, one of the few wives who had been chosen by lot to accompany their husbands to the battle zone. Catherine had to pay her own way out to be with her father, and though he'd forbidden it, she was glad that she had disobeyed him. If she hadn't, they would never have had that last year together, and she would never have met the McNallys. They were servants, and they were so much more. They had been through the perils of war together and that made an enormous difference.

That thought made her think of the article she was writing. She had to get it done. It wasn't only herself she was thinking about. The McNallys were her dependents. If she couldn't provide for them and pay their wages, she didn't know what would become of them. With so many men returning from the war, jobs were scarce, and the McNallys weren't getting any younger. She had to get that article ready for tomorrow.

Spurred to action, she made for her bedchamber upstairs. Though it was August, there was a distinct chill in the air. She donned her tan coat, noting that the frayed black piping on the sleeves and hem had been replaced. This was Mrs. McNally's doing. Her black calfskin boots had been resoled. This was Mr. McNally's doing. She hadn't done anything to earn such devotion. She was her father's daughter, and that's what counted with the McNallys. Still, it brought a lump to her throat.

She glanced at her reflection in the looking glass as she began to don her high poke bonnet, and that glance became a stare, a long hard stare. On her next birthday, she would be twenty-six years old. Did it show? She was an aging spinster. *Spinster.* She hated that word. She studied her reflection anxiously, then became impatient with herself. This preoccupation with her looks was beneath the dignity of a woman who prided herself on her intelligence. Aunt Bea had dinned that into her as she had grown to womanhood. And she wasn't preoccupied with her looks. She wouldn't have given them a second thought if it weren't for this appointment with Amy, beautiful, sophisticated Amy.

She lowered her bonnet, and gazed blindly at her reflection as the memory of the last time she had seen Amy came back to her. Her friend Emily and her husband had taken her to the King's Theater for the performance of *Bacchus and Ariadne*. At the intermission, she had looked up at the boxes as Emily pointed out various personages of note who were present that evening. Catherine rarely went to the theater, and she was enjoying herself enormously when her eyes alighted on a beauty who was holding her own private court in one of the boxes. She was surrounded by admiring males. Catherine craned her neck to get a better look at the lady who was causing such a stir, and then her heart stopped beating. It was Amy.

"That," said Emily, in an undertone, "is Mrs. Spencer, you know, London's most sought-after courtesan. They say the Prince of Wales is one of her lovers."

Catherine had felt too ill to reply to this, and anyway, she would not have said anything. Amy was a subject that was too painful to discuss even with her best friend, Emily.

She shook off that memory and rammed her bonnet on her head, then carefully tucked every strand of her abominable red hair out of the way, concealing it completely. Her hair was sure to betray her identity, and she didn't want Amy's footmen to recognize her until she'd stepped over the threshold. Having tied the ribbons under her chin, she picked up her reticule and slipped the strings over her left arm. There would be no need for gloves. Her mother's fur muff was far more suitable for what she had in mind. It was the perfect hiding place for her pistol.

They made the ride to town in her father's old-fashioned, one-horse buggy. McNally was on the box, and the hood had been raised to protect Catherine from the drizzle of rain. The light was fading. Soon it would be dark and the fashionable set would begin on their round of balls and parties. She had chosen her moment with forethought.

Her ultimate destination, as far as McNally knew, was the King's Theater in the Haymarket. He was used to his mistress embarking on these odd jaunts, and supposed that this one, like the others, had something to do with the scribbling she did for *The Journal*. The McNallys were two of a very select group of people who knew A. W. Euman's true identity. On this occasion, McNally was relieved that Catherine was going to a relatively safe part of town. There had been other jaunts to places that made the fine hairs on the back of his neck stand on end. Newgate, for one. The stews of Whitechapel for another. He knew well enough that Catherine was no ordinary milk-and-water miss. She knew how to take care of herself. In Spain, she'd shown more courage than many a seasoned soldier, as had his Mary. But that didn't stop him worrying about her or wishing fervently that she *were* a milk-and-water miss. Those were the girls who found themselves husbands.

In his opinion, she would have no trouble finding herself a husband if she put her mind to it. Her employer, Melrose Gunn, for one. He'd seen the way Mr. Gunn's eyes followed her in a roomful of people. And she was worth looking at—or she would be if only she would spruce herself up a bit. It wouldn't hurt either if she adopted a more ladylike manner. Gentlemen, as a rule, favored girls who were docile, meek, biddable—and as everyone knew, Catherine was the opposite. His Mary blamed the girl's aunt for Catherine's lack of interest in her looks, and her father for her independence. Martin Courtnay had undeniably allowed Catherine more freedoms than were good for her when she had joined him in Lisbon.

Whatever the reason, the sad truth was that Catherine was a bluestocking, one of those females whose minds were set on higher things than being attractive to men. Her ambition was to change the world. He snorted, then a moment later, chuckled. If anyone could do it, she could.

When they drew up outside the King's Theater, the rain had stopped. Catherine stood for a moment on the pavement taking in the sights and sounds. The Haymarket was one of the busiest thoroughfares in the city. Westminster, where Parliament was in session, was only a short walk away, as was Carlton House, the Prince Regent's magnificent private palace. There were more coffee houses, gentlemen's clubs, and eating establishments in this area than in any other part of the city.

Catherine loved it all, loved the aroma of coffee and

beer that wafted on the air, loved the noise and crush of vehicles that rattled over the cobblestoned streets, and she especially loved the bustle of people of all walks of life who seemed to be in a perpetual hurry. Where were they going? What were their business, their dreams, their pleasures? This last thought sobered her. Everything was not always as it seemed. Scratch the surface and one was likely to find a cesspool of vice. This area was also renowned for its multitude of brothels.

There was a glower on McNally's face as he watched her cross the street and disappear into the King's Theater. She never let him accompany her when she was interviewing her subjects. She insisted that they would never tell her anything if there was a witness present. Though he didn't like her going off on her own, there was nothing he could do about it. She'd been her own mistress for too long.

A hackney driver called out, upbraiding him for taking his spot. McNally let fly with a spate of curses that left the hackney driver gaping. He looked more closely at the hefty Scot and his fierce expression, then looked away.

"Damn foreigner!" intoned the hackney driver under his breath.

McNally kept his spot, and settled in for a long wait.

When Catherine entered the theater's vestibule, she heard the applause and knew that soon the halls would be choked with patrons making their way out. One minute after entering the vestibule, she exited by a side door. This subterfuge was all for McNally's benefit. She didn't want him to know that her destination was the most notorious house of pleasure in Pall Mall, and he would know if he saw her enter it. Everyone knew of Mrs. Amy Spencer, London's most sought-after courtesan, and her house in Pall Mall. She had heard of Mrs. Spencer also, but until she had seen Amy in her box at the theater, she had never connected the two.

Pall Mall was lit up with gas lamps, and the light that came from the many coffee houses and taverns that were interspersed with private residences made it the best illuminated street in the city, as well as one of the safest.

Nevertheless, a woman on her own was always considered fair game. Catherine tightened her fingers around the pistol in her muff and hastened her steps.

She was almost at the house when a coach pulled up at its front door. She stepped into the entrance of an alley, and watched as three young women and their escorts alighted. They made a glamorous picture, the young women in the height of fashion, with high-waisted sheer gauze gowns and jewels glittering at their throats. They cared nothing for the cold night air. The gentlemen matched their elegance. They were in dark frock coats and black trousers. Only their neckcloths and waistcoats relieved their somber looks. There was much laughter as bawdy jests flew back and forth. A couple of the gentlemen were swaying on their feet.

Catherine waited until they had entered the house, gave them a few minutes, then, with a quick look around, squared her shoulders and started forward. She felt quite calm as she rapped with the knocker. She had known this kind of calm in Spain. It was always before the battle that soldiers suffered their worst case of nerves. Once the fighting had begun, nerves steadied. Then why were her knees knocking together?

The door was opened by the same august-looking footman in silver livery who had turned her away twice before. From the floor above came the sounds of a riotous party. This time, she didn't bandy words. She thrust her pistol under the footman's nose and had the satisfaction of seeing the supercilious look wiped from his face. As he fell back, she entered the house and kicked the door closed behind her. So far so good.

"Kindly inform Mrs. Spencer that she has a visitor," she said. "No. Don't raise your arms. I mean you no harm. But if Mrs. Spencer refuses to see me, you may tell her that I shall discharge this pistol and bring the house down about her ears, not to mention the militia. I warn you, I shall scream rape if she refuses to see me. Frankly, I don't think her guests would care for the scandal that would ensue. Tell her I said so."

From the top of the stairs came a woman's voice. "John, who is it?" Amy's voice.

Catherine indicated a door that was just off the entrance hall. "You may tell Mrs. Spencer that I shall be in there," she said. Without waiting to see what the footman would do, she pushed through the door.

The room was lit by two candles strategically placed on either end of the marble mantelpiece. Catherine stood with her back to the light so that she would have a clear view of her sister when she entered the room. And she had no doubt that this time Amy would agree to see her. It was one thing to turn her away when the house was empty, but quite another when she had a house full of blue-blooded gentlemen who might well be hauled off to be interrogated by magistrates. That kind of scandal would be hard to live down, even for London's most notorious courtesan.

She didn't have long to wait. The door opened on a cloud of perfume, and Amy stood there before her. Beautiful wasn't the word to describe her. She was stunning. A profusion of tiny black ringlets framed her face; diamonds glittered at her throat; her eyes were huge and dark. The transparent gauze dress was molded to creamy white breasts and long limbs, concealing nothing. Salome down to the last veil.

Her voice spoiled the effect. It was cold and ugly. "How dare you utter threats and push your way into my house."

Catherine forced herself to speak calmly. "I dare because I want to speak with my sister."

"Your sister?" Amy's nostrils flared. "As I remember, you told me in Lisbon that you never wanted to see me again. So what in hell's name are you doing here, Cat?"

It had been a long, long time since anyone had called her Cat. Her throat thickened and she said hoarsely, "I was angry in Lisbon. Shocked. I blamed you for Papa's death. I said things I shouldn't have said, things I regretted almost at once. But it was too late. I couldn't find you. I don't blame you for what you've become. I blame the men who prey on you. I'm sorry for Lisbon, Amy. I'm so sorry."

Amy showed her teeth. "You may take your pathetic apology and get the hell out of my house. Who do you think you are to pity me? Look around you, Cat. I own this house. I earned it with my own money, yes, and every stick of furniture in it."

"Amy . . ."

"Your sister is dead. That's what you told me in Lisbon. And that's the truth. The Amy you knew doesn't exist."

"I can't believe that it has come to this. Now that I've found you, won't you at least give me a chance?"

Amy took a few steps around the room, stopped and asked abruptly, "What is it you want from me?"

Catherine knew that what she really wanted she was unlikely to get. Amy would never go back to the house in Hampstead, not after living in this luxury. But there must be something else she could do besides prostitute her body for money.

As Catherine groped to put her thoughts into words, Amy exhaled a long exasperated breath. "If you think you can persuade me to give up all this,"—she gestured comprehensively with one hand—"you can think again. I have my own box at the opera, yes, and my own carriage. I give parties and receptions and mix with fashionable society. My gowns are made up by the most exclusive modiste in London. These are real diamonds you see at my throat. Need I say more?"

For the first time, Catherine spoke with asperity. "The only fashionable society you mix with are rakes and roués, yet even these degenerates would not dream of introducing you to their sisters for fear you might contaminate them. And this house, for all its elegance, is still notorious. You are almost thirty-three years old. How long do you think you can continue like this?"

"Rakes and roués?" Amy laughed. "What would you know about rakes and roués? Go home, Cat, where you belong. You were right when you said you had no sister. Neither do I. It's as if she never existed."

In answer to this, Catherine set down her muff with the pistol still in it, and opened her reticule. She kept her eyes on her sister as sovereigns spilled through her fingers and onto the carpeted floor. "You sent me these, didn't you? Why, Amy? Why did you send me money?"

For a moment, Army seemed to be debating with herself, then shrugging, she replied, "I saw you from an upstairs window when you came here two days ago. You looked shabby. I thought you could use the money. I'm sure Father didn't leave you well off."

"You see?" Catherine said eagerly. "You're not as hard as you pretend to be. We are sisters, Amy. That means something."

"Oh, for mercy's sake, just take the money and go before someone finds you here."

"I don't want your money. I want us to be friends again."

"Friends!" The word echoed off the walls. Amy lowered her voice. "You were always the clever one, Cat, but you never did possess a shred of common sense. I see nothing has changed. Go home. Forget about me. I don't want to see you here again."

"Then write to me. Answer my letters."

"What would be the point? Anything I might have to say to you has already been said"

Before Catherine could reply to this, voices were heard on the stairs calling for Amy, men's voices.

"I must go," said Amy, "and so must you. Don't show your face here again." She moved quickly to the door, hesitated, then swept out without a backward glance.

When the door closed, Catherine's shoulders slumped. Deep down, she'd known she was going to be turned away, but it still hurt. But what hurt most was that she really didn't recognize her sister in the hard, mercenary creature she had just spoken to. She didn't feel like crying. She wanted to lash out and hurt the men who were responsible for what her sister had become. Amy hadn't always been like this. She'd been a romantic, dreamy sort of girl until she'd fallen in with the wrong crowd. And Aunt Bea hadn't helped. And neither had she when she'd said all those unforgivable things in Lisbon.

She picked up her muff and reticule, but left the sovereigns where they had fallen. The same footman who had opened the front door to her saw her out, or rather, saw her off the premises. He'd been warned not to take any chances, or so Catherine deduced from his clawlike grip on her elbow. She had hardly stepped out of the house when the door closed behind her with a resounding slam.

She stared at that closed door in boiling resentment. For two pins, she'd write a series of articles on the notorious courtesans of London. Jaw clenched, she marched down the steps just as three men in black silk capes descended from a hackney. *Gentlemen,* she thought with a sneer and wanted to spit on them. It was evident that they were bound for Amy's house. Caution was forgotten as she angrily pushed past them. The first one gave way with a muffled exclamation. The second was not so polite. He caught her by the waist and swung her in a circle.

"Whoa," he said. "Why all the haste? The party is this way, darling. You're going the wrong way." His breath smelled strongly of spirits, and Catherine's head went down.

"Marcus, let her be," said the third man. "She's not one of Amy's friends. Anyone can see she's a respectable lady."

"If she's a respectable lady," said Marcus, "why is she coming from Amy's house?"

His two companions laughed and mounted the stairs. One used his cane to rap on the door.

"Look up, darling," said Marcus. "I want to see what you're hiding beneath the brim of your bonnet. I promise I won't bite you."

Catherine didn't move. She stood there silent and stiff-backed, resisting as he cupped her chin, forcing her head up.

He was tall and lean, and gave the impression of an athlete honed for action. His looks were Irish, dark hair, vivid blue eyes, and a mouth that looked as if it smiled a lot. It was not smiling now.

It was a face she recognized, a face she had hoped never to see again. She was staring at Marcus Lytton, the Earl of Wrotham.

Her husband.

The door opened, and light streamed out, illuminating Catherine's face. "Are you coming, Marcus?" There was no answer, and the two gentlemen on the steps passed inside the house.

The hands on Catherine's waist tightened cruelly. "Catalina!" he said, snarling the word. "Catalina! My God, it *is* you!"

Chapter 2

Catherine fought her way clear of his arms and backed away from him. She was frightened, more frightened than she had ever been in her life, and her breasts rose and fell with each labored breath. If ever a man was bent on murder, that man was towering over her. As he lunged, she took a quick step to the side and whipped her pistol out of her muff.

"Stand back!" Her voice wobbled as much as the pistol in her hand, and she made a supreme effort to steady both. She had never, in her worst nightmares, imagined that this day would ever come. He was supposed to be in Paris. They moved in different circles. Three years had passed since she had last seen him. He couldn't remember her clearly. *He couldn't.* Too many women had passed in and out of his life since then.

"Stand back!" she repeated when it looked as if he would come at her again. When he slowly raised his hands she rushed on, "I don't know who you think I am, but you are mistaken. I never saw you before tonight. I don't know you."

Doubt and uncertainty shadowed his eyes. "You're English," he said.

"Of course I'm English. What did you expect?"

"My wife was Spanish."

"Catalina was your wife?"

He nodded.

"I'm not your wife."

"So it would seem." He made a slight movement that managed to convey regret, then lowered his arms. "I beg your pardon. I hope I didn't frighten you, but of course, I must have done. I apologize most sincerely. Now that

I've had a better look at you, I see that you're not Catalina, though you are very like her."

His words relieved her worst fears, and she lowered
the pistol. When she saw that several curious spectators
had stopped to watch, including the driver of the hackney, she thrust the pistol inside her muff. She was still
trembling, still trying to even her breathing. The tempta-
tion to take to her heels was almost overpowering. It
would be the worst thing she could do. She must appear
natural.

"Apology accepted," she said. "No harm done," and
with a nod and a smile, she turned to go on her way. She
had not taken one step when she was seized from behind
and a strong masculine hand gagged her, cutting off her
scream of alarm. His other arm clamped her muff to her
body, making it impossible for her to get to her pistol.
Kicking, writhing, she was lifted off her feet and hauled
toward the hackney.

"My wife," Marcus told the captivated bystanders,
"hopes to elope with Lord Berkeley. And I would let her,
if it were not for our six children at home."

Catherine bit down on his thumb and he grunted.
When he released her mouth, she cried out, appealing to
their audience, "It's a lie! I don't know this man."

There was a menacing murmur from the crowd
which Marcus silenced with his next words. "Ours was
an arranged marriage. She married me for my wealth and
title. Now, she has come to regret it." Then, in a different
tone, for Catherine's ears only, "Is that not so, my dear
wife?"

Catherine knew she was losing the sympathy of the
people who could help her, and she cried out desperately.
"Fetch the Watch and we'll soon see who is telling the
truth. I'm not his wife, I tell you."

Her words had the desired effect. Someone called
out, "Let 'er be, guv'nor, till we fetches the Watch."

Marcus ignored the warning. He had the coach door
open and was hoisting her inside when the crowd surged
forward, sending them both sprawling to their knees.
Marcus was their target, and Catherine lost no time in

scrambling free. Once on her feet, she took off like a hare.

She glanced back once and saw that the crowd was dispersing. There was no sign of Marcus and that only increased her panic. She turned into a tavern, hovered just inside the entrance, and when a waiter came forward, waved him away and made for the back door.

The mews of Pall Mall were as different from the front as night from day. There were a few lanterns lit, but their light hardly made an impression on the velvety darkness. She struck out toward the lights of the main thoroughfare, but she had not gone far along that dark lane before she was wishing she had remained in the tavern. Walls seemed to close in on her, and at every small sound, her heart stopped beating. She tried to hurry and went stumbling through muddy potholes and heaps of manure that had been cleared out of stables for the scavengers to collect in the morning. She felt in her coat pocket, retrieved her handkerchief, and held it to her nose.

When she came to the junction that led to Charing Cross, she stopped to get her bearings. She didn't think Marcus had given up the chase. He'd been like a man possessed. He'd panicked her, and that didn't happen to her very often. Now that she had got a grip on herself, she was beginning to wonder if she should have held her ground and waited for the Watch to arrive.

She pressed back against the brick wall of a stable while she considered her options. To get to McNally, she had to cross the street. If Marcus was still on Pall Mall, he couldn't fail to see her. It was too risky. She would have to make a detour. If she turned right and went around Charing Cross, she would come out on the Strand. Once there, she could hire a hackney to take her to the Haymarket.

There was one other possibility. The Horse Guards were on Whitehall, just a stone's throw from Charing Cross. The militia, who policed the city streets, would be there. If she could get to Whitehall, she could call out the militia. And of course, they would arrest Marcus Lytton, Earl of Wrotham. The idea was laughable. They would question *her*, and ask all sorts of awkward questions she didn't want to answer.

The detour it was, then.

It took every ounce of willpower to leave the shelter of the mews. With a swift glance to her left to make sure the coast was clear, she stepped out boldly and made a right turn. She walked briskly, staring straight ahead, ignoring the stares of various male loiterers who were looking for female companionship.

When she came to Whitehall, she chanced a quick glance over her shoulder and checked in mid-stride. Marcus! He was a good way behind her, but he was moving with speed, not running, but striking out with long strides, fairly eating up the distance between them.

There was no thought in her mind now of going around Charing Cross to the Strand. She picked up her skirts and darted into Whitehall. Only one thought possessed her. She must escape him. Gasping for breath, she ran headlong the last few yards that took her to the Horse Guards, and she dashed into the courtyard. There were several guards in blue uniform who seemed to be on duty. One of them, the officer in charge, came forward to meet her.

"Please help me." She could hardly speak, she was so out of breath. She pointed with a shaking finger. "There's a man following me. He's insane."

Captain Hailey summed her up in one comprehensive glance as a respectable lady, and he took her at her word. He barked out an order, and he and two of his soldiers stepped into Whitehall. Catherine retreated to the archway that gave onto the parade grounds on the other side of the building. When Marcus came into view, her heart leapt to her throat, and she instinctively edged deeper into the shadows.

"Marcus!" The officer in charge sounded astonished. "I didn't know you were back in London. Oh, there's a lady here who says you're insane."

Catherine cursed her ill luck. She should have remembered that Marcus had been a cavalry officer. These men all knew each other. She would get no help here.

There was much laughter, then she heard Marcus's voice above the others. "She dropped her reticule. I only wish to return it to her. Where is she?"

"She's . . . She must be here somewhere."

Catherine did not wait to hear more. She had passed through the arch. Ahead of her were the deserted parade grounds, and beyond that, St. James's Park. There was no caution now. She heard footsteps approaching, and she made a dash for it. When she reached the gate to the park and found it unlocked, she let out a long sobbing breath. At this time of night, the park should have been closed to the public, but it was no secret that when darkness fell it became the haunt of prostitutes and their patrons. Locked gates were nothing to them, nor to the footpads and thieves who frequented the park at night. She was afraid to enter, but more afraid still of the peril behind her.

She flung through the gate and almost immediately swerved from the path. In the dim light from the buildings on Whitehall, she could just make out trees and undergrowth. With head down and muff protecting her face, she pushed her way into the center of a dense thicket of holly bushes and dropped to her knees. She'd made so much noise when she'd sped across the parade grounds that she knew Marcus would have no difficulty tracking her. The most she could hope for was that he would follow the path in his search, taking him deeper into the park and away from her. Then she would slip away, retracing her steps to Whitehall.

The earth was sodden with rain, and like a dry sponge, her clothes began to absorb it. She removed her pistol from her muff and cradled it in the crook of her left arm. A good soldier, McNally had taught her, always kept his powder dry. Almost at once, she became aware that she was not alone. She'd expected Marcus to come thundering into the park. He'd come by stealth, and was playing the same waiting game as she. She couldn't see him, but she sensed his presence. Fear tightened every muscle and her eyes frantically searched the darkness. After what seemed like an eon, a shadow moved. She heard the quick rasp of his breath, and the soft tread of his steps as he made off along the path. Only then did she begin to breathe. Ears straining, she tried to follow his progress. There were sounds, but those came from the lake—oars plying small boats, muffled laughter, and the drone of crickets and other nocturnal insects.

She didn't know how long she crouched there listening. Satisfied that she was alone, she inched her way out of the thicket. She waited for a long time, then slowly straightened. Careful to make no sound, she crept toward the gate that led to the parade grounds, looking over her shoulder at every other step. Only when she was through that gate did the tension gradually seep out of her.

She inhaled a long breath—and a shadow came hurtling out of the darkness. Instinct took over. She cocked her pistol and pulled the trigger. The report was deafening. She saw him check, but sensed that she had missed her target. He still came on, and she turned to flee. Hard fingers bit into her arm, wrenching her round.

"You bitch!" he snarled.

She opened her mouth to scream and his fist caught her a glancing blow on the chin.

A red mist enveloped her. She went limp in his arms.

She came awake on a moan, and her hand fluttered to her jaw. Then she remembered everything, and she jerked herself upright. He was bending over her, his hands on her shoulders, pushing her back against the chair.

"Here, drink this," he said. "You'll feel better in a moment or two."

She didn't have the will to fight him. Her head was swimming and she felt nauseated. She swallowed a few sips of brandy, but when she began to cough and splutter, he set the glass aside.

Though her mind cleared rapidly, she remained as she was, eyes half closed, head supported against the back of the chair. She was taking his measure, trying to sense what was different about him. Then, it came to her. He was no longer threatening her.

She opened her eyes and glanced around the small room. "Where are we?" she asked.

"In one of the upstairs offices."

"We're at the Horse Guards?"

"Yes."

"Where are the guards?"

"Attending to their duties, I presume. I told them there had been a dreadful mistake, that I'd frightened you half to death, and that you were only defending yourself when you let fly at me with your pistol."

"And that's the truth!"

"So it would appear."

She watched him warily as he pulled a straight-backed chair close to hers and seated himself. He was smiling, and that mobile mouth managed to convey that, really, he was quite harmless. His hand reached for her, and she flinched away, pressing herself as far from him as possible. His hand dropped away.

"I've never seen hair that color," he said. "It's very beautiful."

She touched a hand to her hair. It was falling loose about her shoulders. Her bonnet had been removed, and was sitting on top of a flat-topped desk along with her muff and pistol.

He said abruptly, "Look here, I owe you an apology. The thing is, for a while there, I really did take you for my wife. Now that I've seen you clearly, however, and when I saw that red hair, I realized my mistake. And, of course, you did put up quite a fight. What else was I to think but that you had good reason to fear me?" He paused, then said lightly, too lightly for her comfort, "I'm Wrotham, by the way, and you are . . . ?"

The retort was instantaneous. "I'm the woman you frightened half to death."

"Touché."

He laughed, but there was no answering laugh from her. Her mind was grappling with what approach she should take. One wrong word could be fatal. She debated whether or not she should tell him her name and decided against it. What could she tell him? That her name was Catherine? That she'd been in Spain when *he* was in Spain, when, in fact, he'd married Catalina? True, her hair was red, but there were ways of getting around that. No, she didn't want him to know anything about her.

It might come down to it as a last resort, but not if she could help it. She was a respectable lady and this man had attacked her. That's the approach she should take.

She rose slowly, and he rose with her. "You may take your apology and go to the devil," she said. "I'm going to call the guards. I'm going to lay a complaint against you. You attacked me."

"I could counter with the charge that you tried to *murder* me. You were the one with the pistol. Please, sit down till we have a chance to sort this through."

There was no threat in his tone, but it fairly reeked with self-confidence. "No, really," he went on gently, "you need time to come to yourself. Besides, aren't you a little curious about me? I know I'm curious about you. Do sit down."

Remembering her role, she said tartly, "I know as much about you as I care to know."

"What do you know?"

She knew more than most. She should. She'd followed his career long before he'd become a soldier. It was common knowledge that he'd been blessed with good looks, fortune, and a great title which he'd come into when he was only a boy. He'd been spoiled and pampered almost from the cradle. An army of servants catered to his every whim. The result was inevitable. He'd come to believe that the world revolved around him. He fought duels at the drop of a glove; he flaunted his mistresses. It was said that no woman could resist him if he decided he wanted her. His thoughts went no further than the pleasure of the moment. Even his years as a soldier were the result of a wager. In Spain, briefly, she'd thought she'd met someone special, but that man had been a figment of her imagination. He was unscrupulous and heartless, as she had good reason to know.

She hadn't meant to sit down again, but she found herself doing it all the same. He was too tall, too powerful for her comfort, and without her pistol, she felt defenseless. "You are Marcus Lytton, the Earl of Wrotham," she said. "I know you by reputation."

"Reputation?" He cocked an eyebrow as he seated

himself. "I was not aware that my military exploits were so widely known."

The roguish grin got her dander up, and she couldn't help elaborating. "Your reputation as a rake is what I meant."

"You flatter me."

"Only you would think so."

There was a moment of startled silence, then he said softly, "Touché, again, Miss . . . oh yes, you don't wish to tell me your name. You cannot be suggesting that I have designs on your virtue?"

"It never crossed my mind."

"Didn't it?"

His tone was provocative. She matched it exactly. "You are, are you not, my lord, a *married* man?"

The smile was erased. "What do you know of my wife?" he asked.

She hesitated, shrugged, and said boldly, "Until tonight, I knew only what everyone else knows, that you'd married a Spanish girl when you served with Wellington in Spain."

"And after tonight?"

This time she did not falter. "I know that you hate her enough to kill her."

His eyes burned into hers, then the look was gone and the careless smile was in place. "You have misread the situation. It is my wife who wishes to kill me. She may yet succeed. Oh, don't look so stricken. I believe it happens in the best of families. Divorce is so hard to come by, and for a Catholic girl, the word doesn't exist." His voice turned hard. "So you see, Catalina and I are bound together until death us do part. An intolerable situation."

Her mind was racing off in every direction. There were a million questions she wanted to ask, but she dared not voice a single one. Even now, he was suspicious of her. She could feel it in her bones.

She tried to look amused. "I'm sure, my lord, you are exaggerating."

"Am I? I wonder." His mood changed abruptly. "Enough about me. I am at a disadvantage here. I know nothing about you, and until I know more, I refuse to let you go."

He spoke gaily, as though it were all a great game, but she wasn't taken in by it. She'd seen that darker side of him and knew that the danger wasn't over yet. She intended, if at all possible, to leave this place without his knowing who she was or where to find her.

She moistened her lips. "My lord, I appeal to you as a gentleman to let me go. You see, there is someone waiting for me. If he were to hear of my . . . misadventure, it could prove awkward for me."

There was a strange undercurrent in the silence, as though her words disturbed him in some way. "I see," he said. "And this gentleman, I take it, was someone you met tonight at Mrs. Spencer's house. Did you make a secret assignation?"

Alarm coursed through her veins. "Mrs. Spencer? I know no one by that name."

"Don't you? I could have sworn that I saw you leave her house tonight. What happened? Did you quarrel? Did she throw you out in those rags? I know how jealous women can be. And you are very beautiful. Did you steal one of her lovers? Is that it? Who is waiting for you? Is it Worcester? Berkeley? Whatever they offered, I can do better."

A moment before, she had been trembling in her shoes. Now, a wave of rage flooded through her. Each question was more insulting than the last, and he was doing it on purpose. This time, when she rose to her feet, there was no tremor in her knees. She was Catherine Courtnay and no man spoke to her in those terms. "My business with Mrs. Spencer," she said, "is no concern of yours."

"So, you were there!"

"And if I was?"

There was a moment when she knew she had made that blunder she had tried so hard to avoid. He rose to face her and his eyes glittered brilliantly. Then he reached for her, and hard, muscular arms wrapped around her, dragging her against thighs of iron and a rock-hard chest. She could feel the brass buttons of his coat digging into her. Her arms were trapped at her sides. One hand cupped her neck, then his lips were against her mouth.

She moaned, not with pleasure, but in pain. Her jaw still smarted from the blow he had inflicted. She went rigid, waiting for the kiss to end, and the pain to pass.

He took advantage of her passivity and shifted her more intimately against his body. Catherine gasped, and his tongue swept in to take possession of her mouth. This was nothing like the insulting kiss he had forced on her after their marriage in Spain. He was tasting her, savoring her, with more gentleness than she'd dreamed was in him. A shock of pleasure took her unawares, and for a moment she sagged against him. Then she remembered who he was, what he was, and she kicked out at his shins in a fury of shame. He let her go at once.

Her hand went back, but before she could strike him, he grabbed for her wrist. He was laughing down at her.

"So, you're not one of Amy's friends," he said. "I had to find out."

She struck at him again, but he easily dodged her blow.

"Look, I apologize, all right? If you'd answered my questions in the first place, I would never have put you to the test."

She hated his winsome grin, detested the sparkle in his eyes, and was thoroughly incensed by the laugh lines that creased his cheeks. It was utterly futile to pit her wits against this reckless devil. One way or another, he would discover what he wished to know.

She felt in one coat pocket, then the other, and produced two grubby handkerchiefs, a piece of ribbon, some loose change, and last, but not least, what she was looking for.

"This is my card," she said. "Now we have nothing more to say to each other."

"Miss C. Courtnay," Marcus read, "of Heath House, Hampstead. Now why didn't you save us both a lot of trouble and give me this information when I asked you politely?"

Back straight, she marched to the desk, shoved her

bonnet on her head, picked up her muff, then her pistol, and turned to go.

"You forgot this," he said, holding out her reticule. "There is nothing in it. How strange! Most ladies I know keep their possessions in their reticules and not in their pockets."

She snatched it from him without breaking stride. He stepped in front of her and politely held the door open. "So it's true what they say about red hair," he said, and chuckled. "You really do have a temper."

This taunt was treated with all the disdain it deserved. Head held high, she strode along the corridor. Let him call out the guards and have her arrested for attempted murder. She could argue a case against him. And if he did start digging into her past, he would never find anything to connect her to Catalina.

He coughed at her back, but she ignored it. "I believe," he said diffidently, "you are going the wrong way."

Her steps slowed.

"The way out is this way."

She breathed in slowly, did an about-turn, and sailed right by him. He said no more till they were on the pavement on Whitehall.

"How do you propose to get home to Hampstead?"

As though he were invisible, she raised her hand and flagged a hackney. Marcus held the door for her. "The King's Theater," she told the hackney driver.

"Don't tell me you're an actress," said Marcus, following her inside.

She stared pointedly out the coach window, determined not to be drawn into a conversation. Her participation was unnecessary. He embarked on a flow of chitchat that required no response from her, and which lasted until the hackney pulled up opposite the theater.

He allowed her to pay off the driver and that disappointed her. She would have relished the chance to throw his money back in his face, and his look told her he knew it.

McNally turned at their approach. She allowed

Marcus to help her into the buggy, but the ice in her expression did not thaw. "Home, McNally," she said.

"One moment," Marcus advanced toward McNally. "Miss Courtnay has had a slight accident. No, nothing serious. See that she puts a cold compress on her chin when you get her home. Oh, and if she can be persuaded, get some brandy into her."

"Yes, sir," said McNally. He knew an officer and a gentleman when he saw one, even if he wasn't in uniform, and this one had a familiar look. He glanced over his shoulder at Catherine, but was met with a stony stare.

To Catherine, Marcus said, "I shall call on you within a day or so to see how you go on."

Her features might have been carved from stone. "Drive on, McNally."

McNally looked at Marcus.

Marcus took a step back, surveyed Catherine's frozen profile for a long, considering moment, then he grinned. "Drive on, McNally," he called out.

Only then did McNally click his tongue and bring the reins down on the pony's rump.

Marcus watched the buggy make a turn and traverse the length of the Haymarket, until it turned the corner into Piccadilly. Then his smile faded and a calculating look came into his eyes. He was almost certain that she wasn't Catalina, but there was still a small niggling doubt. For all their differences, the resemblance was uncanny, and he had good reason to believe that his erstwhile wife was in England. When he'd seen Miss Courtnay, he'd made the obvious connection. But when she'd opened her mouth, the cultured accent had thrown him. He'd only wanted to satisfy himself that she wasn't Catalina. But it had infuriated him when she'd tried to shoot him.

He shook his head, remembering his confusion when he'd removed her bonnet and the torrent of fiery-red hair had tumbled around her shoulders. He'd noticed other differences that he hadn't noticed before. Her complexion was fair. There were freckles on her nose. Her features were delicate, refined. And afterward, when she came to herself, she had not possessed a particle of Catalina's sexual allure. That was something about Catalina he remembered very well. She'd seduced him with her unawakened sensuality. And he, fool that he was, had been taken in by it, believing that he had found the love that had always eluded him.

No, Miss Courtnay was no Catalina, though she had made quite an impression on him in her own way. She was remote and cool on the surface, but easily aroused to temper. It made a man wonder if there was passion there too.

He didn't regret the kiss. She'd kicked him, actually kicked him in the shins, and that had never happened to him before. Just thinking about it made him laugh out loud. She amused him, and that too was a first. And she also aroused his curiosity.

There were questions that continued to tease his mind. She still had not told him what she was doing at Amy's house. And there were other things that puzzled him: her panic when he'd first run into her; why she was going alone around London late at night; and most puzzling of all—why she was armed with a pistol. As much as anything, that's what had convinced him that she was Catalina.

Miss C. Courtnay was a puzzle he meant to solve.

His first port of call, he decided, would be Amy. He and Amy went back a long way. She'd once been his mistress, but now they were friends, good friends. If Amy knew anything, she would tell him.

Chapter 3

Marcus remembered the reverie very well. He'd been hiding out in *El Grande*'s mountain retreat, recovering from his wounds, and his mind had wandered to England. He'd dreamed of balls, and beautiful English girls in their pale, transparent gauzes, with fragrant hair and soft skin.

And here he was living the reverie, propping up one of the pillars of Lady Tarrington's magnificent ballroom, and he was bored out of his mind. Nothing had changed in the five years he'd been out of England, fighting the French. The same tedious conversations went on around him; the same beautiful girls hung on his every word; the same tawdry *affaires* flourished among the married set. Only the names and faces had changed. If his hostess had not been his godmother, he would have turned on his heel and made his escape.

Welcome home, Marcus, he thought ruefully, and drained the champagne in his glass.

He remembered that it was on an evening just such as this that he'd had a notion to do something different with his life. His twenty-ninth birthday had loomed on the horizon, and he'd felt as old as Methuselah. He'd seen everything, done everything, and that was a sad state of affairs for a young man who had yet to come into his prime. Everything was too easy. There was nothing to strive for. His financial affairs were managed by the best professional minds money could buy, and his half brother, Penniston, ran the day-to-day operation of the Wrotham estates as well as any steward they could hire. There was no need for him to marry and beget heirs if he chose not to. If anything happened to Marcus, there were two half

brothers who could succeed to the title. Gaming, drinking, and wenching had become his way of life. He'd had
everything that could make a young man happy, only he
wasn't happy, he was restless, and there was no explaining it.

He couldn't remember who had first made the wager.
He remembered there were four of them, and that they
had decamped none too graciously from Lady
Castlereagh's ball. They'd ended up in some high-class
brothel and had just been serviced by the best whores that
money could buy. *The best that money could buy.* That
thought had been running through his mind. He hadn't
wanted the best that money could buy. Just once in his
life, he'd wanted something that couldn't be bought. He'd
voiced the thought aloud. One thing led to another.
Someone mentioned the hard lot of a soldier's life, and
before the night was over, his friends had wagered that if
he could endure a soldier's life for as long as six months,
they would eat their curly-brimmed beavers with the
sauce of his choice.

It was meant as a joke. No one expected him to take
the wager seriously. In fact, the wager had nothing to do
with his decision. The novelty of a soldier's life had suddenly appealed to him, and he had acted on impulse.

It was an impulse he had come to regret many times
during that first year. After a while, he'd simply ceased to
think about it. He was a soldier. He had a job to do. It
became a matter of honor to drive the French out of
Spain. Two months ago, it had culminated at Waterloo,
and after that his country no longer required his services.

He'd come full circle, only now he was five years
older and had acquired a little wisdom. He didn't want to
take up the old life. Surviving when thousands of one's
comrades had fallen could do that to a man. He wasn't a
monk, by any means. His perspective had changed,
though, and so had his tastes.

For no apparent reason, there came to his mind a vision of a red-haired termagant. Amy had been no help to
him there. In fact, she'd had a good laugh at his expense
when he'd described the girl. No respectable ladies ever
attended her parties, she'd told him. He hadn't told her

the girl's name, or pursued the matter, not wishing to cause Miss Courtnay any embarrassment. He'd waited a day, to give her temper time to cool, then he'd gone out to Hampstead to see her.

She'd tried to order him off the premises, but he was as stubborn as she, and eventually she'd thrown up her hands and allowed him to enter. He'd spent a good hour with her, and had learned a great deal just by observation. The house, itself, told its own story. It was in decline, fading away like some aging belle. Money was obviously in short supply. From chatting to her woman as she'd served tea and cakes, he'd learned that Miss Courtnay's Christian name was Catherine, that her father, the good doctor, had served in the Peninsular Campaign, that Catherine had been with him, briefly, in Portugal, and had returned to England when he'd died suddenly in some tragic misadventure.

Catherine's look had challenged him to make something of it, but he was beyond suspecting her of being Catalina by this time. She was too English, too demure, too genuine. His godmother would have called her an aging spinster, but that's not how he thought of her. Her tongue was as tart as a lemon, but her eyes could very easily be induced to simmer like hot coals. Temper. He wondered just what he'd have to do to turn that temper into passion.

There wasn't much point in thinking about it. Their acquaintance would be fleeting. For one thing, they didn't move in the same circles, and for another, she'd made it quite clear with those eloquent eyes of hers that the Earl of Wrotham was definitely not one of her favorite people, which disappointed him, because Miss Catherine Courtnay was quite possibly the most interesting woman he'd met in a long, long time.

He came to himself with a start when a country dance was announced. A footman with a tray of champagne glasses approached. Marcus relinquished his empty glass, and shook his head, indicating he did not want another. From the corner of his eye, he observed his godmother bearing down on him with a vision in pink, a young, gawky girl who looked to be about eighteen or

nineteen. In his younger days, he would have run before
he would have partnered one of the shy young wallflow-
ers. He'd preferred the dashing flirts or the more worldly,
married ladies with complacent husbands. He was mel-
lowing in his old age, decided Marcus, and he turned
with a gracious smile to do his duty.

Some time later, he made his way downstairs to the
all-male sanctuary of the billiard room. He wasn't interested in a game of billiards, but in escaping what passed
for conversation in the ballroom. He could relax with
men, especially those, like himself, who had seen active
service, and there were plenty of those about.

He avoided Captain Gronow, who was regaling his
audience with a thrilling account of the Battle of Waterloo. Out on the terrace, several gentlemen were smoking
cigars. Unlike Gronow, who had entered the war in its
last stages, these men were veterans. They'd served with
Wellington so long that they'd come to think of themselves as professional soldiers. They didn't talk much
about their war experiences.

One of those gentlemen caught sight of Marcus and
waved him over. Freddie Barnes was a year or two older
than Marcus, the kind of man who seemed always cheer-
ful. He never whined, never complained, and Marcus
liked him for it. They had much in common. They had
both joined Wellington at the start of the campaign, and
served as Observing Officers—spies in uniform who rode
deep into enemy territory, to report on the movement of
French troops. They weren't the cloak-and-dagger boys
who mingled with the population, but crack cavalry officers who could ride like the wind. They had to be. More
often than not, they were chased back to their own lines
by French lancers.

It was on one of those missions that Marcus had run
into a French patrol and *El Grande* had rescued him.
Something similar had happened to Freddie. When
Marcus was brought in, Freddie was already there and
had been one of the officers who visited him while
Marcus was recovering from his wounds. He had also
been present at Marcus's marriage to Catalina.

Freddie nodded in Gronow's direction. "To hear him

speak," he said, "anyone would think he had been everywhere at once. All I saw of Waterloo were horses' arses and bloody hedges."

This started a spate of humorous anecdotes, each more farfetched than the last. It served to distract their thoughts from their more harrowing experiences.

During a lull in the conversation, Freddie asked, "What news of your wife, Marcus? Is she in England now, or does she remain in Spain?"

This was a question that Marcus had been parrying all evening. It seemed that everyone was eager to make the acquaintance of Lady Wrotham. The rumors that circulated about his marriage were romantic but not unusual, for many English soldiers had married Spanish girls. In his own case, Marcus said as little as possible. How did a man explain to the world that he'd misplaced his wife? Even his own family had been kept in the dark. If he revealed the truth, he knew what would happen. He'd be deluged with girls all claiming to be Catalina, or there would be scores of people offering to tell him where she could be found—for a price. He chose to find her in his own way.

"Oh, she's still in Spain," he said, "but she'll be joining me shortly," and to cover the vagueness of his reply, he accepted the cigar Peter Farrel offered him, and turned aside to light it.

His delaying tactic worked, and the subject of Catalina was dropped. But he could not dismiss her so easily from his mind. The year before, when Napoleon was exiled on Elba and there was a lull in the fighting, he'd gone to Spain to try and find her. By this time, he was half convinced that something must have happened to her, that she and her brother must have perished in the fighting, else why had there been no word from either of them? He'd returned to the monastery where he'd first met Catalina without much hope of finding anything. To his great surprise, he'd found the monks rebuilding it.

From one of the monks, Juan, Marcus learned that *El Grande* was in fact el Marqués de Vera el Grande, a Spanish nobleman. His great villa on the outskirts of Madrid was a ruin. He and Catalina were the only survivors in their family. The French believed they'd slaughtered them all, and that's where they had made a costly blunder. On hearing of his family's fate, *El Grande* had taken his sister and gone into hiding. Shortly after, he had emerged as the legendary leader of the partisans. Juan had told Marcus something else. *El Grande* had escorted Catalina to England.

Marcus hadn't known what to make of this. By his reckoning, that meant they had arrived in England almost two years ago. He would have expected Catalina to stay with his family in Warwickshire or at least to demand as much money as she could squeeze out of them. He'd even looked forward to meeting up with her again so that he could punish her for what she had done. Since he'd last seen her, he'd spent many pleasurable hours inventing suitable punishments for a scheming adventuress who had forced him into marriage.

Catalina was wiser than he'd given her credit for. Evidently, she had no desire to fall into the hands of a husband who hated her.

From shipping records, he had verified that el Marqués de Vera el Grande and his sister had arrived in England. Since then—nothing. It was as though they had vanished into thin air. Strangely, Catalina hadn't used her married name. What was she up to? When was she going to show her hand?

Then a few weeks after he had arrived back in England, something happened that turned his thoughts in a new, more sinister direction. There had been a vicious attack on him. It suddenly struck him that if he were to die, Catalina would be a very wealthy widow.

Marcus was more determined than ever to find her. There must be a way to lure her into the open.

His mind snapped back to the conversation in progress when he heard a name he recognized. "Lieutenant William Harris?" he said to Freddie. "Wasn't he the young ensign who was with us at *El Grande*'s hideout?"

"That's the one," said Freddie. "A damn shame."

"What is?" asked Marcus.

"To make it through the war, only to be killed in a boating accident." He looked more closely at Marcus.

"Didn't you read about it in *The Journal*? It happened in St. James's Park some nights ago. He and his friends had been drinking."

Marcus had an impression of the monastery in Spain, and a beardless youth who would sit silently on Catalina's writing commode while Freddie and he talked. They'd tried to include Harris in the conversation, but he'd been too shy to say much.

"That leaves two of us," said Marcus, voicing a stray thought.

"What does?" asked Freddie.

Marcus realized he had unwittingly piqued everyone's interest. He said easily, "Of the five officers who were rescued by *El Grande*, only two of us are left. You and I, Freddie."

"What happened to the others?" asked Farrel.

Freddie answered, "Well, first, when we left *El Grande*'s lair and tried to cross the border into Portugal, we ran straight into a detachment of French cavalry. In the skirmish, one of the Riflemen was killed, I forget his name. I didn't see what happened to the other one."

"I forgot about the Riflemen," said Marcus.

"Shortly after, Major Sheppard accidentally shot himself while cleaning his pistol. Tragic business."

"And," said Marcus, "right after that, Captain Brinsley's horse kicked his brains out. It was a freak accident."

Someone said, "And Brinsley, I presume, was with you at *El Grande*'s hideout?"

"He was," said Freddie.

Farrel exhaled a long plume of smoke. "Didn't some footpad take a potshot at you in Hyde Park, Marcus? I thought I heard something to that effect."

Marcus turned to look at Farrel. He was over six feet tall and gave the impression that he was a slow, plodding kind of fellow. Marcus knew that this impression was deceptive. Of all the soldiers who had served with Wellington, Major Peter Farrel was most often mentioned in dispatches.

"That's right," said Marcus. "Damn fool shot my hat clean off my head when I was walking on the bridge over the Serpentine. Naturally, I jumped in after it. It was a damned expensive hat."

After the laughter had died down, Farrel asked, "What about this *El Grande*? Who is he anyway?"

"That," said Marcus, "is el Marqués de Vera el Grande, my brother-in-law."

Freddie Barnes left Lady Tarrington's house in a troubled frame of mind. Though he'd told a small lie, which bothered him, there was more to it than that. He hadn't known about the attack on Marcus. Now that he did know, his mind was sifting through everything, trying to find a connection. Perhaps there was no connection between the accidents to Sheppard, Brinsley, and Harris, as well as the attack on Marcus. But it seemed an odd and frightening series of random events.

As the first heavy drops of rain splashed on his face, he turned up his coat collar and hailed a hackney. His rooms were in St. James's, but the hackney did not stop there. It turned the corner into Piccadilly, and made for Bond Street. Freddie knew that he wasn't expected. They had an understanding that they should meet only by appointment, but he felt that these were exceptional circumstances.

The moment he entered the vestibule, he could smell the sex. He heard a woman's voice, crying out in pleasure, and the guttural sounds of her partner. He was enraged, and at the same time he was sick to his stomach. This was the real reason his lover didn't want him to come to his rooms uninvited. He was a faithless, promiscuous libertine. All he cared about was the money Freddie Barnes supplied to keep him in style. There was one other thing his lover required from him and that was his silence.

He was turning to leave when the door to the bedroom opened, and his lover stood framed with the light behind him. He was dressed in a maroon brocade robe. When he saw Freddie, he closed the door with a snap.

"Freddie," he said in a cajoling way, "I thought it might be you. You shouldn't have come here like this."

"No," said Freddie, and couldn't prevent his bitterness from showing. There was no remorse on his lover's face. He didn't even have the grace to look embarrassed. Freddie said, "Now that you're here, I might as well return this." He held out a key.

His lover came forward to within a pace of him. "Why? Because of the woman? Freddie, Freddie, you know she means nothing to me." He placed a hand on Freddie's shoulder, and squeezed gently. "I was lonely without you. She was there. It's as simple as that."

Though he despised himself, Freddie felt himself relenting. Love did this to a man. It made him weak. And he was a man, a real man, in spite of the scorn his friends would heap upon him if they knew of his secret life. He'd been an Observing Officer. He'd fought hand to hand with his enemies. He'd commanded men in battle. He was a man, but not man enough to finish with a young lover who made a fool of him.

He felt suddenly, desperately weary. "Look," he said, "I met Wrotham tonight. No, I haven't told him anything, not yet, but that's not the point. There's something strange going on. It's probably nothing at all, but I thought you should know. There have been accidents, attacks. I'll explain later. Just be on your guard, all right?"

"I don't understand. You're not making sense." The young man looked over his shoulder at the closed door, then looked back at Freddie. "I'll get rid of the woman. Why don't you go on home and wait for me? I'll be along as soon as I can. Then we can talk."

A bitter retort formed on Freddie's tongue, but he couldn't bring himself to utter it. He hesitated, nodded, and turned to go.

"Freddie?" There was a moment of silence, then his lover said, "Does he know about me?"

Freddie stiffened. "I wouldn't break your confidence without your permission."

Those words were rewarded by a devastatingly sweet smile. "That's what I like about you, Freddie. You are a man of your word. Go along, now. I'll be with you very soon."

Freddie was drooping with weariness when he entered his own rooms. Why hadn't he told his lover to go to the devil? Because then it would be over between them, and he couldn't face that. Had he no pride, no dignity? He'd been thoroughly humiliated. God, what was the matter with him?

He poured himself a glass of brandy and drank it back in two long gulps, then he settled himself in front of the empty grate, brandy bottle in hand, and contemplated his future. He was thirty-five years old. He should get married and raise a family. That would please his mother. He gave a hollow laugh and poured himself another brandy. Sometimes, he wished that he were dead. His eyelids felt heavy and he closed his eyes for a moment.

He dreamed that he was drowning. Seaweed was wrapped around his throat. The pressure tightened horribly. When it came to him, finally, that this was no dream, and that someone was murdering him, it was too late to do more than put up a feeble resistance.

Ransom's Bank was on the east side of Pall Mall, close to Charing Cross. Moments after the doors were opened for business, a hackney pulled up and a young gentleman of fashion descended to the pavement. When he entered the bank, he conferred with Mr. Stevenson, the under-manager, and was soon shown to a windowless room in the basement of the bank, just off one of the strong-rooms. Shortly afterward, a trunk was delivered and the customer was left to examine the contents in private.

It was a small trunk, and though the leather was old, it was well cared for. Brass studs decorated the sides and top. There was an oval brass plate on the lid, engraved with three initials, P.R.L. The young man used his key to open the trunk. This wasn't the first time he had examined the contents. Everything was in order—everything that could propel him into the kind of life he had always dreamed of. One major obstacle stood in his way, and when he removed the obstacle, his patience would finally be rewarded. Three years he had waited, and now he could almost taste success.

His fingers delved into letters and documents and

came up with a white velvet pochette, yellowing with age. It was the sort of thing a lady might carry to a ball if there were no pockets in her gown. He emptied the pochette into his hand, and a bracelet nestled in his palm.

There were five cameos on it, all of ladies' heads, all of them different and carved from different precious stones. The one thing that was uniform was the setting for each cameo. This was of filigreed gold, overlaid with vines and roses. It was an exquisite piece of workmanship, but more the point, it was his passport to a life of ease and wealth.

He replaced the cameo bracelet, then the pochette, and after emptying his pockets, threw several letters into the trunk also. Having locked the trunk, he called for the clerk to take it away.

Moments later, he left the bank. Soon, he promised himself, very soon everything would be in place, and he would remove the one obstacle in the path of his ambitions.

Chapter 4

Catherine could not make up her mind whether her ride on Hampstead Heath was for pleasure or because she enjoyed torturing herself. It was early on Saturday morning during one of the warmest spells they'd had all summer; she was mounted on Vixen, a sweet little goer if she knew anything about horseflesh, and she was constrained to ride sidesaddle and hold her mount to a sedate trot. What she wanted was to throw caution to the winds, toss off her bonnet, loosen her hair, and ride pell-mell for the summit of Parliament Hill, the highest point on the heath.

Should she follow her inclinations, she would become the talk of Hampstead. People would wonder how she came to be such an accomplished rider, and McNally would explode in righteous wrath. This was not how ladies conducted themselves. Already, she was in his black books for her little escapade the night she'd met Marcus.

She looked over her shoulder and nodded at her burly, bad-tempered chaperon. McNally was mounted on Derby, the old pony that pulled her buggy, which explained McNally's foul temper. It was long past time that Derby was put out to pasture, but she couldn't afford to replace him. Vixen was the horse of a neighbor who paid Catherine to board her while he was away.

She turned her head when someone hailed her. Emily Lowrie, a pleasant-faced, dark-haired young woman, detached herself from a group of riders and trotted over. The two women had been friends since Emily had come to live in Hampstead some six years before. Though Emily had recently married, she and Catherine still had a great deal in common.

"Don't forget Thursday evening," Emily called out. "There's to be a special guest of honor."

On the third Thursday of every month, Emily hosted a small gathering of friends at her house on the other side of Hampstead Heath. Catherine enjoyed these informal affairs. Emily's husband was a member of Parliament, just starting out in his career, and so the mix of guests was always interesting. There was usually a guest of honor, someone with thought-provoking views. Many an article had been inspired by a conversation Catherine had engaged in at these parties.

"I wouldn't miss it for the world," she said. "Who is this special guest of honor?"

"The Earl of Wrotham," said Emily with a big smile on her face.

"*Wrotham?*"

Emily was delighted by her response. "That's how I reacted when William told *me*," she said. " '*Wrotham?*' I croaked. 'But the earl is so far above us. William, are you sure he accepted an invitation to one of our little affairs? Perhaps you misunderstood him.' And William replied that the earl had practically invited himself."

"I wasn't aware that William knew Wrotham," said Catherine weakly.

"He didn't, until last week. A mutual acquaintance introduced them. Oh, Catherine, isn't it wonderful? If Wrotham were to take an interest in William's career, there's no saying how far he might go. Wrotham knows all the right people. Oh, don't tell William I said that. You know how he feels about patronage."

And on that jubilant note, Emily trotted off to tell the good news to someone else who had caught her eye.

Wrotham! She'd been so sure, the last time she'd seen him, that she'd finally convinced him she wasn't Catalina. Then why had he invited himself to Emily's little party? Damn the man! Did he never give up?

Her first impulse was to beg off, but on thinking it over, she decided to brazen the thing through. Obviously he was still curious about her. What she must do was satisfy that curiosity so that there wasn't a shadow of a doubt in his mind that she really was who she said she was. Then, he would stop pestering her.

She dressed carefully that evening. As she turned this way and that, studying her reflection in the long cheval mirror, she was quite taken aback by the transformation in her appearance. Mrs. McNally had swept up her hair and fastened it to her crown with a cluster of silk rosebuds. Her skin seemed softer, somehow, with a faint blush to it. And as for what the new high-waisted, low-cut ivory muslin did to her figure . . . she shuddered to think what Aunt Bea would have to say if she were here now.

It wasn't vanity that had made her splurge on a new gown, she told herself. True, she'd been annoyed that first night by the remarks he'd made about the "rags" she was wearing, and something about her being the mother of six children. *Six children!* She spread her hand against her abdomen. *Flat,* she told her reflection. And what difference did it make if he'd summed her up as an aging dowd? All she wanted was to look as different from Catalina as possible, as *English* as possible.

She tried not to think about Aunt Bea when she slipped her new high-heeled satin slippers over the white silk stockings that had cost her ten shillings. Ten shillings for a pair of silk stockings! That shocked her more than the cost of the gown. A gown could be made over and could last for years. She'd be lucky if the silk stockings lasted the night. All this finery just to throw Wrotham off the scent? She must be out of her mind.

She was out of her mind in more ways than one. Everybody would take one look at her and think that she was setting her cap for the earl. Before she could decide whether to change, there was a knock on the door and Mrs. McNally entered.

"It's as good as new," said Mrs. McNally, indicating the newly pressed cloak she carried over one arm. She'd found it when she was cleaning out the attics, in a trunk of old clothes that had once belonged to Catherine's mother. The trunk had been deposited in the attic during

Aunt Bea's regime, and Mrs. McNally had a fair idea why.

From all Mrs. McNally could gather, Beatrice Courtnay had been a relic of a former era, a Puritan who had damned vanity in all its manifestations. There had been no pretty clothes for her nieces, no parties, no dancing or trips to the theater. Religion, hard work, and booklearning had taken their place. She'd had no use for the pretty things Catherine's mother had kept about her. The attics had told an interesting story. When she and McNally had arrived on the scene, they'd found them choked with pictures, mirrors, ornaments, and boxes of "unsuitable books" as well as trunks of old clothes, pretty clothes, such as the green satin cloak she had just pressed.

Without fuss or bother, she and McNally had gradually distributed the pictures, mirrors, and ornaments throughout the house. Catherine had been pleased; the house, she'd said, was more like it was in her mother's day. After that, Mrs. McNally had decided to make over some of the clothes she'd found in the trunk, and Catherine had been happy to wear them.

As she looked at Catherine now, a lump formed in her throat. She was a beautiful, vibrant young woman and it was no thanks to the aunt who had raised her. Beatrice Courtnay had a lot to answer for, and so had Catherine's father. When his wife had died, he'd turned his daughters over to the care of a woman who had no notion of how to be a mother to them. She'd driven off one girl and tried to make the other into a replica of herself. Fortunately, Catherine's character had been formed long before the straitlaced maiden aunt had come into her life. And now that Aunt Bea was gone, Catherine—the real Catherine—had come into her own again.

There was only one thing that would make Mrs. McNally's joy complete. She wanted Catherine to meet the right man, a gentleman who would appreciate Catherine's fine mind and, at the same time, put his foot down and stop her reckless visits to places no lady should even know about.

She held the cloak as Catherine slipped into it, then turned her around and did up the buttons. Taking a step back, she assessed the girl from head to toe. In her broad Scottish brogue she said, "Ah, lass, ye're a bonny sight for these old eyes. Ye sly puss, with never a word to McNally or me. Go on with ye. He's waiting downstairs."

Catherine was still turning this little speech over in her mind as she descended the stairs. Halfway down, she almost lost her footing. It wasn't McNally who was waiting for her at the bottom of the stairs, but Marcus.

"I thought I'd surprise you," he said, grinning up at her. She looked flustered, and that pleased him. He'd only just had time to recover his own balance. When he'd first caught sight of her, he'd been struck speechless. "No sense taking two carriages when I have to pass your door to reach our destination. I met McNally on my way in and I told him not to bother with the buggy. I hope you don't mind?"

As if on cue, McNally entered and stood to one side beaming up at her. From the upstairs landing, Mrs. McNally watched with a bemused smile. Catherine descended the stairs and took a moment to draw on her gloves. For the benefit of anyone who might be eavesdropping, she said coolly, "And does your wife go with us this evening, Lord Wrotham?"

"My wife?"

"Lady Wrotham," Catherine prompted. She glanced meaningfully at McNally, then at Mrs. McNally. "I've been looking forward to meeting her."

"Ah, no. Perhaps next time."

The silence sagged with the weight of disappointed hopes. Satisfied that her servants had taken the point, Catherine sailed out the front door.

As soon as Marcus entered the carriage, he said, "That was a fine piece of horseflesh I saw McNally leading into your stable as I arrived. He tells me you stable it for a neighbor who is visiting America."

"It's hardly a visit. Admiral Collins will be away for a year, if not longer."

"So you have the use of the mare?"

"Why do you ask?"

"I thought we might go riding together sometime."

It wasn't hard to see where this was leading. He must have seen her riding in Spain. Was he testing her, still trying to determine whether or not she was Catalina?

"I do have the use of Vixen," she said, "but I'm afraid I don't much care for riding." She thought of her wild midnight rides across the heath, when there was no one there to see her, and she turned her head away to conceal the laughter in her eyes.

"Then who exercises the mare?"

Did the man never give up? "McNally, mostly, though I do take her out once in a while." Before he could probe further, she said, "You deliberately invited yourself to this party because you knew I'd be there."

"True," said Marcus.

"How did you know the Lowries were my friends?"

"You mentioned them in passing, last time we met. Don't you remember?"

Now that he mentioned it, she did remember, and she cursed herself for her stupidity. Her lashes swept down and she took a moment to compose herself. As far as possible, she should be herself, but she mustn't provoke or challenge him. And most of all, she mustn't let him see how utterly she hated him.

She looked at him steadily. "You're hounding me, my lord. I don't like it. What is it you want from me?"

One brow shot up and he let out a quick laugh. "More than either of us has bargained for, but I'd rather not go into that right now. You puzzle me, Catherine. There are so many questions about you that remain unanswered. I can't get you out of my mind."

"And if I answer your questions, do you promise to leave me alone?"

There was a heartbeat of silence, then he shrugged and folded his arms across his chest. "If that's what you want."

How could he doubt it? She nodded, took a deep breath, and said calmly, "What is it you want to know?"

"Have you ever slept with a man?" He couldn't resist it. He had to try shaking up her composure.

Her head whipped up, and when she saw the grin on his face, she exploded. "You crude oaf! I should have expected something like that from you! Have you no manners?"

He caught her wrist as she reached for the door handle and he yanked her back. "It was a forlorn hope," he told her, laughing.

She shook off his hand. "A forlorn hope? What does that mean?"

He shrugged. "You live alone. You travel without benefit of chaperon in a closed carriage with a gentleman of—so you say—unsavory reputation. In my circles, that usually means the lady is open to, shall we say— suggestion?"

"I, thank God, do not move in your circles. I've never required a chaperon until I met you. I'm not a high-born lady, Lord Wrotham. I'm a decent, respectable girl who works for a living, and the gentlemen who move in *my* circles are decent and respectable too."

He let her go when he was sure she wouldn't throw herself out of the carriage. "I won't apologize for the question," he said. "It makes things simpler between us." He abruptly shifted focus. "You said you work for a living. What kind of work?"

It makes things simpler between us. She gave up trying to puzzle out his odd way of expressing himself. She had more to worry about than that. He enjoyed provoking her, which made her nervous. If he got her dander up, she might betray too much.

She'd already decided that there was no point in hiding the fact that she wrote for *The Journal.* The sooner he realized that she was exactly who she said she was, the sooner he would bow out of her life.

"I write for *The Journal,*" she said, "articles, essays, that kind of thing."

"I don't think I understand."

For what remained of the drive to Emily's house, Catherine explained it to him. He was torn between admiration and shock. "A. W. Euman," he said. "That's very clever. It means 'a woman,' of course. Damn, I've even read some of your articles. I didn't know women thought about such things."

It was the sort of compliment she despised, but she kept her tongue between her teeth. "Thank you," she said.

"But *The Journal*! I'm truly impressed. It must have been difficult to convince the publisher—Melrose Gunn, isn't it?—to take you seriously. No offense, but you are a female."

Catherine said sweetly, "On the contrary, it was Melrose who convinced me to allow my essays to be published. You'll meet him tonight. He's Emily's cousin. That's how we met—at one of Emily's Thursday-night receptions. You do realize, my lord, that I'm telling you this in confidence? No one must know that A. W. Euman is a female." And she wouldn't have told him if she hadn't been desperate.

"Why not?"

"Because no one takes a female seriously."

"Melrose Gunn takes you seriously, doesn't he?"

"Melrose is an exceptional man," she said.

They talked at length about the kind of articles she wrote, and at one point, Marcus asked her: "On the night I met you, is that what you were doing, research for one of your articles?"

"It was," she said.

"That's why you were at Mrs. Spencer's house?"

Amy had written to say that Wrotham had been asking questions and she had denied all knowledge of the lady he had described. "It was a hoax," she said. "Someone, quite deliberately, sent me to the wrong house. It happens sometimes. That's why I carry a pistol."

In mounting confidence, she answered each question he put to her and a few he hadn't thought to ask. She didn't want him returning later when something else occurred to him.

When the carriage pulled up in front of Emily's house, she gave him her most appealing smile. "I've answered all your questions, my lord. I trust you will keep your side of the bargain."

He helped her out, and held her wrist when she would have taken a step away from him. "Our bargain," he said, "was that I wouldn't see you again if you didn't wish it. Before the night is over, I hope to make you change your mind."

He loved the worried look that came into her eyes, and was even more tickled when she bared her teeth at him. "I wouldn't bet on it," she snapped, snatched her wrist back and marched ahead of him toward the front door.

Catherine needn't have worried that anyone would pass judgment on her finery. She was in good company. It seemed everyone had donned their best to meet Wrotham. Some of the ladies were so dressed up she hardly recognized them. Pale white gauzes were very much in evidence, as were white silk stockings at ten shillings a pair, and elaborate coiffures held together with posies of silk flowers. She felt quite ordinary. The gentlemen, meanwhile, were sporting the oddest-looking waistcoats, some striped, some heavily embroidered, and some she couldn't begin to describe. It turned out that Marcus was the most conservatively dressed person there, which annoyed her. She felt as if he'd deliberately set out to make fools of them all.

She felt a surge of relief when Melrose Gunn came forward and swept her away on his arm. Melrose was in his late thirties, a very distinguished looking gentleman with silver threads in his dark hair. He was the most eligible bachelor in her circle, and in many ways, the sum of everything she admired in a man. He respected her intelligence, was interested in the things she was interested in and encouraged her to write about them. Catherine had known him almost as long as she had known Emily. He had asked her to marry him and Catherine had refused— and not only because she wasn't free to marry anyone. The truth was, Melrose was too tame for her, and if he really knew her for what she was, the poor man would take to his heels.

"I see you arrived with Wrotham," he said.

She accepted the glass of punch he got her. "Yes. He brought me here in his own carriage. Wasn't that kind of him?"

Melrose, hearing something odd in her voice, gave her a sharp look, then returned his gaze to the group surrounding Marcus. "I suppose women find him attractive," he said carefully.

"Very." This was no lie. She couldn't understand his appeal, but she knew she wasn't immune to it, in spite of the fact that she neither liked nor respected him. That's what made him so dangerous.

Melrose sipped his punch slowly. At length, he said, "They say he is a womanizer, as his father was before him."

She patted his arm affectionately. "If you want to warn a woman away, Melrose, you're going about it all wrong. Don't tell her that a man is a womanizer. She always thinks *she* will be the one to reform him. What you have to do is remind her that he is a *married* man. That will do the trick every time."

Marcus saw them laughing together from across the room. He was too polished to let his curiosity show, too honest to deny that he felt a stab of annoyance at the gentleman's proprietary air. Before an hour had passed, he'd discovered discreetly from Emily all there was to know about Melrose Gunn and his relationship to Catherine Courtnay. Catherine was her dearest friend, Emily told him, Melrose was her cousin. She had reluctantly accepted that the two would never make a match of it; they'd been friends too long.

As the evening went on, he continued to probe for information about Catherine. What he discovered was that she'd lost her mother when she was twelve; she'd been raised by a killjoy, horror of an aunt; and that her sister had eloped never to be heard of again when Catherine was fourteen years old. He already knew about her father's untimely death in Portugal.

He thought of the other women he knew and tried to image them in Catherine's place—living alone, forced to earn their bread—and he couldn't do it. It surprised him that she had not taken the easy way out and married Melrose Gunn, who clearly would have jumped at the chance to make her his wife.

He wasn't able to say more than a few words to Catherine all evening. As the guest of honor, he was very much the focus of attention. In contrast to his godmother's ball and all its boring, insipid conversations, here religion and politics were argued with relish, even by the ladies. Everyone had an opinion on everything. By the end of the evening, he began to think there was something to be said for boring, insipid conversations after all.

He did not come face-to-face with Melrose Gunn until he and Catherine were leaving. Catherine introduced them. Each man studied the other with carefully concealed dislike, but managed to be polite. Marcus knew that Gunn was staying over at the Lowries', so there was no question about who was taking Catherine home. Marcus thought that was too bad since he would have enjoyed besting the man.

He chuckled when he entered the carriage and took the seat opposite Catherine's. He rapped on the roof and the coach moved off at a sedate pace.

"What's so amusing?" she asked. Her hair was falling down and she began to rearrange it.

"Mmm? Oh, territorial rights. I thought I was above that sort of thing."

"I don't understand."

"No. You wouldn't."

"Why wouldn't I?"

"Because you're a female."

There was an odd silence. Something came and went in his eyes. Catherine stopped fussing with the cluster of flowers in her hair. His breathing was audible. A breath caught in her throat and held.

"What is it about you?" he asked softly.

He'd barely taken his eyes off her all evening. He'd never seen such coloring in a woman. An artist could not have captured that warm halo of hair, the subtle tint of her skin. He'd watched the fluid way she moved, studied the animation on her face, and the way her hands gestured when she was discussing something that interested her. He knew he was drawn to her. He admired her, respected her. She appealed to the chivalrous side of his nature. But here, in the intimacy of the closed carriage, with her flowery perfume filing his nostrils, something moved in him, something dark and primitive that made him want to reach out and take. Only one woman had ever held him enthralled like this. Catalina.

"I must be going out of my mind," he muttered, and reached for her. "No, don't fight me. I'm not going to hurt you. Just be still and let me . . . let me . . ." He drew her to his side of the banquette and lowered his mouth to hers.

Her eyes had been drawn to him all evening, and she'd tried not to be taken in by his careless charm. She'd watched that mobile mouth smile a lot, and the blue in his eyes become vivid when he was amused by something. She'd tried to remain immune, really tried, but he had a way of combing his fingers through a lock of dark hair on his brow, brushing it back, a gesture she remembered from Spain, and something inside her had softened. Now, in the warm cocoon of the darkened coach, she found herself softening even more. She didn't feel like Catherine. She was Catalina again, and he was Marcus, before she'd discovered who he really was.

Her lips yielded beneath the pressure of his, then parted to the gentle persuasion of his tongue. His fingers brushed through her hair, dislodging pins and flowers, and he wrapped thick strands of silk around his hands, binding her to him. Her scent, her taste, her flavor filled him so completely that he wanted to drown in her.

She couldn't think, couldn't breathe. Nothing in her experience had prepared her for this quickening of the senses. There was a roaring in her ears, her heart was thundering against her ribs; her head was spinning. With a helpless moan, she wound her arms around his neck and clung to him.

His hands slipped inside her cloak, kneading her waist, her hips, her thighs. It wasn't enough for him.

He wanted to get closer. The kiss became wetter, hotter. It was too intense. They were going too fast, too soon.

He drew away, and their eyes met and held as they looked at each other in silence. The coach swayed, bringing them closer, and she drew his head down to renew the kiss.

He hauled her across his lap, and his hands raced over her, learning her intimately. She went limp in his arms, allowing him whatever he desired.

He knew what it was to want a woman, but never like this. This wasn't easy; this wasn't pleasure. This was madness. He wanted to take her here, in the coach, and possess her so completely that she would know she belonged only to him. She would always belong to him.

He felt like a man rushing headlong toward the edge of a cliff. This wasn't him, or if it was, he didn't recognize himself. She had never been with a man before. He couldn't take her with all the finesse of a rutting bull. He had to get a hold of himself. He had to slow down and make this right for her.

His fingers curled around her hands and drew them gently from his neck. Her long-lashed eyes blinked up at him. He tried to smile. "Catalina . . ." he began.

In the next instant, she had thrown herself to the other side of the coach as far from him as possible. "I'm not Catalina! I'm not your wife," she cried out. "I'm not."

Marcus pressed a hand to his eyes. "Forgive me. It was a slip of the tongue. Your names are so similar. I meant 'Catherine' of course."

He wasn't sure if he was telling the truth. Somewhere in that fervid embrace, Catalina and Catherine had merged together in his mind. It was an unforgivable slip, one that had never happened to him before, and it left him feeling as awkward as a callow youth caught in the act with his first woman.

Her voice was throbbing with emotion. "You shouldn't have kissed me. I shouldn't have let you." She breathed in a steadying breath. "Oh God! How could I have forgotten you are a married man?"

He wasn't going to go into that right now. He said, "You have nothing to be ashamed of. The guilt is all mine."

Tears were shimmering in her eyes, and he wanted to gather her in his arms and kiss them away. He could well imagine her response if he dared lay a hand on her now. "Bloody hell!" he muttered, and raked a hand through his dark hair, brushing it impatiently from his brow. He stared at her long and hard, fisting and unfisting his hands. He wanted to kiss her again, touch her, finish what he'd started. His body was still heavy with desire, still aching.

Suddenly rising, he reached for the door handle. "We've got some talking to do," he said, "but not here. We'll talk when we get to your house, where there are chaperons."

She cried out when he pushed through the door, and cried out again when he swung himself up on the roof of the carriage. For one harrowing moment, she'd thought he was going to throw himself onto the road. When he slammed the door shut with one foot, she sagged back against the banquette and cupped her burning cheeks with both hands.

He was dangerous, far more dangerous than she remembered. She hadn't even tried to turn him away. She'd been putty in his hands. How could a man do that to a woman? Not just any man. This was *Wrotham*!

She touched a hand to her bruised lips. She was still trembling in the aftermath of that kiss. No man had ever made her feel like this, made her ache with wanting him. She didn't want Wrotham. Wrotham, she feared and hated. But Marcus . . . Oh God, she was so confused.

She heard the crack of a whip, and the coach suddenly shot forward. She made a grab for the window frame to steady herself. Above the thundering of the horses' hooves, the whip cracked again. Outside the coach window, shapes and shadows slipped past, as they headed down the hill to Heath House.

When they came to a halt, the door opened and Marcus helped her alight. He saw that her eyes were smoldering again. If they had been alone, he would have given her something real to smolder about.

He hid his smile as he escorted her to the front door.

Chapter 5

"You want me to do *what*?" In her agitation, Catherine jerked her hand, and droplets of tea spilled down the front of her gown. She was hardly aware of what she was doing when she set down her cup and saucer and began mopping the spilled tea with a handkerchief she'd found in her pocket. Her eyes never left Marcus. She couldn't have heard what she thought she'd heard. It was too bizarre. In fact, everything he'd told her was too bizarre.

At her outburst, Marcus had risen from his chair. He was the one who had left the door open in the interests of propriety. Now he closed it and returned to his seat. They were in Catherine's study. A fire had been lit to take the chill off the air, and both chairs had been pushed close to the grate.

"I want you to play the part of my wife," repeated Marcus.

Catherine was slumped in her chair, looking up at him with eyes rounded with incredulity. Alarm licked through her and she could hardly breathe. He'd told her, only moments before, that he suspected his wife was trying to murder him, and now this. What game was he playing, and how should she respond? Did he or didn't he know that she was Catalina? She had to get a grip on herself; she had to continue with the charade that she wasn't his wife.

"Are you out of your mind?" she demanded. "Do I look like a Spanish girl? Merciful heavens, I don't even know the language."

Marcus patiently listened to the stream of incredulous objections that followed. His problems had nothing to do with her. She didn't know if she believed him. Partisans? *El Grande?* He thought his wife was trying to murder him? It was all so farfetched. She had her own life to lead, thank you very much. It was one of her cardinal rules never to get between a husband and his wife. Was what he proposed even legal? Besides, she had her articles to write. He should be locked up in an insane asylum for even suggesting such a thing. She could never pull it off.

When she paused, he said quietly, "I'll make it worth your while. Five thousand pounds, Catherine." He cast a disparaging glance around the shabby interior. "Don't tell me that you can't use the money, because I know that isn't true. Just hear me out, all right?"

Though her shock was genuine, she had to know more. "Five thousand pounds is quite a sum," she responded noncommittally.

"I thought that would get your interest," said Marcus dryly.

As he spoke, he reached for the bottle of brandy McNally had provided and topped off his glass. He then explained the circumstances surrounding his marriage to Catalina, ending with, "Perhaps she only married me assuming I would be killed in the war, and she would inherit a considerable portion of my fortune. But instead, I survived, which has now put her to the inconvenience of having to finish me off herself. And she may very well accomplish it—if I don't find her first."

When he paused to marshal his thoughts, she said, "But surely you could simply have the marriage annulled? It sounds like a completely trumped-up affair. I would think it wouldn't even be a legal marriage in England."

"Then you'd be wrong," said Marcus. "This was wartime, remember, and in the battle zone. The marriage was witnessed by English officers. Many other British soldiers married Spanish girls in unusual circumstances, and their marriages are considered legal. Why should mine be different?"

"But if the marriage wasn't consummated?"

She asked the questions only because she felt he would expect it of her. In fact, she already knew the answers. When she'd returned to England, she'd done some research and had discovered, to her dismay, that it would take an army of lawyers and judges to untangle the legalities of her Spanish marriage. Even the fact that she'd used a false name wasn't grounds for an annulment. She'd counted on Wrotham to use his money and influence to buy his way out of it.

He said, "How could I prove it? Besides, contrary to what most people think, a marriage is still legal even if it isn't consummated. And getting a marriage annulled for a man in my position is very tricky. The verdict could go either way, and if it went against me, I'd be tied to Catalina for the rest of my life. And I have the succession to consider. At any rate, all of that is irrelevant if she manages to get me murdered first."

"Then what's to be done?"

"A divorce, Catherine. Oh, not an English divorce. These things are more easily arranged in Scotland. I've looked into it, you see. It could be done if Catalina were willing. But she has to be here in person before I can proceed."

Catherine understood at last why Wrotham had not taken any steps to have the marriage annulled immediately after leaving the partisans' base. In Spain, she'd wanted to punish him for what he'd done, for deceiving her, for making her fall in love with a simple cavalry officer when all the time he'd been the Earl of Wrotham. The Earl of Wrotham whom she hated with all her heart. It was because of Wrotham that Amy's life had been destroyed.

She'd wanted to make him suffer, to clip his wings for a while, to make him wonder if and when his Spanish "wife" would turn up on his doorstep. It had never occurred to her that that's what he was waiting for her to do.

Ironically, in punishing him, she had also punished herself. Not that she had any romantic ideas about finding love and marriage with the right man. Quite the opposite. At six-and-twenty, she was well aware that she was considered a confirmed spinster, and that suited her just fine. She had no desire to have her own wings clipped—and that's exactly what would happen if she were married, really married.

Wrotham was her husband, and that gave him enormous power over her, something she hadn't thought of at the time. A man could do almost anything he wanted with a wife. The law gave him that right. He could take her house away from her, or stop her writing, or lock her up in his castle. Wrotham, in particular, would be looking to punish her for what she'd done in Spain.

She studied him, surreptitiously, and understood how Amy had been taken in. A man like him, a womanizer from his schooldays, knew how to charm a woman off her feet. Catherine, too, had been susceptible. He had caught her off guard, of course. She wondered if that's what had happened to Amy.

Just thinking about Amy revived the old hatred. She tried to suppress her feelings, reminding herself that with this man she couldn't afford to give in to hot emotions; she needed all her wits about her. Perhaps he, too, was playing a game, a more sinister game than she.

Before she spoke, she reached for the china teapot, refilled her cup with piping hot tea and took a long swallow. "What makes you think your wife wants you dead?"

Marcus studied her face, and wondered what she had been about to say before she'd taken a swallow of tea. "There was an attack on me in London," he said. "In Hyde Park to be precise. Footpads were lying in wait for me, hiding in the bushes."

"Footpads? What does that have to do with your wife? Attacks in the city are commonplace."

"Random attacks are commonplace. I was deliberately set up. I received a hand-delivered note from a lady, asking me to meet her at the bridge that crosses the Serpentine. It turns out she never wrote the note."

"Perhaps it was just a prank gone wrong, or," she added sweetly, "perhaps it was the lady's husband who had taken you in dislike."

A faint smile touched his mouth. "I never take up with married ladies. Even if I did, gentlemen in my circles settle their quarrels on the field of honor."

"Duels!"

He ignored the scathing tone. "This was an ambush. My attacker or attackers were quite determined to get me. I, on the other hand, didn't even have my pistol with me. I did the only thing I could. I vaulted over the railing of the bridge, swam to the opposite bank, and took cover in the undergrowth."

She shook her head. "But still, what makes you think your wife was behind the attack? You must have other enemies. Why not—well, your heir?"

"Penniston?" He laughed. "The only thing my half brother is interested in is horses and farming. No," he stopped her as she made to interrupt, "I'm not saying Catalina or *El Grande* pulled the trigger, but they could have hired thugs to do their dirty work."

She couldn't defend Catalina and *El Grande* without rousing his suspicions, so she said instead, "Wasn't there anyone there to help you? Hyde Park is usually crowded."

"It was twilight, just before the park closed. After the shooting, people came running, but no one saw anything or anyone."

She said weakly, "I still find it hard to believe that your wife is behind it."

"My wife and her brother. Don't forget *El Grande*. And recently I've discovered some other things that add to my suspicions."

He rose, glass in hand, and began to stroll around the room. When he came to the French windows, he pulled back one velvet curtain and looked out on the heath. It was too dark to see anything, and the room behind him was reflected in the dark pane of glass.

Suddenly turning, he said, "A week ago, a good friend of mine was murdered in his rooms. Colonel Frederick Barnes. Did you hear of it?"

She nodded wordlessly. The report of the murder had been on *The Journal*'s front page.

His eyes smoldered like the hot coals in the grate. "He was one of the witnesses to my marriage to Catalina. There were seven English soldiers in *El Grande*'s mountain hideout when I was there, five cavalry officers including myself and two Riflemen. Now there are only two of us still alive—myself and one of the Riflemen." His fingers tightened around his glass. "The other Rifleman died in battle. The four other officers died in suspicious circumstances, though Freddie is the only one whose death is unquestionably a murder. Are you with me so far?"

"No. What suspicious circumstances?"

"Accidents—or what appeared to be accidents. Accidents without any witnesses."

"I see. Go on."

"Apart from the fact that we were all English soldiers, the only other thing that connects us is that we were at *El Grande*'s base at the same time."

She remembered the English soldiers who had been at the monastery with Marcus, but she remembered them vaguely. She had kept well out of their way on the chance that one of them might have recognized her, or might recognize her again. She would have done the same with Marcus if he had not been so badly wounded when he was brought in.

He was waiting for her to say something. "It might be nothing but coincidence," she said.

"Then again, it might not. Having been attacked once, I'd be a fool not so suspect so many coincidences."

"And you think *El Grande* and Catalina are responsible for—what?—these four, five deaths?"

"Well, he did once threaten to kill my comrades if I didn't marry his sister."

"He threatened—?" She had a vague recollection of *El Grande* threatening something when she'd accused Marcus of trying to rape her, but she didn't remember it as clearly as Marcus. "But you did marry his sister. Surely, if he'd wanted to, he could have killed all your comrades there and then."

"Perhaps it was a warning for the future."

Realizing that nothing she could say was going to change his mind about *El Grande,* she went on to something else.

"What about the Rifleman who is still alive? How has he managed to escape being killed or attacked?"

Marcus took a sip from his glass, then returned to his chair. "I don't know who he is or where to find him. For all I know, he, too, might be dead."

"But you said he was at the guerrilla base when you were. You must know who he is!"

"That's the damnable thing. I never got to know either of the Riflemen. They were enlisted men, and as a rule, enlisted men don't mix with officers. Remember that I wasn't billeted with the others. Because of my wounds, I was given a room to myself, Catalina's room. Just these past few days since Freddie's death, I've tried to discover who these Riflemen were, but there are no records, and the only people who would know are all dead."

She thought about this for a moment, then said cautiously, "I don't see how this fits in with what you've already told me. If your friends were witnesses to your marriage, wouldn't it be better for Catalina if they were alive and could support her story?"

"It seems that way," said Marcus. "There's obviously more here than meets the eye. I haven't figured out Catalina's game yet, but I don't intend to simply wait for her to make the next move."

A thought was revolving in her mind, and she voiced it hesitantly. "I should think *El Grande* would have more enemies than you. What if he is the target? From all I've heard, many private accounts were settled in the *guerrilla*, the partisans' little war. Perhaps someone has a grudge against him."

"Believe me, I am not discounting any possibility."

There was something in the set of his face that made her go cold all over. Her throat was so dry, she had to swallow before she could find her voice.

"You said that you wanted me to play the part of your wife. What could you possibly hope to gain by that?"

His eyes were pinpoints of light when they focused on her. Gradually, they warmed. "What I hope to gain," he said, "is to draw my wife and her brother into the open. I traced them to England. I know they are here, and I'm hoping to find them. When they realize that someone is posturing as Catalina, my long-lost wife, it should completely throw them off course, and draw them out of hiding. It's high time I gained the upper hand. I've been playing it their way for too long. So, will you consider it?

Will you play the part of my wife? Five thousand pounds, Catherine. It's nothing to sneeze at."

She rose to her feet and stared at him in astonishment. "After what you've told me? Are you out of your mind? Or perhaps you think I'm the crazy one? I wouldn't play the part of your wife for all the gold in England! Strange as it may seem, I like being alive. You may take your preposterous proposition, Lord Wrotham, and go to the devil." She marched to the door, opened it, and held it for him.

"That's what I expected you to say," he said.

Which was exactly why she'd said it. If he'd taken her at her word, she would have had to find a way to bring him back.

"Ten thousand pounds," he said softly, "if we apprehend them. That's a tidy sum of money for anyone, Catherine, even for a man in my position."

It was a fortune. She could live in luxury for the rest of her life.

She closed the door and returned to her chair. "I'm not promising anything," she said, "but . . . all right, explain to me how you think this would work. Maybe if I understand it better . . ."

There was a different look about him now. The charm had flown out the window and he was staring at her with barely concealed contempt. What had she said? What had she done? Then a mask came down and the look was gone.

Marcus leaned forward in his chair, his arms resting on his thighs, brandy glass cupped in both hands. "You won't be in any danger Don't you see, the last thing they would want is for anything to happen to you, else Catalina's designs on my fortune would be thwarted, because she would, to all appearances, be dead. There would also no longer be any point in killing me since you would be the one to claim my fortune as my widow. Either way, they lose."

"But *El Grande* and Catalina could prove that I am an impostor!"

"It will never come to that. What Catalina wants is money, and I am prepared to pay handsomely to buy her off." To her raised brows, he elaborated, "The divorce, Catherine. I'm willing to pay whatever she asks for the divorce."

She couldn't conceal her scorn. "Are you saying that to save your own skin, you would pay her off, a murderess? What about your good friend, Freddie Barnes? What about those others, your fellow officers, who were murdered? Won't there be any justice for them?"

He said mildly, "You're a fine one to talk when your sole motivation for even listening to me is money. You're quite a mercenary little . . . witch."

Catherine lifted her brow. "You're not my friend, Lord Wrotham. I don't owe you anything. You're lucky that I'm even hearing you out."

He let out a breath. "You're right, of course. And you're right that I won't let Catalina and *El Grande* off so easily. But once I have them in my power, your part ends. I won't go into how I intend to deal with them afterward."

She said, without much hope of convincing him, "What if you're wrong? What if *El Grande* and Catalina are innocent? What if there's another reason for all those murders—if they really are murders."

"If I'm wrong, I lose nothing. If I'm right, I'll make damn sure that justice is done."

Eyes closed, she leaned her head against the back of her chair. He was on the wrong track or he was playing her along for some sinister purpose of his own. But she couldn't make this decision by herself. Others were involved and she needed to consult them.

Marcus watched her in silence. He didn't know what to make of her. Perhaps it was truer to say that he didn't know what to make of himself. In the coach, she had enthralled him. Now, he felt contemptuous. She was just like every other woman—she could be bought if the price was right. Perhaps he'd been wrong about her. Perhaps she was Melrose Gunn's mistress. The thought irritated him, but not half as much as his body's automatic response to her.

"In addition to the money," he said, "you may keep

the wardrobe and jewels that will be necessary to pass you off as my wife."

She opened her eyes. He was using that tone of voice again, the one that barely masked his contempt. She would ponder that later.

Before she could respond, he went on, "I could hardly expect you to do it because it's the right thing to do, now could I? Besides, you'll earn your money. This may take several months. We'll spend some time in London, just to show you off and spread the word that my wife has arrived from Spain. That should give Catalina and *El Grande* a jolt." His smile showed just how much he enjoyed that particular prospect. "Then we'll retire to Wrotham, where my family resides."

"Wrotham?"

"My estate in Warwickshire. Don't look so alarmed. We won't even embark on any of this until you've learned your part."

"It's just too farfetched," she said. "How can I play Catalina? What about my hair? What about the language? I know only a few words of Spanish."

"We can deal with all that."

"What about my friends? If they see me, they'll recognize me."

"Your friends don't move in my circles. And, in my experience, people see what they expect to see."

Testing him, she went on, "Why me? Why not someone who already has black hair? Why involve me in your affairs?"

"You look like her. That may or may not be important, but it will certainly be more convincing to *them*."

There was a long silence, then she exhaled a slow breath. "I need time to think about it," she said.

"How much time?"

She did a quick calculation in her head. "A week. No, don't try to press me. If you do, the answer will be no."

He gave in gracefully, sensing that she was already halfway persuaded to help him, and he didn't want to tip the scales the wrong way. At the front door, he waved McNally off as he came to assist him with his coat.

"Melrose Gunn," he said casually. "Will he be a problem?"

"Why should he be? I can write my articles anywhere."

"I wasn't thinking of your articles."

"What were you thinking?"

"You seemed rather taken with him." His expression was guileless, blank.

"I am taken with him. He's an intelligent, articulate man who has dedicated his life to improving the lot of others."

"I heard something tonight to the effect that he is courting you?"

"That won't be a problem," she said. "Melrose and I are friends, and that's as far as it goes."

"Mmm," said Marcus, and opened the front door. "Do women find that sort of thing appealing?"

"What sort of thing?" she asked, mystified.

"You know, men like Gunn, intelligent, articulate, dedicated."

Comprehension slowly dawned. "Not all women," she replied, smiling up at him, "but to a woman who appreciates the finer qualities in a man, he is almost irresistible."

Pleased with his scowl, she bade him a civil goodnight, shut the door on him, and returned to her study.

Chapter 6

Her smile soon faded. He had given her a lot to think about. It would have been so much simpler if they had been able to sift through everything together. But that was assuming that Marcus had been open and aboveboard with her. She shrugged, thinking of her own duplicity, which far surpassed his.

Staring into space, she reviewed everything that Marcus had told her. Intuitively she felt he had been telling the truth, that his object really was to draw Catalina into the open so that he could proceed with a Scottish divorce. One option was to simply tell him that she was Catalina. But she was afraid to do that. He was out to punish Catalina, and there was no saying what he might do. No, she wasn't quite ready to go that far yet.

The next thing she did, as she always did after an interview, was make notes. Ten minutes later, she set down her pen, rested her elbows on the flat of her desk and cupped her cheeks with her hands. Major Carruthers would have to be informed of everything Marcus had told her tonight. And *El Grande,* of course. Would he be interested? Would he care? Would it be enough to draw him back to the land of the living? There was only one way to find out. She must write to them both. For a long, long time, she remained as she was, thinking of *El Grande* and the year she'd spent with the partisans.

It had all started in Lisbon, not long after she'd buried her father and was making plans to return to England. That's when Major Carruthers approached her. A crisis had arisen in British Intelligence and he was short of one Sketching Officer to send into the field. These were spies who went behind enemy lines to sketch military targets so that there would be no unpleasant surprises when Wellington deployed his armies. Major Carruthers had seen some of the sketches she'd done of Madrid, before the retreat, and though she'd sketched only for pleasure, he knew she had the talent for this particular mission. And so she was recruited as a British spy.

She'd met *El Grande* on that first mission, when he and his band of guerrillas accompanied her to the target, a bridge that the British wanted to blow up to secure their position. It was the first time she'd changed her appearance to make herself look Spanish, the first time *El Grande* had claimed she was his sister as a ruse to infiltrate French lines. It was a ruse they were to use many times, until fact and fantasy became blurred in everyone's mind.

One mission led to another, and before long it made more sense for her to remain with the partisans. The McNallys were asking too many awkward questions about her strange absences. In the end, she told them she was returning to England as companion to an elderly English lady she'd met in Lisbon. It was the only way she could explain that lost year of her life, the year she'd lived with the partisans.

At first, she'd felt aimless, and hadn't much cared what became of her. She was just getting over the trauma of her father's sudden death and the horrible quarrel with Amy. In time, she'd come to care about the partisans and their struggle against the French. She'd learned their language and shared their hardships.

It wasn't long before she was doing a lot more than sketching military targets. She became a true partisan. Their cause became her cause. She learned to shoot, ride, and fight as well as any of them. It wasn't that she liked war, but she looked back on that time as one of the most rewarding periods of her life. She'd known the kind of freedom few women ever experienced, especially English ladies. Oh, to ride with *El Grande* and the partisans once again, and camp under a canopy of stars, and tell stories around the campfire to pass the time! There had been a darker side to it, the fighting and bloodletting, but that's not what she remembered best. And as far as possible, the men had kept the women out of the worst of it.

By comparison, her life in England was pale and placid, though she supposed she had it better than most. She was her own mistress and came and went as she pleased. Her work at *The Journal* took her into all sorts of places, some of them truly seamy. She still wanted to improve the lot of others, but oh, how she missed that sense of oneness with the partisans.

She lifted her head and kneaded the stiff muscles in her neck, trying to loosen them. A slight movement brought her gaze to one of the bookcases. It looked no different from the other bookcases in the room, but that was deceiving.

Lifting the candle from the desk she crossed to the bookcase. Her hand moved along the wall, feeling for the molding that was loose. When she depressed it, there was a grating sound, and she swung the bookcase away from the wall with the pressure of one hand.

The bookcase didn't conceal a room so much as a large windowless closet. Her father had once kept his specimens and poisons here, and other medical supplies that he'd wished to keep out of reach of small fingers. There were no jars or bottles here now. This was where she kept her Spanish sketches, hidden away from curious eyes.

She absorbed everything in one long look. There wasn't much to see—rows of open shelves and a few artists' portfolios, some old diaries, and an odd assortment of boxes containing papers and documents, and relics of her days with *El Grande*'s band. She grasped one of the portfolios, slipped it under her arm, and carried it to her desk.

There was very little in it. Almost all of her Spanish sketches had gone directly to British Intelligence. The portfolio contained only those sketches that were personal to her, and most of those were portraits of partisans or peasants she'd encountered on her missions. This was the record of her year with the partisans, and she thought of it as a testament to them. There were faces here she would never see again.

She thumbed through the sketches till she found the one she wanted. It was a black-and-white portrait of Marcus. Once again, she was struck with the Irish cast to his looks. He looked like a rogue, but a likable rogue, with no real harm in him. She'd done the sketch from memory, after the "Isabella" episode, when he'd kissed her. But he wasn't a likable rogue. He was beneath contempt.

Captain Marcus Lytton—that's how she'd thought of him then. She'd fallen in love with him, of course, but she'd fallen in love with someone who didn't exist. She could still remember her shock and nausea when she'd discovered that the man she loved was really the Earl of Wrotham. She knew all about Wrotham. He was part of the crowd that her sister, Amy, had taken up with when Aunt Bea had come to live with them. Wrotham loved her, Amy had told her, and she had thought Amy the luckiest girl in the world. Until she'd found her one night in the stable, distraught, bleeding, terrified their aunt would find her. Then Amy had told her that Wrotham had raped her. Not long after, she'd eloped with someone else, and that was that. Later, much later, she'd heard that Amy had become Wrotham's mistress. Perhaps, by ruining Amy, it's what he had intended all along.

At *El Grande*'s headquarters, when she heard that name on the lips of the young ensign and the jest that accompanied it, suggesting that *El Grande*'s sister was ripe for the plucking, she'd been filled with a murderous rage. She'd wanted to punish the earl for what he'd done, not only to Amy, but also to her. He'd been trifling with her—that's all their cozy conversations had meant to him, while all the time she'd been falling in love with him.

She'd punished him for both Amy and herself, and she didn't regret it. She refused to regret it.

She replaced the sketch of Marcus and selected another. This was the face of a young man in profile, darkly handsome, ascetic, passionate. At the time she'd done this portrait of *El Grande*, there had been a price on his head. A thousand French crowns had been a phenomenal sum, but there wasn't a partisan or peasant alive who would have dreamed of betraying him. *El Grande* had inspired a fanatical devotion among his followers.

Now there were no followers, no more battles to fight, and no passion left. He had escorted her to England, and then had withdrawn from the world. She'd expected him to return to Spain, but it was the one place he didn't want to be. He'd told her he was not sure that he would ever go back. She didn't know what would become of him.

Other memories tried to intrude but she pushed them away. She wasn't up to examining them right now. It had been a long night, and her head ached from thinking so much. Unfortunately, she wasn't done yet. She still had those letters to write.

She went through the sketches systematically, but it was just as she remembered. Except for Marcus, there was nothing here of the other English soldiers who had been in the monastery at the same time as he. She'd kept well away from them and wouldn't recognize any of them if she saw them again.

The thought made her wince. She wouldn't be seeing any of them again. They were all gone, all but Marcus and one Rifleman. Oh God, what did it mean?

She closed the portfolio, returned it to its hiding place, then stilled as her eyes came to rest on the box of relics of her year with *El Grande*. These were her partisans' clothes, divided skirts, and a short pelisse that had once belonged to a French soldier. She stood for a long time looking at that box of clothes. Then she laughed softly and began to remove the confining pins from her ruined hair. As the tresses fell to her shoulders, she shook them out and let out a sigh of pure pleasure. A moment later, she began to strip off her muslin dress.

She used no lantern in the stable, but Vixen knew her scent. The mare neighed softly as though she, too, understood the need for stealth. It took only a moment or two to saddle her, and a few minutes after that to lead her to the track that gave onto the heath. Catherine mounted up male fashion, and pulled gently on the reins, restraining the mare. Confident that no one was around to see them, she kneed Vixen to a slow walk and then to a canter. When they came out of the trees, she gave her horse its head.

There was no balking on the mare's part. She knew the way, knew what was expected of her. They had made this ride in all kinds of weathers. In the daylight hours, she was kept to a slow, ladylike trot, unless McNally was riding her. At night, with Catherine, she ran the race of her life.

The mare hurtled down the first incline and leapt over a stream. Her hooves clattered on the pebbles, but she did not falter. Up, up they went, toward the highest point on the heath. The wind came rushing headlong to meet them and Catherine relished the contest. She laughed and looked up at the stars.

Chapter 7

Amy Spencer, formerly Amy Courtnay, kept her expression gracious as she ushered the last of her callers out through her front doors. They were all under the impression that she had an appointment with some eminent gentleman who wished to keep his identity a secret. She had fostered that impression. For a woman in her position, style, beauty, and wit were not enough. She must always appear to be in demand, exclusive, a prize worth capturing—for a price.

As soon as her footman shut the doors on her departing guests, her smile slipped. Today was her birthday, and there wasn't a soul in the world she wanted to share it with. The night before, her box at the theater had swarmed with young nobleman who were eager to kiss the tips of her fingers or bask in the warmth of her smile. This afternoon had been no different. But they didn't care for her as a person. They didn't even know her. She was the rage, and to be seen with her driving in the park, or in a restaurant, or in her box at the theater was regarded as an accomplishment. To receive an invitation to one of her parties was considered an enviable distinction.

That's what she was. A distinction. She couldn't get any higher, not in her world. She wasn't received in polite society, but that didn't stop polite society from beating a path to her door, if they were males. Right this minute, she could have her pick of six titled gentlemen, each of them eager to take her under his protection. Yet, not one of them loved her. What they wanted was the distinction of having Amy Spencer as their mistress. Happily, she was her own mistress, and since she didn't care a straw for any of her suitors either, she was quite content for the moment to live like a nun.

She entered the little parlor at the back of the house where Eliza, her maid-companion, usually went when there was no company in the house. The room was empty. Amy wandered over to the sideboard, poured herself a generous glass of Madeira, and settled herself on one of the stuffed sofas flanking the fireplace.

"Many happy returns, Amy," she said, and took a healthy swallow from her glass.

There were no presents, no letters of congratulation. She never told anybody about her birthdays. Dates always made her feel uneasy, and she'd stopped counting after her twenty-sixth birthday. Twenty-six was an excellent age for a woman, she'd long since decided, and she had made up her mind to halt there for the rest of her life.

You're almost thirty-three years old. How long do you think you can continue like this?

"A damn sight longer than you would imagine, Cat," she told the empty room, but the thought prompted her to lay aside the glass of Madeira.

She couldn't afford to indulge herself as other women did. Her face and figure were her fortune. Youth. It was such a bore, but that's what men wanted in a woman. Every morning, she spent hours at her toilette to achieve the desired effect. With each passing year, it took a little longer to achieve.

The thought soured her. In fact, ever since Cat's unwelcome visit, she'd felt restless and irritable. That her prissy little sister should actually think she ran a brothel in her house! She gave parties, entertained, introduced her "friends" to gentlemen who wanted something different from the prim little misses and wives who made up their social set. What her friends did after they left her house was no business of hers.

She was thirty-three years old. She should be savoring her success. It had been a long hard climb from the day the lover she'd hoped to marry had cast her off without a penny to her name. Many women in her position had ended their days as drabs in St. James's Park, selling themselves for a shilling. By choosing her lovers carefully after that, with an eye to the future, she'd reached the top of her profession.

As for the future, she had no qualms there. She'd learned to be careful with her money. She knew when to be frugal and when to splurge. Her parties never cost her a penny. The morning after, her footman would present her with a tray of envelopes, each stuffed with fifty-pound notes and the card of the giver. She would then write to each gentleman indicating that though a gift was unnecessary, she accepted her benefactor's generosity in the spirit in which it was intended.

Her own money went mostly on clothes, servants' wages, and the upkeep of the house and carriage. Everything had to be up to the mark. To appear shabby was to court disaster. Then people would start to wonder if she were slipping, and if once the rumor got started, they would desert her for the next rising star.

She was thirty-three years old. It was her birthday. Where the hell were her friends?

She laughed mirthlessly. What had got into her? She was her own best friend and had known it for a goodly number of years.

With a touch of defiance, she reached for her glass of Madeira. "A toast to Amy Spencer," she said, and drank deeply.

The door opened and Miss Collyer, her maid-companion, entered. She was a handsome lady approaching forty who had fallen on hard times, and had been in Amy's employ for over a year. Amy felt sorry for her, and at the same time, amused. She was convinced that the poor woman had hopes of snagging herself a rich husband from her mistress's coterie of gentlemen friends. What Miss Collyer had yet to grasp was that the older men got, the younger and prettier the women they chased after.

Miss Collyer said, "Mrs. Bryce is here. Will you see her?"

"Why not?" said Amy. "Julia is my closest friend." Or what passed for a friend in their circles. "No, I won't receive her in the drawing room. This little parlor is more intimate. Show her up."

The young woman who entered a few moments later was dressed in the height of fashion. Amy could not help reflecting, as they kissed cheeks, that her rival was not looking in top form. And that's what Julia was, her rival—or she hoped to be. She had a rented house in Charles Street, and kept a box at the theater. But she had not yet reached that pinnacle of popularity where her parties were attended by men of the highest rank and fashion. Like Amy, she understood the need to appear exclusive and sought after.

After Miss Collyer had left to arrange for tea and biscuits, they talked of mutual acquaintances. Amy sensed there was another reason for Julia's visit, something particular. She seemed distracted and on edge. It was not until the tea and biscuits had been served and they were alone that Julia came to the point.

"Wrotham has quite deserted me," she said with her silvery little laugh. "In fact, I've been displaced."

The laugh grated on Amy's nerves. Lord Melbourne had once complimented Julia on her charming manner of laughing, and she had never forgotten it. "Men were ever fickle," replied Amy.

"So you do know something," said Julia, pouncing on her. She tossed her head in another affected gesture and her dark ringlets bounced. "They are all saying that they met on your doorstep. Who is she, Amy? Who is my rival?"

"I know of no rival, unless . . . could it be that Lady Wrotham has arrived from Spain?"

"Oh no, that's not it. It's rumored that he's set his mistress up in a little house in Hampstead. He never takes her anywhere. Nor does he go anywhere. I've sent round several notes to his house in Cavendish Square. He has not answered any of them. This is so unjust. I turned down Leinster because I was so sure I had Wrotham in my pocket. Now, everybody is laughing at me, saying I counted my chickens before they had hatched."

A peculiar sensation was unfurling in Amy's stomach. "Hampstead?" she said. "And they met on my door-step?"

"You didn't know?"

Amy didn't hear the question. She was remembering Marcus describing Catherine to her, wanting to know who the girl was and why she had come from her house. He had accepted her answers without pressing her, and had led her to believe that he had lost interest. Clever, clever Marcus.

Without a pretense of civility, she interrupted Julia's monologue. "Who told you about the house in Hamp-stead?"

"Bertie Lamb, last night at the theater. He said his coachman had it from Wrotham's coachman."

Amy decided to put a stop to this before it got out of hand, and she knew just how to handle Julia Bryce. "Bertie Lamb is an old woman. He likes nothing better than to cause trouble. I've seen the way he looks at you. It wouldn't surprise me if Bertie wants you for himself. Don't you see, it would suit him very well if you were to cut Wrotham. Then you might turn to him."

The pout vanished, and a speculative look lit up those lovely green eyes. "Bertie? You think he's taken with me?"

"Of course he's taken with you. Isn't every man?"

The silvery laugh rang out. "But Bertie doesn't have a penny to his name."

"Nor manners, nor scruples. You'd be much better off with Wrotham."

"But why hasn't he answered my notes?"

"There could be any number of reasons. Only he can tell you."

Julia looked down and carefully stirred the silver spoon in her cup. When she looked up, the calculating glint was back in her eyes. "You and Wrotham were very close at one time, were you not?"

It was common knowledge, so Amy didn't try to deny it. "I was his mistress once, but that was more than ten years ago. We parted as friends, and we have remained on good terms since then."

"Do you know what I admire about you, Amy? You

don't have a jealous bone in your body. If I were you, I'd want to scratch out the eyes of any woman Wrotham looked at." Julia forgot the silvery laugh and giggled. "Only, it's the other way round, isn't it? It's women who can't take their eyes off him."

"Jealousy," said Amy dryly, "is something women in our position cannot afford. Only wives are allowed to be jealous. Remember that before you begin to spread rumors about Wrotham. You wouldn't want to make an enemy of him."

"No indeed," said Julia.

She did not remain long after that, and when she left she was more like herself—in short, full of herself.

From an upstairs window, Amy watched her enter her carriage, then she went immediately to her escritoire in her bedchamber where she began to compose a letter to Catherine. Her thoughts were chaotic, and she started over several times. She'd just begun on her fifth attempt when a footman brought a large package that had just been delivered to the house. Inside, there was a framed watercolor of Hampstead Heath, with a note attached. *Happy birthday, Amy,* she read. *Love, Cat.*

She stared at that note and watercolor, feeling as though her heart would break. When she had control of herself, she called for her footman and ordered her coach to be brought round. A few minutes later, she sent another footman after him to cancel the order. For this journey, she preferred the anonymity of a hackney coach.

Chapter 8

Catherine watched *El Grande* in silence as he used the tongs to add coal to the fire in her study. Major Carruthers had chosen to sit at the desk, and he was absentmindedly drumming his fingers as he reviewed the facts of the case. They had been talking for more than an hour, going over things in much the same way as she and Marcus had done the week before.

This wasn't the first conference she'd had with Major Carruthers. They'd met earlier in the week in a back room of a ladies' dress shop. But it was the first time she had seen *El Grande* in a long while. She knew that Marcus was fishing at a friend's place in the country for a few days. There were no servants in the house; she had encouraged the McNallys to visit their daughter in Twickenham, and they would not return until the next day.

El Grande caught Catherine's stare and he smiled. "English summers are hard to get used to," he said, pointing to the fire in the grate.

"Autumn has arrived early," she said. He was a year younger than she. But he had a presence that had nothing to do with age. Still, it was not the same presence he'd possessed when he was the leader of the partisans. He'd been everything his legend said he was and more besides. But that was before they'd driven the French from Spain. Now he was only a shade of his former self. It hurt her to see him like this, but what hurt her most was that she didn't know how to help him.

When Major Carruther's fingers stopped drumming, his companions turned to look at him. He was a commanding figure even though he wasn't in uniform. His height was well above six feet, his face was handsome and in spite of his forty-eight years, there was no gray in his crop of thick brown hair.

"Interesting," he said, "very interesting. Did I mention that Wrotham's war record is outstanding? No one in his regiment has anything but good to say about him."

Catherine said, "So you think he is telling the truth?"

"I didn't say that. Appearances can be deceiving. Where was I? Oh yes. Now that I've done a little digging and have more to go on, here's how I see it. Colonel Barnes was murdered. There's no doubt about that. As for the other 'accidents,' frankly, I don't believe they were accidents. I'm with Wrotham on that, and for the same reasons. It's too neat and tidy. There were no witnesses. So where does that leave us? I'll tell you where."

He went on at some length, going over the same ground that she'd gone over with Marcus. He always came back to the same thing: if all these men had been murdered, it was logical to assume that one of the survivors was responsible, either Marcus or the Rifleman.

"But if Wrotham is the murderer," said Catherine, "why would he draw attention to the deaths of these men? It doesn't make sense."

Carruthers replied, "What better way to throw us off the scent should he be the last survivor and people begin to ask questions? But all this is speculation until we know more."

Then without warning, he pounced on her. "And we mustn't forget you, Catherine," he said. "You have a motive for doing away with Wrotham."

Color bloomed in her cheeks. At their last meeting, she'd had to tell Major Carruthers that she was the woman Marcus had married in Spain. She'd told him only that she'd done it out of anger, because Wrotham had been trifling with her, and that she'd assumed he would annul the marriage once the war was over. It had never occurred to her that the major would conclude that her vendetta against Wrotham might be a murderous one.

Then she caught the twinkle in his eye and remembered that Major Carruthers liked nothing better than to shake people up. Relaxing, she said, "I suppose you'll say next that I've involved British Intelligence just to throw you off the scent."

Catherine looked at *El Grande* and found herself responding to his smile. For a fleeting moment she saw the old *El Grande*, the man who had been her friend and mentor.

Carruthers was frowning down at his fingers, which had started to drum again, and he clenched them into a fist. Looking up, he said, "I can't investigate the Rifleman when I don't know who he is. As I've already told you, there shouldn't have been any Riflemen there at the time. They must have been deserters who had the bad luck to run into a French patrol. We may never find out.

"In any event, all we have to go on is Wrotham." His eyes were trained on Catherine. "Whether or not he knows that you are Catalina doesn't matter. We want you to accept his proposition and find out what he's really up to, if anything. Gather as much information as you can. Who does he see? Where does he go? Work your way into his confidence and see what he knows. If he's innocent, well and good. Then we'll know the Rifleman is behind everything. But, for the moment, let's proceed on the assumption that Wrotham is guilty. It's safer that way.

"If he's the killer, remember he has struck many times. It goes without saying that you will take every precaution. You know how to take care of yourself."

"I understand," she said quietly, "and I accept."

As soon as she said the words, she began to feel the blood pumping through her veins. She was on a mission again, and all her senses and faculties were sharpening. She had wished for a little more excitement in her life—but not this much excitement.

Major Carruthers said, "You must never drop your guard. You must always suspect the worst. *Always*. I hear Wrotham is a charming, presentable gentleman. He has a way with woman. Don't let him get too close to you."

"Let me reassure you on that point," she said. "I know what Wrotham is, and I completely despise him."

She flashed a look at *El Grande*, but this time, he did not return her smile. He said, "If you betray your dislike, he may become suspicious."

"I know how to do my job," she said.

"Good girl." Major Carruthers rose to his feet. "Barnes was one of my best Observing Officers. He was also related to the Minister. I'm under great pressure to get to the bottom of this. There are still details to be worked out—your contact and so forth."

"What about Robert? Doesn't he have a part to play?" She and *El Grande* had always worked together.

"Absolutely not, but I'll leave him to tell you why. I know you want some time together. Shall I wait for you, Robert?"

"Thank you, no. I'll find my own way home."

"As you wish."

When Catherine returned to her study after seeing Major Carruthers out, *El Grande* rose from his chair and held out his arms. She walked into them without hesitation.

"Oh, Robert, I . . ." She was too overcome to say more.

"I've missed you too," he said. "You're well? Happy?" He held her at arm's length.

"I'm fine. And you?"

"I don't have the nightmares any more, and Father Mallory says that's progress. But Catalina, why did you agree to take this mission?"

She pulled out of his arms. "Because Major Carruthers is right. This is the perfect opportunity to solve the mystery. No one else could get as close to Wrotham as I can. No one else could play the part of Catalina."

He had a way of fixing his gaze on people that made them question the truth of what they were saying, what they were thinking, what they were feeling. That look always made her squirm.

He said, "You're not still trying to punish Wrotham for what he did to your sister?"

"I don't know why I ever told you about Amy," she said crossly.

"For the same reason that I told you about my family. We are friends."

"That's not the reason. It's because you have a talent for making people tell you their darkest secrets."

"You haven't answered my question."

She let out an exasperated breath, then laughed. "No. It's not for revenge. It's for all the reasons I gave you, and . . ."

"And?" he prompted.

"I don't know if I can put this into words. My life lacks something, but I don't know what. Oh, not a man. In fact, a husband would only spoil things for me, take away my liberty." She shrugged helplessly. "Life, of late, has become too tame. Am I making sense?"

He touched a hand to her cheek. "Poor Catalina. Poor me. The war has changed us. It seems we are both making our souls in our different ways."

She didn't want to pursue that subject because there was something that was bothering her. "Robert, you don't really think Wrotham is the murderer, do you?"

"No. I keep remembering that threat I used to force him to marry you."

"Wrotham mentioned that, too. You threatened to kill all his comrades."

"It seems to me that if he'd wanted his comrades dead, he would have called my bluff."

She shook her head. "You and Wrotham think alike. He thinks you meant what you said and now you are acting on it."

"*Dios!* And why should I do that?"

"That's what he wants to discover."

They both smiled. "I wish," said Catherine, "that we could do this together, just like the old days."

"Carruthers won't allow me to be a part of this. He knows my days as an agent are over."

When she began to protest, he went on quietly, "You know, yourself, my heart wouldn't be in it. I'm not the man I once was. I'm not *El Grande*. I'm a man who doesn't see much point in anything. I wouldn't be a help to you. I'd make mistakes, and that could prove disastrous. Major Carruthers knows that—which is why he won't allow me to be a part of it."

Before she could respond to this, the knocker

sounded on the front door. It took a moment for Catherine to remember that there were no servants to answer it. When she rose, he rose with her.

In his grave way, he said, "We've said everything that needs to be said, haven't we?"

"No, don't go. It's such a long time since we've seen each other. I'll get rid of whoever is at the door, then we'll talk about the old times. All right?"

He was very gracious. He always was. "I'll take a turn in the garden," he said.

Chapter 9

She watched him leave by the French doors, then she hurried to answer the knocker. At first, Catherine didn't recognize the lady who stood on her doorstep. She was dressed in black and a heavy net veil concealed her face. Then the lady pushed past her and entered the house and recognition dawned.

"Amy!"

Catherine wasn't sure what she had hoped for, but almost at once, Amy's harsh reply dashed her hopes. In a low, terse voice she said, "I wish to speak with you in private, Cat."

Amy's eyes darted around the hall, as if to assure herself that they were unobserved, and before Catherine could stop her, she quickly crossed to the study and entered it.

The candles had yet to be lit, but a welcoming pool of light spilled onto the hearth from the fire in the grate, suggesting intimacy. Amy was blind to everything except her purpose in coming here. She took a few steps into the room, threw back her veil, and cut Catherine off in midsentence.

"This is not a social call. I have no wish to be entertained in the parlor. What I have to say to you is best said here in the privacy of your study. I want to talk to you about Wrotham."

The name deflected Catherine from what she was about to say. "What about Wrotham?" she asked cautiously.

Amy made a gesture of impatience. "I wasn't born yesterday, Cat. I know when a man has taken a fancy to a girl, and Wrotham fancies you. He described you to me. I saw his face. How far has it gone? That's what I want to know."

Catherine was frozen to the spot. The thought that was going through her mind was that Amy knew or suspected that she was married to Marcus.

Catherine's silence unleashed a torrent of words in Amy. "You little fool! Don't you know you're playing with fire? He won't marry you. He'll marry a woman from his own class. They always do."

"What are you talking about?" asked Catherine, lost in a maze of misunderstandings. "Marriage with Marcus is the farthest thing from my mind."

The color washed out of Amy's cheeks and she inhaled a shocked breath. "You don't know what you're saying. You're not cut out to be a man's mistress. You don't understand what can happen to a girl when a man grows tired of her. I know what I'm talking about. Do you want to end up like me? Because if you do, you are going in the right direction. One false step, Cat, that's all that is necessary and you can bid farewell to your chance for a home and children." Her face hardened. "Think about it, Cat—no husband, no home, no children. Only a succession of protectors. Is that what you want? Don't be a fool. No man is worth the sacrifice."

As the spate of words continued unchecked, Catherine's bewilderment quickly gave way to comprehension, and at the last, she understood far more than Amy realized she was telling her. Her eyes felt hot and no words formed in her mind to express what she was feeling inside.

"Amy," she said finally, breaking into her sister's harangue, "you are quite mistaken. Wrotham means nothing to me. He saw me coming from your house and mistook me for—for someone he knows. He's curious about me. That's all there is to it."

Amy absorbed her words in silence and some of the fire went out of her. "You don't love him?"

"I hardly know him."

"Don't lie to me, Cat. Not about this."

"I'm not lying."

All the fight seemed to go out of Amy. She turned away, then stiffened again as a gust of wind rattled the French doors. With one swift glare at Catherine, she called out, "Do come in, Marcus. You've been found out. No need to skulk like a thief."

When nothing happened, she reached for the French doors and threw them open. The man who entered was tall and dark but the light made it impossible for her to see his face clearly. Then, as he came closer, she saw that he wasn't Marcus and a little of the tension went out of her. He was young, about Cat's age, and his clothes suggested a country barrister or schoolmaster.

Her eyes lingered on the stranger's face and she thought him the most beautiful man she had ever seen. He wasn't smiling, yet she sensed an inner radiance that seemed to be directed at her personally. His eyes, under a thick fringe of lashes, were almost black. She wondered how much he had heard of her conversation with Catherine, and color swept up her throat and ran into her cheeks.

"You must be Catherine's sister," he said. "Forgive me for not making my presence known before. I didn't mean to eavesdrop."

Catherine caught Amy's look, half questioning, half accusing, and, inspiration failing her, she fell back on the truth—or as much of the truth as would smooth over the awkwardness of being caught alone with a handsome young man and no one to chaperone them.

"Robert is a priest," she said.

Amy stayed for half an hour. She hadn't wanted to stay that long, but Cat had produced a bottle of sherry and a plate of plum cake and insisted on making a celebration of her birthday. She'd been touched, of course, but what she'd really wanted to do was run away and hide. The young priest, Father Robert, made her feel transparent, as though he could see right through her, and it was a feeling she did not like.

She'd hoped for a private word with Cat so that she could question her further about Marcus, but the priest's presence prevented it. Not only that, but he'd also invited himself along on the return drive to town, and there was no rational explanation for refusing him. She didn't understand why she felt uncomfortable in his presence. He hadn't alluded to her conversation with Cat. In fact, he'd said very little. But every now and then, she'd felt his eyes on her.

She allowed her eyes to stray to him now. They were in the hackney she'd hired to convey her to Hampstead, and he was on the opposite banquette. Her own carriage was so distinctive, so dashing with its yellow satin trimmings that she'd feared someone would recognize it and start asking questions about Cat. She didn't care what people said about her. She was immune to gossip. But Cat was different.

He was looking out the window and she seized the opportunity to study him. He was very different from the men who moved in her world. He was young, much younger than she was. His clothes were shabby. Though his accent was flawless, she could tell he wasn't a Londoner. She put him down as Irish. He was a priest. He was unworldly, innocent, chaste, and all the things that she could never be again. She didn't know why her throat was so scratchy, then he looked at her and she did know.

"I'm not ashamed of what I am," she said.

"What are you, Amy?" he asked softly.

Her dark eyes blazed at him. "You know what I am. You were listening on the terrace when I spoke to Cat. I think you knew what I was before I opened my mouth. I think Cat has told you all about me. What are you, her Father Confessor?"

"Why are you so angry?"

"I hate people who judge me. I don't need a Father Confessor."

He let out an odd little laugh. "Believe me, I'm the last person who should judge anyone."

His words sounded sincere, and she couldn't help asking what he meant.

He shrugged. "People have strange ideas about priests. They think we are saints, but we're not. We are flesh-and-blood men, and subject to the same temptations as other men. I was a priest once, a long time ago. Catherine misled you there. I'm not a priest now. I discovered that I didn't have the vocation for it. Fortunately, I had never taken my vows. I was a postulant." He spread his hands. "Now, I'm not even a postulant. I'm a lay brother and I live with the monks at Marston Abbey."

There was a prolonged silence as Amy considered his words. Finally, she said, "How does Catherine know you?"

"We are a Benedictine order, and the lay brothers are allowed to do good works in the community. Catherine supports these good works. She gives money, donates clothes, and gives shelter from time to time when some destitute person has nowhere to go."

Amy looked out the window. "That sounds like Catherine," she said.

He laughed. "We're always looking for benefactors." When she was silent, he said in a more serious vein, "There's so much suffering in the world, so much that needs to be done. I could make it my life's work and hardly make an impression."

She gazed at him with cold eyes. "Leave me alone, Brother Robert. Find yourself another benefactor. I have nothing left to give."

"I wasn't talking about money."

"Neither was I."

It was too late to turn back the clock. Amy rubbed her hands along her arms and repeated the litany as she paced back and forth before her bed. *It was too late to turn back the clock.*

She stopped pacing. She wasn't sure whether it was that brief interview with Cat or the carriage ride with the priest that had set her back on her heels. Probably a combination of both. Add to that a strange, intermittent restlessness that had plagued her for the last year, and she was a prime candidate for going into a decline. Why was she so miserable? She had everything she wanted.

Catching sight of her reflection in the looking glass, she turned away so that she wouldn't be forced to look at herself. She knew she was beautiful. That's how all her troubles had started.

Cat thought she was little better than a common prostitute, and perhaps she was right, but that's not how she saw herself. She'd had four or five protectors in her time, and a series of lovers, and there was nothing common about any of them, except perhaps for the first.

It had all started with Ralph. She'd eloped, thinking he was going to marry her. It's what he'd promised to do. But he hadn't married her. He'd cast her out. They weren't all like Ralph. Marcus had been kind, and he'd never lied to her. And Clive . . . she'd almost fallen in love with Clive.

Major Clive Barron had set her up in Lisbon where the British Army languished, waiting for money and supplies to go on with the war. She'd had her own little house. Everything was idyllic until the day her father saw and recognized her as she was alighting from her carriage. They'd fought terribly. Clive had only been defending her when he'd pushed her father out of the way. He hadn't even known that it was her father. Then tragedy had struck. Her father had fallen heavily and hit his head on the pavement. He'd tried to rise, staggered, and fallen on his face, never to rise again.

She'd had to face Cat, whom she hadn't seen in years, with the news of their father's death, and what Cat had said to her had scourged her worse than any lash. There could never be anything between Cat and her after that.

God, how had it all gone wrong? All she had ever wanted as a young girl was to be loved. Then she'd met Ralph and she'd thought herself the luckiest girl in the world. She'd had a rude awakening, a savage awakening. She'd given up everything for him, and he'd cast her off without a penny. She wouldn't make the same mistake twice. Her life's work was to look after Amy Courtnay.

She wasn't going to let Cat or some unworldly priest deflect her from her course.

It was too late to turn back the clock.

After removing her robe, she blew out the candle and climbed into bed. The oblivion of sleep eluded her. Restless, she turned on her side.

Chapter 10

A week after she agreed to play the part of Marcus's wife, Catherine found herself in a rented hunting lodge near Stamford in the wilds of Leicestershire. It was only now that she realized she had not really thought out all the implications of what she had agreed to do.

She was supposed to be preparing for the part she must play. Marcus wanted her to learn Spanish, or enough of the language to convince everyone that she was indeed Catalina. There were also riding lessons and pistol practice for the same reason. It wasn't easy pretending to be inept when she was, in fact, accomplished in all the things he wanted her to learn.

There was one last thing she was dreading—she had not yet dyed her hair black. So far, she was sure Marcus was convinced that she was Catherine. But the final test would come when she altered her appearance, before they set off for London. She was walking a very fine line: she had to convince the world she was Catalina, and at the same time convince Marcus of the opposite.

"Me llamo Catalina Lytton," said Catherine in her cultured English accent.

Catherine's tutor, Señor Matales, repeated her words back to her several times, trying to improve her intonation. He was under the impression, which was fairly close to the truth, that Catherine was an actress who was trying to perfect her latest role, with her husband's help, far from the distractions of London.

The servants, who had come with the lodge, had been told what Señor Matales had been told, that Mr. and Mrs. Lytton were theater people and would be spending no more than a week or two in their rented lodge. Once she and Marcus left here, they would never see any of them again.

Marcus's family believed that he had gone to Spain to fetch his bride. Her own absence was more difficult to explain. What she'd finally hit upon was the same fictitious widow whose companion she'd once claimed to be to explain the year she had spent with the partisans. Mrs. Wallace, she'd told the McNallys and all her friends, had invited her on an extended tour of the Continent, now that there was peace in Europe, and since all expenses were to be paid by the widow, she had leapt at the offer.

"*Me llamo Catalina Lytton,*" intoned the tutor encouragingly.

"*Me llamo Catalina Lytton,*" repeated Catherine, mimicking his intonation, but not too perfectly. Though she spoke Spanish fluently, she didn't want anyone to know it.

"*Buenas noches, mi esposo,*" said Señor Matales.

"*Buenas noches, mi esposo,*" repeated Catherine back to him.

There was something else she hadn't taken into her calculations. Marcus was supposed to be her husband. From the start, she made sure that she had her own bedchamber and Marcus never entered it uninvited. But she couldn't keep him at arm's length when others were present. Marcus insisted that they behave like a happily married couple. Consequently, he touched her a lot, stole kisses, teased her unmercifully. He had a playful side to him as she should have remembered from the Isabella incident in Spain. That very morning, in the breakfast room, he had pulled her onto his lap and kissed her just as the maid entered with a fresh pot of tea. Catherine had wanted to hit him, and the twinkle in his eyes had told her he knew it. She couldn't hit him with the maid there, and after a while, she hadn't wanted to. She touched her fingers to her lips, remembering that kiss.

At that moment, Marcus appeared in the doorway and he paused for a moment to study Catherine before she noticed him. He'd found himself studying her now and again during the last week, and had discovered, to his chagrin, that she was more similar to his wife than he'd bargained for.

Catherine shied away from him at every turn, tried to keep him at arm's length. It aroused the hunter in him. Only Catalina had ever evoked that primitive side of his nature. And now Cat.

But Catherine was different from Catalina in other ways. Her intelligence, the scope of her interests, her wry wit were uniquely hers. She amused him, and that was the last thing he could have said about Catalina. Even Catherine's cool, intimidating stares amused him. She might not know it yet, but she wanted him. Beneath that cool exterior, he sensed a reckless, adventurous side to her, and he wanted to be the one to offer her that adventure.

Since he was a married man and she didn't want to be married, the only solution was to take her as his mistress. He'd already established there was a mercenary side to her and he was willing to pay handsomely for the privilege.

But first he would give her time to become accustomed to his touches, his kisses, what he wanted from her. When he felt his body harden in anticipation, he strode into the room.

"Buenos días, mi esposa."

Marcus's voice brought Catherine's head whipping round. He was dressed in skintight doeskin breeches, black topboots, and a gray riding jacket, and seemed quite unconscious of the elegant impression he gave. As she continued to stare, a small smile touched his lips.

Recalled to her senses by that smile, she responded tartly, *"Buenos días, mi esposo."*

"It's time for your riding lesson," he said.

She grimaced, and after making her excuses to her tutor, she followed Marcus out of the room.

The last thing she needed was riding lessons, but this was something else she couldn't tell Marcus, for how could she explain? The only horses her family had owned were placid ponies to pull her father's one-horse buggy. A country doctor could not afford a stable of horses, and Marcus would know it. He also knew that she had been boarding Vixen for only a few months.

She'd learned to ride in Spain. *El Grande* had taught her how, along with her instinct for self-preservation. Anyone could learn to ride if it was a case of life or death, and it had been just that, quite literally, on more occasions than she cared to remember. Right this minute, she longed for a good gallop . . . but that was impossible with Marcus.

As the groom led out Daisy, the horse Marcus had chosen for her, Catherine began to act her part. She'd done a lot of playacting since they'd arrived at the lodge. It was becoming second nature to her now. In a voice that only he could hear, a plaintive voice, she said, "Is this really necessary? You know you'll never make me an accomplished rider in the short time we'll be here."

"I'm aware of that. All I'm hoping for is that you'll learn to handle your mount better, improve your seat, and so on."

She became indignant. "I know how to ride! Ask McNally. Ask Emily Lowrie. I've even been out on Vixen."

"Poor Vixen," said Marcus, and laughed. "I suppose you think you're a crack shot too?"

He was referring to the time he had set up a target and asked her to shoot at it. More playacting on her part. She'd loaded the pistol with the precision her father had taught her, but she'd been very careful to aim wide of the mark. Marcus had hooted with laughter.

"I do know how to shoot," she said now. "You made me nervous. That's all it was."

"Oh, I'm not finding fault," he said. "If you'd been a crack shot, you might have killed me the night we met. If you'd been Catalina, you wouldn't have missed."

"Catalina, Catalina, always Catalina. Is there anything this paragon of a woman can't do?"

Evidently her words had startled him. "What?"

"It sounds to me as though you are still in love with her."

His face darkened. "Don't be absurd. I was never in love with her. Catalina Cordes is a devious, scheming bitch who deserves everything she is going to get. Now, would you mind if we went on with the riding lesson?"

She smiled to mask her contempt. So he *had* been trifling with poor Catalina. No, she didn't regret her Spanish marriage, not one whit, and he could roast in hell
before she would help him out of it.

With hands on her waist, he lifted her into the saddle. "No, don't clutch at the reins," he scolded her. He
demonstrated, not for the first time, the correct hold so
that she would not ruin her mount's mouth. "Relax," he
told her. "Daisy is a docile as a lamb."

She didn't want to overdo it, so she followed his in-
structions but managed to look uncomfortable.

"Where are we going?" she asked.

"I thought we'd ride to the folly," he said.

"The folly?"

"You remember the little house that overlooks the
valley?"

"Oh, that folly." It wasn't a house so much as a shelter for anyone caught by a sudden storm. It also had the
best view for miles around.

"We shall take it at a slow canter," he said.

She wondered what he would say if she told him
she'd outrun countless French cavalry patrols in the hills
of Spain. "I'll try to keep up," she murmured.

It was a slow, boring ride and Catherine wasn't sorry
when they reached the folly. She was feeling distinctly uneasy with the way Marcus was looking at her, the way he
touched her, making her hold the reins just so, or sit
straighter in the saddle. There were no servants to see
them now.

What had she expected? He was a rake and she was
a woman. Did he think she would be the next woman in
his bed? The gall of the man! It was no more, no less than
she expected.

"What is it, Catherine? What are you thinking?" He
had dismounted and was tethering his horse to the folly's
rail.

The look in his eyes reminded her to be careful. He
was uncanny at reading her mind, and that made him
doubly dangerous. "I'm worried about meeting your family. I guess I'd be a fool not to be."

He was standing beside her mount, eyes narrowed as

he stared up at her. "Put your hands on my shoulders," he said.

When she obeyed, he lifted her down from the saddle. He didn't let go, and her heart began to race. His body was brushing against hers and his eyes were on her mouth.

As his head descended, she quickly gasped out, "Your family, Marcus ... How do they feel about the fact that you married a Spanish girl?" She pulled out of his arms. "Tell me more about them so I'll know better what to expect."

There was a faint smile on his face as he tethered her mount. "Is is really the thought of my family that put that look on your face?"

"What do you mean?"

"I think I unnerve you," he said, and grinned.

In her primmest voice, she said, "Though it may be difficult for you to understand, I'm not really your wife. We are playacting, Marcus." She raised her voice. "*Playacting*. If you once overstep the line, I promise you I'm going straight home to Hampstead. Do you understand?"

"Quite," he said, but he was still grinning.

She swung away from him and pretended an interest in the view. "I'm nervous about having to mix with the aristocracy," she said, "not to mention playing the part of a Spanish girl."

He came up behind her and stretched one hand around her shoulders to rest on the upright post, boxing her in. "My stepmother is not from the aristocracy. She was a tailor's daughter. She isn't received in polite society. I thought everyone knew."

"Not received?" she asked, astonished.

"I take it you don't know the story of my disreputable family?"

"No." What she knew was the story of his disreputable self.

"I hardly remember my father," he said. "He died when I was just a boy. From all accounts, I didn't miss much. Even when he was married to my mother, he was an inveterate adulterer and seducer of young women. When my mother died giving me birth, he lost all discretion, all decency. He caught sight of Helen Shore, my stepmother, in a London street. She was eighteen and he was close to forty. He was completely taken with her. She refused to have anything to do with him, but that didn't stop my father. He simply abducted her and carried her off to his castle in Warwickshire."

"What a charming man!" said Catherine acidly, thinking, *Like father, like son.*

Marcus smiled faintly. "He wasn't the first nobleman to consider himself above the law. This all happened in the last century, in 1785 to be precise. Things are different now. Catherine, don't look at me like that. I have never yet abducted a young woman. This is my father and stepmother I'm telling you about. I assure you, I am nothing like my father."

Her tone was dry. "Perhaps you should start comparing yourself to someone else."

"Who, for instance? Melrose Gunn?"

She frowned at him. "Marcus, just tell me what happened when your father abducted your stepmother."

The heat in his eyes gradually cooled. "They were married in the chapel at Wrotham. In time, she bore him two sons and a daughter."

He paused, then said, "This new marriage did not improve my father's character. He continued to be as unfaithful as ever, and died in a duel over another man's wife."

"Your childhood must have been quite unhappy."

"Not at all. My father's saving grace as a parent was that he never was there. And so when he died, I hardly missed him."

Catherine felt a surge of pity for Marcus. When her mother died, it seemed as if her world had ended. "Why isn't your stepmother received in polite society?"

His profile was to her and he seemed absorbed in the scenery. Below them, the valley with the river running through it was spread out and the trees were ablaze with color. He turned his head to look at her. "People didn't want to believe he had married her, a tailor's daughter. They preferred to believe she was his mistress. As a result, when his friends came calling, their wives stayed at home."

"But that's cruel."

"Yes, isn't it? I was too young at the time to know what was going on."

"But your father *did* marry her?"

"Oh yes. Helen had an excellent witness in my father's chaplain, and the marriage was entered in the chapel register."

"Then how could anyone doubt their marriage?"

"There was a bracelet, the Wrotham bridal bracelet, a family heirloom that has passed to each earl's bride in turn. The tradition began with the first earl. My mother wore it, for instance, but my father never gave it to his new bride, and no one knows what became of it."

There was a long silence as she digested his words. Amusement kindled in his eyes. "What?" he said. "No more questions?"

She shot him a sharp look. "I need to know these things if I'm pretending to be your wife. Now what about your half brothers and sister. You haven't told me about them."

"There's no point in going into that. You'll meet them all soon enough. In the last six years, remember, I have hardly been at home. I've been off fighting a war. We're almost like strangers. Now don't worry, Cat. You'll have no problem handling my family. You can handle anything."

He'd taken to calling her "Cat" and she found it disturbing. Only Amy had ever called her that. It was too cozy, too intimate for her liking, but she hadn't voiced her objections, knowing he would disregard them anyway.

"Not I, Marcus. *Catalina*. I hope I can live up to your expectations."

"You and Catalina are not so different."

This wasn't what she wanted to hear. "Oh, come now," she scoffed.

She didn't resist when he cupped his hands on her shoulders. She was sure he suspected nothing, but alarm rippled through her all the same. She couldn't afford to make a wrong move.

"Your looks are deceiving," he said. "On the surface, you look like a very proper lady. No one would guess that you are A. W. Euman, *The Journal*'s most respected commentator, or that you go around town with a pistol concealed in your muff. Catalina's looks were deceiving too. No one would have suspected that she was a partisan and could fight as well as any man."

As casually as she could manage, Catherine eased out of his grasp. She didn't know what alarmed her more, the admiration in his eyes or the way he was putting two and two together without being aware of how close he had come to hitting the mark.

She managed a light laugh. "If I'm to pass myself off as Catalina, I'd better get back on Daisy and practice some more." She turned away and made for the tethered horses. Marcus followed her. "I've been thinking about this, Marcus, and I wonder if we're going about it the right way. I'll never learn to ride as well as a Spanish partisan. Couldn't we come up with a good reason why I should stay away from horses?" She wasn't speaking out of nervousness, but because she wanted to convince him that she and Catalina were nothing alike.

"What reason?"

"I'm sure if we put our heads together we can come up with something. As for the language, I've been thinking about that too. I'm not going to say a word in Spanish if I can help it. I shall tell everyone that I was raised by an English governess and that's why my English is so fluent and my accent so polished."

"Catalina's English was very sketchy."

"Well, no one will know that, will they? Marcus, if you don't think I can pull this off, perhaps we should forget the whole idea?"

He almost smiled when he saw the hopeful look in her eyes. Forget the whole idea? Not if he had anything to say about it. He was no longer thinking only of bringing *El Grande* and Catalina to justice. He was thinking of having Catherine under his roof for the next few months. It was a tantalizing thought.

With hands on her waist, he hoisted her into the saddle. "I have every confidence that you can pull this off," he said. "I don't know why you're worrying. You're a born actress."

Her eyes slid away from his. "You may be right," was all she could find to say.

Later that night, Catherine completed her notes, then used the pounce pot liberally to dry the ink. Though these notes were meant for Major Carruthers, at this stage she didn't need to hide them. Anyone reading them would take them for the pages of a lady's diary. Tomorrow, sometime during the day, she would leave them, as though by accident, in the conservatory. By the next morning they would be gone. And if she ever needed help, all she had to do was include their password in her notes. In an emergency, she could go to Crewe, one of the gardeners who'd been put into place even before she and Marcus had arrived.

So far, everything had gone off without a hitch but the real test would come when she darkened her hair. There must be a way of throwing Marcus off the scent. She stared into space—thinking, planning, plotting.

Catherine gazed at her reflection in the looking glass in horrified fascination. Catalina gazed back at her. Her hair was dark, though not as dark as she'd made it in Spain. Her ploy would never work! Marcus would take one look at her—and he would know. He'd already knocked on the door, wanting to come in and see her handiwork. She dared not unlock that door and let him see her like this.

"Catherine?"

She had to unlock the door. She had to go through with it. What else could she do? She picked up the basin of hair dye and began to slop the contents on covers, chairs, even on her own garments. It was all part of her plan—and it now seemed hopelessly inadequate.

"Catherine, let me in."

She finished by dipping her hands in the basin and wiping them on a towel. The third time he called her name she took a deep breath, ran her fingers through her mane of rapidly drying hair, and went to unlock the door.

The smile on his face froze when he saw her. For one, heart-stopping moment, their eyes locked. Then Catherine's instinct took over.

"I could kill you for this!" she cried, and flinging away from him, she stalked to the mirror. "Just look at me!" she wailed. "I could pass for one of the witches in Shakespeare's *Macbeth*. This isn't me! I never knew, never guessed . . . I was a pretty girl once. Now look at me! Oh God, what have I done?"

Marcus had recovered his wits. There had been a moment of electrifying recognition, but it was fleeting. Catherine was right. The dark hair was not flattering.

"A witch?" he said. "I wouldn't go that far." It was then that he saw the state of her room, and he began to laugh. "Cat, what the devil have you been up to? This place looks like a slaughterhouse."

She scowled at him. "Oh, it's easy for you to laugh! That horrid stuff drips everywhere. I should have dyed my hair while I was bathing, not at the washstand. Oh Marcus, this is never going to work. I don't look like a Spanish girl. All I've done is turn myself into an ugly English girl."

"It's not as bad as that."

She said with a shade of incredulity, pointing at her reflection, "Is this what your wife looked like?"

Hand on chin, the other hand cupping his elbow, Marcus studied her.

She could hardly breathe. "Well?"

He shook his head. "When I try to think of Catalina now, I can't see her face clearly. All I can see is your face."

"That's hardly flattering!"

"But I do remember that she had a mole right here." He touched the corner of her mouth.

"A mole?" There had been no mole. Was he testing her?

"Then again, perhaps not. I just can't remember."

She turned to face him. "It would seem that your wife didn't make much of an impression on you." She didn't know why she was so angry. "Has *any* woman ever made an impression on you, Marcus?"

He smiled wickedly. "You have, Cat." He took her in his arms. She slipped her hands inside his coat and spread them wide against his chest.

"What the devil!" He dropped his arms and took a step back. "Your dressing gown is soaking wet!" He looked at the stains on his hands.

Catherine gasped. "There's dye on your shirtfront, and on your coat. No, don't touch it. This stuff spreads so easily." She dived for a towel and began to mop at the stains her hands had made.

"For God's sake, Cat! You're only making it worse!" He quickly retreated to the door.

She was standing there with that unruly mop of hair sticking out in every direction. "You'll have to do something with that hair," he said. "Oil it, I don't know. Something. Don't forget, we have an early start tomorrow."

When the door closed behind him, Catherine heaved a sigh and collapsed against the bed.

Chapter 11

The following morning, Marcus and Catherine started out for London. They left as Mr. and Mrs. Lytton and arrived at Marcus's house in Cavendish Square as the Earl and Countess of Wrotham. This would be Catherine's debut into Marcus's social world and her first real test as Marcus's wife before he introduced her to his family in Warwickshire.

Their first social engagement was a small dinner party at his godmother's house in St. James's Square. Lady Tarrington's idea of a small dinner party was thirty people or so.

"Don't be nervous," Marcus said. "You can hold your own anywhere, Cat."

He helped her into the carriage then climbed in after her.

"I can't help being nervous," Catherine replied. "I have friends in London. What if someone recognizes me?"

"Who, for instance?"

She was thinking of her sister. "My friend, Emily, and her husband, or Melrose Gunn."

"They wouldn't be at a party like this. If they happen to see you at the theater or some other public place, it will be from a distance. They will see what they expect to see—my wife." Misunderstanding her silence, he went on, "We've gone over it all already. The best way to spread the news that my wife has arrived from Spain is to show you off. That ought to give *El Grande* and Catalina something to think about. After that, we shall retire to Wrotham."

Marcus believed, or said that he believed, that it

would be much easier to control the situation at Wrotham where anyone or anything out of the ordinary would be instantly obvious. He wasn't going to leave everything up to Catalina and *El Grande*. He was going to make them come to him.

She said, "I understand all that. But it's still nerve-wracking to pretend to be Catalina. What if people see through my disguise? I have blue eyes. Did you ever think of that?"

"You worry too much. Catalina's eyes were blue. As for pretending to be Catalina, there are times when even I could believe that you really are my wife, and I *know* you are an impostor."

"Truly?" She smiled into his eyes.

"Truly." He grinned. "Except when you open your mouth. Your Spanish leaves much to be desired, as I'm sure you already know."

She pretended annoyance at his flippant tone. "I speak Spanish as well as you. Better in fact."

"Yes, but that's not saying much, is it?"

As it turned out, it wasn't as much of an ordeal as she had feared. Marcus hardly left her side, and his godmother and friends were determined to enjoy everything she said or did. They avoided asking her any awkward questions, though it was no secret that Marcus had met her under extraordinary circumstances. Many of Marcus's friends were out of town, at their country estates for the hunting season, and this made things easier too.

During the week that followed, they went to the theater and she caught sight of Amy in her box surrounded by admirers. Marcus acknowledged Amy with a bow, but he did not leave Catherine to visit her, as many men would have. Respectable ladies simply ignored what their husbands were doing in front of their noses. Marcus was right about one thing. Though Amy's eyes frequently strayed to Catherine, there was no shock of recognition.

As the days slipped by, she was surprised to find that she was enjoying herself. It would have been easy to confuse reality and fantasy if not for the fact that she was on a mission and could never forget that Marcus, too, might be playing a part.

Major Carruthers wasn't sitting idle either. While she played her part, he was investigating all the circumstances surrounding the other murders, trying to find something that was common to them besides the fact that all the victims had been at *El Grande*'s base at the same time. Catherine found herself hoping that they would soon find evidence that would clear Marcus. It was one thing to punish him for what he'd done to Amy, but she did not hate him enough to want to see him hang—unless, of course, he had actually committed the crimes. In fact, she was afraid she was beginning to like him all too well.

Almost every afternoon, weather allowing, she and Marcus went out for a drive in his curricle. They were never alone, for there was always a groom trailing them on horseback, and she knew he was armed. All the coachmen were armed. When she duly reported this to her superior, adding that it seemed to support Marcus's version of events, she received a terse message to the effect that Marcus might be merely trying to throw suspicion off himself, unless, of course, she and *El Grande* really *were* the villains.

She was mulling this over in her mind as they turned into Hyde Park when Marcus said, "I saw you talking to one of the gardeners this morning, before breakfast. What were you talking about?"

The gardener was Crewe, Major Carruthers's man. She said lightly, "That was Crewe. He's such a dear. He served in the Peninsular Campaign, did you know?"

"Yes, I did know," said Marcus. "That's why I hired him."

His gaze was fixed on his team of chestnuts and she wasn't sure if he was suspicious or merely making idle conversation.

"Since I'm Spanish," she said, as though *she* were making idle conversation, "he thought I should know it. Naturally, I thanked him for saving my country from French domination."

Marcus flashed her a smile. "You did well," he said, and some of the tension went out of her.

A moment later, he pulled on the reins and they drew to a halt. "Tristram," he called out.

Catherine turned her head and saw a young man mounted on a handsome bay. He immediately separated from a group of riders and trotted over. Just by looking at him, she could tell he was related to Marcus, though he didn't have Marcus's powerful physique yet. Tristram, she remembered, was Marcus's younger half brother.

"Catalina," said Marcus, "allow me to present my brother Tristram."

There was an edge in Marcus's voice that made the young man color up. "Charmed, I'm sure," he said. "That is, welcome to England. I mean—"

"We know what you mean," said Marcus. "What I want to know is what you are doing here. The new term has started. Why aren't you at Oxford?"

"How do you do, Tristram?" Catherine said, "I have been looking forward to meeting you," and she extended her gloved hand.

Tristram accepted it, saw that something more was expected of him, and blushing hotly, dutifully kissed it.

Marcus shot her a look, then immediately resumed the conversation. "Well?"

"The thing is, Marcus," said Tristram, tugging at his collar, "I'm not cut out for the university." He began to stammer. "Latin and Greek—I just can't get the hang of them."

"You mean you failed your term examinations. I see. We'll have to talk about that later. But why haven't you shown your face at Cavendish Square? How long have you been in town?"

"Oh, a week or so. I just thought . . . well, that you wouldn't want company—not when you're just . . . that is . . . I thought you might want to be by yourselves for a while."

Marcus snorted.

Catherine smiled and said, "How very thoughtful."

"Where are you staying?" asked Marcus.

"At the Carillon. I'm with Cousin David. He's here

somewhere." He threw a hopeful look over his shoulder. "At any rate, David came over from Ireland to buy stock for his stud." His voice took on an eager tone. "We've been to Tattersall's and, oh, all over the place. It's not easy—" He broke off and exclaimed in a relieved tone, "Oh, here he is!"

The man who came toward them was older than Tristram. He looked to be in his late twenties, had finely chiseled features and fair hair that was long on the collar. Though his garments were conservative, he had a certain presence. Catherine found herself responding to his smile.

When the introductions were made, Marcus said, "It's good to see you again, David. It must be all of— what?—twelve years?"

"Oh, longer than that," said David. "Your stepmother says fifteen years."

"You've been to Wrotham?"

"Yes, before we came up to town. It was good to get to know the Lytton branch of the family again." He laughed. "I took the opportunity to look over your horses, but couldn't come to terms with Penn. Now that I have seen what Tattersall's has to offer, I realize Penn was offering me a bargain."

Marcus smiled. "Perhaps I shall offer you an even better bargain. You are, after all, my only cousin. What are your plans?"

David put a hand on Tristram's shoulder. "Oh, this is mostly a business trip, and Tristram has been a great help to me. He knows all about horses, and he knows all the best breeders."

"Yes, Tristram certainly knows about horses," said Marcus dryly. "We'll have to get together, a dinner perhaps, before Catherine and I go off to Wrotham."

"I'd be delighted," said David, and he inclined his head gravely. He then turned to Catherine and said something in Spanish.

"Tris, I expect to receive a visit from you tomorrow morning," said Marcus.

"Beg pardon? Oh yes, of course. I'll be there."

"See that you are."

When the gentlemen moved off, Marcus flicked the

reins and his team broke into a canter. Catherine looked away, thinking of Tristram and the projected interview with Marcus. She didn't think it was her place to comment, so she said neutrally, "That's a long time since you've seen your cousin."

"David lives in Ireland."

"Ireland's not the end of the world."

"We're not a close family."

"I see."

"What did he say to you? I couldn't follow his Spanish."

Catherine gave him an arch look. "He said that I was the most beautiful woman he'd ever met, that I was charming, intelligent, and witty, and that you are a very lucky man."

Marcus grinned. "Minx! He said no more than three words to you."

"That's the thing about Spanish. One can say a lot in a few words."

Marcus glanced at her through half-lowered lashes. She was flirting with him. There was a sparkle in her eyes and her cheeks were delicately flushed. Her brown hair was covered by her bonnet, which was fine with him because he didn't like her with brown hair. He missed the halo of flame. As he turned back to his horses, he fantasized that he was drawing the pins from her hair and spreading her glorious tresses across his pillow. Then he began to divest her of her garments.

He would go slowly with her, very slowly. He would do nothing to frighten her. Each caress would become more intimate than the last. Then, when she was ready for him, he would show her what all this flirting was leading to. He would bury himself inside her delectable body and give her her woman's pleasure before taking his own release.

He glanced at her again. Their eyes met and held. He felt the rise and fall of her breasts, felt his own breathing become harsher. His loins tightened.

She said quickly, "He said, 'Till we meet again.'"

It took a moment for him to get his body under control, and another even greater effort to change his train of thought. He said finally, "How wise of you to remember. I won't always let you turn me away, Cat. One of these days, it's not going to work."

She looked away. "I don't know what you mean."

"Don't you? Do you think I don't know what you're feeling right now?" He paused as he carefully guided his team between two stationary vehicles. "Your breathing is difficult. Your skin feels hot. You want my hands on you." His voice became hoarse. "I know, because that's how I feel too."

"I won't listen to any more of this," she cried.

"Cat—"

"Please, Marcus! Don't!"

He flicked her a look and saw the fear-bright eyes and the pulse leaping at her throat. "Ah, damn!" he said.

They returned to the house in silence. He set her down at the front door, while he went off to stable the horses in the mews. Catherine shut her bedroom door, locked it, then sagged against it. She was trembling all over, aching, aching . . .

She shook her head. She was on a mission. Marcus was the prime suspect. Major Carruthers had warned her what to expect. He was a rake. He had a way with women.

Gradually, her breathing slowed.

They delayed their departure for Wrotham by one day because the gowns that Marcus had ordered for Catherine were not quite ready. These were garments that had been ordered when they'd taken up residence in Cavendish Square. Catherine had had no part in it really except to stand there and be measured. Marcus and the modiste had decided everything between them and Catherine had been happy to leave them to it.

He had already provided her with a wardrobe, but it was modest. Those were gowns that had been rejected by a sober society matron who was one of Madame's best customers, gowns that Marcus had said would do in a pinch. Now, as Catherine fingered a blue and silver confection of froth, she felt her mouth begin to water. She picked up another gown that still had pins in it. This one was of white silk with tiny white roses embroidered on the square-cut bodice and along the edge of the train. When the silk slipped through her fingers, she gave a sigh of pure pleasure.

Almost at once, as if on cue, she had an impression of Aunt Bea, lecturing her on the perils of the senses. It was a sin to want to look pretty and to covet pretty things, she'd said. That's why Aunt Bea had always worn black. Catherine no longer accepted everything her aunt had told her, but she couldn't suppress a certain misgiving when she deliberately flaunted her aunt's rules.

It was absurd. She was a grown woman. She must make up her own mind about what was right and what was wrong.

Marcus had observed her eager expression turn pensive and now faintly defiant, and he wondered what she was thinking. "Why don't you try it on?" he said.

She looked up at him. They had not been on the best of terms since the last time he'd taken her out in his curricle. They didn't quarrel; they just circled each other like two wary dogs. As she looked at him now, she sensed that he was over his ill humor, and her own lips turned up in a smile.

"Why not?" she said, and allowed Madame to lead her to the changing room.

When she returned, Marcus was sitting in an upholstered gilt chair on the far side of the room. She was quite dazed at the change in her appearance and waited expectantly for Marcus to say something complimentary. Behind her, Madame clapped her hands and exclaimed her approval.

Marcus said, "Well, don't just stand there, Cat. Walk toward me. Let's see how you move."

She'd never had a dress with a train before, and though it was awkward, she managed quite well by taking small, mincing steps. Her brows lowered when she saw that Marcus was hiding his mouth behind his hand.

"Madame," said Marcus, "would you mind leaving us for a few moments? There is something I wish to say to my wife."

"What?" asked Catherine when the modiste had closed the door on them.

"Cat, you are supposed to be a Spanish girl, not some terrified English maiden who has been made to walk the plank." He made no attempt to hide his amusement. "Think yourself into the part. You're Catalina. Spanish girls move with feline grace. They do it deliberately, to attract the notice of men. Catalina most of all."

Now this was an insult that was almost past bearing, not to Catherine, but to Catalina. She longed to put him right, but of course, this was impossible.

She smiled through her teeth. "I don't think I follow you. Perhaps you'd care to demonstrate?"

His mischievous eyes glinted up at her. "Ah no. I'd never get it right. This is something that only a woman could do. I don't have the hips for it."

"What have hips got to do with it?"

"A Spanish girl sways her hips as she walks. Try it, Cat."

Catalina had never swayed her hips in her life. Catalina had worn divided skirts. Catherine picked up her train and strode down the length of the room just as the real Catalina would have done.

Marcus shook his head. "You look gauche. Try again."

Jaws clamped together, she rolled her hips in the manner of Juanita, a prostitute in whose house she and *El Grande* had once taken refuge when the French were searching for them.

"Not bad," said Marcus. "I think you're getting the hang of it. It's too bad that you're so skinny. Catalina's curves were more generous."

"Catalina's curves—!" She stopped herself just in time.

He was obviously enjoying himself enormously. "And she had a way of looking at a man, from the side of her eyes, that could stop him dead in his tracks."

She was hanging on to her temper by the skin of her teeth. "Marcus, I've been around Spanish girls. They're shy. That's all it is."

He gave her an amused look. "Cat, take my word for it, they're not shy."

"You must have been acquainted with Juanita," she said.

"Who?"

In answer, she circled around him, swaying her hips and batting her eyelashes.

Marcus eyed her speculatively. "There's something missing. It's more than just the way you move. Catalina oozed—"

"What?" she demanded when he hesitated.

Marcus shrugged. "Whatever it was, it's obviously something that can't be learned. Don't worry, you'll be fine, Cat."

She knew that he was teasing her, but she couldn't help being annoyed. He might have said something nice about her appearance.

With her head held high, she marched toward the changing room calling for Madame. Then a cold gust of air swept through the front door and Catherine turned to see who had arrived. On the threshold stood a beautiful and fashionable young woman wearing a blue pelisse. She was smiling brilliantly at Marcus.

Madame Demeurs, who had come running, stared at the newcomer in open dismay.

"Mrs. Bryce," said Madame faintly.

"Julia," said Marcus. "What the devil are you doing here?"

Julia Bryce let out a silvery laugh and quickly went to Marcus. She'd heard about Marcus's bride and what she'd heard had resurrected her hopes.

Her friend Harriet Harding had been watching the Wrothams' arrival in town and considered the Spanish girl about as exciting as curds and whey. It was only a question of time before the earl set up a new mistress. Julia had made up her mind not to give him up without a fight. She did not see Catherine watching from inside the changing room.

Julia did a little pirouette. "Oh, Marcus," she said rapturously, "how can I ever thank you? And Madame, also? This is the most beautiful outfit I've ever had."

Then she flung herself into his arms and fastened her mouth on his.

Catherine's eyes flicked from Julia to Marcus. Though she could tell that the passion was largely on the lady's part, Marcus wasn't putting up much resistance. In fact, he wasn't putting up any resistance at all.

Madame was wringing her hands, protesting that Mrs. Bryce had not made an appointment.

Marcus untangled himself from Julia. "This *is* a surprise," he said.

A quick glance over his shoulder told him that Catherine had seen everything and had correctly added two and two. He quickly crossed to her and said with a sheepish grin, "Wait for me. I won't be gone long."

His sheepish grin was met by a stony stare. Cursing under his breath, he returned to Julia, offered her his arm, and swept her out of the house.

Chapter 12

Marcus's carriage was stationed outside the door. He told his coachman that he would be back soon, then he walked Julia toward Baker Street and hailed a hackney. "How did you know where to find me?"

She resisted as he tried to usher her into the cab of the hackney. "I saw you from across the street, from Harriet Harding's house. Marcus, what is it? Where are you taking me?"

"What I have to say to you is best said in the privacy of the cab."

She sensed a rebuff coming, and she wasn't going to let that happen again, not after what she'd heard about his wife. Marcus was a demanding lover, violent in his passions. If his wife knew what he was really like, she'd run home screaming to her duenna.

As soon as they were seated, she said, "Don't try to tell me you don't want me, because I won't believe it. When I kissed you back then, you went as hard as a rock."

The graphic words had his blood pounding, and his body hardening. She laughed softly, knowingly, and placed a hand on his thigh. "Do you remember what happened the last time we were alone in a carriage, Marcus? You took me right here, on the banquette." When she saw the heat in his eyes, she tossed her head. "You won't get what I can give you from another woman, least of all a dutiful little wife. Admit it, Marcus, your wife doesn't hold a candle to me."

The heat in his eyes rapidly cooled. He looked at her, really looked at her, and he felt repelled. She was so utterly different from Cat. Julia knew how to ensnare men, but every smile and gesture was calculated. He doubted that even the passion was genuine. He'd always known it, and that made him no better than she.

With a violent oath, he brushed her hand from his thigh. "I don't discuss my wife with anyone. But I will say this: Catherine never bores me."

When his meaning finally registered, her mouth twisted in fury. "You were going to make me your mistress! You were going to set me up in style!" And that's what rankled. She'd become the envy of all her friends. She'd already chosen a fashionable house in Knightsbridge and had spent hours in Rundell and Bridge poring over trays of expensive trinkets.

"Oh, no," said Marcus. "I said nothing about making you my mistress. An *affaire* is what I wanted, and you know it."

"I lost Leinster because of you," she railed.

"And I paid you handsomely for your loss. That's all you care about, isn't it—money? I'm not a miser. Tell me what I owe you and we'll consider our accounts settled."

A hard, calculating look came into her eyes. "There's someone else. That's it, isn't it?"

"Julia, I'm a married man."

"You never gave a thought to your wife before now." When he shrugged, she said vengefully, "Don't think you can come crawling back to me after this. I never want to see you again."

"You've taken the words right out of my mouth."

She started up and pulled on the check string to halt the coach. Marcus opened his mouth to try and diffuse a situation that had suddenly turned ugly, and received a slap that jarred his teeth. She was out of the coach before he could stop her.

He half rose from his seat to go after her, then sank back when he realized they were on the Oxford Road. It was a very busy thoroughfare and she would be perfectly safe. Besides, blood dripped from a cut on his lip and he dabbed at it with his handkerchief. He would have been angry if it was not all so absurd. They'd had an *affaire*, and that's all it amounted to, an *affaire* which he'd ended shortly after he'd met Catherine. As far as he knew, their parting had been friendly. Then what the devil had got into the woman? He shook his head, reflecting that the thought processes of females were beyond a mere male.

He watched her from the window as she crossed the road and hailed a hackney. Once she had entered the cab, he put his head out the window to tell his own driver to return to Portland Square. That's when he caught sight of someone who looked strikingly familiar. It was a young man on the other side of the road, and he was looking back at Marcus as though he couldn't quite place him either.

Recognition came to them both at the same moment. *El Grande* flashed Marcus a cold, hard stare before he turned and disappeared into an alley. Marcus flung open the cab door, shouted to the driver to wait for him, and ran across the road, dodging carriages and riders.

He hared down that alley like the sprinter he'd been in his Oxford days, and he came out on Soho Square. There were plenty of people around, but not the man he was looking for. He struck out along Frith Street, but soon decided it was hopeless. Still, he wasn't ready to give up yet. He turned right, came out on the Oxford Road and found his driver still waiting for him.

"Go down Charing Cross Road," said Marcus, "then make for Piccadilly. And hurry."

Inside the coach, he cursed himself for not taking one of his own coachmen with him. Two hunters were better than one.

He'd grown careless lately, and spent far too much time thinking about Catherine when he should be remembering the purpose of having her pose as his wife.

On that sober thought, he removed his pistol from his coat pocket and cradled it in the crook of one arm.

When the footman advised Amy that Mr. Robert Cordes was waiting downstairs, she was not well pleased. This was the third time Cat's priest, or whatever he was, had called on her in the last month, and each time he'd been told she was not at home. He was pestering her, and she made up her mind there and then that she was going to put a stop to it.

"Show him up," she told her footman.

Miss Collyer, her companion, set aside her knitting and began to fuss with her muslin cap. Amy would have laughed if she hadn't been so nervous. Her companion had watched, from an upstairs window, each time Mr. Cordes had been turned away, and the silly twit had taken a fancy to him. The old saw was right: there was no fool like an old fool.

Amy said, "Perhaps, Miss Collyer, you wouldn't mind waiting in the parlor?"

"Shall I bring tea and cake?"

"Oh no. Mr. Cordes won't be staying long."

"No?"

Amy smiled at the disappointment that one word conveyed. "He's a priest, Miss Collyer, or a monk. I'm not sure I know what the difference is, but you can take that speculative gleam out of your eye. Not only that, but he's young enough to be . . . well, he's years younger than you or I."

"That handsome young man is a priest?"

"So I understand."

"What a waste!"

"Yes, isn't it? I'll call you if I need anything."

Miss Collyer left the room, and moments later Mr. Robert Cordes was announced. Amy greeted him coolly and invited him to be seated.

"You'll join me in a glass of sherry or Madeira?" she asked.

"Madeira," he responded. "Why do you look so surprised?"

She went to the sideboard where she poured out two glasses of Madeira. "I had an aunt who was very religious. She said that strong spirits were the invention of the devil. I never thought a priest would drink anything stronger than coffee or tea."

He accepted the glass she offered. "I told you before you have a strange idea of priests. I also told you that I was not a priest. I'm not even a monk, and now I know

I won't ever be one." He sipped his Madeira. "I have another life waiting for me when I leave the Abbey. One day, I'll tell you about it."

This was becoming too cozy for Amy's peace of mind, and she said abruptly, "This is all very interesting, but would you mind telling me why you are here?"

"I have a letter for you from Catherine."

She took the letter from him and broke the seal. "Why did she send it with you?"

"She was afraid that if she sent it by the post, you would return it unopened."

Without replying, she sat down and quickly scanned the two pages he'd given her, then she read them again. Looking up at him, she said, "It says here that she's gone off to France with some widow woman. Did you know about this?"

"Yes, I knew."

"Well, at least that will keep her out of Wrotham's way for a month or two, though I don't know why I'm worrying. His wife has arrived from Spain, so that should keep him occupied."

He said, "You don't care for Lord Wrotham, do you, Amy?"

She heard something in his voice that caught her attention. Squinting up at him, she said, "Marcus, that is, Lord Wrotham, has been a good friend to me, a very good friend. But that doesn't mean I want my sister to take up with him. Catherine is . . . well, she's the sort of girl who should be married and raising a family. Marcus is already spoken for, so that's that."

He was looking at her oddly.

"What is it?" she asked.

"You need someone to look after you, Amy."

"So that's it! Cat sent you here to save my soul."

"You know that's not true."

"Then she sent you to spy on me." She abruptly rose, moved to the sideboard, and picked up a tray to show him. Nestled on the tray were a dozen promissory notes all made out to Mrs. Amy Spencer. "This should please Cat," she said. "She thinks I'm a whore. Well, of course,

I *am* a whore, and this proves it. Now I come to think of it, she thinks I run a brothel. Why don't I show you over the house, and you can tell her how right she is?"

He merely said, "How did you get these notes?"

He had a way of looking at her that made her want to tell him her darkest secrets. She fought the power of that look and tried to say something flippant, but she couldn't quite manage it.

"I give parties," she said at last. "Gentleman pay for the privilege of being my guests."

"Parties where men meet women who are not their wives?"

"Parties where they meet my friends. I'm not responsible for what they do once they leave here."

"Aren't you?"

His rebuke made her blush. "You sound just like my aunt Bea. She was a killjoy too."

"This brings you joy?" he asked incredulously, making a sweep with one hand that encompassed far more than the room.

Tears suddenly clogged her throat, something that hadn't happened to her in years, and that made her angry. She tried to give him the same speech she'd given Cat, about her fine clothes and jewels, and her financial security, but the words stuck in her throat.

"I'm not like your aunt Bea," he said. "She didn't know how to live. You're right. She was a killjoy. She should never have had the charge of two young girls. But that's in the past. You are a grown woman now. You can choose your own life."

"Like Cat, I suppose."

"Yes, like Catherine. Why not?"

"My, my! You and Cat appear to be in each other's confidence. I suppose you think you know all there is to know about me. I don't want your pity, Robert Cordes. In fact, I don't want anything from you. Now, if you'll excuse me, I'm rather busy at the moment."

"Don't go, Amy. Please, won't you talk to me?"

She should run from the room, and didn't know what held her. "What is there to talk about?"

He shrugged helplessly. "Nothing. Everything. I don't know London well. I thought you might show it to me. Perhaps next week? For the next little while, I'll be on retreat, progressing through the spiritual exercises my spiritual director has set for me."

Spiritual exercises? Spiritual director? The words terrified her. She shook her head. "What would be the point?"

He gave her one of those looks that made her feel transparent and terribly, terribly guilty, then he smiled, and that smile made her heart turn over. "Do you think God has a sense of humor?" he asked.

She stared at him blankly.

He rose and faced her. "I thought there was to be no more joy for me. Then I walked into a room and there you were. I'd been praying, you see, for a sign that God really exists. And He answered my prayer. I'd lost my faith and God restored it, but I never expected him to restore it in quite that way. No, don't look frightened. Am I going too fast for you? Forgive me, but I don't know how to go about courting a woman. You will have to teach me, Amy."

"I'm not frightened. I'm *horrified*. You know what I am. And I'm years older than you. There can never be anything between us. Look away from me, Robert Cordes. Look to someone your own age, someone like Cat."

She backed away from him, and with a choked sob turned on her heel and ran from the room.

A few minutes later, *El Grande* exited the house, but surprised the footman by using the back door. In the mews, he took a quick look around before stepping out. At odd intervals, he stopped to make sure that no one was following him.

For the next little while, he put all thoughts of Amy out of his mind and focused on Catherine and her mission.

He'd been overconfident. He'd never expected to run into Wrotham. Carruthers had told him that the earl and Catherine were on their way to Warwickshire. Something must have delayed them. Next time, he'd make sure they were gone before coming to London.

When he came out on Charing Cross, he hailed a hackney. There was still no sign of pursuit. Relaxing against the banquette, he closed his eyes and thought of Amy.

Chapter 13

Marcus arrived home in a temper. Not only had he lost *El Grande,* but Catherine had not waited for him at the modiste's. For her own safety he needed to know where she was at all times, and she knew that.

As he entered his front door, he heard laughter coming from the drawing room upstairs, Cat's laughter. For a moment, he felt intense relief. Then the anger returned.

As he took the stairs two at a time he heard a masculine voice answering something Catherine had said. Another rule broken—she wasn't supposed to entertain guests without him.

When he entered the drawing room, he found her with Tristram and their cousin David. There was a crystal goblet in everyone's hand, and it appeared to him—he glanced at the unstoppered decanter on a side table—that they were making short work of his prize sherry. No one noticed that he had entered the room. Tristram was sitting silent with a bemused expression on his face, staring intently at Catherine, while she carried on a lively flirtation with David.

"Ireland sounds fascinating," she said with just a trace of a Spanish accent. "I can't believe Marcus has never been there. Naturally I shall try to persuade him to accept your very kind invitation. You'll have more cake?"

David declined, but at Tristram's nod, she rose gracefully and moved to the side table against the wall. Marcus couldn't take his eyes off her. She wasn't walking, she was gyrating, swaying her hips like a woman of the streets. He looked at his cousin and brother. They couldn't take their eyes off her bottom either.

"Marcus!" exclaimed Catherine, and all heads turned to look at him.

He greeted everyone cordially, but the look he gave Catherine spoke volumes. She ignored it, fluttered her eyelashes, and offered Tristram the plate of cake. Marcus caught the amusement in his cousin's eyes; David seemed to know something was going on between husband and wife.

Catherine said, "David has invited us to visit him in Ireland. Isn't that kind of him?"

Marcus answered curtly. "I'm afraid that won't be possible at present. There's too much that needs to be done at Wrotham."

"Then," said Catherine, addressing David, "you must visit us."

"Oh, I will," he said, smiling up at her. "I'm holding Marcus to his promise. Unless, of course, you were joking with me, Marcus, about giving me a better bargain than Penn."

"Oh, Marcus would never go back on a promise," said Tristram.

At the side table, Marcus was pouring himself a glass of sherry, and his temper was not improved when he discovered there was hardly enough sherry left in the decanter to half fill his glass. He looked at Tristram. "Didn't we decide when we last spoke that you were going to concentrate on your studies so that you can return to university at half term?"

"Oh, but I have. I do."

"So what are you doing here?"

"I am paying my respects to Catalina."

"Marcus, how can you be so severe?" said Catherine, bestowing a brilliant smile on Tristram. "Who could be bothered with Latin and Greek on such a beautiful day!"

"This is a family matter, Cat," Marcus snapped. "I'd advise you not to interfere."

The amusement vanished from David's face. Tristram threw Marcus a look of reproach, and Catherine looked daggers at him.

Regretting his outburst, Marcus said, "Why don't we

all go down to Wrotham together—tomorrow or the next day? And Tristram is right, David. I always keep my promisees. I'd be happy to show you our stock."

In spite of Marcus's attempt to make amends, conversation became awkward, and David and Tristram soon rose to leave. Marcus repeated his invitation, and it was agreed that they would all travel to Wrotham together the following morning.

There was a long silence after their departure. Then Marcus said, "Didn't you think how I would feel when I returned to the modiste—only to find you gone?"

"Hah! You should have thought of that when you took off with that woman. I'm not a parcel you can leave and pick up at your convenience."

"I left you where I knew you would be safe. I left footmen and coachmen to protect you."

"Protect me from what?"

"From *El Grande*. In fact, I saw him out the coach window. I tried to chase him down, but I lost him."

The paralyzing tension that gripped her mind eased. "You saw *El Grande* and lost him? When? Where?"

Marcus told her what had happened, ending with, "So now you know what kind of danger you were in. And I would like to know," he went on sharply, "why you were entertaining guests against my express orders."

"David and Tristram are hardly guests. They are family. How could I turn them away?"

She had a point, which infuriated him even more. "And was it necessary to conduct yourself like Haymarket ware?"

She showed him her teeth. "Would you care to explain that remark?"

"Batting your eyelashes. Swaying your hips. Dazzling poor Tristram with your smiles. Anyone can see he's besotted with you. Does that please you? Well, it doesn't please me. You were making a spectacle of yourself. I don't expect my wife to act like a loose woman."

"I was only doing what you told me to do! You told me to think myself into the part of the *incomparable* Catalina. Didn't I do it right?"

His hands clenched. "That was only a game we were playing. I was only teasing you."

"Perhaps I wasn't amused." She examined her manicure. "Actually, I thought it was David who was taken with me. And you say Tristram is too?"

It was the last straw. When he reached for her, he thought he was going to shake some sense into her. He was as surprised as she when he grabbed her in a bear hug and took her lips in a voracious kiss.

She didn't struggle, didn't try to fight him off. She was going to show her utter contempt for him by offering a passive resistance. And she would have resisted him forever if a wave of pleasure had not taken her unawares.

Marcus soon sensed that she wasn't resisting him and the fierce pressure of his arms eased; his lips softened; he began to taste and tease. His lips moved to her eyelids, her throat, her chin, then returned to her mouth. At his urging, she opened her lips to him, and he entered her. Soft. Moist. Pliant. When he kissed her, his little spitfire became putty in his hands.

He pulled back his head to get a better look at her. In a low, husky voice, he said, "Cat, tell me what you are feeling."

Confused. Dazed. Worried. Those hands, those clever hands were brushing with tantalizing slowness from her waist to the swell of her breasts. Breathing was becoming difficult. Her skin was so sensitive that her clothes hurt. She moved restlessly in his arms. "I feel . . . dizzy." She moaned, and clutched at his shoulders as the room began to spin. "What . . . ?"

She was swept up then set down on the sofa in front of the grate. Marcus eased down beside her and gathered her close. She made a feeble attempt to rise but he forestalled her.

"Feel what you do to me," he said, and eyes holding hers, he slowly unbuttoned the front of his shirt and placed her hand on his chest.

The beat of his heart against her hand made her own pulse leap in response. Warm masculine flesh tensed beneath the pads of her fingers. She began to tremble as need rose in her.

She shook her head. "I shouldn't be doing this. *You* shouldn't let me." She sucked in a sharp breath as his hand closed over her breast.

"It's all right," he soothed. "I just want to kiss you, hold you, touch you. Don't you like what I do to you?"

Her neck felt boneless and her head lolled in the crook of his arm. "No. Yes. I don't know. I can't think when you touch me like this."

She gasped when he kissed her breasts through the thin fabric of her gown. He began to work at the buttons on her bodice and when she tried to stop him he kissed her again. She was giving in to him. He could feel her surrender all through his body, and his blood began to pound.

Unrestrained now, he pressed her back among the cushions and he stretched out beside her. His hands moved on her, calmly, deliberately, taking an intimate impression of the softly flaring hips, the supple waist. When he rubbed his thumbs over her nipples and she jerked, he soothed her with kisses, but he didn't stop what he was doing.

She whimpered when he slipped one hand under the hem of her gown and began to brush along the inside of her leg.

"Easy," he said. "Easy."

He waited a moment to give her time to become accustomed to his touch, then he parted her knees. She made no move to stop him, and he gritted his teeth as his control began to slip. He slid his hand higher and into the opening of her drawers. His fingers found her and stroked the entrance to her body, then slipped inside. She was panting softly. His breathing was strident. She was ready for him, and he was so hard he ached with it.

Catherine couldn't keep pace with what was happening to her. All her senses were focused on the brush of his lips, the touch of his hands. She wanted . . . she didn't know what she wanted.

"Marcus, oh Marcus," she said, pleading with him.

"It's all right," he said, hardly knowing what he was saying. "I'll take care of everything, even if Catalina never agrees to divorce me."

Her voice was thick in her throat. "What are you saying?"

"I'll always take care of you no matter what."

Catherine's scattered thoughts suddenly snapped together. He couldn't be suggesting what she thought he was suggesting. "How will you take care of me?"

"I'll set you up in your own little house."

"As your mistress?"

"It's the only way for us."

The wallop took him completely off guard, and for the second time that afternoon, his teeth jarred together. Shock held them both immobile; then, with a gasping cry, Catherine pushed out of his arms and scrambled to her feet. She lost no time in buttoning and straightening her disheveled clothing. This done, she rounded on him, and, hands on hips, bosom heaving, glared down at him. Marcus would have roared in frustrated desire if he'd been able to unclench his teeth. Hands cupping his sore jaw, he glared back at her.

"What the hell was that for?" he demanded through his teeth.

Her eyes sizzled. She couldn't credit how close she had come to disaster yet again. Her body ached for him, burned for him, yearned for him, and this in spite of her knowing who and what he was.

Mistress. That one little word had brought her to her senses. He was married to Catalina, or he thought he was, but that didn't stop him trying to seduce another woman. She was a female and it was enough. A passing fancy, that's all she was to him, a potential mistress.

"Well?" demanded Marcus.

"I don't take up with married men."

"Dammit, Cat, I don't feel married. I haven't seen my wife for three years."

"That's irrelevant! I am a respectable woman. If you ruin me, no man will have me."

His face set in stubborn lines. "I would have you."

"Indeed?" Her nostrils quivered. "As you had Julia Bryce?"

"No, dammit. She's not in the same class as you. I don't think of you in that way."

She said frigidly, "Wasn't she a virtuous girl once?"

"She chose her way in life, and I'll be damned if I'll let you lay her sins at my door. Women like Julia sell their favors for money, Cat. You are too inexperienced to understand."

When he rose, she took a quick step back.

"Cat—"

"Don't!" If he touched her now, she would fight him. Tears gathered, not for herself but for Amy. So this was how he had seduced her sister. Poor Amy hadn't stood a chance. Just thinking about Amy and Marcus together in that way made her cringe. It was a pity that she hadn't remembered before she let him kiss her.

"Decide," she said, "right now, whether or not we are to go on with this. I won't play the part of Catalina unless you swear to me that you won't try to seduce me. I mean it, Marcus."

"You think that was a seduction? If that's the case, I'd like to know who was doing the seducing." He combed his fingers through his hair. "You were as hot as I was."

She ignored the taunt. "That's not all."

"Oh?" His eyes narrowed on her.

"I'm supposed to be your wife. You said that we're supposed to give the impression that ours was an impetuous love match."

"I did. What of it?"

"Only this. I won't be humiliated by a husband who takes up with other women. I won't have people laughing at me, Marcus, or pitying me, even if I am only playing a part."

"I see," he said. "I can't have you, and I can't have other women. Is that it?"

"That's it."

"How long do you expect me to remain a monk, Cat?"

"How long do you expect me to play the part of your wife?"

Not another word was spoken, but she saw that he had taken her point, and she left the room.

• • •

Marcus drove the coach with a reckless disregard for the lashing rain or the gathering dusk. Beside him, his coachman shriveled into his sodden greatcoat. Marcus knew what James was thinking. He thought that his master had been tipping the brandy bottle after a lover's tiff with his wife. It's what all the servants thought. No sober gentleman would drive out on a wild night like this just for the pleasure of it, and they would be right, up to a point. It would never occur to them that this wild drive to Hampstead was a distraction, something to relieve the agonies of unsated desire. Only by pitting himself against the elements could he find a release of sorts.

Catherine. He couldn't believe how mistaken he'd been in her. He'd thought that behind the ladylike façade she was courageous and daring. He'd thought she'd had a sense of adventure. What other kind of person would agree to help him entrap his wife and *El Grande*? He didn't know what to make of her. But one thing was clear: she wanted him as much as he wanted her. Damn the woman! What was it about her that he found so appealing?

He tried to bring Catalina's face into focus, but he found that he couldn't do it. His real wife was becoming more and more of a shadowy figure. It was Catherine who was responsible for that. Whenever he tried to think of Catalina, it was Cat's face he saw, Cat's way of moving, speaking, looking at him. His wife's memory was fading into oblivion.

He cracked the whip and sent the team of chestnuts careering down a hill. James closed his eyes and prepared to meet his Maker.

Chapter 14

They stopped for the night at the Falcon in Stratford-upon-Avon, twelve miles from Wrotham. The following morning, when they started on the last leg of their journey, Tristram and David decided to ride on to Wrotham, just to exercise their horses. That was, at least, what they told Marcus and Catherine. In private, they candidly admitted they'd had enough of being cooped up with a married couple who were barley on speaking terms.

Catherine was sorry to see them go. Now that she and Marcus were alone in the coach, their long silences would become more noticeable. The next twelve miles were going to be the longest twelve miles in her life. Marcus had brought a book with him and had become engrossed in it before they'd even left Stratford behind. She had only her thoughts for company.

Fine. She would begin by dissecting the character of the boor who shared the coach with her. That he was an unprincipled rake had been established beyond question—Amy, Julia Bryce, Catalina, and now Catherine Courtnay, and these were only the women she knew about! She wasn't the least bit sorry that she'd entrapped him into marriage. In fact, she was proud of herself. She had belled the cat, and now all women would know that he was only trifling with them. To be forewarned was to be forearmed. Then how could she explain how narrowly she had escaped succumbing to him? He was a practiced rake, and that's where the danger lay, so practiced that he knew how to make a woman forget her own name.

Narrowing her eyes, she turned slightly to look at him. It wasn't difficult to imagine Marcus as a soldier.

Such men unconsciously exuded an aura of command. Major Carruthers had told her he had a distinguished war record. She couldn't fault him there. In Spain, he'd been an Observing Officer, riding deep into enemy territory to gather information. He'd been a spy, but a spy in uniform. The French regarded these spies as men of integrity, and because of this, no harm would have come to Marcus if he'd been captured.

It would have been different if the French had captured her or *El Grande*. They were the true spies, concealing their identities, carrying out their missions in stealth. Just thinking about *El Grande* made her throat ache. If only he'd been the old *El Grande,* he would have taken charge of this mission. He wouldn't have allowed Marcus to call all the shots. He would have conceived his own plan, and *he* would be trying to draw Marcus into the open. Major Carruthers was all right in his way, but he was cautious. *El Grande* wasn't reckless but he never shied away from a calculated risk.

And he was never careless, as she had been careless. She should have warned him that their departure for Wrotham had been delayed by a day. She'd known that *El Grande* didn't spend all his days at the monastery, that he worked among the destitute of London. Then why hadn't she warned him to stay out of sight for one more day?

She knew the answer. She'd become far too personally involved in this mission. It was something that had happened to her only once before—in Spain, with Captain Marcus Lytton.

Cards on the table, Catherine, she told herself sternly. Admit it! In spite of everything, you're attracted to that cad sitting next to you. You were jealous of Julia Bryce, jealous of Catalina, and that's why you went off like a rocket, trying to make him jealous, too, when he walked in and found you with David and Tristram. And because you have been thinking like a woman and not like an agent, you put the whole mission in jeopardy. Even these long silences come from hurt pride. You're an agent. Marcus is the prime suspect behind a series of murders. You have a job to do. Do it.

She let out a long sigh, then turned her head to look at him. "Marcus," she said softly. When he looked up from the book he was reading, she went on, "I apologize. I'm behaving like a silly little schoolgirl."

He tossed the book aside and smiled ruefully. "Are you, Cat?"

She was making the overture, just as he'd known she would, and already his mind was grappling with the logistics. He could lock the carriage doors and pull the blinds down, and then—

"I shouldn't have asked you to give up other women when this isn't a real marriage. After all, it's been more than three years since you married Catalina. People change. I don't think anyone will be shocked if you take a mistress. In fact, I think they may be shocked if you don't." There! She'd said it, though the words had almost choked her.

Marcus replied in a low, enraged tone. "Thank you, but I have more scruples than you. How dare you suggest that I treat my wife so shabbily?"

The woman in her rose to the surface. "You were going to make me your mistress, weren't you? What's the difference?"

"If you don't understand it, I can't explain it."

"But—"

"No, Cat. We're going to play this my way. You will hang on my every word, and I will be enthralled with you."

"I don't know if I'm that much of an actress."

"Try," advised Marcus.

"As you wish."

She stared out the window in stony silence, and Marcus picked up his book.

She heard the baying of the hounds before she saw the castle.

Marcus said, "There have been hounds at Wrotham since Norman times. First they were for hunting stag, but now they're only for foxes. Penn has been restocking the park with fallow deer, but they are off limits as yet, until the herd becomes established."

As Marcus pointed, she looked out the window, following the progress of the hunt as riders and hounds went leaping over hedges and across fields. "Why are all these people wearing yellow coats?" she asked.

"That's the Wrotham colors. And there is Wrotham," said Marcus, and Catherine moved to the other side of the coach to take in the view.

It was a fortress, a massive, rugged presence looming over the country town which went by the same name.

"From here," said Marcus, "it looks as if the town is built around the castle. But that's deceiving. The castle is actually on the other side of Wrotham, and is much older than the town."

"How old is it?"

"The original keep was granted to my ancestor, Robert FitzBrant, in 1153. Over the centuries, various lords of Wrotham added towers and battlements. Wrotham is not actually our principal residence—we've always looked on it merely as a hunting lodge."

"And where is your principal residence?"

"Lytton, in Worcester. It's only a manor house, but it's more comfortable. Castles, as you'll discover soon enough, tend to be drafty, uncomfortable places."

She said no more, but fixed her eyes on the horizon, taking stock of the massive stone edifice that had stood sentinel over the valley for over six hundred years. Faced with the concrete evidence of Marcus's enormous wealth, she felt a good deal subdued.

The town might not have been as old as the castle, but it wasn't exactly modern either. It was Tudor and very similar to other towns and villages they'd passed on the way. Half-timbered wattle buildings with thatched roofs lined the cobbled streets.

"Wrotham parish church," said Marcus at one point, indicating a Norman building on the north side of the town. "It's worth a visit. My ancestors are buried there."

Comparisons were odious, but she couldn't help thinking of her own family. Her grandfather on her father's side had once farmed a few acres in Hampshire. On her mother's side, her grandfather had been a vicar. Before that, her people had been soldiers. That's all she knew.

"What are you thinking?" said Marcus.

She spoke more tartly than she meant to. "Your ancestors and mine had one thing in common at least."

"Which is?"

"They all ended up in church graveyards."

The lines around his eyes crinkled, and he smiled, not one of his provocative smiles, but one that made her feel less nervous. "You'll do just fine," he said, and after a moment, she smiled too.

The approach to the castle took them through dense, leafless woodlands which gave way to fallow fields and well-tended farms. Marcus kept up a flow of anecdotes as they drove by various points of interest. They passed a country house which, as it turned out, wasn't a country house but the Wrotham kennels and stables. Then, too soon for Catherine's comfort, they were through the great stone gatehouse, with the Wrotham coat of arms above it, and soon after they pulled up at the front doors of the main building. As she alighted from the carriage, Catherine glanced at the small knot of people who had gathered on the stone steps. Instantly she picked out the lady she assumed was the dowager countess.

She'd expected Helen of Troy, a woman whose face had launched a thousand ships. The lady who came forward to greet her was certainly pleasant to look at, but she was no Helen of Troy. She had dark hair that was rapidly running to gray, a sweet face, and a figure that could only be described as stout.

As servants came forward to unload the baggage, Marcus said, "Helen, come and meet your new daughter-in-law."

Shining brown eyes met Catherine's. "Catalina," said the dowager Countess of Wrotham, "I've waited for this moment for three long years," and she embraced Catherine warmly.

Catherine found herself responding to that warmth and was horrified to find that her eyes were stinging. She didn't feel like a woman or a British agent, but like a little girl who wanted her mother because her heart was breaking. She disengaged from that embrace with the greatest reluctance. *This isn't real,* she reminded herself, *I'm only pretending.*

"Please," she said, and her voice was hoarse, "call me Catherine. I want to be English. I want to learn English ways."

"Oh, Marcus, she's so lovely," said the dowager, and she embraced him too.

"And this is Samantha," said Marcus.

Catherine knew that Marcus's sister was older than Tristram, but the young girl who smiled at her shyly as she curtsied looked as though she belonged in the schoolroom.

"And last but by no means least," said the voice of the gentleman who was waiting to be introduced, "is the black sheep of the family. I'm Penniston, but everybody calls me Penn. How do you do, Catherine."

This was Marcus's other half brother—and his heir. If Samantha looked younger than her years, Penniston looked older. The resemblance to Marcus and Tristram was there, but lines of dissipation were carved deeply in his handsome face. He'd been drinking. She couldn't smell the drink on him, but she remembered how it had been with her father. Penniston's smile was just a shade too warm. His stance, his movements, were just a shade too relaxed.

"How do you do?" she said with a curtsy.

"Where are Tristram and David?" asked Marcus.

Penniston said, "They're trying out the new Andalusians I bought from Colonel Herriot. But I'm warning you, Marcus, I don't want David to have those. Strike any bargain with him you like, but the Andalusians stay at Wrotham."

There was a moment of silence, then the dowager said quickly, "Have you had breakfast? I've given you and Catherine the lord's chamber, Marcus, and moved my own things to the blue chamber. How was the drive?"

Catherine sensed undercurrents eddying below the surface and wondered if she was being fanciful.

With the dowager leading the way, they entered the Great Hall. It was a long, dark room, two stories high, with bare stone walls hung with tapestries and stags' heads. Every alcove, and there were many of those, seemed to be guarded by a ghostly knight in a suit of armor.

"My father," said Marcus, "had two passions in life, hunting and his armory collection."

In Catherine's ear, Penn murmured, "He had another passion, but we don't refer to it in polite society."

"What was that?" Marcus asked the question without heat, but Catherine could feel those eddies rushing around like a treacherous whirlpool.

Penn flashed a smile. "I was pointing out Father's portrait." He nodded at the portrait that hung above the fireplace mantel and which dominated the room. The fifth earl, in hunting regalia, stood with one foot on the neck of a glassy-eyed stag his hounds had brought down. His sword was bloodied.

"They say," said Penn, "that we sons are made in the image of our father."

Catherine shuddered. "I hope not," she said vehemently. Heads turned in her direction.

Marcus smoothed over the awkward moment. "Come on, Cat. The sooner we get settled, the sooner I'll show you around the place."

They separated at the bottom of the stairs. Catherine didn't look back, but she was conscious of three pairs of eyes following her.

The moment she entered the lord's bedchamber, the tension began to drain out of her. It was only now that she realized just how much she had been dreading this meeting with Marcus's family.

Marcus waited until the footmen had deposited their boxes in the middle of the floor then, after dismissing them, he threw off his cloak and sprawled in a big old-fashioned armchair in front of the fire. Catherine removed her bonnet but kept on her pelisse. The room was enormous, and the fire had yet to take the chill off the air. She moved to the window and looked out. From there, it was impossible to tell that she was behind the walls of a medieval castle. Broad meadows fell away to stands of willow that grew thick on the banks of the river Avon. In the near distance was the town of Wrotham. Poised above it, like a ball of dirty cotton, was a cloud of smoke that had spewed out of the multitude of chimney stacks.

Turning, she said, "Tell me why your family isn't close. Is there a reason?"

"It's not because of Helen," he answered. "She's no wicked stepmother."

"I can see that. But the rest of you don't seem very affectionate, though I think Tristram would be, if you gave him half a chance. Then there's David. If I had a cousin and he lived in Ireland, I wouldn't wait fifteen years to see him."

"I suppose we're no better or worse than other families of our class. We boys spend most of our time in boarding school, and only come home for the holidays. I also served six years as a soldier."

"But what about when you were children . . . ?"

"I didn't live here as a child. When my mother died, I went to live with my aunt. My father visited me sometimes. But the first time I met Helen and her brood was at my father's funeral."

"But that's . . . sad."

He looked at her curiously. "You don't need to feel sorry for me. My aunt was like a mother to me. You were raised by an aunt, too, weren't you?"

"Aunt Bea," she said, with so much distaste that Marcus laughed, and after a moment, she laughed with him.

He said casually, "Your friend Emily told me that your aunt was very straitlaced."

She shot him a sharp look. "Now don't *you* get the wrong idea. I'm not at all like my aunt."

"Who are you trying to convince, me or yourself?"

She drew in a sharp breath and let it out slowly. "It's not because of my aunt that I refused your insulting offer. You are a married man, and even if you weren't, I still wouldn't become your mistress."

He said impatiently, "I wasn't thinking of that."

"Then what were you thinking?"

"I was thinking that when I look at you I see more

than one woman. There's more to you than you want me to know."

She hoped her shock didn't show. "You're not making sense."

"You're passionate about things and reckless too . . . then a mask comes down, and you're like ice."

"Well, I'm playing a part, of course."

"But which part is the real you?"

This conversation was too close for comfort. It was time to change the subject. Her eyes fell on their trunks and boxes.

Frowning up at him, she said, "Where is your room, Marcus?"

He slouched down in his chair and grinned. "Ah, yes. My room. What would you say if I told you there is a Wrotham tradition that the lord and his lady always share a room?"

"I'd say I don't give a fig for Wrotham traditions."

"Somehow, I thought you'd say that."

He rose and made for the door.

"Marcus?"

"Yes?"

"I mean, that is, what are you going to tell them?"

"If anyone asks, I shall say that my wife is convent bred and is too modest to share a room with a man, even if that man is her husband. That's not far off the truth, is it?"

And with that question hanging between them, he left the room.

Chapter 15

Penn was the last to arrive for dinner that evening. When he saw Marcus seated at the head of the table, the seat he, Penn, usually occupied, he muttered something under his breath, and took the empty chair beside his mother. One look at Penn told Catherine all she needed to know. She knew the signs. Penn had been drinking again. He was past the expansive stage and into the silent one. With her father, the next stage was either a bout of weeping, or he would turn on those closest to him and rail at them for all his troubles. When Penn called the footman over to pour him a glass of wine which he immediately raised to his lips for a long swallow, her heart sank.

"*Tus ojos son azules.*"

Catherine let out a startled, "*¿Qué?*"

David Lytton, who was seated at her right, was smiling at her. "Your eyes are blue," he repeated in flawless Spanish.

She flicked a look at Marcus. This was what she feared most—to be confronted by someone who spoke the language fluently. Marcus did not appear to have heard his cousin.

"*Sí,*" she replied softly.

Again he spoke in Spanish. "Where did a Spanish girl come by those blue eyes and fair skin?"

She spoke with the Spanish accent she'd adopted since she'd made her debut as Catalina. "From an English ancestor. Speak English, señor. I wish to practice my English."

Marcus broke in. "Where did you learn to speak Spanish, David?"

There was a pause. David looked down at his plate, then looked up to see everyone staring at him. Everyone could see that Marcus's question had embarrassed him.

"One of my friends is married to a Spanish girl," he said lamely.

"Oh yes," said Penn, snickering. "One of your friends! Marcus, how can you be so gauche? How did you learn Spanish? Not from a tutor, I'll wager."

"Penn," said the dowager, smoothing things over, "why don't you tell Catherine about the horse you've set aside for her use?"

The dowager had an anxious look on her face, and Catherine's heart went out to her. She remembered so well trying to placate her father on occasions just such as this. She'd felt so helpless.

"Let Marcus tell her," said Penn sullenly. "They're his horses. My opinion counts for nothing around here."

Marcus ignored Penn. He called one of the footmen over and said something quietly in his ear.

The dowager looked back to Penn in appeal, and he said finally, "She's a spirited little filly who comes from your own neck of the woods. Her name is Magazin."

"One of the Andalusians?" asked Catherine, feigning delight. She'd been expecting the offer, and she and Marcus had already decided how to get out of it.

Tristram said, "That one is a lady's mount! I'll wager Catherine is used to something better. I'd be happy to lend you Charon—also an Andalusian, but not nearly so tame as Magazin. In fact, Charon is the best that Wrotham has to offer."

"Oh, I couldn't accept such a sacrifice," said Catherine. "You'll want to ride Charon yourself."

Tristram made a face. "My time is going to be occupied studying Latin and Greek with Mr. Reeves, our chaplain."

"All the same," said Catherine, "I think I shall stay with the filly, but thank you for the offer."

This was Marcus's cue, and he said, "I'm afraid I can't allow it, Catherine. You know the doctor has forbidden it."

The dowager's face lit up and she said impetuously, "You're with child! Why, that's wonderful news!"

Catherine's hand fluttered to her throat. "Ah, no." No one blinked. Not a muscle moved in any of the faces that were turned to her. They might have been carved out of stone. Color rushed to her hairline, and her eyes flashed to Marcus. "Marcus?" she appealed faintly.

Marcus made a small sound of exasperation. "It's nothing more than an old riding injury that acts up once in a while."

"My hip," said Catherine quickly. "It always pains me when the weather changes. Oh, not enough to lame me, but enough to make riding awkward."

There was a moment of profound silence, then everyone began talking at once. Catherine looked at Marcus, who answered that look with an imperceptible shrug. No one believed them. To argue the point would only make matters worse.

It was then that Penn looked around for a footman to refill his wine glass. There were no servants in sight, nor bottles of wine or decanters. He turned his head to stare at Marcus, then, leaning heavily on the table, he rose to his feet.

The eyes of the two brothers locked, battled, and moments later, with a snarl of rage, Penn knocked over his chair and stumbled from the room.

"What was that all about?" Catherine asked David in a shocked undertone.

He did not raise his eyes from the food on his plate. "Marcus ordered the footmen to remove all the liquor," he said, "and Penn has just discovered it."

Later, three very subdued ladies entered the drawing room while the gentlemen remained in the dining room. Catherine wondered whether Marcus would allow the usual port and brandy and she thought not. He'd had that hard, inflexible look about him when Penn had tried to stare him down. Marcus was determined to break Penn of his addiction even if he had to smash every bottle of liquor in the house. But that's not how it worked. A drunkard always knew where he could find his next drink.

The dowager looked at Catherine, tried for a smile, failed, and said, "This is a fine welcome to Wrotham, Catherine. I'm sorry. Penn isn't always like this. It's just that, well, he was angry with Marcus for offering David better terms on the brood mare he wanted."

Samantha said the first words Catherine had heard her say since they'd sat down to dinner. "I don't blame Penn for being angry. Marcus should have known better. Penn is the one who knows everything about running Wrotham—Marcus is more like a visitor!"

"Samantha!"

The girl colored. "Well, it's true, Mama." Though the words were defiant, she was looking at Catherine with an appeal in her eyes.

Catherine said, and meant it, "No, that wasn't well done of Marcus, and"—she paused, groping for the right words—"I understand, truly I do." And she did, far more than these ladies could possibly know.

Now that she had a chance to study Samantha, she saw that her first impression hadn't been completely true. She'd summed her up as a quiet little mouse, but now she saw that she was also loyal to a fault. It was more than loyalty. The girl loved Penn, and if Marcus did not watch his step, he would find his mouse of a sister had turned into a lioness.

"Do you play whist?" asked the dowager.

"No, ma'am." Cards, according to Aunt Bea, were an invention of the devil. Of course, just about everything, according to Aunt Bea, was an invention of the devil. The thought arrested her. Was it possible that in some ways, she was still unwittingly under her aunt's thumb? "But I'm willing to learn," she added.

The dowager beamed. "Splendid!"

"Drat!" said Samantha. She had spread the pages of a newspaper on top of the piano and was going through them systematically.

"What is it, dear?" asked the dowager.

"A. W. Euman's column isn't in this edition of *The Journal* either. She must still be on holiday."

Catherine had just been lifting the first card the dowager had dealt her, and she dropped it. "A. W. Euman?" she said. "But surely he is a gentleman."

"That's what I used to think," said Samantha, "but Mama has convinced me that she's a female."

Catherine was astounded, and couldn't help showing it. To her knowledge, no one had ever guessed that A. W. Euman was a female. "Whatever gave you that idea?" she asked the dowager.

"It's just a feeling I have." When she saw that Catherine wasn't really interested in the cards, she set them on the table. "Do you read A. W. Euman?"

Catherine nodded.

"Have you ever noticed that she sees everything through a woman's eyes? There are times when I think she's seeing things through *my* eyes."

"Really?" said Catherine faintly. "But she, that is, he has been to Newgate and to parts of the city that no decent lady would dare visit." Not to mention the brothels that proliferated in and around Covent Garden.

"This is no conventional lady," said the dowager with enthusiasm. "That's what I like about her. She's intrepid, and reckless. She never lets anything stand in her way. When she wants a story, she goes after it. It wouldn't surprise me if she disguises herself as a man."

And she'd thought of it, but she didn't have the height or build to pull it off.

"And you're not shocked?" Catherine looked from mother to daughter.

The dowager's eyes dropped away. "I envy her," she said. "I suspect she's a woman who lives on her own—well, she must be or the men in her life would never allow her so much freedom. She comes and goes as she pleases." She seemed to be enthralled at the idea. After a reflective moment of silence, she continued, "Such a woman would know how to take care of herself. She wouldn't depend on any man for anything."

"I think you have the wrong idea about A. W.

Euman," said Catherine, not altogether sure whether she was flattered by this portrait.

"Don't you approve?" This was from Samantha. "You were once a partisan. I would think that you and A. W. Euman would have much in common."

Admiration was shining in the girl's eyes. Catherine opened her mouth then shut it. *Hell and damnation,* as McNally would say. She'd found two kindred spirits—in Wrotham, of all places.

"Yes, I approve," she said, "though I wouldn't want Marcus to hear me say so."

Above the laughter that followed, a voice from the door—Marcus's voice—said, "What wouldn't you wish me to hear, *mi esposa*?"

The men entered, but Penn was not with them.

David took the chair next to Catherine's. "A dry house," he whispered, and winked at her.

Catherine pretended not to understand. "Helen believes that A. W. Euman is a female."

"A. W. Euman?" said Marcus. "Oh, the fellow who writes for *The Journal*. I've met him a time or two."

"You've met him?" said the dowager, astonished. "And he's not a woman?"

"Oh, he's womanish, I'll give you that. Come to think of it, he puts me in mind of a spinster."

The dowager and Samantha couldn't hide their disappointment. Catherine was more successful at concealing her fury.

"Well, don't stop there," she said. "We're all ears. Do tell us more."

Marcus obliged. "He's very straitlaced, very moral. He doesn't drink, doesn't play cards, and doesn't run around with loose . . . that is, let's just say he is very moral." He kept a straight face.

"I see nothing wrong in that," declared Catherine, and all the gentlemen chuckled.

Shortly after, tea was served, and the conversation became general. The men decided to go hunting early the next morning—and Tristram only if he made up the lost hours of study. One by one, people made their excuses and retired for the night.

When Catherine made to leave, Marcus walked her to the door. "Wait up for me," he said.

She gave him a startled look, nodded, and slipped through the door.

He found Penn in the estate office, which was in the stable block, outside the castle walls. Penn was standing at his desk, studying his ledgers. There was an opened bottle of brandy on the desk, and in one hand he was cradling a filthy glass that was empty. At the sight of Marcus, he reached for the brandy bottle and filled his glass to the brim.

"Here's to the return of the Prodigal," he sneered. He drank deeply, then wiped his mouth on the back of his sleeve.

Marcus said, "I'm sorry about David. He caught me by surprise. Once I'd given my promise, I couldn't go back on it. I give you my word that it won't happen again."

It was obvious from Penn's expression that whatever he had expected to hear, it certainly wasn't this. Coming to himself, he said, "Apology accepted."

Marcus leaned one shoulder against the lintel of the door. "When did your drinking habit become an addiction?"

"Ah. Now this is more like it. Marcus, you are not my father. I won't be lectured by you. And I'm not addicted."

"I'm your brother, and I feel responsible for you."

"Half brother," corrected Penn. "And since when did you start feeling responsible for me? There was never any love lost between us. I was just a convenience, someone who managed your estates while you went off to war. Are you finding fault with the way I run things?"

"Of course not. You've done an excellent job. But what about the future, Penn? You can't go on like this. You have to pull yourself together and make something of your life. I've been thinking about it ... supposing you take over that place of ours in Cornwall? I'll deed it to you. You can do whatever you like with it. I think you would enjoy the challenge."

"I don't want your charity."

A muscle tensed in Marcus's cheek. "You never expected me to return, did you, Penn? You thought I'd die out there in Spain, and you would have inherited everything."

Penn began to laugh, then stopped abruptly. "I never expected to hear you say such a thing." He reached for his glass and took another swallow. "Not to me."

Marcus realized that nothing he said was going to make the slightest difference. He could praise Penn or he could insult him, and either way, his words would have no effect.

"This conversation is leading nowhere," he said. "But I'd like to make one thing plain: I will not put up with drunkenness in my own home. Every bottle of spirits has been locked up and I have the key." When Penn said nothing, he went on, "If you won't think of yourself, think of your mother. Can't you see you're breaking her heart?"

"Damn you! I'm not a drunkard! I'm not! I can stop any time I want."

Marcus stared at him hard. "Are you sure of that?"

Penn looked at the glass in his hand. "I can stop any time I want."

The sight that met Marcus's eyes when he entered the lord's chamber riveted him. She was seated at a small table in front of the fire, completely absorbed in her task, unaware of the man who stood transfixed, watching her dip pen into ink and begin to write. She had changed into her nightclothes, and she was wearing something soft and dark, something feminine that molded itself to her curves. Her dark hair was subdued in a severe knot and emphasized her strong features. For a moment, a fraction of a moment, he could almost believe that he'd taken a step back in time and he was with Catalina again in that small priest's cell in *El Grande*'s hideout in Spain.

But, of course, it wasn't Catalina he was remembering. Cat's face and form had become so etched on his mind that it was impossible now to see Catalina clearly.

When he could breathe, he said softly, "What are you doing?"

She answered absently, "I'm making notes of my impressions of your house and family."

"You keep a diary? A journal?"

The pen stopped scratching. She was smiling when she finally raised her eyes to his. "Not a diary, Marcus. Just notes. I'm a writer. We writers never trust anything to memory. Who knows? I may find inspiration for an article for *The Journal* while I am here. Please." She indicated a chair on the other side of the table. "What is it you wished to say to me?"

He took the chair she indicated. "Nothing in particular. Oh, don't go getting that look in your eyes. We're supposed to be married. What will everyone think if we don't spend time alone together? I won't stay long."

She saw the logic in this and nodded.

He let out a long sigh, stretched out his legs, and propped his feet on the brass fender. "I apologize for that scene with Penn. I knew he sometimes drank to excess, but I've never seen him so offensive with it. It won't happen again. I had my steward lock up every bottle of wine and spirits in the house, and the key to the cellar is now in my pocket."

"I didn't take offense. I felt sorry for him."

Reacting to the reproachful note in her voice, he replied abruptly, "I've already apologized to Penn for not consulting him about the mare David wanted. Dammit, Cat, I was within my rights. I am the master here."

"And I'm sure Penn knows it. I don't mean to criticize you . . ."

"Go on. I know you have more to say."

He was looking at the notes she'd made and she couldn't see his expression, but his words were all the encouragement she needed. "I don't think you're handling this the right way. You humiliated him publicly by having the servants remove the wine and decanters, and now that you've locked everything away, he'll only be more stubborn. Until he admits he's a drunkard, there's not much anyone can do. Perhaps if you tried to be his friend—"

"His friend? Cat, we are brothers."

"Yes, but as you told me yourself, you're not a very close family. Perhaps that's part of the problem."

He suddenly looked up and pinned her with blazing eyes. It was one thing to reproach himself for his sins, but quite another to hear it from someone else, especially her.

"You've been in my home for less than twenty-four hours, and just like that"—he snapped his fingers—"you think you know better than I how to manage my family?"

"You asked for my opinion. And I do know what I'm talking about. When one member of a family is addicted to alcohol, the whole family suffers."

He said carefully, "A moment ago, you said you were making notes of your impressions of my house and family for an article for *The Journal*. What kind of article?"

"Country sketches, that sort of thing." Her hand went involuntarily to her notes and covered them.

"May I see your notes?"

She shook her head, and said lightly, "I never permit anyone to read my notes. You'll have to wait until you read my piece in *The Journal*."

His voice was like ice. "Let me see the notes, Cat."

She moistened her lips. "They're not complete."

Abruptly reaching forward, he wrested the pages of notes from her and scanned the title. " 'A Drunkard's Progress,' " he read aloud, and his expression became livid. He stood up, towering over her, and she shrank back into her chair.

When he saw the look of fear, he swung away from her, putting some space between them, then he turned to face her. He articulated each word slowly and precisely. "You are not going to make my family fodder for that tawdry little column you write for *The Journal*. Do I make myself clear?"

"But I wasn't—"

He silenced her with a sweep of one hand. He knew his reaction was extreme, but he couldn't help what he was feeling. He'd just come from his confrontation with Penn, and his frustration was keen. Moreover, in his mind, by finding fault with his brother, she was finding fault with him.

A warm, passionately caring woman couldn't behave like this. She wasn't a warm, passionately caring woman. She was a cold, unfeeling witch who cared only for the pieces she wrote for *The Journal*.

It came to him then just how deeply he had come to care for her, and the thought made him writhe. She didn't care for him. For all he knew, even the passion was a sham. She certainly never had any trouble putting a stop to things before they'd gone too far.

"I thought you were different," he said, "but I see I was wrong. Other people are just potential subjects to you to be analyzed and then documented for the world to read about. Perhaps they'll be amused, or perhaps they'll shed a tear. It's all the same to you as long as you titillate your readers. Well, you won't do it with my family. I'm paying you well for your time, and every second of your time belongs to me. As long as you're employed by me, you're going to forget that you are a writer. And one more thing. When this is over and you've gone back to your life in Hampstead, I shall be reading *The Journal* in minute detail. If you write anything that embarrasses any member of my family, I shall bankrupt not only you but your employer also. Do you understand?"

"Marcus," she cried passionately, "I wasn't writing about Penn. I was writing about anyone who drinks to excess. You see—"

"Don't lie. His name is right here in your notes."

"But I'm not writing about him in particular."

"No, but you'll use him as an example."

He looked at the paper in his hand and threw it on her writing table. Then, with a savage oath, he flung out of the room.

She felt shattered. He'd never looked at her before with such contempt. But he didn't understand. She did care about people, she cared deeply, but caring wasn't always enough. It was because she'd felt so helpless to change things that she'd become a writer in the first place. Perhaps she didn't do much good, but it was better than being a complete spectator at the world's misery.

She stared into the glowing coals in the grate and wondered why she should care what he thought of her.

Chapter 16

A week later found Catherine walking the ramparts of the south wall. This was where she came to exercise when no one was free to accompany her on her walks. This morning, Marcus and David were out shooting with some local gentlemen, Tristram was at his studies, she wasn't sure about Penn, and Samantha and Helen, to Catherine's intense envy, were riding somewhere on the moors. She might have gone walking with an armed footman in tow, but Marcus and she had agreed that it would look odd. In any case, she enjoyed these solitary walks along the ramparts.

The sun went behind a cloud and she looked up in some surprise. When she'd come out on the walls there hadn't been a cloud in sight. Though autumn was almost over, these last few days they'd been enjoying warm weather. Now, dark clouds that seemed to be a reflection of the darkness in herself were gathering overhead. There were shots in the distance and she presumed they came from the gentlemen who'd gone out hunting.

She propped her crossed arms along one of the battlements, and rested her chin on them. As far as the eye could see, for miles around, these lands belonged to Marcus. For centuries, the citizens of Wrotham had paid their feus to the lords of Wrotham. Until she'd come to this castle, she'd never really thought of Marcus as a peer of the realm. She'd thought of him as a soldier, then again as an unscrupulous rake, and sometimes as a mischievous rogue. She was seeing another side of him now. He was very much the lord of his domain.

Since their quarrel, there had been no more cozy chats. He never came to her room; anything that had to be said was said in passing. He never teased her any more, never tried to get her dander up. He was polite but distant when they were alone, and when company was present he was merely polite. Though she hated to admit it, she missed the old Marcus.

If anyone noticed that theirs was not a perfect marriage, no one mentioned it. It was Penn's unpredictable behavior that was on everyone's mind. One moment, he'd be laughing and joking as if he didn't have a care in the world. The next his mood had turned ugly and he was looking to pick a fight. It was always a great relief when he left to work on estate business.

There wasn't a drop of liquor in the house. Penn never complained, or mentioned it, but everyone knew that he was getting it somewhere. According to David Lytton, Marcus had only succeeded in punishing the innocent by locking up all the liquor in the house.

She felt sorry for David. He'd never meant to stay on so long, and clearly felt a bit out of place, but the dowager wouldn't hear of his leaving so soon. In a few days, there would be a ball in honor of Marcus and his bride, and she wanted him to attend. David had given in gracefully. If Catherine had been David, she would have invented an ancient uncle whose dying wish was to look upon his nephew's face one last time.

Well, perhaps that wasn't completely fair. Marcus's family wasn't really so bad. She was becoming rather fond of them, more than fond, even of Penn. There were times she saw something in his eyes that made her want to reach out to him. As for the dowager and Samantha, it was impossible not to like them; they were so eager to learn about the ladies in Spain and London, the current fashions, and the parties she'd attended. And Tristram was her most devoted admirer.

To Marcus, on the other hand, she was a cold-hearted, mercenary adventuress with whom he'd made a bargain. And if he knew the truth he'd think even worse of her.

This was dangerous thinking. Major Carruthers would be appalled if he knew how she was wavering. *Never let your feelings get in the way of doing your job* was what he always said. She hoped the major was doing *his* job. For herself, she was beginning to think she'd come on a wild-goose chase.

It had begun to rain. After a few minutes, she headed for the door to the tower staircase. It was dark inside the tower. This was unusual and she stopped. Because so little natural light entered the tower from the arrow loops set in the wall, lanterns at each flight of stairs were always lit. She saw at once that one of those lanterns had gone out. This hardly bothered her. Though the stairs were dangerously steep, she'd descended them often enough to be sure of her footing. As she started down, she heard a faint sound. Someone had either just entered by the door to the bailey, or had just left by it. From one of the arrow loops close by, a gust of wind buffeted her, bringing the rain with it. She hardly felt it. Her hand had gone automatically to her pocket where she kept her pistol.

The minutes slipped by, and still she remained motionless. She sensed something wrong. First the lantern and now something else. But what? And then she had it. The door to the bailey had rusty hinges. It was impossible to open it without the thing wheezing like an old bellows. But now it seemed to be working smoothly as if the hinges had been . . . oiled.

She took the stairs one slow step at a time, pressing herself against the outside wall, her eyes scanning the gloom. At every other step, she stopped and listened. Suddenly, her foot went from under her. She flung back to prevent herself from pitching forward, and she landed with a thud on the stone stairs, her pistol still clutched in her hand. She heard something go rattling down the stairs, then the sound of breaking glass.

Her back had taken the brunt of her fall, but it was the pain in her left elbow which made her gasp. Hunched over, she rocked herself, waiting for the pain to recede.

When she tried to rise, her foot slipped and she fell heavily on her bottom. She touched the sole of her shoe, and her hand came away covered in oil.

After pocketing her pistol, she used her petticoat to wipe her shoes clean, and when next she descended the stairs, she felt her way with her hands. One step down, she came upon a pool of oil, and beyond that, the broken pieces of a lantern. It looked as though the lantern had fallen from the wall and spilled its contents over the steps. That's what everyone was meant to think, but she was unconvinced.

She heard it again, the faint sound of the door opening, and her head lifted.

"Catherine?" Marcus's voice. "Are you sure she's here?"

Another voice, Tristram's. "I saw her on the walls not ten minutes ago."

"Catherine?"

She heard Marcus and Tristram taking the stairs. "I'm up here. No, don't come up. I'm coming down."

When she reached the bottom of the stairs, Marcus said, "I looked for you on the walls when I came in, but couldn't see you. Where were you?"

It never entered her head to tell him the truth—that someone had deliberately tried to hurt her, or even kill her. He would only put the blame on Catalina and *El Grande,* and she had no reply to that. But someone had tried to hurt her, and she didn't know what to think.

She tried not to sound as shaken as she felt. "I came in out of the rain and just sat on the top step thinking about things. I'm sorry. I forgot the time. Oh, I should tell you, one of the lanterns fell from the wall. It's broken, and there's glass scattered on the stairs."

"I'll get one of the footmen to see to it," said Tristram.

Marcus was watching her closely. "Cat, are you all right?" he asked softly. "You're very pale."

She wanted to believe that the concern in his voice was genuine, but the suspicion that Marcus may have just tried to hurt her had taken possession of her mind, and she was numb with the horror of it. Perhaps he'd known all along that she was Catalina. Perhaps she had walked right into his trap. Her hands were trembling. Somehow, she had to hide what she suspected or the game would be up.

"Cat?"

"I'm fine. Really. I can't think why you're making such a fuss."

Tristram held the door for her, but she managed to brush her fingers casually along one of the hinges. Just as she suspected, she found oil.

"You may not have noticed, but there's a storm brewing," Marcus said curtly. "I was told you were walking on the ramparts and came to fetch you. Don't you know that when lightning strikes, the worst place to be is on the castle walls? I thought you had more sense."

She saw, then, that he had her cloak over one arm. And just as though he commanded the heavens, lightning streaked across the sky, the thunder rolled, and the rain came down in torrents.

He flung her cloak around her shoulders, and flanked by Marcus and Tristram, she crossed the bailey at a run.

Since Catalina was a Catholic, it made perfect sense for Catherine to go occasionally to the priest of the small Catholic church at the edge of town to make her confession. Sometimes he came to the castle to talk to her. What no one knew was that Father Granger was Major Carruther's man and Catherine made her reports to him.

She left her carriage in the lane and entered the church unescorted. With the exception of Father Granger, the church was empty. His back was to her, and she saw that he was replenishing an iron stove with coal from a blackened scuttle. The weather had turned cold and she was wearing a warm pelisse with a sable collar that matched her muff. Her gaze wandered, taking in the marble statuary, the stained-glass windows, the candles on the altar. Then, after dipping her fingers into the font of holy water, she made the sign of the cross and entered the confessional. Father Granger followed her at once.

His face was obscured by the screen but she could hear the rasp of his breathing. The time had come for her to tell him that there had been an attack on her. They would assume, of course, that Marcus was behind it. It was what they'd been waiting for, a sign that Marcus had been lying to them all along, that he was, in fact, the man who had murdered all those English soldiers. It meant he knew that she was Catalina, and that this elaborate scheme of his was a ploy to lure *El Grande* out of hiding so that he could kill him too. Once she made her report, it would all be out of her hands. Whatever the consequences to Marcus, it was none of her business.

"What is it, child?"

The priest's voice brought her back to where she was. She stared at the screen with panicked eyes. She knew how she was supposed to think. Logic. Deduction. Putting two and two together to come up with the right answer. But where Marcus was concerned she found it impossible to be logical. Everything in her recoiled from the thought that he was a murderer. It wasn't true. It simply couldn't be true—and she was willing to stake her life on it.

"I have nothing to report," she said.

There was a moment of silence. "And that's all you have to say?"

It was all she had to say to *this* priest. If *El Grande* had been here, it would have been different. He wasn't like Major Carruthers. He saw to the heart of things. He would understand why she couldn't betray Marcus, and he would trust her instincts. Someone else had to be behind this attack on her, and if *El Grande* were here, they would sort things through together.

Names came to her mind, but as quickly as they came, she discarded them. She couldn't believe a member of Marcus's family wished to harm her. Then who—

"My child," said the priest, and paused.

Catherine's thoughts snapped together. "That's all I have to say," she said.

Chapter 17

It was early morning, very early, and Amy Spencer never, *never* rose from her bed before noon. None of her friends ever did. Yet here she was again, donning her plainest coat and bonnet just so that she could go around town, unrecognized, with the man who had turned her life upside down. She'd stopped giving parties. She rarely went to the theater. And her carriage with its distinctive trimmings was never allowed out of the coach house. As a consequence, her popularity was slipping, and she could not seem to care.

She glanced out the window and saw that it was raining. Perhaps he wouldn't come for her. It would be better if he didn't. There could never be anything between Robert and her, and she never tired of telling him so. She was too old for him, too experienced, too jaded. Besides all that, she'd learned that he was Spanish and not Irish as she'd assumed at first. They were too different. They had nothing in common. Then what in hell's name was she doing going out with him again? This could only lead to heartbreak.

She didn't care. At least she now knew that she had a heart to break. He made her feel—not young again—but untouched by all the sordid circumstances of her life. He'd told her that soon he would be returning to Spain to take up his life there. It was for the best, but until that day arrived, she would cherish their few days together.

That didn't sound like Amy Spencer. What the hell had got into her?

Miss Collyer poked her head around the door. "He's here," she said in the tone of a breathless schoolgirl.

Miss Collyer wasn't the only one who felt breathless around Robert.

He was waiting for her in the vestibule. She'd known many handsome men in her time, but no one had ever matched Robert. Of course, looks meant nothing to her—she knew better than anyone that beauty did not bring happiness. It was Robert, the man, that drew her with his beautiful wise eyes. Sometimes it seemed to her that he knew far more about life than she.

"I thought we'd go for a picnic," he said, and before she could draw on her gloves, he pressed a kiss to her bare wrist.

Another chaste kiss that inflamed her. Oh God, she was playing with fire. She didn't mind getting burned but she was determined that when this was over, Robert was going to return to Spain unscathed.

She smiled up at him. "Haven't you noticed? It's raining cats and dogs."

He laughed. "The English have such quaint ways of expressing themselves. You mean it's a downpour."

"That's exactly what I mean. So how can we go on a picnic?"

"Have a little faith in me, Amy. I know what I'm doing."

He had a way of bringing a conversation from the trivial to the profound. He was doing it now.

She answered him seriously. "Let's not talk of that now. Let's just enjoy these few hours we have together."

They came out of the door hand in hand. He said, "I've hired a carriage to take us to Chelsea. We can have our picnic inside while we watch the boats on the river."

It was a closed carriage, but she knew he hadn't chosen it only because of the rain. They both wanted the anonymity. He wasn't free to tell her what his reasons were for secrecy, and as for her, she did not want any ugly gossip to touch Robert because of who she was.

When they were on their way, he removed one of her gloves, then laced his fingers through hers. "Now don't be frightened," he said.

She looked at their joined hands and felt the power of his touch all through her body. It had never been like this. Still looking at their joined hands, she said softly, "Robert, you've never been with a woman in that way, have you? I mean—"

"I know what you mean. And the answer is no." She looked up and caught his smile. "Priests don't as a rule," he went on. "And afterward, when I left the seminary, there was no woman I wanted to marry."

"And with you marriage would have to come first?"

He grinned. "For me it must be marriage or nothing."

He'd relieved her worst fears. He was safe from her. Now he would go home to Spain, meet some nice young girl, and they would live happily ever after. She couldn't bear it.

"Now it's your turn," he said. "Tell me why your life took a different direction from your sister's."

She didn't mind the question. From the very first, it had seemed so natural, as if they had known each other all their lives, to share their innermost feelings about things. Last time they were together, he'd told her why he'd lost his faith. He'd been studying to be a priest when the French had tortured and murdered every member of his family. He'd become a partisan. And later, when the war was over, he'd been sickened at the man he'd become. He hadn't been able to remain in Spain. There were too many painful memories.

She answered him matter-of-factly. "I wasn't happy at home, and eventually I took up with the wrong set, the fast set. One night, one of those 'friends,' a man I thought I loved, raped me. Later, he apologized, and said that he'd been overcome by his emotions. He wanted to marry me, to make things right, but for complicated reasons it had to be a secret marriage. I still loved him and so I forgave him and we eloped. But he had lied to me—he had never had any intention of marrying me. Instead he set me up as his mistress. And that was the beginning of my career as Amy Spencer."

"Wrotham!" he said with disgust.

A look of surprise crossed her face. "Why do you say that? No. It wasn't him. He came into my life much later than that. I didn't even know Marcus at the time."

"Then why does Catherine hate Wrotham?"

He was looking at her closely, not saying anything, not condemning, and suddenly she had to tell him the whole sordid story. "I once saw Marcus at Vauxhall Gardens when I was with these friends. There was talk, you know how it is—everyone thought he cut such a dashing figure. After all, he was young, wealthy, and titled. It happened that when I got home that night, I had a ferocious quarrel with my aunt. She said horrible things to me— that I would never amount to anything and so on. I flung the first name I could think of at her.

" 'As a matter of fact the Earl of Wrotham is in love with me!' I told her. 'So I might yet turn out to be a countess.' And the more she poured scorn on the idea, the more I elaborated on it. Very soon after, I was lying to Cat too."

She touched a hand to her eyes. "She found me the night I was raped. I wasn't a pretty sight. She demanded to know if Wrotham had done this to me. I couldn't bring myself to tell her that the man I loved had done it. Cat kept after me, and finally I said, 'Yes.' It just seemed easier."

He tipped her chin up and gave her a searching look. "You must tell her the truth."

"Why must I? It's all ancient history. Marcus means nothing to her, or that's what she told me." She sat up straighter. "Are you saying that she lied to me?"

"No. I'm not saying that. I'm saying that you must tell her the truth because it's the right thing to do."

There was no disgust or contempt in his eyes, only compassion, and for some reason she could not fathom, she felt tears begin to well.

"I'll tell her," she said.

He smiled. "Why don't we start our picnic now, and when we get to Chelsea, we can walk along the riverbank."

"Walk? In this rain?"

"The sky is clearing. Have a little faith, and you'll move mountains. Trust me in this."

He was wrong. It was still raining when they got to Chelsea.

"I did warn you," she said, delighting in teasing him.

It didn't stop him. He dragged her, squealing and protesting, out of the coach, and set her on her feet.

"We walk," he said.

And so they did, in the rain, and Amy had never enjoyed anything more. Everything amused them, everything delighted them.

"We're mad," said Amy at one point, laughing up at him.

"No. We're in love."

The smile left her face. "Oh, Robert, I wish it were that simple."

A man's strident voice drowned out his response. "It *is* her. I told you it was her. Amy! Amy! Don't you remember me?"

Four young gentlemen of fashion were descending boisterously from a carriage that had stopped on the Chelsea Road. They seemed to have been out all night and were now on their way home.

"Don't you remember me, Amy? It's Harry Simpson. My cousin brought me to one of your parties." He hiccuped. "Why don't you join us and we'll have a little tipple and jaw over old times?"

This last suggestion won a roar of approval from his friends. Amy was seized by two of them, and they began to drag her to the carriage.

"Let go of her!" said *El Grande* in a voice that immediately cast a pall on the riotous young men. They turned to stare at him.

"Good God!" exclaimed Simpson. He looked *El Grande* up and down, taking in the plain, serviceable garments that had never seen the hand of a London tailor. "What are you?" he demanded. "A lackey? Be on your way, man, before I take my whip to you."

Although Amy was struggling and protesting, she wasn't frightened. She knew how to manage young bucks who'd had a few drinks too many. But she wasn't given a chance to charm them out of their deviltry. She stumbled, and when she was wrenched roughly to her feet, she cried out.

With a roar of rage, *El Grande* lunged for the ringleader and they went tumbling to the ground. His fist smashed into Simpson's face and blood spurted on both men. There was a moment of stunned silence, then Amy was shoved aside, and three men rushed at *El Grande*. One had a cane and brought it down on his head. As he lay there stunned, another kicked him in the side.

Amy screamed and rushed to his defense. A strong blow sent her sprawling. Screaming hysterically, she came at them again. One man held her off, while the others hauled *El Grande* to his feet. As she watched frozen in shock they beat him mercilessly with their fists, each blow more savage than the last. It was over in a matter of seconds, but those seconds were the longest in Amy's life. When they let him go, he sank to his knees then rolled on his back.

Amy was beside herself. "You'll pay for this," she screamed. "I know you, Harry Simpson. I'll set the magistrates on you."

"Do that," he said and sneered. "What magistrate would listen to you? You're nothing but an old whore."

A coach that was passing had stopped, and a man jumped out and came racing down the riverbank toward them. He had a pistol in his hand.

El Grande's assailants backed off and made for their carriage. Amy stumbled after them and came to a halt. "Savages! You won't get away with this! You won't! I swear it!"

"Old whore!" came the reply.

Another took up the refrain and soon they were all chanting it. "Old whore! Old whore! Old whore!" And they kept on chanting it as their carriage bowled along the Chelsea Road.

Sobbing uncontrollably, she walked to *El Grande* and knelt beside him. The man who had come to their aid was bending over him.

"He's not seriously hurt," he said. "There are no bones broken." He looked at Amy. "I say, aren't you Amy Spencer?"

She nodded, but she was looking at *El Grande*. His face was filthy and smeared with blood and dirt. It had stopped raining, but Amy wasn't aware of it. She felt in her pocket and brought out a handkerchief with which she began to dab at his face. When his eyes opened and he stared up at her, she wept in deep uncontrollable sobs.

She blamed herself for everything that had happened. She knew she'd been playing with fire, but she'd never expected anything like this. If there was a price to pay, she'd been willing to pay it. But not this, *not this*. She felt naked, soiled, and exposed for the fraud she was. *Old whore*. The ugly words were still ringing in her ears. She'd been living in a fool's world and this was the result. It must never be allowed to happen again.

He raised to his elbows and groaned. "Amy?"

"Put your arms around my shoulders," said their rescuer.

When their coachman saw them approaching, he jumped down from the box to help them. Unfortunately he hadn't been in a position to see the fight, for his view had been obscured by a stand of willows.

Inside the coach, *El Grande* came to himself slowly.

"How do you feel?" asked Amy.

He flexed his jaw. "As though a carriage had just run over me. I'm out of practice, and they surprised me." He saw the look on her face and he fell silent, waiting for her to speak.

"This could ruin me," she said at last. "I didn't need your help. It's young men like Harry who keep me in pocket. I'm giving a party tomorrow night. Now, goodness only knows whether I shall have any guests. He doesn't look like much, but Harry Simpson has influence."

He said quietly, "I want you to marry me and come with me to Spain."

"Spain?" She laughed, though the laugh almost choked her. "And what would I do in Spain?"

"Be my wife. Have my children. Help me to rebuild everything I've lost."

"Everything I want is here. I thought you understood that." *Oh God, please forgive me.*

"I hear your words, Amy. But I don't believe that's what's in your heart."

"If you really knew me, Robert, you would know that I never allow my heart to rule my head."

When the coach pulled up outside Amy's house, she was out the door before he could stop her.

"This is goodbye, Robert," she said, and that was all she said. He knew that this time she meant it.

Chapter 18

Catherine stood on the gallery of the Great Hall looking over the crush of people on the floor below. The reception in her honor was in full swing, and the county for miles around had turned out to pay their respects. At her side was Tristram rambling on about horse breeding.

Her eyes were trailing Marcus. The dancers shifted and she saw him dancing with a beautiful woman who was sheathed in gold and white tissue. It was the second time he'd partnered her.

"Tristram," she said, unaware that she had interrupted him in mid-sentence, "who is that woman who is dancing with Marcus?"

He looked over the dancers, then looked back at Catherine. There was a twinkle in his eye. "That," he said, "is Mrs. Elizabeth Proudfoot." When he saw that the name meant nothing to her, he folded his lips together, and the twinkle in his eye faded.

Narrowing her eyes suspiciously, she turned slightly to look at him. "And who is Elizabeth Proudfoot?"

He stuttered, then said, "She's the woman who jilted Marcus. I thought everyone knew."

She turned away to conceal her shock. "Oh," she said.

"It happened years ago," said Tristram quickly. "They were betrothed when Marcus was my age or so. Elizabeth jilted him when a better offer came along."

"A better offer?" She couldn't imagine a better offer than Marcus.

"A duke," said Tristram, wishing he had kept his mouth shut. "But she didn't marry him. Before the wedding, the duke, who was ancient, suffered a stroke and that was the end of that. She ended up marrying one of our neighbors."

"Which gentleman is her husband?"

"Oh, old Proudfoot died years ago. Now Catherine, don't look like that. If there's one thing Marcus despises, it's women like Elizabeth. I've heard him call her a mercenary . . . um . . . witch."

Catherine laughed, then stopped abruptly when she realized what she was doing. Ever since the episode on the tower stairs, she'd warned herself endlessly to trust no one. Yet here she was again, taking everyone and everything at face value.

She slanted a sideways glance at Tristram. She just couldn't see him as a murderer. The same could be said for everyone at Wrotham. She couldn't go on like this, in an impasse, helpless to make a decision about what she should do next. She was courting disaster.

Suddenly conscious that Tristram was watching her curiously, she said, "I hadn't thought so many people would turn out to wish us happy."

"The county has certainly done Marcus proud," agreed Tristram. "The last time I saw such a crush was at Marcus's coming-of-age. I was only a boy at the time, but I still remember it."

"But haven't there been other balls since then?"

He shifted from one foot to the other, looked away, then said, "You know how it is with my mother. If it were not for Marcus, half the people here would have found some excuse not to attend. Not that it matters," he added staunchly. "Mama doesn't care much for their society either."

Catherine's eyes found the dowager, and she said impulsively, "But she looks radiant."

Tristram followed the path of her gaze, and he saw Penn partnering his mother in a country dance. "Oh, that's because Penn is on his best behavior tonight, and Samantha has made quite an impression on the local swains."

The country dance ended, and moments later, she

saw Marcus ascending the stairs toward her. He never once took his eyes off hers, and her pulse began to race.

He stopped in front of her. "The next dance is a waltz," he said. "I want to dance it with my wife." He wasn't smiling. He was very grave, and very, very handsome.

She put her gloved hand into his gloved hand, but the gloves did not protect her from the sensation of warm flesh embracing warm flesh. If it was all in her imagination, it was a convincing fantasy. She was so aware of him, she had difficulty breathing.

It got worse on the dance floor when he held her in his arms as they waited for the music to strike up. She could hear his heart thudding against her breast, feel his warm breath on her cheek. He was staring at her with an unsmiling, fixed intensity, and she began to tremble. She remembered that look. They'd be talking quietly in the priest's cell at *El Grande*'s base, and suddenly they would have nothing to talk about. His eyes would fasten on hers, with that same fixed intensity, and her mouth would go dry. She'd known what he was thinking because she was thinking it too. She wanted to be in his arms. She wanted him to make love to her.

She swallowed hard as she strove to remain rooted in reality. She couldn't— She shied away from the thought, but in spite of her best efforts, the thought completed itself. She was in love with him. That's why she was jealous of Elizabeth Proudfoot. That's why her reports to Major Carruthers contained nothing of any significance. And that's why she was so sunk in misery that some mornings she didn't want to get out of bed. She was in love with Marcus.

The orchestra struck up, and he swung her in a circle. He was holding her close, too close, but either he or the music had taken her beyond wanting to protect herself. She could feel her skirts brushing against his legs, feel the suppleness of his movements as he took her where he wanted her to go. They might have been alone on the dance floor. Everything seemed to recede. Even the music became muted. She was aware of nothing but the tall dark man who held her in his arms and made love to her with his eyes.

At length, when the music stopped, he let her go. It took several moments for her to get her bearings. For the first time in a long while, Marcus was smiling at her and the smile reached his eyes.

He said, "We must talk. You know that, don't you? I'll come to your room tonight."

She was too shaken to respond, and by the time she came to herself, Marcus had surrendered her to her next partner.

The rest of the evening had a dreamlike quality to it. Catherine was aware on one level that she played her part with flair, but on another level, her mind was in a turmoil. For the second time in her life, she had fallen in love with Marcus, and the thought appalled her.

By the time the last guests had departed, panic had set in and she couldn't stop shaking. One thought consumed her: she must begin to sever her ties to Marcus.

When Marcus came to her room, she pleaded a headache. After one searching look, he crossed the hall to his own room and shut the door with a snap.

She allowed her maid to prepare her for bed, but as soon as she was alone, she rose and donned her warm robe. Just doing something, even if it was only pacing in front of her bed, had a steadying effect.

She tried not to dwell on her feelings for Marcus but it was impossible. She recognized, now, that in spite of Amy, in spite of everything, she had never stopped loving him. How was it possible to love a man she despised?

That was the trouble. She didn't despise him. By slow degrees, she had come to admire him until she'd begun to doubt her own sister. She couldn't believe that Marcus had ravished Amy. At the same time, she couldn't believe that Amy would lie to her. She didn't know what she believed.

She was going in circles. What she needed to do was think of a way out of a situation that had turned into a nightmare. Her mission was over. She had to get out of here.

She moved to the window and looked out. Across the water meadows, the lights of the town winked back at her. There were moors out there, and the best riding to be had in three counties, if Tristram was to be believed. She longed to take out Vixen, and feel the wind in her hair as they galloped across the heath. She'd been shut in too long, a prisoner of the part she was playing.

She'd done her own discreet investigating of everyone's whereabouts during the time she was walking on the ramparts. None of the men had an alibi, not even Tristram. His tutor, the chaplain, had been called away to the bedside of a dying parishioner. The gentlemen who'd gone out hunting had separated, and Marcus and David couldn't account for anyone. Only Helen and Samantha could vouch for each other.

She'd then considered whether any of the servants could be involved, but they were all local people or they had been with the dowager for years. Nothing suspicious there. And of course, besides Marcus and herself, no one had ever set foot in Spain, or if they had, no one was saying anything. All of which brought her full circle. Who else would wish to harm her but Marcus?

She lay down on her bed to think things through, but only grew more confused. She must have dozed, for when she came to herself, her mind was as clear as a bell, and she knew exactly what she must do. She would make up an excuse to go to London and then confront Major Carruthers. They must take Marcus into their confidence, she would tell him, and *El Grande* must be brought into it too. They would lay all their cards on the table. She would tell them all about the accident. And—somehow—she would have to tell Marcus that she was really Catalina. Then, together, they could decide where to go from there.

Swiftly rising, she paced to the window. She ran her finger through her hair and lifted her face, imagining the sensation of galloping across the heath.

She stared out that window for a long time. Suddenly filled with resolve, she began to dress.

• • •

Marcus reined in, and his mount reared up, powerful forelegs pawing in the air for an instant, then he touched spurs to flanks and his horse shot forward. They took the hedge at full speed, with a disregard for the night conditions that would have been arrogant had Marcus not known every detail, every nook and cranny, every rock and boulder on that treacherous course. Both he and Tarquin had run this course many times before.

When they came to the top of a rise, the chestnut automatically veered to the left in a half circle. A touch on the reins brought his head up and he came to a quivering halt. Marcus looked out over the valley. On one side were the lights of the town; on the other side lay the castle, though there was little to be seen of it now that night had fallen. The way down led over the old stone bridge that crossed the Avon, then through dense woodlands and lush farmlands that now lay fallow. Behind him were the moors. This was his domain, his home. It was a good feeling.

On the lower slopes, two grooms astride prime Wrotham horses waited patiently till Marcus joined them. Beyond a greeting no other words were spoken. They were becoming used to their master's odd penchant for riding out late at night. Marcus supposed they thought him either reckless or deranged or both, and they might well be right. All he knew was that unless he drove himself to the point of exhaustion, he would be awake half the night. Awake. Restless. And aching with unsated desire—a sad state of affairs for a man who was used to getting just about any woman he wanted.

He was experienced enough to know that he could have Catherine too. But that wasn't what he wanted, not if he had to seduce her. He wanted her to come to him without regret. If he could find Catalina, he would divorce her tomorrow, or he would arrange for her to obtain a Scottish divorce. Cat knew all this and it made no difference. She had scruples and she would never take up with a married man.

The trouble was, though he respected her scruples, it

didn't improve his temper. Frustration was riding him hard, making him cool and distant, making him find fault with her at every turn. He'd been furious at the article she'd written based on Penn, but when he'd had time to think about it, he realized that what he'd really been afraid of was that she saw him as a subject too. He didn't so much care if she saw Penn as a subject, just as long as she saw him, Marcus Lytton, as a man.

The way she had responded to him tonight, when they'd waltzed together, had convinced him that he hadn't been wrong about her. They'd made love on that dance floor, in front of a hundred people. She'd been pliant in his arms, and susceptible to his every move. His mind hadn't been on dancing, but on bed, and she had known it too. The air between them had been charged with sexual energy. For a moment, he'd lost his bearings, and he was transported to the priest's cell in that burned-out monastery in Spain. He remembered Catalina stopping in mid-sentence when he forgot to guard his expression, then a moment later, she would leave the room.

It bothered him, this confusion he sometimes experienced between Cat and Catalina. They were the only two women who had ever aroused that primitive side of his nature, making him want to reach out and take. Not that he would ever do such a thing. He might not be the most moral man in the world, but he had his code of honor. That was the difference between Cat and Catalina, too. The one was honorable, the other was a conniving little bitch.

Just thinking about Catalina made him angry all over again. His patience was running out. More than a month had passed since he had introduced Cat to society, first in London and now here in Wrotham. Not once had Catalina or *El Grande* tried to get word to him.

It was time to move on to the next step in his plan. Catherine, as Catalina, must lay claim to *El Grande*'s estates. He hadn't thought everything through yet. They would work through lawyers so that she wouldn't have to go to Spain. If that didn't force Catalina and her brother into the open, he didn't know what would.

He savored the cold blast of air that ruffled his hair. Tarquin danced beneath him, straining against the bit. Marcus laughed and slackened the reins, then horse and rider bounded forward. The grooms cursed under their breath and started after them.

Chapter 19

Catherine made her way out of the castle without too much difficulty. There were still people coming and going, mainly tradespeople and servants, but in her serviceable garments, she blended in well, especially with the hood of her mantle half covering her face. If she was stopped at the gates, she would tell the porters that she was a village girl whose sweetheart was one of the temporary chefs especially brought in for the ball. Fortunately no one stopped her. No one even gave her a second stare.

She ran into trouble at the stable and kennel block. She'd expected it to be dark there, but when she turned the corner of the U-shaped building, she found that several outside lanterns were lit, and in the yard, beside a tethered horse, three men were arguing. Two of them were Tristram and Penn, the other was dressed in Wrotham livery—evidently one of the grooms. Catherine pressed into the shelter of a darkened doorway, debating what she should do next. As she watched, Penn went sprawling, and Tristram and the groom helped him to his feet. She realized Penn was highly intoxicated.

"Don't want to go to m'bed," Penn yelled, trying to shake himself free. "Want to go to the village. I've run out of brandy, damn you! Got to get another bottle. Smollet, you're a damn tat ... tall ... informer, that's what you are. I've a good mind to turn you off."

"Yes, sir," replied the groom respectfully.

Tristram's voice was furious. "You should be thankful that Smollet refused to let you ride out. One of these days you'll break your neck, not to mention the neck of a good horse."

Supported by Tristram and the groom, Penn was half

carried, half dragged out of the yard. Catherine did not wait for them to come near her. She did an about-turn and quickly went down the length of the kennels, turned the corner and waited. The argument between Tristram and Penn had made the dogs restless. Now, as the men reached the kennels, the hounds broke out in an unholy uproar, dashing themselves against the gates of their wooden enclosure. They were still barking when the men moved off into the shadows.

For a long time after, Catherine remained motionless, her heart thundering against her ribs. Then, moving quickly and silently, she returned to the yard where the horse was tethered.

At her approach, the gelding lifted his head. He was a glossy black with ears pricked forward and nostrils flaring. His big black eyes were curious rather than wary. Catherine had the sense that he was weighing her up in much the same way that she was weighing him.

"You beauty," she breathed. "You're Tristram's Charon, aren't you? The Andalusian. Are you as good as he says you are?"

When she ran a hand along the long, smooth neck, the horse whinnied softly. Catherine checked the girth and tightened it. With a swift glance around, she swung into the saddle male-fashion. A slight pressure with her knees was obeyed instantly, and the horse moved off in a slow walk. A few paces took them out of the light and into the shelter of darkness. Behind them, the dogs continued to bark. It would be some time before the hounds settled, and some time yet before Smollet would return to check on Tristram's horse. When he found Charon missing, she hoped he would conclude the horse had bolted when the dogs went wild. Later, when she returned to the castle and set the gelding free, the groom would presume the horse had found his own way back.

When she came to the water meadows, she pulled on the reins and turned her mount. On a gentle rise, she checked. A breeze ruffled the surface of the river, and the air smelled pristine pure and as cold as the moon that floated above them. In the distance glowed the lights of the village.

Charon was impatient with the delay. He stomped and pulled on the bit, dancing to the side when Catherine tried to restrain him. It was as if he were telling Catherine not to be so craven, that he was bold enough for the two of them.

She laughed as she felt the excitement begin to build in her. It seemed like an eon since she'd been mounted on a horse of Charon's caliber. Muscles rippled and tensed, and she could feel the sheer power waiting to be released at her signal. He was hers to command. How could she resist?

She slackened the reins and let the Andalusian have his head. With a whinny of pure delight, or so it sounded to Catherine's ears, he pranced and danced, then broke into a canter and finally lengthened his stride till they were soaring above the sward like swallows in flight.

There was no doubt in Catherine's mind that Charon knew where he was going. In all probability, he and Tristram had made this ride many times. If it had been Penn's horse, it would not have surprised her if the Andalusian had trotted into the courtyard of the Black Boar in Wrotham and deposited her outside the taproom door.

This thought again brought to mind the pitiful scene she had witnessed in the stable yard. Penn needed help, but she didn't know how to help him. Nothing seemed to work with him. In her father's case, he had finally stopped drinking when one of his patients, a young woman, had died. It hadn't been his fault, but he had blamed himself. After that, he wouldn't allow alcohol in the house.

Suddenly, without warning, a dark, silent shadow hurled itself toward them. Her response was quicker than conscious thought. She checked, gathered her mount, then touched her heels to his flanks. Beneath her, Charon bunched and strained, then soared effortlessly into the air.

"Damn! A hedge!" breathed Catherine, and she let out a shaky laugh. When Charon made a perfect landing on the other side, she pulled to a stop, then slowly turned to face the hurdle they had just cleared.

Though it was dark, there was enough light from the moon to make out shapes and shadows. She saw that they had left the familiar bridle path and were following a parallel route. Obviously Tristram and his horse preferred a more hazardous course.

She patted Charon's neck. "Let that be a lesson to me," she said. "It's never wise to let your horse have its head, especially if that horse is a jumper."

Charon's ears twitched as if he were trying to make sense of what Catherine was telling him. Suddenly tossing his head, he whinnied and looked toward the river. A pair of deer came leaping out at them, then veered away toward the castle. There was no time to enjoy the spectacle for hard on the heels of the deer came the crashing sounds of what had startled them. Then the darkness seemed to part and three riders emerged. Catherine's response was reflex. She curled her hand around the butt of her pistol and withdrew it from the inside pocket of her mantle.

"Who goes there?" A man's voice.

Not a man's voice—Marcus's voice. There was a moment of stark disbelief, then Catherine pulled on the reins to turn Charon's head.

Everything seemed to happen at once. A pistol shot rang out, and stones and turf kicked up at Charon's hooves. The gelding reared up, almost unseating Catherine, then leapt forward when she touched her heels to his flanks. One of the riders tried to intercept them, and Catherine fired a warning shot over his head.

"Kenyon, Harley, spread out," yelled Marcus.

Instinct took over. Catherine knew that Marcus would win in a straight race. She had to go for the high ground where there were obstacles to get around.

She had to get back to the castle before Marcus recognized her. If she failed, he would know that she was Catalina. Catherine would never have taken the Andalusian out.

She couldn't reveal her identity, not yet, not until Major Carruthers gave her permission. At the back of her mind, the old doubts began to take shape, electrifying her, and her whole being was possessed with the absolute need to escape from her pursuers.

As Charon hurtled toward the trees, Catherine traced

in her mind the route she had to take. On the north side of the castle, there were cliffs that fell away to a sheer drop. To get round those cliffs, she would pass through woodlands and marsh and steep hills with little cover except for a few stunted trees and patches of broom and berry bushes. Close to the castle, there was a stream with a wooden footbridge across it. Once she crossed that footbridge, she would be safe.

They vaulted a dry stone wall, and in a few leaping bounds gained the cover of the trees. At this point, it wasn't much of an advantage, for the trees were thin and leafless. The going was rougher here and Catherine was forced to slow Charon's tearing pace.

They plunged down banks and leapt over ditches and hedges, and ever at her back, Catherine was aware of the thundering clamor of pursuit. It was a wild, reckless ride and at the same time it was intoxicating. Excitement seemed to surge through her bloodstream, heightening all her senses.

A long time later, when she came to the edge of the trees, she reined in. By her reckoning, they had circled the base of the cliffs and were on the other side of the castle. From here, the way wound up through marsh and undergrowth. She took a moment to think out her next move. Before she could urge her mount forward, the night air was severed by the snarl of a predator and the petrified screams of its prey. Catherine cried out. Charon plunged and stamped and bellowed in terror.

"Halt!" Marcus's voice came from their right. Then, "I have you now."

The threat of discovery drove Catherine on. They burst from the shelter of the trees like an arrow shot from a bow. Behind them, men cursed and Marcus bellowed out orders. Catherine crouched low in the saddle and clung like a burr. The night and all its shadows hurtled toward them in a confusion of shapes.

A shot from one of their pursuers whizzed over their heads as Charon was vaulting a ditch. He foundered, sending Catherine spinning. She hit the ground with a thud, attempted to rise then fell back in a daze. Charon quickly recovered and took off like a hare. Moments later, Marcus and his companions went thundering by in a fury of flashing hooves.

She was battered and bruised but otherwise unhurt. Sucking air into her lungs, she rolled to her knees. She didn't have the strength to pull herself to her feet, so she stayed bowed over, trying to get her breath back.

Night sounds began to filter through the fog in her brain. An owl screeched, a twig snapped, some small creature passed within a few feet of her. After a few minutes she sat back on her heels and tried to get her bearings. She was in a clearing, but she wasn't out of the woods yet. The inadvertent pun brought a shivery, humorless laugh. Oh God, this wasn't the moment to give in to hysteria. Besides, as a partisan in Spain, she'd been in worse fixes than this. Partisans didn't panic. They picked themselves up and went on.

El Grande had taught her that a soldier always looked first to his weapons. She felt for her pistol, stumbled to her feet, and went limping into the nearest stand of trees. Once there, she sank down in a thicket of juniper and propped her back against a fallen log. Now that she had started to think like a partisan, she felt a little better.

From the inside pocket of her cloak, she removed an oilskin pouch containing steel balls and powder horn. Though her father had shown her how to use a pistol when she'd first arrived in Portugal, it was *El Grande* who had taught her how to reload and fire off three shots a minute. It was a useful skill when facing Napoleon's crack units. The motions had become second nature to her so that she could reload blindfolded.

She held the pistol and ball in her left hand and poured powder from the horn into the barrel with her right. After inserting the ball, she quickly disengaged the steel rod from under the barrel, rammed the ball home, once, twice, then replaced the ramrod before pulling the cock back with her left thumb. A little powder in the pan was all that was necessary to prime the piece.

She transferred the pistol to her right hand, then stared at it for several long moments. She wasn't going to use it on Marcus, of course. It was a defense, a threat to be used as a last resort if they cornered her.

A shiver ran over her, then another. In the desperate run for freedom, it hadn't occurred to her to wonder why Marcus was out riding so late at night. As she thought about it now each answer that came to mind was more sinister than the last. She tried to force herself to think rationally. He couldn't have been setting a trap for her because he couldn't have known she'd go out riding. Besides, he hadn't known who she was, and he never would if only she could get back to the castle before he did and discovered her missing.

Spurred by that thought, she dragged herself up and began to make her way through the trees. She tried to hurry, but her limbs were stiff and sore. At one point she stumbled and heard something tear, but she didn't stop to examine her skirts.

Gradually the trees thinned out and she paused beside a stand of mountain ash. At this point, the track plunged down a steep incline to the wooden footbridge that crossed the stream. The stables and kennels were far below her, but it was too dark to see them. Once she crossed the footbridge, she would be within a stone's throw of the castle walls. After that, it should be clear sailing.

Something, some feeble sound from the depths of the woods carried to her. She tilted her head, listening. The sound came nearer, and finally she recognized it. It was the sound of the hounds baying. Marcus had set the dogs on her trail.

She couldn't cross the footbridge now. She had to throw the dogs off her scent and there was only one way to do it.

Picking up her skirts, she slithered down the bank toward the stream. Her teeth were chattering even before she plunged into the icy deluge. Water swirled around her knees. Hiking her skirts to her thighs, gasping, she stumbled over pebbles and climbed over boulders as she made her way downstream toward the bridge. She had not gone far when she heard voices and the tread of horses' hooves. A lunge took her to the shelter of the bridge. Flattening herself against the center post, she clamped her teeth together to stop their chattering.

"What's 'e doing then, down there?" said a voice that Catherine recognized as belonging to young Harley, one of Marcus's grooms.

It was Kenyon, Marcus's head groom, who answered him. "What His Lordship is doing is fetching some of the hounds to track our poacher."

"Poacher?" Harley made a derisive sound. "That was no poacher. That was Master Penniston in one of 'is drunken binges."

"Master Penniston would never shoot at his brother."

" 'E might if 'e was drunk. And that was 'is 'orse we caught, wasn't it?"

The head groom said frigidly, "Can't you tell one horse from another yet? Sometimes, I think you'll never amount to anything. That was Master Tristram's horse. Besides, they told us at the stables that Master Penniston never left the castle tonight. And it's not our place to question Lord Wrotham. We're paid to do as we're told. So let's get a move on and flush out that bloody poacher so we can get to our beds. He must be here somewhere."

After what seemed like an endless interval, the riders passed over the bridge and made for the high ground. Catherine couldn't wait any longer. The pain in her legs was excruciating. She had to get out of the water. She lunged for the bank and flung herself facedown on the hard turf. Her breathing would have betrayed her if she had not muffled her mouth in the suffocating folds of her mantle.

It wasn't enough to escape detection.

"Who goes there?" The strident demand came from the head groom. When there was no answer, he said, "Harley, go down and see what's there."

There was the creak of leather as the groom dismounted. Instinct made Catherine freeze where she lay, facedown, as though she were part of the landscape. When she heard the tread of booted feet, she stopped breathing altogether. The sheer effort of controlling herself made her tremble in reaction. She knew she was on the verge of panic, and bit down hard on her lip.

Harley let out a bellow of laughter. "So that's it," he said. "Bleedin' Wrotham deer. Just what our poacher is after."

"What?"

"Deer," he yelled. Under his breath, he said, "One o' these days, m'beauties, I'm going to 'ave m'self a nice saddle o' venison, see if I don't."

Catherine didn't dare raise her head until she heard horses and riders move off. A quick glance around revealed a group of fallow deer drinking from the stream on the far side of the footbridge. When she moved, they raised their heads to look at her. Suddenly, the silence was torn by the baying of the dogs and the deer started up then darted into the trees.

Catherine gathered herself slowly and got to her feet. Her legs were so numb she could hardly hold herself up. Sheer desperation forced her on.

The ivy and saplings that grew densely along the castle walls seemed to reach out and gather her in. She laid her cheek against that hard, granite bulwark as though she were embracing a long-lost lover. Then, with heart pounding, she picked her way carefully downhill toward the south gateway.

Her entrance into the castle bailey was as easy as her exit had been, easier in fact, for she slipped by the porters just as a coachload of musicians were making a noisy exit. Servants were still clearing up in the Great Hall. Snatching up a candle, she sped up the stairs.

When she entered her own chamber, she locked the door and sagged against it. She wasn't capable of rational thought, not yet. Now that the danger was over, she felt all the physical discomfort of her sodden garments and her aching limbs.

After setting down the candle, she peeled out of her wet clothes and slipped into a lacy nightgown. Her hair was tumbled around her shoulders in a mass of tangles. Brushing it back off her face, she secured it with pins. It was as she was locking her pistol in the bottom drawer of her excritoire that she sensed something odd. There was a small sound, the merest whisper of cloth on leather. She stiffened, then slowly turned to face the wing chair by the hearth.

"So it was you, Catalina," said Marcus softly.

Chapter 20

For a moment she simply stared, stunned at seeing him in her chamber. He was out hunting with the dogs. She'd heard them. Then how had he come here?

He had risen to his feet and his powerful physique made her feel all the disadvantages of her femininity. His face looked as if it were carved from a block of ice, and there was self-derision mixed with the fury that blazed from his eyes. Though his words were softly spoken, there was never any doubt in her mind that he was dangerously angry.

"Would you believe I left my grooms in charge of the hunt and came here in person simply to assure myself that you were safely tucked in for the night? I didn't want to take any chances, not when someone shot at me on the bridle path less than an hour ago. It never occurred to me that it was you." He paused then went on, "It was you, wasn't it, Catalina?"

He wanted her to protest her innocence. He wanted her to call him every vile name under the sun. Even now, when he was convinced of her guilt, he was willing to hear her out and accept any reasonable explanation she could offer for the sodden and torn riding habit and the pistol she'd dropped into the drawer of her writing table.

She stood there like a porcelain figurine, her face set and white, her eyes blank as she gazed at him. He felt his fingers curling into fists, felt the sizzling heat of betrayal rise in him. It would take very little to smash her into a thousand pieces.

At last he understood his confusion when he'd tried to separate Catherine and Catalina in his mind. There was no confusion now. Only Catalina could have ridden Tristrams's horse the way this woman had ridden it tonight. And it was only when she'd walked into her chamber that everything had come together in his mind with blinding clarity.

She had made a fool of him every step of the way, first in Spain as Catalina, then later, in England, with his own connivance, when he'd persuaded her to play the part of his wife. And that's what galled him. It had all been done with his own connivance.

When he took a step toward her, the numbness in her brain cleared. "Marcus, listen to me," she cried out, involuntarily retreating a step. "You must see now that *El Grande* and Catalina pose no threat to you. All these weeks we've been together, if I'd really wanted to, I could have murdered you a dozen times over."

"You damn near murdered me tonight."

"I fired over your head, to warn you off."

"Where were you going tonight? What were you doing? Where is *El Grande*? Who are you and what do you want with me?"

He had backed her into a corner. Instinct made her hold up her head and return his stare. She said quickly, "I really am Catherine Courtnay. In Spain, I was a British spy. Catalina was only a role I played. *El Grande* pretended to be my brother."

He registered no shock at her words. When he took another step toward her, she cried out, "If you'd only give me a chance to explain!"

"You can begin by telling me where your accomplice is."

"He's not here. He's with the brothers at Marston Abbey."

"*El Grande* is a priest?" he asked incredulously.

"He was a priest once, before the French invaded Spain. Now he's a lay brother with the monks."

"Then who were you meeting tonight?"

"No one. I was restless. I went down to the stables and found the Andalusian tethered to a post. I couldn't resist taking him out for a ride. That's all it was, Marcus."

He breathed deeply. "I'm not sure I believe you, but you'd better begin at the beginning and explain to me what the hell is going on. Go on. Begin from the beginning. I want to hear exactly how you became involved in this."

All her senses were alive to her danger. He knew that she was Catalina and he knew about *El Grande,* and that's all he knew. She wasn't going to exacerbate matters by bringing Major Carruthers's name into it. She wasn't going to tell him that she was working for British Intelligence.

"Someone murdered all those English soldiers," she said. "*El Grande* and I thought you might be trying to throw suspicion on us. When you asked me to play the part of Catalina, we thought it would give us a chance to discover what you were up to."

Her explanations were disjointed, going back and forth in time with little regard for sequence. Marcus interrupted frequently, and in a matter of minutes, he had grasped the gist of her story. It was obviously going to be a long night, for as they spoke, he added several lumps of coal to the embers in the grate.

"Why in hell's name wasn't I told the truth?" he demanded at one point.

She swallowed hard. "We had only your word that you were attacked in London. You were a suspect. We couldn't tell you the truth."

His eyes flared. After a long silence, he said, "Let's forget that for the moment. Let's return to Spain. Why did you force me to marry you? Why did you pretend I'd tried to ravish you?"

He was towering over her, thirteen stones of solid masculine bone and sinew. She lifted her chin. "I overheard two of the English soldiers talking about you. That's when I learned you were not the simple captain you pretended to be, but the Earl of Wrotham. It suggested to me that you were trifling with my affections." She certainly wasn't going to tell him about Amy.

A boiling sea of rage erupted in a roar. "Don't lie to me! You weren't the person you were pretending to be either. It was more than that. You heard I was an earl and you made up your mind to have my wealth and title for yourself."

At that, she moved. With the back of her hand she pushed against his chest and brushed by him. She opened the door of the great oak wardrobe, removed her warm cerise robe and slipped into it. When she turned to face him, her eyes shimmered with fire. "Let me tell you, Marcus Lytton, there isn't enough money in Christendom to tempt me to marry you. When I learned that you were the Earl of Wrotham and had been trifling with me, I decided to pay you back in your own coin. I thought you would have our marriage annulled before the month was out. I never thought of your heirs. I wasn't even sure that our marriage was legal. I didn't discover how difficult it would be to get out of until I came back to England."

When she made to move away from him, he grabbed her by the arms and wrenched her around. "You're my wife," he said. "All these months, you've kept me at bay by reminding me that I'm a married man. But, dammit, you are my wife. I could have had you any time I wanted."

And that's what rankled. While he had mooned over her, suffering all the torments of unsated desire, she had been secretly thumbing her nose at him. He had allowed her to set the rules between them, and all the time she had run rings around him.

"You ride as well as a trooper," he said with enough inflection to make it a question. Before she could answer, he answered himself. "Hell, you damn well ride like the wind, as I saw with my own eyes tonight."

His control was slipping, and that frightened her.

He exhaled a slow breath. "And you're a crack shot."

"I told you I knew how to use a pistol."

He caught her chin in the cup of one hand and she winced. "You speak Spanish fluently."

"Yes," she whispered.

"God, is there no end to your lies?"

He still wasn't sure that he believed her, wasn't sure what her game was. He writhed to think that twice in one lifetime, this woman had made him fall in love with her, and he had no doubts now that he was in love with her, else why did her betrayal hurt so much? He had dreamed of this moment, fantasized about how he would take his revenge. Now there was a double betrayal to avenge.

His fingers dug into the soft flesh of her arms. "I warned you in Spain that one day there would be a final reckoning between us. You tricked me into marriage. Fine. You got what you wanted. Now it's time to pay the piper."

"What does that mean?"

"It means that you are going to act like a wife."

She strained against him, both hands splayed against his chest. "Don't be ridiculous, Marcus. You're not going to . . . to take me against my will. I can't believe such a thing of you."

That was something else that rankled. He'd been so bloody scrupulous, keeping his hands off her, when he'd known that he could have her any time he wanted.

"Against your will?" he gritted. "Madam, you've been ripe for the plucking since I first clapped eyes on you. It won't be against your will."

She gasped and jerked free of him. "You conceited clod! Do you know what your trouble is, Marcus?" As she retreated, he advanced, stalking her. "Your trouble is that women come too easily to you. There are a lot of women in this world who are impressed with a title and a fat purse."

He bared his teeth in a ferocious grin. "I could not have put it better myself, and of all such women, you, my sweet, take the honors. But I'm not one to argue with the hand of fate. I've dreamed of this moment ever since the night you forced me to marry you, and now that it has arrived, I'm going to take my revenge."

She had taken refuge behind one of the armless chairs, and her fingers were curled around the wooden backrest. "Marcus, stop this!" she commanded. To her great surprise, he stopped an arm's length away. She inhaled a shallow breath. "Now," she said, smiling a little, "why don't we sit down and discuss this like two reasonable, civilized people?"

When he swept the chair aside, sending it crashing to

the floor, she flattened herself against the wall. Her breasts were rising and falling in her agitation. A pulse beat frantically at her throat. Her eyes were wide and unfaltering on his.

Looking at her now, he could hardly believe that he had allowed her to convince him she was not Catalina. That same charge of sexual tension sizzled between them. She aroused the same primitive feelings, the burning sense of possession. His woman. His wife. He'd never felt that for any other woman. God, if he couldn't have her now, he would go insane.

"Don't be afraid," he whispered, "I won't hurt you."

He reached for her, and with a cry of rage, she sent her hand flying across his face. They both recoiled at the blow. He stared at her long and hard, then suddenly pivoting, he stalked to the door. It wasn't what she expected him to do, and for a moment she watched as though she were turned to stone. When she realized he was leaving, that he wasn't going to hurt her, she darted after him. He had his hand on the door when she slammed against it, preventing him from opening it. With her back pressed against the door, arms splayed wide, she faced him.

"Marcus, no. I'm sorry. All this time, I've misjudged you. Please don't be angry with me." Something else had occurred to her and it made her heart sing. Marcus wasn't the person who had broken the lantern on the tower steps. He was angry, but he wouldn't hurt her.

"Get away from that door," he snarled, "or I won't answer for the consequences."

"You don't mean that; I know you don't mean that."

With teeth clenched, he put his hands on her waist and lifted her out of the way. No sooner had he turned back to the door, when she slipped under his arm and barred his way again.

"Cat, I'm warning you."

"Marcus, you don't frighten me."

"Well, I damn well ought to," he roared.

She'd hurt him, she could see that she'd hurt him, and it was the last thing she had expected to do. He'd always seemed so sure of himself, so in command of every situation. How had she come to have such power? It moved her, as nothing else could have moved her. She stopped thinking of herself and thought only of him.

"I'm sorry," she whispered. "I'm so sorry."

"I was only trying to frighten you a little. You deserved a lot worse than that. The slap was quite unnecessary. I've never forced myself on any woman. I'm not about to start with you."

"I know, I know. We're both overwrought. It's been a horrible night, a horrible night."

"Will you stop repeating yourself like a damn parrot and get away from that door?"

She started to laugh.

"Cat."

"Oh, my love, my love."

She fell into his arms and fastened her lips to his. Marcus, wide-eyed and disbelieving, tried to pry her loose, but he could not budge her. After a moment or two, he stopped trying.

She felt the change in him, and kissed him again, softly this time, provocatively, seducing him to yield to her.

"Cat," he said shakily, pulling his mouth from hers.

"Mmm?"

"Don't do that."

"Don't do what?"

"You know."

"This?"

Her fingers had undone the buttons of his shirt, and her hand slid inside the opened edges to caress bare flesh. "Don't you like it?" she crooned. "I've wanted to do that for a long, long time."

"That's not the point ... ah ... ! Cat, would you mind if we did this on the bed?"

She led the way, clear-eyed, unprotesting, as eager for him as he was for her. Just knowing that she wanted him made his blood thunder in his ears.

Her lips were soft and full, and the taste of them was intoxicating. There was passion there, untutored, waiting for the right man to unlock it. But she had to choose this. There must be no regrets later.

"Cat, are you sure this is what you want? You'd better make your mind up now, for in another moment or two, you won't have a choice."

She stretched languidly. She'd never felt so sure about anything in her life. She knew she wasn't thinking rationally, couldn't think rationally after the terrors she'd just been through. But there was something else at work in her. She was doing it for him.

"Marcus, stop talking and start showing me what I've been missing all these years. You've been trying to seduce me for weeks. Fine. Seduce me."

He sounded shocked. "I haven't been trying to seduce you."

"Have it your own way. Just get on with it."

He laughed and rolled with her on the bed. She lay perfectly still as he began to disrobe her, looking up at him with darkening eyes. "Marcus," she said, and there was a catch in her voice.

He divested her of her nightgown, then he methodically removed his own clothes.

He hadn't counted on the effect her nakedness would have on him. Her breasts were perfect, the large crests like overripe berries. He touched a finger to one nipple and swallowed as it came erect. He couldn't resist setting his mouth to it. When she shifted beneath him, and spread her legs in artless appeal, he had to grit his teeth against the waves of lust that roared through him. Forcing his desire to recede to manageable proportions, he brushed his fingers through the auburn triangle between her thighs to penetrate, though not deeply, the entrance to her body. Catherine moaned and arched into the caress.

He pulled back to look at her. Her eyes were wide and luminous; her breathing was quick and shallow. Her fingers curled into the muscles of his shoulders.

He laughed softly, pleased with her response to him. "You were made for this," he said. "No, don't be shy. Look at me, Cat. I'm only a man."

She came up on her knees, and allowed her gaze to travel over him. Where she was pale and soft, he was dark and hard. Powerful was the word that came to mind. His broad shoulders tapered to hard, muscular thighs. His sex was long, thick, and jutted from a dark nest of coarse hair. She swallowed hard.

"Oh, Marcus," she said in a shaken whisper. "Oh, Marcus."

Marcus saw the confusion in her eyes, heard the pulse of desire in her voice, and he took instant advantage. "Lie with me," he said, and with eyes on hers, he brought her down to lie with him.

He began to caress her, only this time with less restraint, using his lips and tongue in his war to master her senses. He wasn't going to give her time to think. He wasn't going to give her time to change her mind. When she began to tremble beneath him, crying his name, he rose above her.

He planted himself firmly between her thighs but he didn't take her, not yet. He waited until her lashes lifted and those expressive blue eyes were fastened on his. He gave her a moment so that there could be no misunderstanding between them. This was what they both wanted.

"Ah, Cat," he said, then he took her mouth in a voracious kiss just as he took her body.

She jerked and cried out, protesting the painful intrusion. Gritting his teeth, he forced himself to stop but he ignored the press of her hands as she tried to push him away. When he felt her sheath grow moist and supple around him, he drove into her, embedding himself deep inside her.

She moaned, and he kissed her. "It's all right," he said in a soothing whisper. "It's all right."

She was feeling numb and a little battered from the force of his entry. His words hardly soothed her. Marcus saw the sizzle in her eyes, but he didn't give her time to speak. He began to move, slowly at first, then with increasing confidence as he felt her move with him, instinctively enticing him to a greater passion. He wanted to go slowly, to give her pleasure so that next time she would be eager for his lovemaking, but his body had been too long denied. He began thrusting heavily.

As he withdrew, then lunged again, filling her completely, scorching waves of sensation drowned her in pleasure. Her skin was hot; an ache grew in her loins. Her awareness was centered on his movements as he drove into her. She felt herself hover on a crest, reaching for something that was beyond her ken.

Marcus could hold off no longer. He kissed her fiercely, hotly, then cupping his hands around her bottom, he lifted her to him and drove into her again and again. At the last, when his climax burst upon him, he emptied himself deep inside her in hard convulsive thrusts.

In the long silence that followed, Catherine lay beneath him like a stone. She couldn't summon the energy to throw him off. She felt bruised and shaken, but most of all she felt cheated by a tantalizing promise that had never materialized. She'd abandoned the prohibitions of a lifetime to reach for something that apparently didn't exist ... and now that she'd recovered her senses, she was beginning to burn with an odd mixture of shame and embarrassment. How had it happened? What could she say to him? She was sprawled on the bed, legs splayed wide, with Marcus planted solidly between her thighs, and his huge sex still buried inside her. She was ruined and all because she had wanted to be nice to him! She hadn't understood anything. Seduction didn't come from the outside, but from within.

Marcus shifted his weight to allow her to draw breath. He knew there was a big smile on his face. When she sniffed, he lavished her with soft kisses. "It will be better next time," he promised.

He was roused from his inertia by a sharp blow to the ribs. Groaning, uncoupling their bodies, he rolled to his side. Catherine lost no time in slipping from the bed. When she saw the streaks of blood on her thighs, she let out a long teary sob, then dived for her robe. Having belted it, she turned to face him.

He'd raised to his elbows, but he made no move to cover his nakedness. Catherine emitted a soft sound, reached for the clothes which were thrown haphazardly on the floor, and threw him his shirt.

"Have you no modesty?" she hissed.

His brows rose, but he answered her mildly. "With you? None whatsoever. You may not believe this now, but the day will come when you won't be modest with me either."

She waited until he'd donned his shirt, then she said in a low, passionate voice, "Have you any idea what we did here tonight?"

His mouth curved in a slow, sensual smile. "Why don't you remind me?"

It was all she could do to look at him, knowing that only moments before she had lain naked in his arms. She cleared her throat. "What we have done by consummating our marriage is complicate things beyond belief."

"I didn't 'consummate our marriage,' as you put it."

"What did you do?"

"I had you," he said bluntly. "At long last, I had you. God, I don't mind telling you that you had me worried for a time. I thought, hoped, you had a passionate nature, but a man can never really be sure until he takes his woman to bed. You, my pet, were worth the wait."

Marcus didn't see the effect his words had on her. He had vaulted from the bed and was adding coal to the blazing fire in the grate. He was in the mood to hum a bawdy ditty he'd picked up while soldiering in France, but he refrained, not wanting to sound too smug in case it got her dander up. But he was smug. A woman like Catherine didn't surrender herself to a man unless that man meant something to her. And just to make sure she understood what he had claimed not minutes before in that very bed, he was going to claim it again and again until the memory of this night was impressed upon her for all time. It was going to be a long night. Time and enough when dawn came to talk things out. His smile intensified.

She tried not to sound surly. "I'll wager you've said that to a goodly number of women in your time."

"What?"

"That she's worth the wait."

He came to her and looped his arms around her shoulders. "You're wrong, love. No woman ever made me wait before."

"What colossal conceit!"

He grinned. "I'm being honest."

"You should try for modesty, Marcus."

He cocked his head, trying to gauge her expression, then he said very seriously, very quietly, "I'm not going to justify my past, not to you, not to anyone. So don't ask me."

She pushed out of his arms. "I'm sure your past is fascinating, Marcus, but frankly, I'm not interested. It's the future that concerns me. Now that you know about *El Grande* and me, there are things we should discuss, but not now, not right this minute." She pressed a hand to her temples. "I have a headache. This has been a harrowing night, to say the least. I'd be obliged if you would get dressed and leave me in peace to sort things through."

He jerked her back when she tried to slip by him. His eyes moved over her slowly, observing the flushed cheeks, the glitter in her eyes, the provocative tilt to her chin. "You're not sorting anything through," he said. "Everything is out of your hands. From now on, I'm the one who will be making the decisions. Not you, and not *El Grande*. Do you understand, Cat?"

Through set teeth, she said, "I won't go on playing the part of your wife, not after what happened here tonight."

"Cat, you *are* my wife, and there's no getting around it."

"And you can have me any time you want, I suppose?"

"What's wrong with that?"

"Not if I have anything to say about it."

"What the devil is the matter with you?" demanded Marcus, staring at the tears that were welling in her eyes.

"I'll tell you what's the matter with me. I hate you. That's what's the matter with me."

Marcus blazed with anger. "You have a strange way of showing that you hate me."

"You've had what you wanted. Now go."

"It's what you wanted too, isn't it?"

"I must have been out of my mind."

Baffled at the change in her, Marcus reached for his clothes. He glowered at them for a moment then flung them aside. His eyes held hers. "If that was hate," he said, "I can live with it."

"Marcus, I'm sorry about Spain. More than sorry. But you've had your pound of flesh. Enough is enough."

"So that's it," he said. "Cat, revenge was the last thing on my mind when I made love to you tonight."

She was unconvinced. "Was it?"

"Please trust me, Cat."

She couldn't think when his hands were massaging her shoulders. She licked her lips. "I want to trust you, Marcus."

"Cat," he groaned, and swept her into his arms. He laid her on the bed and came down beside her.

When he kissed her, she put out a hand in a half-hearted attempt to delay things. She wasn't sure if this was what she wanted. He captured her hand and brought it to his groin, curling her fingers around his swollen shaft. She could sense the rising need in him and it made her own need burgeon out of control. Then he wasn't asking, he was taking, and she reveled in it.

When he tasted the surrender on her lips, without breaking the kiss, he slipped off her robe. His hands moved possessively over her body, taking, giving, and infinitely arousing. When she began to tremble, he mounted her.

This time, he was determined not to take his own pleasure till he had brought her to climax. He drew her up with the slow, steady rhythm of his body moving on hers. He kissed her endlessly, plunging his tongue deeply, carefully building the passion between them. He felt the tension grow in her, felt the tightening in her loins as he drew her to the crest. When she began to convulse beneath him, Marcus threw off his restraints. Bracing himself on his hands to make his penetration as deep as he could make it, he moved with the ferocity of a jungle cat. At the end, her shocked cry of pleasure was the sweetest sound he had ever heard.

This wasn't the end of it. He let her sleep for a while, but he felt like a man driven. She was his. After tonight, she would never deny him again.

She wasn't fully awake when he entered her. A flurry

of protests flew from her lips. Marcus disregarded every one of them. "So go to sleep," he said, and worked on her till sleep was the last thing she wanted.

Much later, he decided he didn't want a passive lover, not after she'd responded with such abandon those first few times. He showed her how to give him pleasure, then wondered if he was crazy to put so much power into her hands, when she ruthlessly used her newfound knowledge to make him writhe with wanting her.

Toward dawn, they slept. Marcus was first to awaken. He lay with his eyes closed, savoring the feel of her in his arms. When he thought about how she'd kept him at arm's length by continually casting in his teeth the fact that he was a married man, his temper began to heat. It ebbed when he remembered the night just past. In one night, she'd gone a long way to making up for the last few months.

There were still many questions he wanted answered. The sooner he met with *El Grande,* the sooner he could begin to fit some of the pieces of the puzzle together. It exasperated him to think that it meant starting over. He'd been on the wrong track all along, and all because Catherine had lied to him. There were going to be no more lies, no more secrets between them. She was his now, and her loyalty belonged to him.

She came awake slowly. She felt his breath, his warmth. Blue eyes locked on blue eyes. He kissed her, and she slipped her arms around his neck.

"Marcus," she said in a breathy murmur. "Marcus."

His hand slid up her leg to her thigh. "Love me, Cat."

She began to tremble, feeling the familiar quickening inside her. "This isn't right," she whispered. She wanted so much more.

"There's no right and wrong between us. Not now."

As his weight came down on her, she whimpered in sheer animal arousal. She had the strangest feeling of being mastered, then her own passion blazed up to match his.

When it was over, Catherine burst into tears. Marcus seemed to understand that he was the source of her unhappiness but he did not console her or make false promises.

"From now on, we're going to do things my way," he said, then he began to dress.

Chapter 21

"Tell me about *El Grande*."

Catherine took a moment to smooth her white linen napkin over her lap before considering Marcus's request. Three days had passed since Marcus had found her out. They were now in London, in his house in Cavendish Square, about to eat breakfast before going to Marston Abbey to meet with *El Grande*. The rest of the family was still at Wrotham.

She spooned some marmalade onto her plate. "I've told you all I know."

"Then tell me again."

Catherine knew he wasn't deliberately trying to needle her. It was just that every time she told the story, she remembered something she hadn't mentioned before. It was tedious, and at the same time it was unnerving. She was left with the distinct impression that Marcus was trying to trick her into revealing something she wished to conceal. And she had plenty to conceal. She did not want to tell him about Major Carruthers, and her role as a spy, making her reports to British Intelligence. Somehow, it didn't seem so disloyal when only she and *El Grande* were involved.

When she told him about the lantern on the tower stairs, he'd seen immediately that she had kept quiet about it because she had suspected he was responsible. He'd made her describe the episode a dozen times, and had finally dismissed the idea that either a member of his family or one of the servants had done it deliberately. In his hearing, Penn had ordered one of the gillies to oil the hinges and accidents did happen. On the other hand, if it wasn't an accident, it would have been simple for an outsider to steal the Wrotham livery, sneak into the castle precincts, and take advantage of his opportunities.

It was all so confusing. Even the problem of their marriage had yet to be resolved. She couldn't go on playing the part of Catalina forever. She wanted to go back to being herself, but before that could happen, they had to decide what story to tell his family and the world to explain Catalina's disappearance. These problems hadn't stopped Marcus from exercising his conjugal rights every chance he got. She seemed to spend her nights in a sensual haze, and her days waiting for night to fall.

"Why are you frowning?" asked Marcus.

She erased the frown. "What do you wish to know?"

He stared at her for a moment, then said slowly, "Are you all right, Catherine?"

"Why shouldn't I be?" When he gave her one of his narrow-eyed stares, she said impatiently, "I'm fine, Marcus, really. Now, what is it you wish to know?"

"Tell me about *El Grande*'s early life."

She had it down by rote. "He was the youngest son of el Marqués de Vera el Grande, and being the youngest son, he was destined for the church. It's not uncommon even in English families. The eldest son inherits the title and estates, the next in line goes into the army, and the younger sons either go into the church or scramble for a living as best they can."

Marcus cut into a piece of ham. "That doesn't describe my family."

"No, I'm well aware of it."

His eyebrows rose in a questioning arc. "Meaning?"

"Meaning your family is . . ." She stopped when she remembered their quarrel, when he'd found her writing notes for an article on what he'd thought was Penn's drinking habits. "It doesn't matter," she finished lamely.

"Go on, Catherine, I really want to know."

"I was only going to say that Wrotham is all they know. It wouldn't hurt them to expand their horizons."

He looked at her for a moment, then leaned back in his chair. "All right. Out with it. What do you think I should do?"

"Well," she said cautiously, "if I were you, I'd bring them to London; introduce them to society. Especially Helen and Samantha. Samantha needs to have a London season like other girls her age. And now that the war is over, Tristram should go on a grand tour after he graduates from university."

"You've left out Penn."

"I really don't know what the answer is for Penn. Perhaps he could go with David to Ireland and help him develop his property."

She glanced up at him. "That's something else I don't understand. It seems so sad that David is your only cousin, yet he's merely an acquaintance. You've never mentioned his father, who must have been your uncle."

"I believe he was," returned Marcus with a smile. "Well, as I've said before, we are not a close family. I know my father went to see his brother every few years, and sometimes my uncle came to England with David, but I remember only vaguely." He was eyeing her curiously. "What makes you so passionate about families, Cat? What about your own family? What happened there?"

Her eyes suddenly felt very hot and she looked down at the toast on her plate. "I'll tell you what happened. I thought I was walking on solid ground, and it turned out I was walking on thin ice."

She didn't know where the tears were coming from except that she'd become very teary in the last little while. It didn't take much to set her off.

"Go on."

She swallowed before continuing. "I was twelve years old when my mother came down with a fever. I never thought about it. It never occurred to me that she wouldn't get better. After all, it was only a fever, and my father was a doctor. I went to bed one night without a care in the world. When I awakened the next morning, my life would never be the same again."

He said quietly, "Your mother died during the night."

She nodded. "I don't really understand what happened to us after that except that we seemed to stop being a family. My father started drinking. My aunt came to live with us. Ours was not a happy household."

"Your father drank to excess?"

"He was a drunkard," she said bluntly.

"But he overcame his addiction?"

She nodded. "A patient died, and he blamed himself. He never touched another drop after that."

"I see." After a long silence, he said, "You had an older sister, I believe."

Her head snapped up. "Who told you that?"

"Your friend, Mrs. Lowrie."

She didn't want to tell him about Amy yet. It was just one more problem, one more lie, that lay between them, and she was too fragile to deal with it right now. There was one thing, however, she no longer doubted. Amy had lied to her. Marcus was incapable of raping a woman.

"Yes, I had a sister once. She eloped, and after that my father would never allow her name to be mentioned in his hearing." She saw that she was mangling her table napkin and took a moment to smooth it out. "When he wasn't there, my aunt had plenty to say. I used to lie in my bed at night, worrying that my father would turn against me, too. I was determined never to put a foot wrong, which is a terrible burden for a child to bear.

"Oddly enough, the only time I came close to feeling I was part of a family again was when I was with the partisans."

Marcus gazed at her reflectively, trying to fit the pieces together. The aunt, he knew from Emily Lowrie, had been a puritanical ogre of a woman. The older sister had rebelled. Catherine had conformed, and now he understood why. Now he understood a lot of things he hadn't understood before.

For the first time, he began to see her as she really was. He'd always admired her, but he was seeing a different side to her, one that stirred him profoundly. It was like looking through a glass darkly and seeing himself. They'd both been lonely as children.

"I suppose," said Marcus, "you looked upon *El Grande* as a brother?"

"Hardly. *El Grande* was our leader." Her expression was almost challenging. "He made decisions that weren't always popular. Sometimes, he executed those who collaborated with the enemy, Spaniards, like the partisans. Some of them might well have been their own sons or brothers."

"I remember his reputation. 'Barbaric' some called him."

She visibly bristled. "It was a barbaric war, and *El Grande* was fighting to win. What would you have had him do when you know yourself that the French behaved like wild animals? I'll tell you this: there wasn't a man or woman among us who wouldn't have laid down his life for *El Grande*. That's the kind of loyalty he inspired."

"I'm not finding fault with the man. I'm simply trying to understand him." He spoke the truth, and yet it didn't sit well with him that she so obviously hero-worshiped *El Grande*.

"What is he doing here in England?" he asked. "Now that the war is over, why doesn't he go back to Spain and take up his life there?"

She patiently repeated what she'd told him before. "Spain holds too many painful memories for him. The French murdered his whole family. He likes England, likes the English." She shrugged. "I don't understand all the subtleties myself, Marcus. *El Grande* says he's making his soul. He'll go back to Spain when he's ready. Or he may never go back."

"Making his soul? Are we talking about penance?"

"I think so. Marcus, try to understand, before the war, he was in a seminary, studying to be a priest. He was, *is*, a man of God. The things he did to help win the war have weighed heavily on his conscience. Why do you continue to suspect him?"

He evaded the question by looking at his watch. "We'd best be on our way," he said.

Catherine nodded and tried not to look nervous. She hadn't had a chance to get word to either *El Grande* or

Major Carruthers that Marcus had found her out.
Marcus never let her out of his sight. She knew he wanted
to take *El Grande* unawares, and that was the last thing
she wanted.

"What is it, Catherine? Why do you look like that?"

She looked up to see Marcus staring at her with that
hard, watchful expression she'd come to hate. The truth
of the matter was that neither of them could completely
trust the other.

"I was thinking of *El Grande*," she said, and was
glad when he let it go at that.

Marston Abbey was only a half hour from London on the
main road to Sevenoaks. They were met at the gate by a
monk in a white habit, a great bull of an Irishman who
reminded Marcus of a prizefighter he'd once bet heavily
on, and who had won him a tidy sum of money.

The monk took their names and left them at the gate.
It was a good ten minutes before he returned to say that
Brother Robert was free to meet with them.

Since Marcus knew next to nothing about the mo-
nastic life, he kept up a stream of questions as Brother
Fineas escorted them to the main building. They learned
that the abbey was originally a manor house and had
been purchased by the order and converted for use as a
monastery.

"We are Benedictines," said Brother Fineas. "The
monks wear white habits, and the lay brothers wear
brown. We divide our time into prayer, study, and labor."

"Correct me if I'm wrong," said Marcus, "but I understood that Henry the Eighth sold off all the monaster-
ies when he quarreled with the Pope."

"That," said the monk, flicking Marcus a dry look,
"was almost three hundred years ago. Times change."

The path led downhill through an avenue of old
yews to a cobbled yard. There were many brothers in
brown or white habits crossing the yard to the various
stone buildings.

"A working farm," observed Marcus as they passed

a flock of sheep that some monks were herding into a pen.

Brother Fineas veered neither to left nor right, but forged ahead on the flagstone path. The manor itself rose up suddenly in front of them. He led the way through an arched porch with a coat of arms above it, across an inner courtyard and through another door. Here, they came to a cavernous hall, two stories high, with a dozen trestle tables, each accommodating four or five monks who seemed to be absorbed in their books.

Brother Fineas had them wait in the vestibule. Women were not allowed in the monks' inner precincts, and in the outer precincts they were allowed only if suitably dressed. That's why Catherine was robed from head to toe in unrelenting black, with a black silk veil concealing her face.

Marcus watched Brother Fineas's progress through the aisles of tables, anticipating the moment when the monk's hand would fall on the shoulder of *El Grande*.

"Señor, señora, this way, please."

The softly spoken greeting came from behind him. Surprised, Marcus pivoted. A monk in a brown habit was leading Catherine toward a door at the side of the stone staircase. He went after them.

The room they entered was almost bare of furniture except for a plain trestle table and four armless chairs. There was a massive stone fireplace, but the fire wasn't lit. Marcus registered these things only dimly. His eyes were fastened on the young monk who was now embracing Catherine. When they separated, and Catherine explained, rather disjointedly, why they were here, Marcus took a moment to study him. He'd caught only a glimpse of *El Grande* in London, and he was seeing things he hadn't noticed then. *El Grande* didn't look like the charismatic leader of his legend, the man he'd met in Spain. He looked exactly what he appeared to be.

But he wasn't a simple monk. The little charade with Brother Fineas that had caught them off guard was an elementary exercise that all Intelligence officers were taught before they went into the field: distract the enemy and come at him from the quarter he least expects. Already, Marcus was beginning to feel like a rank amateur in the presence of a master.

"I think," said Marcus, "you have found the perfect hiding place."

Catherine looked at him suspiciously. *El Grande* smiled, and Marcus held out his hand. "We were never formally introduced," he said. "I'm Wrotham."

Genuine amusement glowed in those dark eyes. "And I'm Robert," said *El Grande*.

His handclasp was firm but that wasn't what impressed Marcus. He could feel the hard calluses on the palm and fingers. It was a laborer's hand.

"Please," said *El Grande*, "won't you be seated?"

Marcus did not waste words. As soon as he was seated, he plunged right in. "I cannot reconcile in my mind," he said, "what Catherine has told me about you. What kind of man deals in lies and deceit and at the same time devotes his life to God?"

Catherine had positioned herself at the window. She was still standing. In the act of throwing back her veil, she gasped, and rounded on Marcus. "You promised not to lose your temper!"

"I'm not angry. It's a serious question and I want a serious answer."

"But . . ."

El Grande silenced her with a look. "It's all right, Catherine. I owe him an explanation." He looked toward Marcus. "The short answer to your question is—a man who has no real vocation. I'm not a priest, Lord Wrotham, and I know now I shall never be one. There is too much of the world in me."

Marcus stared long and hard into *El Grande*'s unguarded eyes. Unsure of what he read there, he said, "What about Spain? You are the last of your line. Surely you will want to return and take up your life there?"

El Grande's smile was fleeting. "Anything is possible."

Catherine said softly, "Robert is a stone mason, Marcus. They are building a church for their order. There is a quarry nearby. You should look around while you have the chance."

There was a silence, then *El Grande* spoke in a dull, flat voice. "Lord Wrotham has other things on his mind, Catherine. Now, sir, how may I help you?"

Marcus felt as though a shutter had descended, that he'd had his chance and he'd thrown it away. He looked at Catherine and she stared back at him with huge, appealing eyes.

He shifted uncomfortably, feeling out of his depth here. He was only a simple soldier. He hadn't fought the kind of war the partisans had fought, where there had been hostage taking and massacres of the civilian population. He couldn't begin to imagine what *El Grande* had been made to suffer. Catherine was right. He had no business judging other people when he'd no conception of the life they'd led.

Catherine's eyebrows were flexing eloquently. Marcus sighed and held out an olive branch. "I'm not sure if there will be time to see everything, but I would enjoy a tour of the manor, if you can be spared from your duties."

The austere expression gradually softened. "I can be spared. Now, how may I help you, Lord Wrotham?"

Marcus came straight to the point. "You may begin by telling me all that you remember of the English soldiers who were with me at your headquarters."

What *El Grande* had to say added very little to what Marcus already knew. He had been on a mission to Madrid, he said, for almost the entire time that Marcus and his comrades were marooned in the monastery, and when he'd returned, he'd escorted them to British lines almost at once. There had been very little opportunity to get to know the English soldiers even if he had wanted to, which he hadn't. He was the leader of a group of partisans. He didn't want to be known and recognized by outsiders. It was too dangerous.

At one point, Marcus said, "It always comes back to the mysterious Rifleman who got away. I don't suppose there's any way of discovering who he is and what happened to him?"

"I'm not in a position to say. Perhaps you should ask . . ." *El Grande* looked up to see Catherine, standing behind Marcus, vigorously shaking her head.

Marcus swiveled in his chair, and Catherine stared down at him. "Should ask whom?" said Marcus, still looking at Catherine.

El Grande said, "What do you think, Catherine?"

"Oh, I think we'll never find out anything about that Rifleman. Too much time has passed."

After a long reflective silence, Marcus said, "Why did you want Catherine to play the part of Catalina?"

Catherine said quickly, "I've already told you all that."

"I'm asking *El Grande*."

El Grande's eyes never wavered from Marcus's face. "I suspected you of murdering the English soldiers who were at my headquarters. By asking Catherine to play Catalina, you gave us the perfect opportunity to keep you under surveillance."

"Good God, man, if I had been the murderer, think what might have happened to her!"

Catherine addressed her remarks to *El Grande*. "Marcus doesn't see me as a crack agent. He thinks I'm a helpless female." Then to Marcus, "You may find this hard to believe, but in Spain the French put a price on my head. No one forced me to play the part of your wife. It was my own decision. I never *really* suspected you," she added, not quite truthfully, "but even if I had, I still would have done it. I know how to take care of myself."

"You know how to take care of yourself!" said Marcus savagely. "What about the accident you say was a deliberate act of violence against you?"

"What accident?" asked *El Grande*.

"Marcus thinks it was an accident," said Catherine. "I don't know what to think any more," and she went on to describe what had taken place.

"Perhaps," said *El Grande*, "we are making mountains out of molehills. I was attacked, too, when I was walking with Amy, but it was nothing more sinister than young ruffians looking for trouble."

"Amy?" asked Marcus.

El Grande looked at him coolly. "Mrs. Spencer," he said.

"Mrs. Amy Spencer?" Marcus was frowning. "Not the Mrs. Spencer who lives on Pall Mall?"

"I see you know her too," replied *El Grande*.

Catherine turned away and fussed with the hem of her pelisse. Her brain was reeling. *El Grande* and Amy? She was bursting with questions, but she swallowed them while she waited in pent-up silence for what would happen next.

Marcus said, "I'm acquainted with Mrs. Spencer." He paused. "But I'm surprised that a man who has embraced the religious life should be acquainted with her too."

The transformation in *El Grande* was remarkable. His body tensed. His eyes flashed then cooled to ice. Marcus had seen that same look many times in his rake-hell days, but it was always before some gentleman had challenged him to a duel. *El Grande* flicked a glance at Catherine, and Marcus sensed the tension gradually go out of him.

El Grande shrugged. "I don't spend all my time in the monastery. My work as a lay brother takes me to the city. During the course of my work, I met Mrs. Spencer. Is there anything else you would like to know?"

"Yes," said Marcus. "I want to be quite clear on one thing. Were you and Catherine acting on your own in this? Was British Intelligence or the War Office involved?"

Catherine said nothing.

El Grande said quietly, "You must understand that I have not been involved in intelligence work since I left Spain."

Catherine added, "I told you, Marcus, I wanted to do it."

When he did not reply, and then went on to something else, she released the breath she had been holding.

After a while, a white-robed monk brought them mugs of hot, spiced cordial to ward off the chill. Outside, a light snow was falling and it was evident there would be no time left to tour the monastery. The horses would be chomping at their bits.

"Of course," said Marcus, taking a swallow from the pewter mug he'd been handed, "I haven't had as much time to think about this as you. As you know, I was working on the assumption that you were the villains and I was your victim. Now that I am more enlightened, it occurs to me that we must be witnesses to something."

"But witnesses to what?"

"If we knew that, we'd know who the murderer is."

"I still have my journals and sketches from that time," Catherine said. "Maybe you'd like to have a look, though I haven't found anything significant in them."

Marcus looked at her incredulously. "Why didn't you tell me this before? Sketches? Notes? Of course I want to see them!"

Catherine glared at him. "I couldn't tell you before because then you would know that I was Catalina. Anyway, if anything unusual had happened, I would have reported it. Besides, I never met the English soldiers. As I already told you, I kept well out of their way for fear they would recognize me if ever we met again. I would have done the same with you, if you had not been so badly wounded and I had to nurse you. The only sketches I did were of partisans."

"Reported it to whom?"

"What?"

"You just said that nothing unusual happened or you would have reported it. Reported it to whom, Catherine?"

There was a heartbeat of silence, then she said, "To Major Carruthers. In Spain, he was my liaison with British Intelligence."

Before Marcus could respond, *El Grande* said, "I think it would be a good idea if you went through those journals and sketches. You might see something that Catherine has missed."

They left soon after that. But in the carriage, it was instantly obvious that she and *El Grande* had not fooled him for one minute.

He didn't say anything. He didn't have to. The look he gave her was so cold that she shrank into the folds of her warm pelisse. Not a word passed between them on the way home, but when they entered the house, his fingers tightened around her arm and he did not let go of her until they entered her bedchamber.

Chapter 22

"Listen to me very carefully," said Marcus, "I don't want to repeat myself. You are going to start at the beginning and you are going to tell me the whole story. No more lies. No more evasions. I want to hear about Major Carruthers, and I want to hear about Amy Spencer and your connection to her." The slow, precise diction suddenly gave way to a ferocity that made her shiver. "Make no mistake, if you don't tell me everything, every last insignificant detail, I shall call your *El Grande* out, or I shall horsewhip him to within an inch of his life."

He knew his words had been effective by her sudden pallor. Threats to herself would have been useless. But he had known that she would never see any harm come to her precious *El Grande*. For him, as she'd already told him, she would be willing to lay down her life.

She said in a shaken voice, "You can't mean that, Marcus."

"Try me." When he saw that she believed him, he went on, "Begin with Major Carruthers, or whoever is now your liaison with British Intelligence."

There was a moment of silence while Marcus sat down. He didn't invite Catherine to take a seat, and as she stood there before him, she felt like a prisoner in the dock, looking into the eyes of a judge who had already made up his mind to condemn her.

She felt herself shrinking before that look, not in fear, but in shame and guilt. He'd never once lied to her, not once, in all the time she'd known him, and she had tricked and deceived him from the very beginning, going back to their forced marriage in Spain. There might be some excuse for her accepting Major Carruthers's mission, and her subsequent masquerade, but that ended the night Marcus found her out and she became a true wife to him. She couldn't think why she hadn't told him everything then except, perhaps, that she'd been trained to think like an agent. But she was a woman, and this was the man she loved. She would never lie to him again.

Lacing her fingers together, she looked down at them, and stared long and hard at the wedding ring he'd given her, then she began to speak, beginning with the night he had asked her to play the part of Catalina.

As she spoke, fragments of memories flashed through Marcus's mind. Even then, when he'd put his proposition to her, he'd been taken with her. He'd trusted her, believing her to be honorable. But she'd been deliberately cultivating his trust. More than that, she'd made him fall in love with her. She'd used his need for her to blind him to her true purpose.

When she fell silent, he said, "Now let me see if I have this right. Major Carruthers is your superior. He ordered you to play the part of Catalina. You are an Intelligence agent and you were given the mission of spying on me because Major Carruthers suspected me of murdering my comrades. You communicated with him through other agents who had been placed in my household, except for when we were at Wrotham. Then Father Granger became your liaison with Major Carruthers. Have I left anything out? Oh yes, *El Grande* had no part in this. Is that the substance of what you've just told me?"

"Marcus, there's a lot more to it than that."

"Answer my question."

She nodded, feeling sick inside. This catalogue of her sins made her sound like a coldhearted, scheming adventuress who had been trying to trap him at every turn. "Marcus, I wish you would believe that I wanted to prove your innocence," she said quietly.

"I'm waiting for an answer to my question."

Her eyes dropped away. "*El Grande* played no part in it," she replied.

"So you believe. But I'm not convinced that he wasn't in this up to his neck."

Her head lifted and she said incredulously, "You can't suspect him of murdering all those men!"

"Why can't I?"

"Because—Marcus, I *know* him. Besides, what possible motive could he have?"

He couldn't prevent his bitterness from showing. "What possible motive could *I* have, but that didn't stop you suspecting me. But let's go on now to Amy Spencer. What is your connection to her?"

"Amy is my sister," she said simply.

For a moment, he was at a complete loss, then enlightenment dawned. "The one who eloped when you were just a girl?"

"Yes."

His eyes narrowed as he digested her words. "And how does she fit into this?"

"*El Grande* met her at my house. I was as surprised as you when he said that he'd been out walking with her. They must have agreed to meet again. I can't think why, unless she's helping him with his work among the poor."

Her words registered, but only just. Marcus was still trying to come to grips with this new development. Amy Spencer was Catherine's sister. He didn't know that he'd risen to his feet, and was leaning against a bedpost with one hand wrapped around it. "Your sister," he said. He had a vision of a little house in Chelsea, and Amy wearing nothing but some trinket he'd given her, disposed provocatively on a yellow sofa while he was tearing his clothes off.

His eyes flew to Catherine's and he blushed like a guilty schoolboy.

Catherine read everything in his expression, and for the first time since entering that room, she didn't feel like the guilty party. "Yes, *that* Amy Spencer," she said.

He immediately went on the defensive. "I can't deny that she was my mistress at one time, but that was a long time ago."

She went on the offensive. "As I recall, the first night we met in London, you were going into Amy's house."

"She gives parties, for God's sake. There's nothing in

that. Since she left my protection, we've been friends, nothing more."

"Parties where gentlemen meet ladies of a like mind. Loose women, to be precise."

He combed his fingers through his hair. "I was a single man. I didn't know you then."

"You were married to me. I was Catalina."

"You should have told me."

"Why should I? I had my revenge when I forced you to marry me."

They stood like two statues, glaring at each other. Marcus finally broke the silence. "Revenge? You spied on me for revenge?"

She let out a shaken breath. "No. That's not what I said. That's not what I meant."

"Then what did you mean?"

"I mean that in Spain, when I forced you to marry me, it wasn't only because you'd been trifling with my affections. I was thinking mainly of Amy and what you'd done to her."

He slapped the bedpost with the flat of his hand, making her jump. "Why am I to blame? She had other protectors before me. Why did you decide to punish me?" He let out a low laugh. "What a stupid thing to ask! Blind chance brought us together and you seized the opportunity of taking your revenge. Well, let me tell you something, you sanctimonious little prude." She fell back as he advanced on her. "I'm not apologizing for Amy. She chose her path in life. I had nothing to do with it. I wasn't her first lover by a long shot, and I won't be her last."

When he paused to draw breath, she plunged in. "Will you listen to yourself? *She chose her path in life.* Amy is my sister. Could you dismiss Samantha as easily as that?"

He opened his mouth, shut it, then said in a driven tone, "We shall leave my sister out of this discussion, if you please."

She bared her teeth at him. "I understand. I really do. Samantha is as pure as the driven snow. She and Amy aren't in the same class, are they? The one is destined for the estate of holy matrimony, the other is a toy, a plaything for a rich man's pleasure. And where do I fit into your scheme of things, Marcus? I'd really like to know."

His voice was as cold and grim as his expression. "You are my wife."

"And what about women like Amy? Can't she be a wife too?"

"I repeat, Amy chose her path in life. No one forced her into it, least of all me." His voice changed, became harsher. "For God's sake, Cat! Don't you know your own sister? Amy is a high flyer. She likes the things money can buy. She's not like you. She could never be satisfied with the life you lead."

"And you should know, I suppose?"

"Better than you."

She flung away from him with no clear idea of where she was going, then flung back as another thought occurred to her. "You once asked me to be your mistress. Am I a high flyer? Is that how you see me? Do I remind you of Amy?"

"Don't be ridiculous. You and Amy are nothing alike."

"Who are you insulting—Amy or me?"

"I would never insult Amy. That is to say—"

"Ah, so you're insulting me. Then why did you ask me to become your mistress?"

His frustration was rapidly coming to boiling point. "I thought we would suit. I knew you wanted me and I wanted you."

She gasped. "You thought we would suit! I wasn't good enough to be your wife, I suppose. And did I suit, Marcus?" The words spilled from her lips before she knew what she was saying. "In bed, was I as good as Amy? Was I as good as your other mistresses?"

He ground his teeth. "I'm not going to answer that question, and you shouldn't ask me."

All the passion suddenly drained out of her, and she stared at him in shocked silence. She couldn't believe she had said those words, couldn't believe they were having this conversation. But what horrified her more was that she'd discovered she was jealous of her own sister. Just thinking of Marcus and Amy together scourged her worse than any whip. Amy was beautiful, polished, experienced, whereas she had been sitting on the shelf for years.

His face was pale and he was frowning. "This conversation," he said, "should never have happened. My relationship with Amy is long over. You are my wife. That's the end of it."

His words snapped her out of her reveries, and she remembered her resolve. "There's something else you should know," she said. "It wasn't because Amy had been your mistress that I wanted revenge. It was because she told me you had ravished her. That's why I hated the name Wrotham. That's why I forced you to marry me in Spain."

He could hardly breathe, and he said harshly, "Your damn sister lied to you!"

"I know that now. But I didn't know it at the time. I know you couldn't do such a thing."

"How can I believe anything you say? From beginning to end you've hated me."

"That might have been true once," she whispered, "but it's not true now."

"Oh no, Cat, that's too easy. You'll want proof of my innocence. Well, it just so happens I don't give a damn whether you believe me or not."

He went to her writing table and found a piece of vellum.

"Marcus, what are you doing?"

"You're going to write to Major Carruthers. You mentioned a password. Use it. I want him here immediately. Now."

She wrote exactly what he'd told her to write. He took the letter from her and said, "Don't leave this room until I come back."

He didn't wait for her reply.

Major Carruthers kept his smile firmly in place until His Lordship's butler had closed and locked the doors behind him. It was between two and three o'clock in the morning, and though there were plenty of hackneys coming and going, conveying members of the fashionable set to their next party, no one took any notice of him. Wrotham, he decided, should have had the decency to call out his own coach to take him home. Of course, the man was preoccupied, and he'd given him plenty to think about. Even so, this was not the best of hours to be abroad in the city, especially when one left the hallowed precincts of Mayfair.

He swung his cane in an arc, just in case any stray footpad got a nasty idea in his head, and he resigned himself to the long walk home. An hour later, when he entered his own house, he cheered up a little. It was a small cozy house, with small cozy rooms, much friendlier than that big drafty barn Wrotham called home.

There was no candle waiting for him in the vestibule. When he'd gone tearing out of the house, he'd left his wife in bed, and he was too cautious to leave a flame going when there was no one around to guard it. He mounted the stairs in darkness and pushed into the chamber he shared with his wife. A few minutes later, robed in his long white nightshirt and with his nightcap snug on his head, he climbed into bed.

This was where he did his best thinking, and he sat up, propped against the pillows, sorting things through in his mind. "A bloody fiasco from beginning to end if you want my opinion," he told his wife's sleeping form.

Whether by instinct or training, even in sleep, she murmured something soothing.

"They were two of my best agents in Spain, and now look at them. They're worse than useless. One has fallen in love with the prime suspect, and the other is mooning over a whore." He didn't name names. Though there was no one there to hear him except his sleeping wife, he was ever a cautious man.

Something of what he'd said must have penetrated his wife's dreams, for she repeated, quite distinctly, "A whore?"

"Oh, not that he knows I'm on to him. What did he think—that I'd let him gallivant all over town with London's most notorious courtesan without keeping an eye on him?"

A rote answer.

"Not that I suspected anything. No. I thought we *owed* it to him for all the help his partisans gave us in Spain. The thing is, he's been, well, strange since the campaign came to an end." He heaved a long sigh. "And my prime suspect turns out to be a great disappointment to me. If he were behind things, he would have eliminated my agent. Instead, he's . . . well, let's just say he's taken my agent under his wing."

An incoherent murmur.

"And to think that my agent was withholding information from me!" He yawned hugely. "At any rate, it's out of my hands now. The only suspect left is the Rifleman and he's obviously got clean away. As I told His Lordship, the trail has gone cold, and we can only assume that our villain has accomplished his goal. It's time to call off my men.

"Now, respecting the murder of Freddie Barnes—"

His wife heaved herself up. "For heaven's sake, Charles, go to sleep."

He grinned from ear to ear. "Now that you're awake, love, how about a little kiss?"

"You wakened me on purpose! What are you doing? Oh, you wicked, wicked man! Oh, Charles!"

When Catherine heard Major Carruthers leave the house, she went to the door and stepped boldly into the corridor. A glance to her left told her that the same footman who had been there when she'd tried to go downstairs shortly after the major arrived was still on duty. He hadn't let her pass then, and of course he wouldn't let her pass now.

"Just taking the air," she told the footman cordially. She seethed with resentment at Marcus's methods of controlling her, but she wasn't going to take her anger out on poor William. She just wished Marcus would come upstairs so that she could tell him to his face exactly what she thought of him.

The library door opened and she saw Marcus framed in the doorway. "Giles," he called out, "bring me a fresh bottle of cognac." Soon after, a footman came running with a bottle under one arm.

Catherine whisked herself into her room and banged the door shut. She was avid to know what the major and Marcus had talked about, but the cursed man had evidently no intention of sharing that information with her. She'd been right to be afraid of telling him that she was his wife. As plain Miss Catherine Courtnay, she could come and go as she pleased. As the Countess of Wrotham, she was under her husband's thumb. Major Carruthers was powerless to help her now.

She prowled her room until the prowling got on her nerves. The bed seemed inviting for all of five minutes, then she was up and prowling again. It was impossible to sustain her anger at that pitch, and as it gradually ebbed, she realized that there was more to her anger than Marcus's high-handed methods of controlling her.

She sat down on the edge of the bed and tried to identify exactly what she was feeling. Disappointment? Despondency? It was closer to despair. How could she ever win his trust and respect after what she'd done? How could she ever win his love? It occurred to her that he had never wanted her to be his wife. All he had ever offered was to take her as his mistress.

She stretched out on the bed and stared sightlessly into space. The truth was she couldn't imagine what the future would hold for them, but it looked bleak. She shut her eyes and waited for Marcus to come to her.

As soon as she heard the door latch click, she pulled herself to a sitting position. Many hours had passed and she hadn't slept a wink. The candles were still lit, and she saw that he had discarded his coat and neckcloth, and his shirt was open to the waist. There was a smile on his face, and she knew he had been drinking, but she did not think he was drunk.

A little tremor of fear stirred inside her as he came away from the door. He was a powerful male animal and she couldn't read his mood. When he leaned over her, she could smell the brandy on his breath, but she had the presence of mind not to show her fear.

He said, "I swear on everything that is holy that I did not ravish your sister."

She touched a hand to his lean, harsh face. "I believe you."

"Tell me you don't love *El Grande*."

"I don't love him, Marcus, not the way you mean, and that's the truth."

He leaned closer. "Tell me the passion was real. Give me that much at least."

She swallowed the lump in her throat. "It was real. The passion was always there, even from the beginning."

Those were the last words they spoke. He extinguished all the candles and joined her in the bed. He used her as he had never used her before. There was no gentleness in him, no tenderness. His passion swept everything before it, and there was no restraining him. He was mastering her in some primitive way that found a response in the darkest reaches of her psyche.

When it was over, and she lay shuddering in his arms, he slipped from her body and went instantly to sleep. She lay motionless for a long time after, thinking about the future and how she could bear it.

The following morning, they met in the breakfast room. She'd been downstairs for hours waiting for him to appear. He didn't look like the man who had taken her to bed last night with such savage passion. He looked his usual urbane self.

He dismissed the servants with a nod, went to the sideboard, and poured himself a cup of coffee. "Major Carruthers had some interesting things to say for himself last night," he said as he sat down.

She didn't want to hear about Major Carruthers right now. She wanted him to say something that would make everything right between them, something that would show he felt more for her than physical desire. "What did he say?"

"He said that I'm no longer under suspicion and that he'd reached a dead end."

Pride came to her rescue and she found herself responding automatically. "Why are you no longer under suspicion?"

"Because I didn't kill you when I found you out."

"Then who does he think killed all those English soldiers?"

"Our unknown Rifleman."

He glanced at her and looked away. She didn't look like the woman who had responded to him with such abandon only a few hours ago. Last night, he'd taken her with a merciless passion that shocked even himself. He'd discovered something about himself. He wasn't the civilized gentleman he'd always assumed he was. He'd spent an hour or two in his library after Major Carruthers had left, reliving all the torment of her betrayal. The brandy hadn't helped. It had destroyed whatever it was that kept him civilized. That primitive side of him had beat violently through his blood, making him want to be master of his own woman. He would wipe the memory of *El Grande* from her heart and soul. Now, she wouldn't even look at him. God, what had he done?

"Did you say something, Marcus?"

"I said that Carruthers has a theory. That the reason all those soldiers were murdered was because they would recognize the Rifleman. For some reason that only he knows, he didn't want that to happen. You and *El Grande* and I have been spared because we never came face-to-face with him, and wouldn't be able to recognize him. The Rifleman must know this, or he would have eliminated us too. It seems a reasonable theory, don't you think?"

"What about that attack on you? What about the lantern on the tower stairs?"

"Major Carruthers put it this way: if we hadn't suspected that there was a murderer at large, what would we have thought of that attack on me and the lantern on the tower stairs?"

She stared at him in silence as she reflected on his words. At length, she said, "We'd think that the attack on you was made by thieves who had very cleverly set you up with a note from your ... from your mistress, and that the lantern on the stairs had, in all likelihood, fallen from the wall."

"Exactly. So we can stop looking over our shoulders."

"What if Major Carruthers's theory is wrong?"

"The only reason I didn't suspect the Rifleman from the beginning was because I thought you and *El Grande* were behind everything. If we three are in the clear, who else could it be?"

He buttered some toast and began to munch on it. Catherine stirred the cold coffee in her cup. She looked at Marcus and something in that look put him on his guard.

"What is it?" he asked.

"You see what this means? We are free to do whatever we want. I can go back to being Catherine Courtnay again."

He toyed with his toast. "You are not Catherine Courtnay. You are my wife, my countess. But I do see what you mean. You don't have to go on playing the part of Catalina."

She leaned forward slightly. "I've been thinking, Marcus, and I see a way out."

"Do you now?" He spoke without expression.

"*El Grande* and I can testify that you were forced into this marriage. You have witnesses, now, Marcus. The marriage will be annulled, and we can go our separate ways."

There was such ferocity in the look he flung at her that she jerked back as though he'd struck her. His voice was hard and clipped. "I told you I would be calling the shots from now on, not you, not *El Grande*, but me. Do you understand?"

She jumped to her feet and the words spilled from her mouth in a torrent. "I don't care how you do it, but I want this impossible marriage to end. And I refuse to go on playing the part of Catalina. I hate brown hair. I want my own life back. I want my friends and my own things about me. I want to be myself again." She felt weak at the knees and steadied herself with both hands spread flat on the table. "And I won't have you use me as you used me last night."

His eyes were as black as pitch and his whole face

was clenched. All the torments he'd suffered the night before in his library rushed back in full force. He felt hurt to the quick, not only by her betrayal, but because it seemed to him now that even the passion they'd shared had been a sham on her part.

"A divorce it is, then," he said, and he flung out of the room.

Chapter 23

Catherine returned to Heath House in a sleek, well-sprung traveling chaise. It was a relief to be herself again—no more feigning a Spanish accent, no more lying in her teeth to people she'd come to like, and—most glorious of all—no more dyed black tresses. It had taken her hours to scrub the nasty stuff from her hair.

And no more Marcus—damn the man!

She'd brought with her a jumble of boxes, the supposed booty of her three months with the widow Wallace. Marcus had rehearsed her till she was almost word perfect. They had even mapped out a possible itinerary she and Mrs. Wallace might have followed. Nothing was left to chance. He hadn't sent her home from London, but had made it look as if she had just crossed the English Channel. The last time she had seen him, they were in a posting-house in Dover.

He'd been polite but reserved, and she'd taken her cue from him. They would have to communicate from time to time, he said, if only to discuss the details of their annulment or divorce. But he assured her that whenever they crossed paths, no one would ever know they were more than acquaintances.

"What are you going to tell your family?" she'd asked.

"I haven't really thought about it. Does it matter?"

It did matter, more than she wanted it to. She'd never see any of them again. In the short time that she'd known them, she'd come to feel as though she were one of them. Now she must be divorced from them too. It hardly seemed fair.

"I suppose not," she said. "I'm sure whatever you decide will be fine with me."

Almost the first thing she did after returning to Heath House was to go through her sketches and diaries. These were not really diaries—they were notebooks where she wrote down details that later became reports for Major Carruthers. The sketches, the few that she still had, were all portraits of partisans—except for the one portrait of Marcus.

She stared at it for a long, long time before going on to the next. There was a sketch of Juan playing cards with the padre; partisans, mostly women, coming and going, and one of *El Grande* returning from a mission with some of their comrades. No one had posed for these sketches. They were all done from memory, something to occupy her on those endless stretches when *El Grande* was on a mission that did not involve her.

There had been many of those.

The first time she saw Marcus after she'd returned to being Catherine Courtnay was when he came to look over the sketches. He had sent a note beforehand and arrived at the French doors of her study long after the McNallys had retired for the night.

He looked over her notes and sketches, but found nothing revealing in them.

"I don't suppose it matters now," he said, breaking one of the long silences that had fallen between them.

"No, I suppose not. Marcus, have you seen your solicitors yet?"

"Hardly, I've only been back in town for a few days."

"Of course."

Another long silence ensued. "Would you like some tea? Coffee?" she asked, just for something to say.

"Thank you, no. I really shouldn't be here, alone with you, so late at night."

When she didn't say anything, he inhaled sharply and went on, "Now, don't get the wrong idea, but I've rented a cottage not far from here. Old Dalby's place. Do you know it?"

"I know it," she said carefully. It had been lying empty for six months.

"I've installed caretakers to look after things for me. Mr. and Mrs. Mills they're called. If something comes up and you need to get hold of me, you can reach me through Mills."

"What could come up?"

"Nothing, I hope. But you are still my wife, and I am still responsible for you. That reminds me—how do I give you the money I owe you? Do you want a bank draft?"

"What money?"

"For playing Catalina."

"I didn't do it for money! I was on a mission. I knew I would never see a penny of it."

A sudden tension gripped his face. "Of course," he said. "How could I possibly have forgotten?"

He left shortly after and she spent a sleepless night trying to decipher every look he'd given her, every word he'd uttered, and what he'd been thinking during those long silences.

She slipped into her old life with barely a ripple to mark the transition. It felt as though she had never been away. The itinerary with the fictitious Mrs. Wallace stood her in good stead, but really, no one was trying to catch her out. When she became confused about dates and places, everyone made allowances. They had no reason to suspect that she wasn't telling the truth.

Even when she refused to write about the places she was supposed to have visited, no one raised awkward questions. A. W. Euman was known to write about serious subjects and her holiday with the widow, so she said, was too frivolous for words.

She thought long and hard before she wrote her first piece for *The Journal*. After much soul-searching, she decided that she couldn't allow Marcus's feelings to sway her. She wrote about her own father, but she wrote for Penn, and everything she wrote came straight from her heart. She knew Helen and Samantha would read her column, and she tried to give them a ray of hope.

On her second week back, she met Marcus, as if by chance, when she was out riding on the heath. In one comprehensive glance, he took in Vixen, the sidesaddle, and her pursed lips.

"Oh, my poor Cat," he said, and they both laughed.

He'd been to see his solicitors, he told her. Dissolving their marriage was turning out to be more complex than they'd thought. Messrs. Brown and Armitage were exploring every alternative, and when he had something more to tell her, he would come to her again.

She watched him ride away till he disappeared from view, and she still went on staring for a long time after.

Though she rarely left Hampstead now, the Lowries persuaded her to accompany them to the theater one night. Emily thought she looked poorly and needed to be taken out of herself. Amy was in her box, as beautiful as ever, but it seemed to Catherine that her court of admirers had dwindled. This was explained by Emily, who pointed out another box. Julia Bryce's star was on the rise, judging by the crush of gentlemen with her, and as her star rose, the star of her rival waned.

Emily whispered, "That's how it is in the *demi-monde*. There's room for only one queen. You know, I can't help feeling sorry for Mrs. Spencer."

Catherine nodded. Then the curtain went up, and the play began.

During the intermission, she came face-to-face with Amy in the hallways. To Catherine's disappointment, Amy looked right through her. Not by one look or word did she acknowledge her in any way.

The following morning, however, she received a hand-delivered letter. She recognized Amy's writing, and her heart was pounding when she sat down at her desk and tore it open. It was a long letter, begging for her forgiveness for all the wrong Amy had ever done her. Then Amy made her confession. She had done the Earl of Wrotham a great wrong, she said, and she wished to make amends.

Catherine read on, knowing exactly what Amy was going to say, and as she read, she felt angry and weepy by turns. If only she had known this before she'd met Marcus; if only she'd never found Amy in the stable; if only she'd trusted her heart and confronted Marcus with Amy's lies. And if only there was a way to turn the clock back.

Amy's letter answered one thing that had been puzzling her. She was sure this confession was the result of *El Grande*'s influence. He was a priest, or as close as made little difference. He'd obviously taken Amy under his wing. That must be why he'd been out walking with her.

Amy ended her letter by saying that she was leaving London to spend the winter months in Italy, and though she would never acknowledge Catherine publicly, she wished her to know that she would always love her.

That night, Catherine donned her partisan's clothes and went out on the heath with Vixen.

It was Emily who brought her the latest gossip about Marcus.

"What about the Earl of Wrotham?" asked Catherine, trying to appear casual.

She breathed deeply, filling her lungs with air. Earlier that morning they had gone to church, and afterwards they had decided to go for a walk on the heath.

"For the first time, his whole family has joined him in town—all except the youngest, who has gone off to university. Everyone is talking about it."

"Why?"

"Well, of course you know that the dowager Lady Wrotham's father was a butcher—and she's never been received all these years!"

"He was a tailor," said Catherine.

"Whatever. Don't interrupt, Catherine. The thing is, the earl has spread the word that where he goes, she goes." Emily clapped her hands. "And it's worked. They're seen everywhere."

Catherine wanted to throw her bonnet in the air. She flicked a glance at Emily, then looked away. "What do they say about Wrotham's wife?"

"Oh, she's gone home to visit some sick relative or other. Naturally, there's a great deal of speculation."

"Oh, naturally," replied Catherine dryly.

They had come to one of the natural ponds on the heath, and they stopped for a moment to catch their breath and watch the ducks. There were plenty of pedestrians taking the air, and a few riders exercising their horses.

Catherine raised a hand to rub the back of her neck, and suddenly paused. Pivoting, she scanned the faces of the people behind her.

"What is it?" asked Emily.

Catherine said slowly, "I had the strangest feeling, as though someone were watching me. This isn't the first time I've had this feeling lately."

Emily turned her head to look over her shoulder. "I don't see anyone." She looked at Catherine, cleared her throat, and said, "Catherine, I've found the perfect man for you."

"There is no such person as the perfect man."

Emily ignored the cynicism. "He's just moved into the area and has rented the Smythes' place in Church Row. You'll meet him when next you come for dinner. He's to be the guest of honor. His name is Nigel Dearing."

Catherine came to an abrupt halt. "I like the single life."

Emily walked on past her. "That's because you don't know any other."

And to that, Catherine could find no reply.

As she undressed for bed, she thought about what Emily had told her about Marcus's family. That he had taken her advice touched her deeply. Perhaps, in time, he would soften even more. Perhaps he would come to forgive her for all the lies she'd told him.

Sleep did not come easily. As she began to relax she thought back to the last time she and Marcus had made love. It didn't help to remind herself that he'd been trying to humiliate her. Her body was telling her something different. It ached with unsated desire; ached to feel Marcus's embrace again.

Groaning, she gritted her teeth and started counting sheep.

Chapter 24

Two days later, Catherine came out of the local saddlery where she'd taken one of Vixen's bits to be repaired, and found Marcus waiting for her in a hired hackney. He didn't descend from the coach to help her up. Instead, he extended his hand and pulled her in.

As the hackney moved off, she said, "Is so much secrecy really necessary?"

He shrugged. "I don't want to rouse suspicion. Everyone thinks my wife is off visiting relatives in Spain. If they see me with you, people are bound to start talking. I'm thinking of you, Cat."

She looked up at him, and Marcus continued, "They're going to talk even more when we dissolve our marriage. You know, of course, that everything will have to come out? I mean your identity, Cat. There's no possibility of keeping it a secret." She looked dismayed, and he went on, "You'll have to appear in person. Whom did you think you would be when they questioned you—Catalina or Catherine?"

"I never gave it a thought," she said faintly.

"Well, think about it now." There was a pause, and he said quietly, "We must tell the truth. If we lie and are later found out, our divorce may well be quashed. I can't divorce Catalina Cordes without bringing Catherine Courtnay into it. It was Catherine Courtnay who posed as my wife these last weeks."

She knew that he was thinking of the succession. A man in his position had to be sure that his children were his legal heirs, especially his firstborn son. She looked at the finger which was now bare of his wedding ring, and her eyes began to tear.

"What—?" She cleared her throat. "What do your solicitors have to say about it?"

"So far, I've told them very little. I wanted to make sure, first, that you understood everything would have to come out. However, I did learn that the Scottish divorce is out of the question. It seems that too many English couples have gone that route, and now one has to be Scottish before their courts will give you a hearing. Don't look so forlorn. There are other possibilities open to us."

She wasn't forlorn. Her pulse had quickened and her spirits had lifted. "It doesn't matter," she said. "I'm in no hurry. How did your family react when you told them Catalina had been called away to visit a sick relative?"

Marcus chuckled. "They descended on my doorstep, *en masse,* to demand what the devil was going on. Even Tristram came down from Oxford. They had the idea that all was not right between us. I put them off as best I could. They'll learn the truth soon enough." The smile left his eyes and he looked at her in a way that drove her lashes down to hide her own feelings. He said quietly, "You made quite an impression on them, Cat."

Her heart felt as though it were breaking. She got out hoarsely, "No more than they made on me."

He looked out the window. "I read your piece in *The Journal.* You were right and I was wrong. I hope you will accept my apologies for ripping into you. It was to the point, yet it was compassionate." He turned his head to look at her. "You wrote it for Penn, didn't you?"

Since she couldn't find her voice, she nodded.

"He read it, you know, but I don't think he recognized himself in it. He doesn't think his drinking is a problem. And actually, since he's arrived in town, he hasn't touched a drop."

"Penn came too?"

"Oh, Helen insisted on it. And now I'm insisting that they stay for the little Season. I thought you'd be pleased."

She managed a smile. "You've done well, Marcus. I've heard how you forced society to accept Helen. I think it's wonderful."

"You wouldn't recognize her. Or Samantha either.

They're having the time of their lives. Penn and I, of course, are the ones to suffer. Every afternoon and evening, we take turns doing our duty—escorting our ladies from one engagement to another. I've persuaded David to stay on too. Penn and he spend a good deal of time together looking over horses. At Christmas, Tristram will join us again, then we'll all be together."

Every word he uttered seemed to be aimed straight at her heart. She couldn't listen to more. "When do you intend to tell your family the truth?"

"That depends."

"On what?"

He hesitated, then said flatly, "On whether or not you are pregnant with my child." He gave her a moment to let his words sink in. "It's been almost a month. Cat, are you pregnant?"

She looked up at him with huge, stricken eyes. "No, Marcus," she said. "I'm not."

When Marcus returned to town, he went straight to his club in St. James to meet with his cousin.

David ordered dinner, beefsteak with the obligatory bottle of burgundy. Marcus then asked him how the morning had gone.

David pulled a long face, and laughed. He'd spent the morning with Penn, looking for a stud stallion to go with the mare Marcus had sold him. This was all Marcus's idea. He wanted Penn's every waking moment to be occupied so that he wouldn't have time to think of his next drink.

David said, "I'm sure Penn thinks I don't know a gelding from a brood mare. In other words, he thinks that, as a breeder of horses, I'm a disgrace to the Lytton name. We've arranged to go to Tattersall's tomorrow."

"I'm obliged to you," said Marcus. "And I mean that, David. It's good of you to give up your time for Penn."

"It's no sacrifice. He knows more about horses than I could learn in a lifetime. You're very lucky that he manages your stud for you."

"It's his stud too."

"I don't think he sees it that way. He sounds quite bitter." David looked up. "I beg your pardon. I shouldn't have said that."

Marcus waved his apology away. "I don't know how Penn came to be so touchy. He wasn't always like that. How is the beefsteak?"

They were about ready to leave when Peter Farrel caught sight of them and came over. Marcus hadn't seen Peter since the night of his godmother's ball, the night that Freddie Barnes was murdered.

"Marcus, I'm glad I caught you," Peter said with his usual abruptness. "There's a rumor going around that I think you should know about." His eye fell on David. "How do you do, Mr. Lytton?"

"What rumor?" demanded Marcus.

"They say that you've hidden your wife away because you think her life is in danger."

"Why should I think that?"

"You know, we spoke of it before. Because you're the only English soldier left from that place in Spain."

"What has that to do with my wife?"

"Don't be obtuse, Marcus. If you're a target, she may be a target too."

"Whose target?"

"How should I know? One of the partisans who was with you, one presumes. Or that Rifleman. Just be careful, Marcus. Don't say I didn't warn you. G'day to you, Mr. Lytton." And with that, Farrel sauntered off.

Marcus turned to David. "Have you heard this rumor?"

"Yes, I have, but the story was so convoluted that I didn't know what to make of it."

"I don't know what to make of it either," said Marcus.

Farrel's words stayed with Marcus on the short walk home to Cavendish Square. He was annoyed that the gossip had hit so close to the mark, at least on one point. At the same time, he wasn't afraid that Catherine's life was in danger. Major Carruthers had convinced him that the murderer's object had been achieved when he'd eliminated all those who might recognize him again and place him at *El Grande*'s base. The episode with the lantern on the tower stairs and the attack against him in Hyde Park were not connected. Still, the mystery continued to tantalize him. Who was the murderer and what had driven him to commit so many murders? Was it the Rifleman, or, as Farrel had suggested, was it one of the partisans? He thought of *El Grande* and cursed under his breath. He was jealous of that young man, and that did not sit well with Marcus.

He suspected that once Catherine were free of him, she would eventually marry *El Grande*, and that did not sit well with him either. He had no excuse, really, for the delay in seeing his solicitors, except his own reluctance to proceed with the divorce. A divorce wasn't something to be entered into lightly. He was thinking of Catherine.

Bloody hell! Who was he trying to convince? There was a lot more to it than that. He didn't want a divorce. He missed her. In spite of everything, he actually missed her. A sane man would be glad to be rid of her. But not he! The sad truth was he was bewitched by a woman who had repeatedly betrayed him.

He didn't know why he was angry. He'd stopped being angry a long time ago. This wasn't the first time he'd gone over things in his mind, and he'd come to acknowledge that Catherine wasn't entirely to blame. She was, after all, an agent. She'd been under orders, and couldn't have told him anything, even if she'd wanted to.

Something Carruthers had said came back to him. The major had told him that because Catherine had not reported the incident on the tower stairs, she could no longer be trusted as an agent. At the time, Carruthers's words had only infuriated him. She hadn't said anything about the tower stairs incident because she'd suspected *him* of trying to murder her. When he'd had time to cool down, he came to see what Carruthers was getting at. Catherine's loyalties were divided. Marcus wasn't making any assumptions about her feelings, but at the very least she hadn't wanted to see him hang.

He wasn't blameless either. He'd bullied her at every turn or he'd tried to. And when she'd stood her ground, he'd become as sulky as a schoolboy. He could hardly believe, now, that he'd asked her to be his mistress. The one thing he could say in his own favor was that he hadn't tried to seduce her. She'd come to him of her own free will. Now that he knew about Amy, he realized how much Cat must have forgiven him before she'd taken that step—not because he'd ravished Amy, Cat would never forgive that—but because Amy had once been his mistress.

Just thinking about Amy, even now, made the color rise hotly in his cheeks. He still found it hard to believe that Amy Spencer was Cat's sister. In other words, his sister-in-law was once his mistress. And Cat had been curious about his relationship with Amy. The damnable thing was, so was he. He could remember the house in Chelsea in which he'd installed her, he could remember a yellow sofa, and he remembered he'd been hot for her. And that's all he remembered. He had only been twenty-two at the time, and if Cat only knew it, he'd been hot for every pretty woman who caught his eye. Amy was only one in a long line of mistresses over the years, and not one of them was memorable. It was just his bad luck that he'd once chosen the sister of the woman who would one day be his wife.

A picture formed in his mind. He saw them all sitting down to Sunday dinner, *en famille*, his wife at the foot of the table, as was proper, and his former mistress . . . He said something crude under his breath, and a passerby looked at him askance and turned away in another direction.

Of course, Amy was the least of his problems. There was still the question of Cat's feelings for *El Grande*. She'd put that young man on a pedestal. On the other hand, he'd rather be the man in her bed than the man she hero-worshiped with a young girl's devotion. Of the two of them, he had the better bargain. It was damn cold on a pedestal. And damn hot in Cat's bed.

The passion had been real. He'd relived their last night together many times over, and he was convinced that the passion had been real. She'd been shocked by his ardor, hell, he'd shocked himself, and he had initiated her into too much too soon. He'd done things with her, to her, that he'd never done with another woman, and asked things of her that he hadn't known he was going to ask, but nothing that could be called wrong between a man and his wife. At least, not by his lights. And she hadn't protested, or tried to restrain him. She had given him the freedom of her body as he had done with her, and they'd both reveled in it.

All this was beside the point. Cat wanted a divorce, and he had promised to take care of it. He couldn't delay any longer. Tomorrow. He would set up an appointment with his solicitor first thing tomorrow morning.

Face like granite, he slammed into his house. Giles, the footman, came forward to take Marcus's hat and coat, but one look at his master's murderous expression made him veer off and discreetly disappear behind a potted palm.

Chapter 25

Under the brilliant glare of a thousand candles, Marcus's godmother, Lady Tarrington, surveyed the crush of guests in the ballroom of her house in St. James's Square. Her receptions were always well attended, but this one was exceptional—in spite of the fact that the Season had not begun. This was the little Season that preceded Christmas. And the reason so many had come was because everyone was curious about Marcus and his family.

They had all heard the rumor that had taken London by storm, that Marcus might be the target of a Spanish vendetta, and was forced to hide his wife for her own protection. It added a certain recklessness to the evening, a certain danger in even knowing him. Though privately she dismissed the gossip as nonsense, she wasn't above using it to ensure the success of her ball.

Of course, Marcus wasn't the only drawing card. His stepmother was equally an object of curiosity. Lady Tarrington's eyes searched the small knots of people who were standing at the edge of the dance floor, waiting for the orchestra to strike up. There stood Lady Wrotham flanked by her two sons, Penniston and Tristram. Almost thirty years had passed since the scandal of Wrotham's marriage to a tradesman's daughter, complete with abduction and possible ravishment. In spite of the passage of time, one could still see what had caught the earl's eye. Though the countess had grown a bit stout and her black hair was liberally laced with gray, she had the face of an angel. There wasn't a line on it. It wasn't a beautiful face so much as a sweet face, and when Lady Tarrington thought of the black-hearted devil who had forced that innocent young girl to become his wife, she shuddered in revulsion.

Marcus, thank God, was nothing like his father. The boy had had a shaky start, but time had steadied him. Mary, Lady Tarrington decided, would be proud of her son if she could see him now. He was doing what his father should have done years ago if the old sod had had any decency. He was establishing his stepmother and her family in Society.

In the weeks that had passed since they had all come up to town, they'd been taken up by some of the foremost hostesses of the *ton*, herself among them. This was Marcus's doing. When he set his mind to charm, there wasn't a woman alive who could resist him. It was too bad that his brother Penniston wasn't more like him.

Penniston was aware of Lady Tarrington's scrutiny and he involuntarily squared his shoulders. He still could not get used to so much attention. He didn't make the mistake of thinking he was the object of anyone's admiration. They were watching and waiting for his branch of the Lyttons to fall flat on their faces. Well, he wasn't about to do anything to shame his mother, not in public.

The countess saw the look on her son's face and raised her brows meaningfully. In response to that look, Penn spoke to her in an undertone. There was something on his mind, something he wished to discuss with his mother, but not in front of Tristram.

Tristram missed the exchange. His eyes were trained on a young gentleman whose neckcloth was a vision of intricate knots and folds. Though he would have been embarrassed if anyone had known it, nothing in that ballroom had impressed him half as much as the neckcloths sported by gentleman of rank and fashion. In this instance, he was memorizing every fold, knot, and bow so that he could describe it in detail to his friends in Oxford when he returned the next day.

The countess said, "Penn and I are going to take a turn in the gallery, Tris."

"What? Oh. You don't mind if I mingle?"

"Of course not. I want you to enjoy yourself."

Her heart swelled with pride as she watched him join some friends who were idling their way into the card-room. She was perfectly sure there wasn't a person here tonight who was as happy as she. Samantha had "taken"—and here the countess searched the dancers to see her daughter partnered by the handsome young heir to Sir John Hanton—her youngest son was obviously at ease here, and Penn was behaving as well as she had ever seen him.

As Penn led her through the glass entrance doors, she touched a hand to the locket at her throat.

Penn noticed the gesture. "It's beautiful," he said. "Marcus did well."

She stopped beside a long pier glass to admire the pendant. It was exquisite, a single cameo of black onyx set in rubies. The relief was of her profile, taken from a miniature of herself as a young girl, before her marriage to Wrotham. When Marcus had fastened it around her neck before they'd set off earlier that evening, she'd thought her heart would break.

They had all assembled in the drawing room and Marcus had said in his matter-of-fact way, "The date of your marriage to my father is engraved on the back. I'm starting a new tradition. From this day forward, every Wrotham bride will receive a cameo pendant."

"I wonder what happened to the original bracelet?" Tristram had said.

"I suppose we'll never know," Marcus answered. "Stolen? Lost? I doubt we'll ever find out."

Now, looking at her elder son, the countess said, "Frankly, Penn, I prefer this pendant to the Wrotham bracelet. One day I shall give it to Samantha, and that's something I could never do with the bracelet. It's an heirloom, and if it's ever found, it will go to Catalina."

Penn led her to a sofa in a window embrasure. "I've heard something that I think you ought to know." He remained standing.

"If you mean the rumor about the vendetta and

Marcus, I know all about it, and Marcus says there's nothing to it."

"It's not that. It's . . . I was at the solicitors yesterday, and Armitage said some things that were disturbing."

"What did he say?"

"I got the distinct impression that Marcus had been looking into an annulment."

"Oh, no! But Marcus and Catalina seem so perfect for each other."

Penn said patiently, "Mother, you're not thinking of all the implications. What if Catalina never returns?"

She looked up at him with fear shadowing her eyes. "What will you do?"

"If I'm right, then you know what we must do."

And with those words, all her hopes fell around her ears like a house of cards.

A few minutes later, Marcus checked his watch as he left the house. He'd done his duty. Everything had gone off as well as he'd hoped. The ball would go on till dawn, but he had somewhere else to go.

Now it was time to please himself.

When he emitted a shrill whistle, his coach pulled out of a line of stationary carriages and came to a stop at the edge of the pavement.

"Hampstead," Marcus told his coachman and climbed in.

On the drive to Hampstead, he kept thinking of something Peter Farrel had said to him while they'd enjoyed a quiet smoke in the billiard room. The subject had been the Spanish-vendetta rumor and Marcus had done his best to convince him there was nothing in it. That's when Peter had offered his own interpretation of events.

"In that case," he said, "I'd look closer to home."

"Meaning?"

"Who stands to gain the most if anything should happen to you or your wife?"

"You can't mean Penn!" When he saw that Peter did

mean Penn, he'd said incredulously, "But what about all those other deaths? What about Freddie Barnes?"

"Ah. Now that is very clever. Those other deaths support the vendetta rumor. In short, if anything should happen to you or your wife, no one would suspect your heir."

"But Penn was never in Lisbon or London when those deaths took place."

"Are you sure? In any case, he might have hired agents to do his dirty work for him."

The conversation had ended abruptly, when they were joined by Tristram and his friends. On thinking it over now, Marcus simply could not imagine Penn in the role of a murderer. His brother was no saint, but he was honorable. Penn could have robbed him blind while he'd been at war. Instead, he'd returned to find his estates and tenants as prosperous as ever.

Dismissing Farrel's theory, he turned his thoughts to Catherine. He knew she would be attending one of Emily Lowrie's informal soirées tonight, and he had decided on impulse to see her—not that he had any intention of showing up at Emily's. What he had to say to Catherine was best said in private.

He'd been to see his solicitors, and now he knew there could be no annulment, no divorce, English or Scottish style, no unraveling the knot that tied them together. His solicitors had laughed in his face when he'd told them about this hypothetical friend, naming no names, who had been forced into marriage with one woman, thinking she was another, who had discovered his error and had subsequently not only lived with her quite openly as his wife, but had also regularly exercised his conjugal rights.

He'd left his solicitors' office feeling lighthearted. Catherine and he really were married, and there was no way out of it. It might not be the kind of marriage they wanted, but given time, they might make something of it. Now all he had to do was convince Catherine of it.

It was too bad she wasn't pregnant. That would have solved all their problems at one stroke.

· · ·

As the evening wore on, Catherine found it increasingly difficult to concentrate. She wanted to go home, but she'd no wish to break up the party by having one of the other guests take her in his carriage. She'd arrived with Mr. Dearing, Emily's perfect man, and she couldn't bring herself to tear him away from his perfect woman, a great, statuesque blond he'd taken an instant liking to and from whose side he could not be dislodged. Poor Emily was bitterly disappointed.

Catherine had walked to and from Emily's house many times across the heath, and she made up her mind to slip away without making a fuss. She made her excuses to Emily, tactfully parried her friend's spate of protests, and slipped out the front door.

Though it was dark on the heath, she felt no fear as she crossed the road and struck out along the path. She didn't have far to go and there were still plenty of people about, some of them courting couples, and there was also a party of young people indulging in a late-night picnic.

The sounds thinned out as she made her way to the avenue of trees that led to the track to her own house. Then there were no sounds, only silence, dead silence. Her steps slowed and she came to a halt. Something was wrong.

This was her domain, and she knew that the heath was never silent. There should have been something, the rustle of a fox or badger on its nocturnal prowl, a bird of prey settling on its perch, even a domestic cat looking for a fight or a mate. There was nothing.

Her hand curled around the pistol in her pocket and she stepped off the path. Footpads were not unknown on the heath, but they usually struck in the less populated areas.

From somewhere ahead of her, she heard the merest whisper of sound, the tread of someone approaching or retreating. She leveled her pistol and waited. The silence was unnerving.

She had to move before whoever it was cut her off from the house. Through sheer force of will, she kept herself from running, and walked up through the trees as silently as she could. Her heart was thudding against her ribs and she could hardly breathe when she saw the shape of Heath House loom out of the darkness. With skirts bunched in one hand and the pistol clutched in the other, she sped up that flagstone path then drew back violently as a dark shape came out of the shadows to meet her. A scream hovered in her throat and came out a moan.

"Marcus! You frightened me half to death." She pocketed the pistol. "I thought you were a footpad. I might have shot you."

"As you see, I'm not a footpad."

Now that her fears were explained, she went weak with relief. "How was I supposed to know it was you? Why are you here?"

"I have something to say to you."

He grasped her arm and hustled her around the side of the house to a lane that backed onto the heath. His carriage was waiting, his own carriage, and he hoisted her inside.

When he had climbed in beside her, and the coach jolted into motion, she said, "Where are you taking me?"

"Nowhere in particular. I've told my driver to drive around. This is more private than your house. I don't want anyone to know I've called on you. There's been too much talk already."

"Won't your coachmen know?"

"They won't say anything. They've been with me for years."

She refrained from pointing out that the McNallys were just as trustworthy as his coachmen. Her hair had come undone and was falling around her shoulders. "What is it you wished to say to me?" There was an odd silence, and she looked up to see him staring at her.

"No, don't," he said, as she began to fix her hair. "I like you with your hair down," and reaching over, he pulled the remaining pins from her hair. "Such beautiful hair," he said, and captured a strand.

Her mouth went dry, and she remembered another carriage ride, when he'd kissed her. Her eyes dropped to his mouth.

His voice was low and hoarse. "It's just occurred to me that I've never seen your red hair spread across my pillow. I used to fantasize about it. I still do. But your hair was always brown when I made love to you."

She had her own fantasies, and her body began to throb with awareness. She had no recollection of who moved first. She thought she swayed toward him, and the next moment she was in his arms.

He dragged her across his lap. His chest rose and fell, and for a long time he just looked at her lips. Then his head descended and he covered her mouth with his.

There was a desperation to his kiss that bordered on violence. Just knowing how much he wanted her made her want him too. When she moaned and angled her mouth wider, he crushed her to him with arms of iron.

The smooth swaying movement of the coach set up a rhythm that found an echo in the pulse points of his body. Calmly, deliberately, he shifted her so that she straddled him. When she inhaled sharply and lifted to her knees, he cupped her bottom with widespread hands and eased her down. He was hard for her and he wanted her to know it.

He fettered her with one hand behind her knee and with the other he deftly peeled back her cloak and molded his fingers over first one breast, then the other. When her head dropped and he was sure she was accepting his touch, he brought up both hands and stroked the soft mounds through her clothes.

He said hoarsely, "I'm sorry if I frightened or disgusted you when I came to your bed on our last night together. I won't ever do anything again when you don't want me to. All right?"

On a strangled moan, she got out, "You didn't frighten or disgust me. I was as shameless as you."

He bit her lip, not hard, but with enough force to get her attention. "Not shameless, love. You were perfect. And I was out of my mind with wanting you."

She stopped his mouth with a kiss. Marcus needed no more encouragement. He quickly undid the buttons on her bodice and bared her breasts. When he took a nipple in his mouth and sucked strongly, she threw back her head. He released the nipple he'd laved and went for the other. Catherine was almost delirious with the pleasure of it, and her hips began to move in instinctive appeal, sliding and grinding against his hard groin.

His hand began to stroke beneath the folds of her gown, kneading her hips, her bottom, feeling for the strings of her drawers. Through a daze of passion, it began to dawn on Catherine that Marcus meant to take her right there in the coach.

She brought her hands down and pushed feebly against his shoulders. "We shouldn't be doing this. What if the coach stops? The coachman will find us."

He crooned soothingly into her ear and dealt with her drawers, tearing them apart to give him greater access to her body. In spite of her protests, she didn't try to stop him.

His fingers delved and found her wetness, then he dipped into her, stroking, probing, driving her to her knees.

"Cat?" he muttered. His breathing was harsh and rushed in and out of his lungs as though he had just run a race. He fumbled with the closure on his trousers. "Say yes to me, Cat. Say yes."

She was gasping, quivering from head to toe. Her blood throbbed in a fever of arousal. He always had this effect on her.

"Yes," she said. "Oh Marcus, yes."

She jolted from the shock of his entry. He lay quietly, wanting to give her time to adjust to the fit of his body, but her throaty pleas weakened his control. Clamping her to him, he moved inside her with deep, hard strokes, giving her what she wanted. Shudders wracked her body, driving him mindless with need. When he felt her body tense, hovering on the edge, he surrendered to his own explosive climax, grinding into her till they were both spent and gasping for breath.

It was a long, long time before either of them realized the coach had come to a stop. Catherine looked out the window and saw that they were back at Heath House. She groaned and tried to clamber off his lap. She couldn't believe that she'd been so lost to reason that she'd allowed him to take her in a carriage. At any moment, she expected the door to be thrown open by Marcus's coachman.

"No," said Marcus, tightening his grip on her. "I want to spend the night with you. Oh, not here. Come with me now, to the cottage I've rented."

Everything was going too fast for her. She wanted to say yes, but she didn't know what she was thinking, what she was feeling. "I can't," she whispered.

She came to her feet, and began to adjust her clothing. Marcus said nothing as he did up his trousers, but his thoughts were bitter. He hadn't meant this to happen, but now that it had, he expected her to act like a normal woman. She should be demanding that he make an honest woman of her, and not be slinking off as though she were ashamed of what they'd done. He wasn't ashamed. What the hell had he done wrong?

He couldn't bring himself to tell her what his solicitors had told him. If she couldn't commit herself to him without threats or persuasion, then there was no hope for them.

When they were both ready, he descended from the carriage first, then helped her alight. He walked her to her back door, took the key from her, unlocked the door, then gave the key back into her hand.

As she moved by him, he said her name.

She looked up at him. "What is it?"

"Are you angry with me?"

"No. I'm not angry." Though she didn't know what she was feeling, she knew it wasn't anger. She'd always felt in control of her life, had always lived her life by rules she'd never questioned. Now she felt adrift, with no compass to guide her.

"I must go," she said.

"About the cottage . . ." He hesitated.

"What about it?"

"If you change your mind, I'll be there, waiting for you."

The silence lengthened as they stared into each other's eyes. Her lips parted. His breathing became audible. He lowered his head to kiss her, and she whisked herself into the house.

Chapter 26

The fire was lit; the wine was ready to pour. This time, if she came to him, he wanted everything to be perfect for her. He wasn't going to take her like a rutting boar. He would be restrained, and gentle, and as tender as she could wish. They would drink the wine, and talk, and drink some more. Then he would kiss her hand, and perhaps her lips, but whatever he did, it must be what she wanted. He'd made up his mind that he would never again shock her with his unbridled passions. He had himself completely under control, if only she would come to him.

God, he'd never romanced a woman before. Was he doing it right?

An hour passed before he finally admitted that she wasn't going to appear. He didn't know why he was so angry. If he'd been one of her precious partisans, he would have fared better. She'd committed herself to them come what may—those were her own words.

He poured himself a goblet of wine and drank it back in several long swallows. The air in the cottage suddenly seemed oppressive. Seizing his cloak, he threw it over his shoulders and flung out of the house.

The heath was dark and silent, then not so silent as small sounds began to register. To his right a twig snapped. Branches above his head creaked softly as an easterly breeze bore in from the North Sea, bringing with it sleet and rain. The night was not fit for a dog to be abroad. Cursing himself for a fool, he turned to retrace his steps when he heard something, a sigh, a moan, but whether it came from man or beast, he had no way of knowing.

"Cat?"

The sound that carried to him might have been his name. A shadow hurled itself at him, then she was in his arms, and he was kissing her as if this were to be their very last kiss. They kissed endlessly, with no skill, drinking each other in like lovers dying of thirst. They were no longer aware of their bearings, or that the driving rain was penetrating their garments, molding them into one.

The rain drowned out their kisses and they pulled apart laughing. She whispered so he could barely hear her. "I don't know what I'm going to do about you, Marcus Lytton. You make me feel things I never knew existed, things I shouldn't want to feel."

"What do I make you feel, Cat?"

"*Everything,*" she said helplessly, and he kissed her with abandon because he knew exactly what she meant.

Catching her by the shoulders, he dragged her up the steep incline toward the cottage. They stood in front of the fire undressing each other, laughing nonsensically over trifles. There were no servants to see to their wet garments and they draped them over chairs to dry.

He poured out the wine and they drank from their goblets, then from each other's lips, but they didn't need wine. He was drunk on her; she was drunk on him. They rolled on the bed laughing together, but their lightheartedness slipped away as they threw off the last of their clothes.

When they were both naked, he spread her glorious mane of hair across his pillow. "I have dreamed of this," he whispered, and wound his hands through those fiery tresses, holding her captive for his kiss.

She pulled to her knees and loomed over him. He wanted to touch her, but she wouldn't permit it. All her modesty and inhibitions had slipped away and he reveled in the passion he sensed in her.

She put her hands on him, testing the hard, muscular body that was so different from her own. He was so powerfully made that it was almost frightening. But she wasn't frightened. This was Marcus.

She kissed his mouth, then his throat, and became suddenly teary when she found the scars on his shoulder and on his thigh. These were from the wounds he'd received in Spain, the wounds she had tended in that small priest's cell in the partisans' base.

"What is it, Cat?"

"When they brought you in," she whispered, "you had lost so much blood, I thought you would die. We all did."

"Don't cry. I didn't die. And I can't be sorry that I was so severely wounded. If I hadn't been, I would have been billeted in the crypt and I would never have met you. Are you sorry you met me, Cat?"

"No." She inhaled a teary breath. "No," she repeated.

"Don't sound so sad. Everything will be fine, I promise."

"I don't want to think about the future. I don't want to talk. I just want to make love."

"Then make love to me."

She fell on him, kissing, stroking, driving him wild to take her. It was as if she could not get enough of the scent and flavor of him. There wasn't a part of him she did not touch and taste. He let her have her way until it became too much to bear. Rearing up, he tumbled her on her back, and his hands rushed over her, caressing her breasts, her hips, her belly. He parted her legs and his fingers found and entered her, and he watched her eyes glaze over as he built the pleasure in her. There was a wildness in her that he had never encountered before, and he knew that she would give him whatever he asked of her.

He kissed her breasts, but he did not linger there. His lips and tongue laved her belly, then he put his mouth on her, there, between her legs, and she arched into the caress. A cry tore from her throat, then soft throaty pleas as she urged him to take her.

He positioned himself between her legs and fettered her arms above her head. There was something primitive in the gesture, and he was seized by a sensation he had never experienced before. He wanted her to know—he didn't know what he wanted her to know. She tried to throw off his hands so that she could touch him, but when she felt the steel in him, she stopped struggling and looked up. He read the trust and surrender in her eyes and his heart soared. In sheer masculine triumph, he threw back his head and drove into her, then he went perfectly still when it came to him that he had taken her with all the instincts of an animal.

"Cat!" he said hoarsely.

She was unaware of his distress. Her arms and legs wrapped around him, locking him to her. He laughed softly, then groaned when she moved, driving him deeper into her body. For one moment more, he savored her abandoned response, then he surrendered his control and let the driving pulse in their bodies take them both.

The chimes of a clock somewhere in the house struck the hour. Marcus stretched, reached for Catherine, and came sharply awake when he realized she wasn't in bed with him. He hauled himself up and glanced around the room. There was no sign of her, nothing to show that she'd been with him last night, not a ribbon or a handkerchief or even a hairpin. With a savage oath, he got out of bed and began to dress.

It was what he deserved, he supposed, for a lifetime of mornings like this when he'd escaped before his bed partner had awakened. He'd had good reason. Women were always angling for declarations. They could never be satisfied with the pleasure of the moment. And now, just when he had worked up enough courage to make the declaration every woman wanted to hear, Cat had run out on him.

With another oath, he sat down on the bed and began to pull on his silk stockings. She would never convince him that she did not love him. Other women could give their bodies for the pleasuring, but not Cat. From the very beginning, there had been something special between them, until she'd learned that he was the Earl of Wrotham.

He glowered down at his black pump. What, he wondered, was she running from?

On the drive to town, he fell into a light sleep and awakened when the carriage slowed to a halt. They were in St. James's Street, and carriages that were coming and going to various houses in the square hindered their progress.

Marcus put his head out of the window. "Take the approach from Pall Mall," he yelled to his coachman.

Pall Mall, however, was also choked with vehicles and Marcus decided to walk the short distance to his godmother's house. Halfway along Pall Mall, he passed Amy Spencer's house and he halted.

Though it was after four o'clock in the morning, that wasn't late by London standards, and he would have expected to see every window ablaze with lights. Instead, only two windows in the upper floor were lit up. No one was coming and going through the front doors; there were no sounds of life. The house looked as quiet as a church. On impulse, he crossed the street and mounted the stairs to the front door.

The footman who answered the knocker recognized him and allowed him to enter the vestibule. "Mrs. Spencer is not receiving," he said.

"Is Mrs. Spencer alone?"

"Yes, m'lord."

Marcus's air of indolence slipped away. Giving the footman a hard stare, he said, "Mrs. Spencer will wish to see *me*, Foley. Take me to her at once."

"But sir—"

"*At once!*"

The footman's eyes dropped away. "Certainly, sir," he droned, and led the way upstairs.

Marcus did not wait to be announced. Pushing past the footman, he entered the drawing room. Amy rose from a chair by the fire.

"Marcus," she said. "I was just thinking about you."

All the frustration and torment that he'd been made to suffer because this woman had lied about him swept through Marcus in a sudden tide of fury. "This isn't a social call," he said. "I should like to know why you lied about me to Cat. Your lies have caused more damage than you could ever know."

Amy looked at him without comprehension, then her face crumpled, and she sank into her chair. "I never meant to hurt anyone," she said. "Oh, God, what have I done?"

Marcus stayed for half an hour, not because he wanted to, but because Amy was nearly distraught. She apologized to him over and over again, and couldn't stop weeping. He began to regret he'd given in to the impulse to enter her house. He'd never known Amy to lose her composure, and he was sure there was a lot more to her distress than his angry outburst. He did learn from her, however, that she had written to Cat, exonerating him entirely of her false accusation.

Somewhat mollified, he waited until Amy had got a grip on herself before he took his leave.

He was on the front steps when the door that had just been closed on him opened and Amy stepped out. She was slightly breathless, and the brightness in her eyes did not come from tears.

In a low, vibrating tone, she said; "What is my sister to you, Lord Wrotham? And how do you come to know that Catherine *is* my sister?"

"Because I'm married to her," he said savagely, and began to descend the stairs.

He hadn't reached the bottom when there was a deafening explosion, and something ripped by him and plowed into the door lintel. Amy screamed, and passersby scurried to take cover as horses plunged and reared up.

"Murder," someone shouted, adding to the panic on Pall Mall.

Marcus grabbed Amy by the arm, hustled her inside the house, and slammed the door closed. A few swift paces took him to the window of one of the downstairs rooms. He inched back the curtain and peered out. On the street, pandemonium reigned. No one seemed to know where the shot had come from or who had been the target. People were shouting for the Watch, and coachmen were trying to bring their horses under control.

He heard a sound and turned. Amy had sagged against the door for support, and her face was parchment-white. Her voice shook so badly, he could hardly make out her words.

"Who would want to kill me, Marcus?"

"That shot wasn't meant for you. It was meant for me." Then he shouted, "Foley!"

The footman looked as shaken as his mistress when he answered Marcus's summons.

Marcus was already on the move. "Lock all the doors and don't open them to anyone but me, do you understand?"

"Marcus, you're not going to leave me!" Amy cried out.

When he looked into her panic-stricken face, he softened his tone. "You'll be safe here, Amy. Foley will look after you until I return."

"But where are you going?"

"I'm going to see Major Carruthers," he said, mystifying her. He turned and headed for the back door.

Major Carruthers was an early riser, and he was fully dressed when Marcus finally tracked him down. He ate his breakfast in silence as Marcus told him about the latest attack. Marcus had declined breakfast, but he'd accepted coffee.

"Let me see if I have this right," said Carruthers. "You were at Lady Tarrington's ball, then you went out to Hampstead to talk to Catherine, and finally ended the evening with Mrs. Spencer."

"What of it?" demanded Marcus, not liking something in the major's tone of voice.

"Only this. I wonder why your attacker chose that particular moment to shoot you. Why not when you left the ball, or when you were in Hampstead?"

"If he'd followed me from the ball, he wouldn't have had the opportunity until I left Hampstead, and there were no lights outside my house. I don't know. I honestly don't know. But Pall Mall is well lit. I was a sitting duck, and it would be easy to slip away in the panic he'd created."

"Or Mrs. Spencer might have been the target."

"You don't really believe that!"

Carruthers stared at Marcus for a moment then shook his head. "No, I don't really believe that. As I see it, there are two ways of explaining this. The first harks back to the time you and your comrades were in *El Grande*'s hideout."

"You believe the rumor that's going around? You think this is a vendetta?"

"It's still a possibility in view of this new attack." He looked up at Marcus. "I'm sure you've thought of the other explanation for the attack on you—and the incident with Catherine on the tower stairs."

Marcus said flatly, "I don't believe my heir would do such a thing."

"No? Then let me ask you this. Before Catherine slipped on those stairs, did anyone think she might be pregnant with the future heir?"

Marcus was on the point of dismissing this when he suddenly remembered a conversation at the dinner table at Wrotham. They had used the excuse about Catherine's hip injury so she wouldn't have to go riding. But no one had believed them. Helen had exclaimed, *You're with child!* which was what they'd all been thinking.

Seeing that look on Marcus's face, Carruthers said, "I thought as much."

The silence that followed was broken by Marcus when he burst out, "We can't go on this way. We have to put an end to this business once and for all."

"What do you suggest?"

"I haven't the faintest idea. You're the expert. You tell me."

Carruthers answered, "Short of shipping off to the colonies with Catherine and making a new start there, I haven't the faintest idea either."

"Why Catherine? She should be safe enough as long as no one knows she was Catalina."

"I don't think we can take anything for granted any more."

Marcus jumped to his feet. "Thank you, Major," he said. "At least we agree on one thing. I'm going to keep

Catherine out of harm's way even if I have to gag and tie her down until our murderer is caught." He strode to the door. "But take my word for it—my brother is not behind this." Even as he said the words, he wondered if he believed them.

Chapter 27

Later that morning, Catherine came downstairs to find Marcus waiting for her in her study. She could tell just by looking at him that he hadn't had much sleep the night before. Though Mrs. McNally had told her that Lord Wrotham had something urgent to discuss with her, she'd interpreted that to mean that he wished to haul her over the coals for running away from him while he was still asleep. Now, as he came forward to greet her, she knew it was more serious than that.

"What is it, Marcus? Why do you look so grim?"

He shut the study door before turning to answer her. "I don't mean to frighten you," he said. He waited for her to sit down, then he took the chair opposite. "It's Amy. A few hours ago, someone shot at us. No, she's not hurt, but she's shaken." Briefly he described what had happened.

She stared at him in blind horror. "It's starting up again. My God, there's no end to it. But why Amy? Why would anyone want to hurt Amy? It must have been meant for you, Marcus."

Marcus agreed with her, but he'd decided that the best way to keep Catherine out of danger was to play up the danger to Amy. "We can't be sure of anything. Perhaps the murderer knows Amy is your sister, I don't know. What I do know is that she was badly scared and I want you to look after her while I try to get to the bottom of things."

"Of course I'll look after her, if she'll let me." A thought suddenly struck her. "But *why* did you go to my sister? Did you suspect something? Did she?"

There was a moment of silence, then he said, "I was

returning to Lady Tarrington's ball this morning and happened to pass Amy's house. On impulse, I decided to pay a call on her."

"You were going to a ball at four o'clock in the morning? After . . . after we'd been together?"

"Actually, it was closer to five. We don't keep early hours in the city, Cat."

He was challenging her, but she decided not to take the bait. There was more to worry about here than her petty jealousies. "What does Amy think?"

Evidently, she'd passed some test, for Marcus flashed her a grin. "Amy thinks it could be one of her rivals, or someone with a grudge against her."

"That doesn't seem likely."

"No."

She jumped to her feet and went to the window that overlooked the heath. Everything looked so peaceful and untroubled, while inside her head it felt as though a shell had exploded. There was no coherence. Everything was in fragments.

She turned to look at him. "Amy can't stay any longer in her house in Pall Mall. She must come here to me."

"If the murderer knows Amy is your sister, this is the first place he'll look for her. You and Amy must go somewhere else."

"What about you? What are you going to do, Marcus?"

"What I should have done a long time ago. I'm going to find out exactly what's going on."

"You're going to set a trap for the murderer. That's it, isn't it?"

"I have to try something. We can't just wait for him to strike. He'll succeed sooner or later."

She studied his face. "What are you going to do?"

"I'm going to use your Spanish sketches and notes as bait."

When she started to protest, he interrupted her. "I'm putting my bet on the Rifleman. You and I know there's no sketch of him—but he doesn't know that, does he?

You'll have to help me, Cat. I need you to write an article for *The Journal* about *El Grande*'s base."

"What kind of article?"

"First I want you to get ready to spend a week in the country. I'll tell you everything when we are in the carriage. I've already told the McNallys that you are visiting a sick friend in Richmond."

"What friend?"

"The Widow Wallace."

"But where are we really going?"

"We're going to pick up Amy, and then we're going to my grandmother's dower house in Chelsea, which has been empty for some time."

"Does Major Carruthers know about this?"

"No," he replied emphatically. "I don't want his agents swarming all over the place. I want our murderer to feel very safe. I don't want him to suspect a thing."

"If there's going to be trouble, I want to be with you. Marcus, I was once a partisan. I know how to use a pistol."

"That's why I want you with Amy. I don't want you to let her out of your sight."

He wasn't giving her a chance to think. "But . . . but what have you told Amy?"

"I've told her everything."

"Everything?" she asked, appalled. "You've told her about Spain? About us? About Catalina? About our forced marriage?"

"I've told her everything. Now, where are those sketches and notes?"

She walked to the false bookcase, depressed the lever and swung the door open.

"Very ingenious," said Marcus, and began to gather up portfolios and journals.

If Marcus hadn't been racing against the clock, he would have stayed longer with Catherine and Amy after he brought them to the dower house. They were sisters and that was about all they had in common, that and an odd kind of loyalty that transcended their differences. He wished there was something he could do or say to smooth over the awkwardness, but he didn't have that luxury at the moment.

He got over the awkwardness of his own situation by pretending it didn't exist. He spoke to Catherine as if she were his wife, and he addressed Amy as if she were his sister.

He'd told Amy a lot more than he'd told Cat. Amy was the bait to keep Catherine immobilized while he tracked down his prey. He'd known that Cat would do anything for her sister.

It took him an hour or two to arrange for suitable servants to staff the house. Next he went to *The Journal* offices, just off Soho Square. Though he and Gunn were reserved to begin with, Marcus warmed considerably when he learned that Gunn had just become engaged to Viscount Stranmere's widow.

It took a little longer for Gunn to warm up to him, but when Marcus promised him that *The Journal*, and only *The Journal*, would carry what might turn out to be the story of the decade, Gunn lost some of his reserve too.

"You're setting a trap?"

"It's the only way."

"But how does Catherine come into this?"

"That will all come out, and your paper will be the one to carry the story. Will you do it?"

Melrose Gunn stared at Marcus for a long moment, then a slow grin broke over his face. "I'd do anything for Catherine," he said.

Marcus's brows shot up, then he, too, grinned. "Then that's settled."

He was almost out the door when Gunn called after him, "Good luck, and be careful."

Marcus knew he would find Peter Farrel at White's, his club in St. James's. When they were settled in comfortable upholstered chairs in the reading room, enjoying a quiet glass of Madeira, Marcus came to the point.

"Peter, I have a favor to ask of you."

"What is it?"

The sleepy-eyed look that always gave Farrel the appearance of a gentle giant had disappeared. Instead, a pair of flinty gray eyes was trained unwaveringly on Marcus. Marcus smiled. This was the real Peter Farrel, the veteran of the Spanish Campaign.

Marcus said, "It's about my brother, Penniston."

"What about him?"

Marcus cocked his head. "What do you think of him?"

"To be frank, I thought at first we had a lot in common. He's an expert on horses and he's a keen hunter."

"But?"

"Well, he's not very sociable. He keeps himself to himself. He doesn't make friends very easily."

"I know that," said Marcus. A moment passed, then he went on, "Even so, I'd like you to make a friend of him, Peter. In fact, beginning next Thursday evening, I want you to keep him in your sights at all times. Invite him to your clubs. Introduce him around. It won't be for long. A week should do it. I can't keep him with me every minute of the day. It would be too awkward."

"Why are you asking me to do this?" asked Farrel in his blunt way.

"On the chance," said Marcus, "that Penn may need an alibi."

"What's happening on Thursday?"

"I can't tell you that."

Farrel looked at his friend in perfect comprehension, then he said, "You may count on me."

"I knew I could," said Marcus.

Marcus was exhausted when he returned to Cavendish Square but even so, he could not get to sleep. He kept going over things in his mind, wondering whether he'd overlooked anything. He'd made absolutely sure that his carriage was not followed when he'd taken Cat and Amy to the dower house. If anyone was going to be a target, it was he.

His plan was simple. He was relying on the murderer's ingenuity to track down the author of the article and sketch that were to appear in *The Journal*. He'd thought of laying a trail that even a simpleton could follow, and had decided that would be too easy. The last thing he wanted was for his quarry to become suspicious. The man he was after was clever and tenacious. It might take him a day or two to trace the article to Catherine, but Marcus was convinced he would find a way to do it. And when he did, it was he, Marcus, who would be waiting for him.

Something else kept turning in his mind—his conversation with Peter Farrel. He didn't suspect Penn; he truly was trying to protect him. If anything went wrong, he didn't want Carruthers accusing his brother of something Marcus was quite sure Penn wasn't capable of doing.

That thought led him to *El Grande*.

Neither Catherine nor Major Carruthers would ever suspect *El Grande,* but Marcus was not so sure. *El Grande* had been a ruthless partisan during the war, and Marcus was not convinced he had changed so much since then.

El Grande had come to England. Why? Was he really trying to find his soul with the brothers at Marston, or had he a more sinister purpose in mind?

He thought about *El Grande* for a long time, then he thought of Catherine. He had yet to tell her that he'd been to his solicitors and that there was no hope for a divorce. He couldn't believe, after the night they'd spent together—was it only last night?—that she could still want one.

Then why had she run from him?

It was a long, long time before he fell asleep.

Amy and Catherine did not sit down to dinner until late. They hadn't talked yet about anything important, putting that off until they had time for it. There had been a great deal to do during the day, for the house had been empty for years, and it had to be cleaned and aired.

Now, bathed and changed, they faced each other across a small table that had been set up, at Catherine's suggestion, in the less formal morning room. There was so much to say and Catherine hardly knew where to begin. Though they were sisters, they were strangers, and if it had not been for a bizarre set of circumstances, they might have gone their separate ways without crossing paths again.

"I understand," said Amy, "that this house belonged to Marcus's grandmother?"

She was making small talk only because one of the servants was present.

Catherine said, "She came here when her husband died."

She spoke absently. Her eyes were trained on the footman who was fiddling with a bottle of wine. He didn't look as if he knew how to open it. In fact, he didn't look much like a footman at all. The same could be said of the other two footmen Marcus had installed in his house. They looked like pugilists, as did the cook who had taken over the kitchen—and she was a female.

The cork popped, and Hale, the footman, carefully poured out the wine.

"I'll ring for you if we need anything," said Catherine.

When he closed the door, leaving the two girls alone at last, they both sighed, then they began speaking at once. Catherine stopped and let Amy speak first.

Amy wanted to know all about the Spanish vendetta, and Catherine's year with the partisans, and she had many questions about *El Grande*. Catherine told her everything. She could tell that *El Grande* had made a great impression on Amy, and she began to speculate. Amy's popularity was waning. She no longer gave lavish parties. She was planning to spend the winter months in Italy. Catherine did not go so far as to suspect that Amy might be in love with *El Grande*, but she sensed that *El Grande*, with his priestly gift for seeing into a person's soul, had turned Amy around.

When Catherine had no more to say, Amy looked up. "Do you think he will go back to being a priest?"

"I don't know. He certainly has a gift for it."

"Yes. I'm sure that's true."

When the covers were removed and they were alone

again, a long, companionable silence fell between them. Amy caught Catherine's eyes, started to speak, then cleared her throat before starting over.

"There is something I must say to you, Cat. I want you to know that I bitterly, bitterly regret the lie I told you about Marcus, all those years ago. I didn't even know him then. As I told you in my letter, I did it to make myself appear ... I don't know ... glamorous, I suppose, not in your eyes, but in Aunt Bea's."

"I understand, Amy. I understand how it was."

"Do you?" She searched Catherine's face, and she nodded. "I believe you do. Thank you for that, Cat." She raised her glass. "And now, even if I am a little tardy, I'd like to propose a toast to my little sister and wish her happy with her husband."

Catherine's smile faded. "I take it Marcus didn't tell you that we are suing for a divorce?"

Amy lowered her glass. "Why would you do that?"

"Many reasons, which I'd rather not go into."

A frown knit Amy's brow. "Marcus said nothing to me." When Catherine remained silent, Amy went on carefully, "Is it because of me, Cat?"

"No. I told you, I understand why you lied about Marcus."

"That's not what I mean. Is it because Marcus and I were ... friends at one time?"

"Friends?" said Catherine, brows raised. "Oh yes. *Friends.*"

And with Catherine's snide insinuation, Amy's hangdog demeanor vanished into thin air and she became more like herself. "All right then, if you want it with the bark off, I was his mistress. What of it?"

"What of it?" asked Catherine. "How would you like it if you were married to a man who had taken your sister to bed?"

Amy rested one elbow on the table, and cupped her chin. "I suppose," she said reflectively, "I would always wonder if he was comparing me to her."

Catherine gasped. "No such thought ever occurred to me."

"Didn't it? Then what were you thinking?"

"What was I thinking?"

"You heard me, Cat."

"Well, I was just wondering if Marcus was kind to you. Oh, I don't believe we are having this conversation."

"Let me tell you about Marcus so we'll never have this conversation again."

"I don't want to hear."

Amy let out a theatrical sigh. "He wasn't one of my more memorable lovers. In fact, I think it would be no exaggeration to say he was the least memorable. He was inept and gauche and gave me no pleasure. Frankly, I don't know how he came by his reputation, but it certainly didn't start with me. There was some excuse for him, I suppose. He was only twenty-one or so. Boys of that age don't make good lovers as a rule."

Whey Amy paused, Catherine said incredulously, "Are we talking about *Marcus*?"

"Ah," said Amy with a knowing glint in her eyes. "I see your experience with him is different from mine. Perhaps he has learned a thing or two over the years, but I can assure you, he did not learn with me. In fact, it would surprise me if he can remember anything about me at all, except perhaps that I was very, very expensive."

Her voice changed, and she said, "I swear to God, Cat, I'm not making this up. There is one more thing that I would like to say. Though Marcus was not an exciting lover, he has no equal as a friend, and I've been grateful for that friendship more times than I care to remember. I like, trust, and respect him, and there are very few of my past lovers I can say that about. Does that answer your question?"

Catherine's cheeks were burning. "I never meant— oh, this is so embarrassing." She was staring at her clasped hands. "It makes no difference, Amy."

Amy's patience was wearing thin. "Cat, long before he met you, Marcus had a mistress. Her name was Amy Spencer. That woman had nothing to do with your sister, and now she no longer exists. Can't you let it go at that?"

"I'm not holding that against Marcus or you, not really."

"Then what is it?"

Catherine finally looked into Amy's eyes. "Don't you understand? He never really wanted to be married to me. I forced him into it. Then afterward, when he found me again, I lied to him and deceived him. Good God, I *spied* on him and passed my reports to British Intelligence."

Amy looked at Catherine, and after an interval said, "Well?"

"Well what?"

"Well, surely there's more to it than that?"

"Isn't that enough?" Catherine cried out passionately.

"Not if you love each other."

"Oh, I know he wants me, but I don't think he wants to be married to me."

Amy saw the tears gathering in Catherine's eyes, and she said in a matter-of-fact way, "And I know Marcus, and I know you are wrong. Now, let's talk about something else. Are you really a crack shot, Cat?"

Catherine sniffed and nodded.

"Could you teach me to be a crack shot?"

"No. That comes with practice. But I could teach you how to handle a pistol, you know, load it and unload it, that sort of thing. But I don't advise target practice for the present. Marcus's footmen might get the wrong idea, and we wouldn't want to upset them, would we?"

"Why wouldn't we?"

"Because I think they are crack shots, too."

"The footmen?"

Catherine shook her head. "I know an old soldier when I see one," she said, and both girls began to laugh.

Chapter 28

Catherine's article appeared on the front page of *The Journal* along with a small sketch of the ruined monastery that had served as the partisans' headquarters during the winter of 1812–1813. All over London, the paper was read with astonishment, for the anonymous author described herself as an English girl who had served with *El Grande*'s partisans for a time. It was all verified by the publisher, who also mentioned that this was only the first in a series that would be published in each issue of the paper.

Major Charles Carruthers was one of the first to learn about Catherine's article. He was in his office in Whitehall when his secretary, a recent graduate of Oxford, placed *The Journal* on his desk.

"I haven't got time for this," said Carruthers, giving the paper a quick glance. "Just tell me what it says."

"It says a lot of things," said young Crabbe, "but the paragraph that struck me was the one that says that in future issues of *The Journal* there will be biographies and portraits of everyone who was with *El Grande* at that time. She even mentions the Spanish vendetta."

"Good lord." Carruthers threw aside the report he was reading, picked up the newspaper, and scanned it. When he came to the end of it, he sat in silence with a thoughtful look on his face.

He looked up at his secretary. "She never told me anything about portraits or a journal. Now why wouldn't she?"

Thinking the question rhetorical, the secretary said nothing.

Carruthers pinned him with a steely eye. "Well, come

on, man. You want a career in Intelligence. One presumes you have a brain. Use it."

The secretary, who was in awe of his legendary superior, cleared his throat before speaking. "Why didn't she tell you about the portraits and sketches?"

"That is the question, Crabbe," replied the major.

"Maybe she didn't realize how important they were."

"They're not important. I'm convinced of that."

Working up his courage, the secretary declared, "You can't know that for sure."

"How very true—and neither can the murderer. If you were in his shoes, what would you do?"

Crabbe didn't have to think about it. "I'd go into hiding until I could figure out whether or not these articles could really incriminate me."

Carruthers made a rude sound. "Not bloody likely. Our villain has been masterminding his plot for almost four years. The stakes are too high to bow out at this stage of the game."

"But what else can he do? You don't mean, sir, that he's going to try to kill our agent?"

"That's exactly what I mean. He'll go after those papers and sketches first, of course."

"Then what are we going to do?"

The major stared thoughtfully at the newspaper in his hands. Finally, he folded it and set it aside. "We're not going to do anything," he said. "Perhaps Wrotham can succeed where we have failed. If he wants our help, he'll ask for it. We'll keep out of it, Crabbe. That's what we'll do."

Later that evening, in Watier's club, *The Journal* was passed from hand to hand. Some of the comments were admiring, others derogatory, as they discussed an English girl who had dared to become a partisan. Except for Peter Farrel, no one connected the article with Marcus's wife, though there was speculation about whether or not Catalina might be familiar with the anonymous English girl.

Penn was there, but by this time he was lost in a pleasant brandy-induced haze, and though someone put the paper into his hands, he barely looked at it. He was thinking that Marcus had been wrong to think that he couldn't stop drinking whenever he wanted to. They'd been in town now a number of weeks—he couldn't remember how many—and in that time he hadn't had a single drop of brandy. Tonight was different. This was an all-male party. Not to drink would be rude. He'd have one more and that would be the end of it.

He tried to rise, but his legs buckled under him. His companions thought it was a great joke, and one of them put the brandy decanter on the table right by his elbow. Penn looked around at his smiling companions. Some of them, he decided, were in worse shape than he.

Some of the brandy spilled when he tried to pour it into his glass, and Lord Dowling said, slurring the words, "I can't believe I used to think you were a Methodist."

Everyone laughed at this, and no one laughed harder than Penn. At that moment, he felt as though he had the world in the palm of his hand.

Dowling's joke sparked others, each worse than the last. There was no offense meant, and Penn didn't take offense, since the gist of it was that Penn had surprised them all. He really was one of them. It was a good feeling.

"And I," said Roger Beattie, determined to top them all, "thought you might very well turn out to be a murderer."

"A murderer!" exclaimed Penn, dissolving into laughter. "Whatever gave you that idea?"

Roger's remark was seconded by first one gentleman then another. Peter Farrel said nothing. He was watching Penn intently.

Beattie held the floor, something he didn't do very often, and he made the most of it. "We've all talked about it," he said, looking from one face to another, "and we all have our different opinions. I think this Spanish vendetta thing is a diversionary tactic." When he saw Penn's blank look, he went on, "Some months ago, there was an attack on Marcus in Hyde Park. More recently, he's either sent his wife home to Spain or he's hiding her away somewhere. Obviously he thinks her life is in danger. Well, I ask you, who has the most to gain if Marcus were to die?"

"Who?" asked Penn.

"Why, his heir, that's who, not some Rifleman who would stick out like a sore thumb if he came anywhere near an English officer and gentleman. And the same goes for a Spanish peasant. You, Penn. I'm talking about you."

They went in to dinner on a great gale of laughter. The conversation moved on, but Penn couldn't concentrate. There was something bothering him, something in that last conversation of Beattie's of vital importance, if he could only clear his mind.

He forgot about it when the burgundy was served. Not to accept a glass would only make his friends self-conscious, and he really didn't like to be called a Methodist.

Murderer. Someone had called him a murderer. The thought came to him intermittently as dinner progressed. Fragments of Beattie's conversation came back to him, but it was a long time before his befuddled brain began to make connections.

Suddenly lurching to his feet, he roared, "Call out the militia!"

His companions stared at him in blank shock then went off in peals of laughter. Penn pushed back his chair and stumbled toward the door. He didn't get very far, before his legs buckled under him.

Farrel took him home in a hackney. By this time, Penn could hardly remember his own name. The last thing he remembered as his valet put him to bed was that he had to find his brother and tell him everything.

Catherine read her own article in *The Journal* for what seemed like the hundredth time, then, throwing the paper aside, she sighed, picked up her pistol, checked it for what seemed like the hundredth time, and set it carefully on the table by her elbow.

Amy looked up from the book she was reading.

In reply to that look, Catherine smiled faintly. "I'm probably worrying about nothing. In fact, the more I think about it, the more absurd I think we all are. No one's going to take Marcus's bait. Whoever it is must know that if I'd had anything to go on, I would have done something about it before now."

Amy set her book aside. She wasn't really reading it. She was as restless as Catherine and couldn't settle to anything. "I think you might be right," she said.

This did not pacify Catherine. "At the very least, Marcus should have had the decency to tell me what's going on. After he picked up my article and sketches, he never showed his face here again."

Amy said reasonably, "Cat, he knows what he's doing. He's afraid I may be the next victim. You have your part to play looking after me."

"I know. It's just that I'm so afraid he's going to handle this on his own, with no one there to help him."

"A moment ago you said you didn't think anything was going to happen."

"I know. I know. Shall I ring for tea and biscuits? I know cook has gone to bed, but the footmen are still up."

"I'm not hungry."

"Neither am I."

Their eyes met, smiled, and parted. For three days they'd been confined to the house and gardens while they waited for this particular issue of *The Journal* to come out. They were comfortable with each other now. They'd done a lot of talking in that time, though mostly of their early years. The one thing they had not talked about was the future.

"Talk to me . . . tell me about Wrotham, about Marcus's family," said Amy, not liking the look that had come into Catherine's eyes.

Catherine shook her head. "It's no use, Amy. I must go to him. If anything happened to him and I wasn't there to help him, I would never forgive myself."

Amy started to protest, then thought better of it. If it

were *El Grande,* she would have felt the same way as Catherine.

"Then be careful," she said, and surprised herself by adding, "And God go with you."

El Grande returned to his cell after a night on his knees in the Abbey's chapel. His prayers had been answered. He knew exactly where he was going from here. Tomorrow, he would leave the monks of Marston and never return.

The latest issue of *The Journal* was lying on the small table that served as his desk. He was surprised to see it there, but his surprise lasted only a moment, until he found Catherine's article and sketch.

Seating himself, he began to read.

A few minutes later, when he threw off his monk's habit and began to dress, his face was grim.

In Heath House, Marcus rubbed his eyes, yawned, and stretched his cramped muscles. He had been keeping vigil in the closet where Cat kept her Spanish mementos and now he was ready to give up. Through a crack in the door, he could see through the French windows, and though it was still dark outside, a sliver of light had crept onto the horizon. Soon it would be dawn. It seemed that he had miscalculated. He'd been so sure that the murderer would come tonight that he'd taken the precaution of sending the McNallys away.

He had his hand around the edge of the door when a flickering shadow appeared at the window, then a face. There were no candles lit, for Marcus hadn't wanted to frighten his quarry away, but he'd deliberately banked up the fire, and the glow from the embers gave a weak light. He cradled his pistol in the crook of one arm and waited.

There was a grating sound, then a click, and the French doors swung open, letting in a blast of cold wintry air.

The door was shut, and all was silent. The intruder moved to the desk and systematically began to go through the drawers, then a moment or two later, he passed the closet where Marcus was hiding. Marcus made his move.

"Halt, or I'll blow your brains out," he said, and stepped into the room.

The intruder turned slowly to face him.

"Drop your weapon," said Marcus, "and put your hands in the air."

El Grande's voice said, "I don't have a weapon."

"So, it *is* you!" said Marcus. "You heard me, put your hands in the air."

As *El Grande* raised his hands,. Marcus took a taper from the mantelpiece, lit it from the fire, and proceeded to light several candles around the room.

"You're making a mistake," said *El Grande*.

"Oh, yes, that's what they all say."

"I came to help you."

Marcus smiled. "You came to kill Catherine, but not before you got your hands on her notes and sketches. You should have destroyed them when you had the chance. You counted on us not understanding the significance of what we had in our possession. It was a calculated risk and you lost."

El Grande gave a disbelieving laugh. "I don't know anything significant that I should want to suppress. Let me repeat myself. I came here to help you. It was you, was it not, who sent me that copy of *The Journal*?"

"I sent you nothing."

"Ah, then it must have been Catherine."

"I don't believe you, and even if it were true, do you expect me to believe there's some other reason for you to be here tonight? I caught you in the act. You were going through Catherine's desk."

"I was looking for a weapon. I know she keeps her pistol there."

"A pistol?" Marcus jeered. "That doesn't sound like the lay brother who was so sickened by the war that he never wanted to hurt anyone again."

El Grande said quietly, "I have come to terms with all that. And I've left my religious order now. But I see that nothing I say means anything to you."

The heads of both men whipped round as the French doors rattled. The door swung open and Catherine stepped inside. In her hand, she clutched a pistol, but unlike Marcus's, it was pointing at the floor.

"I could hear you out there in the garden," she said. "What's going on here?"

"Bloody hell!" said Marcus.

With the pistol still pointing at *El Grande,* he positioned himself so that Catherine was not in his line of fire.

El Grande said, "I think he means to kill me. He has this insane notion that I'm the murderer. I came to help him, but he won't believe me."

Though Marcus spoke to Catherine, his eyes were trained unwaveringly on *El Grande.* "He came out here to kill you and steal your sketches. What the hell are you doing here? Stand back, Cat, and for God's sake don't get in my line of fire!"

"Will you listen to yourself!" she cried out. "This is my friend. He saved my life many times, and the lives of countless English soldiers. He saved your life, too, when you were ambushed by French soldiers."

"I'm facing facts, Cat, and you have to face them too."

"What facts?" she scoffed. With one hand on her hip, she stared doggedly into his face.

"You did his portrait. He can't take the chance that it will be published in *The Journal.* I think he's preparing for something that's about to happen, something that will make him publicly known. I think he's going to kill everyone who knows he was once *El Grande.*"

She cried out, "What about all the brothers at Marston Abbey? They've seen him. Is he going to kill them too?"

"To them, he's Brother Robert. They don't know him as *El Grande.*"

"I can't believe you're saying all this."

"Then why is he here?"

"He's here because I bribed one of your servants to take him a copy of *The Journal*. I didn't want you acting alone, and I wanted him to help you. He knows there is nothing in my notes or sketches to incriminate anyone. I told him so when we went to see him together, don't you remember?"

Marcus said viciously, "The *El Grande* I know would have read *The Journal* and gone straight to the chapel to pray about it. He wouldn't have come here, not unless he had a good reason."

When Catherine started to protest, *El Grande* said, "There's nothing you can say, Catherine, to make him change his mind."

She stared at Marcus for a long time, then she turned aside. "Perhaps this will make him change his mind," she said. Stepping right into the line of fire, shielding *El Grande*, she pressed her pistol into his hand.

El Grande instantly pointed the pistol at Catherine's head. "Don't move. Now, Wrotham, put your weapon on the flat of the desk."

Marcus cursed savagely but had no choice but to do as he was told. *El Grande* approached him, the pistol pointing straight at his heart.

Catherine stood back without a word.

"So you are both in it," Marcus said, and the shaft of bitterness that twisted inside him made his voice harsh. "My first impression of you both was the right one."

El Grande spoke softly. "No, Wrotham, Catherine and I were never your enemies. I'm sorry Catherine chose this way to prove my innocence. But you will never question it again."

He flipped Catherine's pistol over and presented it to Marcus with the muzzle pointing at himself. "Take it," he said. "And the one on the desk."

Marcus slowly picked up both pistols. *El Grande* backed away, hands in the air. "If you think I'm guilty, shoot me. Don't hesitate, shoot me."

Marcus dropped both pistols on the table and he gave Catherine a look that froze her to the marrow. "Very clever," he said. "And very brave. *But what if you'd been wrong?*"

Though they'd come at different times and by different routes, Catherine and *El Grande* had both left their mounts at the livery stable in the village of Hampstead. Now, with dawn beginning to appear on the horizon, they felt safe enough to walk openly along the lane that led to Hampstead.

When Catherine saw *El Grande*'s mount, she shook her head. "Where did you get that old nag?"

He smiled at her dry tone. "The brothers don't go in for English thoroughbreds, but Excalibar is no nag. Looks can be deceiving. He suits me very well." He tightened the girth, then stood looking at her when she made no move toward her own horse. "Aren't you coming with me?"

"No."

"I think you should. I think you should give Wrotham's temper time to cool. If you see him now, you'll say things you'll both regret."

"I can't leave him, Robert, not like this. I must make him understand. Will you do something for me? Will you go to Woodside House in Chelsea and tell Amy that everything is all right here? You can't miss the house. It's at the end of the road to the parish church. You'd better be careful though. The footmen are armed."

"Why are the footmen armed, and why is Amy there?"

She explained everything about the attack on Amy and Marcus. He made no comment, but his face was gray and stern.

He said, "I'll wait for you here in case you need me. If you're not back in thirty minutes, I'll leave without you."

It was only a five-minute walk to the house. She didn't enter at once, but turned away to look out over the heath. It wasn't Marcus's last remark that scourged her— *What if you'd been wrong?*—but the one he'd made before that—*So you are both in it.* It seemed he would never trust her. When it came down to it, he would always think the worst of her.

She didn't know how long she stood there, looking into a world that was veiled in shadows, shadows that found an echo deep inside her, but finally she turned and made for the French doors.

Chapter 29

As she entered the house, she automatically squared her shoulders. Marcus was standing by the fireplace. When he saw her, all the color drained from his face.

"I though you'd got away," he said. "I though you'd gone with *El Grande.* Why the hell did you have to come back?"

She took a few steps into the room then stood stock-still when Marcus's eyes jerked to a point behind her. When a voice called her name, a voice she recognized, all her senses sharpened and she could feel the fine hairs on her skin begin to rise.

"Or should I say *Catalina,*" said the voice again, and she turned slowly to face the man behind her.

Marcus's cousin, David Lytton, was only a few feet away, and he was pointing her own pistol straight at her. In his other hand, he held Marcus's pistol.

"Not you, David. Not you." She was stunned, and put a hand on the back of a chair to steady herself. It couldn't be him. It didn't make sense.

"Where is *El Grande?*" he demanded.

"He left, but—"

"Quiet!"

They stood stock-still while David Lytton listened intently. Satisfied that Catherine had returned alone, he said, "What were you doing?"

"We had a lot to talk about," she said. "He's—"

An angry gesture from David silenced her. He was listening again, as though he'd just heard a sound from beyond the French doors.

Catherine's brain was still reeling, and her heart was pounding so hard she was sure the others must hear it.

She was trying to get a grip on herself, weighing her options, wondering what to do next, and she was sure Marcus was doing the same.

After a moment, David relaxed and propped himself against the desk. "Do you know," he said, "I couldn't have arranged things better myself? I'm obliged to you, Marcus, for pressing me into service tonight. I really didn't want to escort your mother and sister to Lady Heathcote's party, but how could I refuse with Tristram back at Oxford and when you've been so very, very kind to me? I was desperate to come here, of course, but the delay served me well. I never suspected a trap. How fortunate for me that *El Grande* walked into it. I didn't even know he was in England. I don't mind telling you that I had a few unquiet moments there. I thought I'd have only Miss Courtnay to deal with. I certainly wasn't prepared to take three of you on. Then, just as I was debating what to do—exit Miss Courtnay and *El Grande*. Oh, this is perfect. When they find your bodies, who else will they suspect but *El Grande?*"

"I can't believe this is happening," Catherine said. "Marcus, what is going on?"

Marcus said, "David was just about to enter the house when *El Grande* arrived. He's been hovering in the garden while we entertained him with our little drama. This is our unknown Rifleman, Cat, only he wasn't a Rifleman. He came out to Portugal with the sole purpose of killing me. He discovered my movements and followed me. I wasn't shot by the French. David shot me. It was his bad luck to be surprised by a running skirmish between an English and French patrol before he could finish me off. Then *El Grande*'s partisans came on the scene, and that was that."

"And he told you all this?" she asked incredulously.

"You might say we were killing time, waiting to see if you'd gone for good."

David cut off Marcus's explanations. "Was *El Grande* mounted or was he on foot?"

"He was mounted." She wasn't sure if that answer was to her advantage, but she could see that he was uneasy, thinking that *El Grande* might be lurking about.

"You won't get away with this. *El Grande* is waiting for me. I only came back to say goodbye to Marcus."

David smiled. "You would say that, wouldn't you?"

"It's the truth."

"Good try, but I heard everything. He won't be coming back."

She sensed that David wanted to make sure *El Grande* was well beyond earshot before killing them both. That bought them a few more minutes. Marcus was too far away to take David by surprise. She had to get closer to him and try to catch him off guard. If only she could keep him talking while she edged closer to him.

"I suppose," she said, looking at David, "you want my journals and sketches? Well, they are not here. They're in a place where you will never find them."

"Another good try," he said, "but I repeat, I heard everything. There's nothing important in your journal and I know you don't have a portrait of me or you would have recognized me when we were first introduced."

"Marcus," she said, without turning around, "why does your cousin want to kill us?"

"That," said Marcus, "has yet to be revealed."

David said, "I was so deathly afraid that you would have worked it out by now. That's why I fanned the rumor that was going around about the Spanish vendetta. I wanted to keep you guessing."

"You succeeded," said Marcus. "But you haven't answered Catherine's question."

"Because I'm your heir, old boy."

Marcus stared at him wordlessly, then exclaimed, "That's preposterous!"

"Yes, shocking, isn't it? No one was more surprised than I when I discovered the truth. My father used to boast about it when I was a boy, but I didn't believe him. I thought it was the drink speaking. Then, when he died, I fell heir to a box of papers and letters that can prove my claims."

"What letters?" asked Marcus.

"Letters from your father to my father. I must thank you for a very informative evening." He was looking at

Catherine. "You know, you were quite safe until you published the article about *El Grande*'s base."

Marcus said, "Who told you that Catherine wrote the article for *The Journal*?"

"No one told me. I worked it out. Oh yes, I knew about Catherine Courtnay, knew you were seeing her, Marcus. But it was only after the article was published that I realized she and Catalina must be one and the same person. There was no English girl at *El Grande*'s base, unless she was posing as someone else. And at Wrotham, when I finally got a clear view of Catalina, it seemed strange to me that she had fair skin and blue eyes. I even mentioned it to her, and she told me she had an English ancestor. Everything came together in my mind when I read the article. Catalina had to be the English girl who rode with the partisans, and I had to get rid of Catalina."

Catherine burst out, "*You* put that broken lantern on the tower stairs!"

He acknowledged this with a slight inclination of his head. "I thought you were pregnant. The last thing I wanted, after everything I'd worked for, was for you to give Marcus a new heir."

"I wasn't pregnant."

"It was quite a blow when you suddenly returned to Spain. But you hadn't gone back to Spain, had you? You were here in Hampstead. When I first followed Marcus out here, I didn't know what to make of the English girl with red hair who had the face of Catalina. I thought you might be Marcus's mistress and that he'd chosen you because you looked like Catalina."

"It was you!" she cried. "On Hampstead Heath, when I was with Emily. You were following me!"

"I had to know how you came into the picture. So, I made inquiries." He smiled. "I probably know more about you now than Marcus does. He was very wise to hide you away from me, but very foolish to allow you to write about the partisans. It told me all I needed to know. You are Marcus's wife. There's no point in denying it. When I heard you with *El Grande* tonight, all my doubts were resolved. Not that it makes any difference. You know too much."

"You attacked Marcus in Hyde Park and in Pall Mall?"

"I did."

"And you were lying in wait for me that night, after Emily's party."

"Oh no. I didn't know you were Catalina then. I was lying in wait for Marcus and would have had him, too, if you hadn't turned up."

Marcus said acidly, "And damn near had me on Amy Spencer's doorstep!"

David smiled. "Pall Mall is perfect. It's so well lit. And there's always a crush of people and coaches coming and going."

"But you failed," said Marcus.

David's smile vanished. "I won't fail now," he said.

Catherine could tell that the waiting was over, that David was confident now that *El Grande* was too far away to hear the sound of a gunshot—two gunshots. Inching closer to him, she said, "Would you satisfy my curiosity about one more point, David? Would you tell me please why it was necessary to kill all the English soldiers who were with you at *El Grande*'s base?"

"Can't you work that out?"

"I'm afraid I can't. You've been too clever for us all along."

He smiled at this. "Marcus almost had it when he told *El Grande* that he was preparing for something that would happen soon, that he thought *El Grande* was killing everyone who knew his identify. Where Marcus went wrong was in thinking *El Grande* had a motive. I'm the one with the motive."

Marcus said, "I understand the part about being my heir. If what you say is true, getting rid of me would mean the title passes to you. But that still doesn't explain why you killed all my comrades."

David clicked his tongue. "You're not thinking, Marcus. I told you I wasn't really a Rifleman. I stole that uniform from a dead man during the confusion, just before *El Grande* rescued me. The only reason that the other Rifleman did not expose me as a fraud was because he was blackmailing me. He signed his own death warrant, as did your friends because they saw my face. We were kept in close quarters. I lied to them through my teeth. I wasn't even using my own name. Until I had rid myself of them, I couldn't dare show my face in London as David Lytton. I had to kill every one of them before I killed you and came into the title."

"You killed Freddie Barnes," Marcus said harshly. "And all the others."

David seemed to be smiling at some private recollection. "Ah yes, Freddie. It's a long story and I won't bore you with all the details. Let's just say your friend Freddie turned up in the sort of place where I never expected to see your friends. We formed a friendship. I told him some cock-and-bull story which he believed. Freddie was very useful to me for a time."

Catherine sensed that Marcus was doing something at her back and to distract David she cried out, "But what about the partisans? They saw you and would recognize you again."

"But they're not in England, my dear Catalina, and I shall certainly make a point of avoiding Spain like the plague."

"What about *El Grande*?"

"He may have caught a glimpse of me once. He wouldn't recognize me again."

Several things happened at once. As Marcus lunged, David Lytton pulled the trigger of the pistol in his left hand. Marcus staggered, then fell to the floor. Before the smoke had cleared, Catherine launched herself at David, trying to wrest her own pistol from his right hand. She heard Marcus moan as he pulled to his feet just as David shook her off. He was taking aim at Marcus again. In desperation, she reached over and grabbed a letter opener from the desk. She brought her arm up in an arc and, with every ounce of her strength, struck at him.

David gasped, sagged, and fell back. Catherine let out a horrified moan. The letter opener was embedded in his chest, just below his shoulder. She'd hurt him, but not enough to make a real difference. Though his face was contorted with pain, and a horrible red stain was spread-

ing out along the front of his coat, he was still holding
the pistol.

Marcus shouted, "Cat, get out of here! Run for it!"

Already, David was pulling himself to his knees. She
quickly crossed to Marcus. "Let's both get out of here,"
she said, and supporting him as best she could, she led
him through the French doors to the path that gave onto
the heath.

Snow was beginning to fall, blurring the outline of trees
and hedges. Catherine thanked God for it. It was to their
advantage, and they needed every edge they could get.
Their pace was so slow that a tortoise could have over-
taken them, and at any moment, she expected to hear
Marcus's cousin hard on their heels. She'd hurt him, but
she wasn't sure how badly.

"This way," she said, and urged Marcus downhill
through a dense grove of oaks.

One of his arms was looped around her shoulders,
and he leaned heavily against her for support. Every now
and again, she could feel his hand move to cover the
wound in his thigh. One part of her mind was sick with
shock. David was Marcus's cousin. She had liked him.
This couldn't be happening. Another part of her mind
was working mechanically, planning a route that would
give them some cover and, at the same time, lead back to
civilization where they could get help. There was no point
in just trying to hide themselves. There were few places to
hide on the heath and she knew that a man who had plot-
ted all these years to get this far would never give up until
he'd found them.

They did not go far before she veered off the track.
On the right, there was a steep bank. It wasn't much protection, but it was enough. She helped Marcus over the
crest, and dragged him along the ditch on the other side
till they came to a ledge of rock with an overhang that offered some shelter from the elements. Here she stopped,
and they both sank down with their backs against the
granite-faced wall.

She wanted to tell him that as a child, this little space

had been her own private domain, where she'd come when she wanted to escape from the world. No one else knew about it, not even Amy. Why was she thinking of this now?

Swallowing against the fear that threatened to overwhelm her, she turned her attention to Marcus. He had removed his neckcloth and was wadding it into a dressing to staunch the flow of blood. She lifted her skirts and tore off a strip of her petticoat, then bound the leg tightly. Marcus did not protest, but she felt his hands clench and unclench at his sides.

"Why have we stopped?" he asked.

She was terrified at how weak his voice was. "If David passes us," she replied as confidently as she could, "I thought we could double back."

She had to dip her head to hear his reply. "What is our situation. Who knows we're here?"

"Amy knows I'm here. And *El Grande* is waiting for me at the local livery stable. He may be gone by now."

Marcus said, "You must leave me here and go and get help. You know that, don't you?"

She didn't argue with him. It might come down to it, but not yet, not until there was no other way. She wasn't going to leave him to his cousin's tender mercies.

She pushed the ugly thoughts to the back of her mind and tried to take stock of their position. She'd knifed David in the shoulder, but that wouldn't slow him down as much as Marcus had been slowed. Then where was he? What was he doing? It occurred to her then that he might be tracking them, following a trail of blood to their hiding place. Hard on that thought came another. If the snow kept falling, their tracks would be easy to follow. But it would be a long time before that happened, and meantime, the snow was their ally, veiling them, though imperfectly, from the eyes of their pursuer.

Signaling to Marcus that she was going to spy out the lay of the land, she pulled to her knees, then to her feet and edged soundlessly to the crest of the bank. A watery dawn was making little headway against an overcast sky and the steady snowfall. The heath was hushed but it wasn't soundless. Catherine heard the trickle of a stream that fed into one of the ponds, and the sounds of animals either stirring from their lairs or going to ground. There was something else she couldn't quite identify, and she tilted her head, straining to catch the sound.

Suddenly, she flattened herself against the hard packed earth. A horse and rider had come into view. She saw David check his mount as he turned in the saddle to look around him. Now she knew why he had taken so long to come after them. He'd taken the time to saddle Vixen. That meant he must have hidden his own horse some distance from the house, too far for him to get to it easily, and she thanked God for this small mercy. There was a pistol in his hand and she did not doubt that it was loaded. He wasn't panicked as she had been panicked when she'd run from the house with Marcus. He was taking his time, doing things thoroughly. And why shouldn't he? They weren't going anywhere, not when Marcus could hardly walk.

"Catherine." David's voice was low and muted and seemed to float to her on the falling snow. "Catherine, I won't hurt you. All you have to do is tell me where Marcus is, and I'll let you go."

She turned quickly away from that unholy voice. Marcus had started to his feet, but as he took a step toward her, his leg gave way and he fell headlong. The sound of his fall and the groan of pain brought a roar of triumph from David.

There was no point in silence now. Catherine jumped over the ditch and made a desperate attempt to help Marcus rise. Fear gave her strength, and she pulled him to his feet, then half dragged, half propelled him along the edge of the ditch. The sounds of pursuit pushed them onward. Even through her terror, Catherine was aware that David did not have everything his own way. The ditch was a trap for the unwary. Rocks and small stones littered their way, as well as rotting branches and potholes. It was hard going, but even harder for a man on horseback.

They burst through a dip in the ground and came out onto an avenue of trees. There was nothing to slow their pursuer here. Catherine knew that Marcus was weakening. He was almost bent double and his breathing was frighteningly hoarse. Without pausing, she left the path and pulled him into a dense stand of saplings and vines. It was just in time. As they crouched down, horse and rider vaulted onto the path and thundered by. Then suddenly—silence.

Marcus whispered, "Cat—"

She put a finger to her lips, cautioning him, then whispered one word. "Trick."

Marcus nodded, and listened as she listened, head cocked to the side, ears straining. Nothing could be heard but their labored breathing and the rapid pounding of their hearts. Gradually, his eyes closed.

Catherine let out a small, shaken breath, and looked at Marcus. His eyes were closed and she could hear his teeth as he clenched them against the pain from his wound. She'd nursed him in Spain and knew just how much he could tolerate without complaint.

Pulling to her knees, she examined the makeshift dressing. In that half-light, the blood on it appeared to be black ooze. When she touched his leg, tightening the bandage, he drew in a sharp breath and opened his eyes.

Very softly, he said, almost mouthing the words, "You know you have to leave me. I'm holding you back. You must get help."

Unsure, wavering, she lifted her head and met his eyes.

A twig snapped and she jerked round. The silence mocked her. She knew that he was out there, waiting as a cat waits for a mouse. He'd waited four long years. He would never give up now.

But the heath was her domain. She knew it intimately, as he could not possibly know it. If she kept her wits about her, she could still escape with Marcus.

She felt on the ground and came up with several small pebbles. *Up.* She mouthed the word, and Marcus nodded. Grinding his teeth together, he heaved himself to his feet. Her arm went back and she tossed a pebble clear across the grove where it struck a tree and went rattling into the undergrowth.

Silence.

"Let's get out of here," she said, and with that incautious remark, the silence was blown apart.

He charged them from a clump of pines not more than twenty yards away. A bullet gouged a hole in the trunk of a tree hard by Marcus's head. Catherine didn't have time to think. He was almost on them. She drew back her arm and let fly with all of her pebbles. They caught Vixen on the chest like pellets from a shotgun. The terrified beast checked, reared up, then lost its footing on the slick ice and slithered into the underbrush.

Without waiting to see more, she grabbed for Marcus. "This way! This way!" and she dragged him into the cover of the trees.

The way down was perilously steep, but the saplings helped to check their headlong descent. Marcus's breathing was rough, and one hand was clamped against his flank where the bullet had entered. From time to time, Catherine flashed him an anxious look but she didn't slacken their pace, not when she knew David was right behind them. She, herself, was gasping for breath, and the stitch in her side stabbed at her like a red-hot needle. When she realized it had stopped snowing, she sobbed in fear. Oh, if only *El Grande* would come back for her.

"What is it?" asked Marcus.

She shook her head, but in another moment, Marcus saw why she was so mortally afraid. They'd come to the end of their cover and, now that it had stopped snowing, they could see for miles over the heath. In front of them was a stretch of water, one of the small lakes or so-called ponds that proliferated on the heath. In the center of the pond was a small island. On three sides, it was hemmed in by hills with no cover to shelter them.

Marcus was hanging on to one of the saplings, struggling to even his breathing. His eyes were searching in every direction, looking for a place to hide. The only cover was back the way they'd come or on the island in the middle of the lake. He heard a horse neighing and that decided him.

"We don't have a choice," he said. "We can't outrun him, but we might outwit him."

"What are you going to do?"

"Depends whether he has reloaded. Have to take the chance. Distract him, Cat. Leave the rest to me."

A few minutes later, David and his mount emerged from the cover of the trees. When he saw his quarry, he gave a whoop of triumph. They were on the heath, and Catherine was stooped over Marcus's inert form, wringing her hands. David slid from the saddle and advanced toward them. Catherine's heart sank when a quick furtive look revealed a pistol in his hand. It wasn't her pistol or Marcus's. That meant it was his own pistol and loaded.

"Don't leave it too late," murmured Marcus.

"Don't worry, I won't."

She waited till she heard the click of the pistol's lock, then she flung round to face him. Her little paper knife had done a certain amount of damage. She was sorry she hadn't aimed a little lower, closer to his heart. There was a stain along the front of his right breast.

Remembering the part she was playing, she cried out, pointing to Marcus, "If we don't get him to a doctor, he'll die. He's lost so much blood."

"Let him die. It will save me the bother of killing him."

David's eyes flicked beyond her to the boneless huddle that was Marcus, then they focused on Catherine again. She was edging away from him, and he followed after her.

"You won't get away with this," she cried out.

"Make this easy on yourself, Catherine. Don't run away. If I wound you, I'll have to kill you with my bare hands, and you wouldn't want that, would you?"

"Don't flatter yourself! I wounded you. I struck close to your heart. In a few minutes, you'll be dead." She knew this wasn't true. Her one aim was to keep his back turned on Marcus.

He looked down and touched a hand to his bloodied chest, and in that moment, Marcus flung himself on him. Both men went rolling to the ground, but for all the surprise, Marcus did not have the strength to hang on to him. They rolled again, and when they stopped, Marcus was prone on his face, and David was straddling him. He had the gun in his hand. Catherine moved like lightning, kicking out with all her strength. The blow struck David's arm and the pistol flew wide and disappeared into a cushion of heather. She would have gone after it if David had not grabbed Marcus's head in a wrestler's lock. She cried out when he smashed Marcus's face into the ground once, twice, then she flung herself at him.

Marcus was no longer resisting, and David turned on her with a snarl. In one ferocious, backhanded blow, he sent her sprawling, then he went after the gun. Catherine shook her head to clear her vision,. Marcus was groaning as he came to himself. She looked up to see David with the gun in his hand. His lips were pulled back in a grotesque grin and the breath tore out of his throat in a horrible dry rasp that reminded Catherine of a death rattle.

But it was her own death she was facing.

She threw herself in front of Marcus, instinctively shielding him.

David smiled. "You first?" he said.

Her voice was calm, and that surprised her. "Better me than Marcus."

He was so close she could smell his sweat.

He leveled the pistol, then spun round when an unholy roar of rage rent the silence. It came from a rider who was descending one of the slopes at a furious pace.

"El Grande!" Catherine whispered, and tears started to her eyes. She would recognize that figure anywhere.

As she watched, others came over the rise, a small detail of militia in red and white uniforms, but El Grande's mount was well in the lead. Catherine turned to look at Marcus. He was wiping the blood from his face, but he had seen them too.

David Lytton spared them not one word or look. He turned and lurched toward his own horse. El Grande came on, and his expression was murderous. Catherine could see him clearly now, and he wasn't armed. He was almost upon David Lytton when David turned and leveled his pistol.

"No," she cried out. "Oh, God, no!"

She heard the report of the pistol, saw El Grande go

tumbling from his mount, then Excalibar plowed into David in a flurry of flashing hooves, cutting off his cry of terror.

Catherine screamed and ran for *El Grande*'s lifeless form. Then the militia came up, and it was all over.

Chapter 30

The door opened to admit Penn, and the dowager countess turned from the window that looked out on the square. Samantha broke off what she'd been saying.

Penn addressed his mother. "Marcus wants to see you."

"I saw the physician leave. Is everything all right?"

"Yes. The bullet was lodged in a fleshy part of his thigh. He suffered a good deal of pain when it was removed, but he's comfortable now, or he will be as soon as he takes the laudanum the physician ordered. He won't take it till he sees you."

She moistened her lips, nodded, and began to follow him out. When Samantha tried to come with them, Penn shook his head. "Not yet. He'll see you later," he said.

He waited until they had begun to ascend the stairs before saying to the countess, "Don't be frightened, Mother. I'm not sorry he's found out. In fact, it comes as a great relief to me."

She wasn't frightened so much as stunned. She was confused and horrified by everything she had learned that morning. That David Lytton had tried to murder Marcus, and now David was dead, that Catalina had been there too, only she wasn't Catalina, she was an English girl, and she had also escaped being murdered by David. The young man who had saved them both was seriously wounded; no one knew whether he would survive. They were in Hampstead right now, in Catalina's house, and a very nice man, Major Carruthers, had brought Marcus home. The major had insisted on speaking to her in Penn's presence, which was awkward since Penn had been feeling out of sorts and had to be roused from his bed. So far they had kept the worst of it from Samantha. Marcus would decide what she must be told.

She glanced at her son; he looked like death warmed over. She was sure he'd been drinking again, but she couldn't worry about that now. Marcus wished to speak with her, and she didn't know how she could face him or her children.

Outside Marcus's door, she put a hand on Penn's sleeve, halting him. "Don't leave me," she whispered.

He replied gently, "I'll be right there beside you, Mother," and he pushed into the room.

Marcus was sitting up in bed. When they entered, two footmen withdrew. Penn led his mother to a chair on one side of the bed and seated her. He stood at the foot of the bed, leaning against the carved post on the other side so that his mother could see him at all times.

Marcus looked as though he'd been beaten by a prize fighter. His face was swollen, and there were bruises on his cheeks and temples. Sweat beaded his brow. He gave the countess a ghost of a smile. "Don't worry, Helen," he said. "What I found out from David Lytton makes no difference to us. You and Penn and the others are still my family. But I must know where we stand. I've asked Penn to explain things but he says it's not his story to tell."

"Yes. Penn told me."

He said gently, "Why don't you begin at the beginning and tell me what happened."

She looked at Penn and he nodded. For a moment or two, she hesitated, then she swallowed and began to describe an episode in her life that was obviously very painful. She couldn't look at Marcus. Instead she stared at the lace handkerchief that she was twisting and untwisting.

"I never wanted to marry your father," she said. "I was in love with someone else. I was only eighteen. Your father was almost forty. I knew of him by reputation. He drank too much. He was . . . well, he wasn't the kind of man any decent girl would want to marry. You know what happened. He abducted me and carried me off to Wrotham Castle. He didn't want to marry me. I wasn't of his class. He wanted to make me his mistress, but I would have none of it. I might not be of his class, but I came from a decent family. My father had several shops in London. I was well educated.

"When your father saw that he could not persuade me he offered marriage, and I laughed in his face. I was so sure that my father would rescue me. Instead, my father wrote me a letter saying that if I refused to marry the earl, he would wash his hands of me.

"What could I do without money or friends to help me? So, we were married—at least, I thought we were. Your father's young chaplain performed the service and registered the marriage. I was too naïve to know that without a license, without banns called, the marriage wasn't legal."

For the first time, she looked directly at Marcus. "John was only eighteen. He wasn't a priest—he had yet to take holy orders. And your father threatened him—made it clear that if he did not do as he wanted, he would never be a priest. Years later John confessed everything to me."

"John? Do you mean John Reeves, my chaplain?" demanded Marcus. "Why didn't anyone ever tell me? Why was John never dismissed?"

"I didn't want anyone to know. I didn't want my children to bear that shame. And as for John, he was as much your father's victim as I was. Since then, he's always been a true friend to me."

There was a silence and she took a moment to compose herself before going on. "For all those years I suspected nothing. It never occurred to me that a man would install his mistress in his family's ancient seat. And your father always insisted that everyone address me as his countess. He liked nothing better than to snap his fingers in the world's face. *Look at Wrotham*, his cronies would say. *He lives by his own rules.*

"I should have known, I suppose, when he did not give me the bridal bracelet. He said it was lost, and I believed him. And when his friends came to call, and they did not bring their wives or daughters with them, your father had a glib tongue. His friends were of noble birth, he told me. They looked down on me because I was only a tailor's daughter. More than ten years were to pass before I learned the truth."

Marcus looked at Penn. "But surely this wasn't generally known? I never heard anything to suggest—" He broke off.

"Yes," said Penn. "There were rumors, but for the most part, they were discounted. After all, we were living in Wrotham Castle, and you acknowledged us as your family. You can have no idea what a burden that was. I'm glad you know. I wanted to tell you years ago."

"It wouldn't have made the slightest difference," said Marcus emphatically, "not to me. Go on, Helen. How did you learn the truth?"

She shook her head. "Suffice it to say, I discovered the truth by accident. Our marriage was a fraud. When I confronted him with what I knew, he laughed in my face. I wanted to leave him, but where could I go? He refused to let me take my children with me, and even if he'd agreed to let them go, how could I support myself? And so I stayed on."

"I'm sorry," said Marcus. "I'm so bitterly sorry."

She looked down at her hands. "So you see, all this time, David Lytton was your heir. I never saw any reason to enlighten you. I assumed you would marry and have children. Then no one would ever know."

"And if something had happened to me, what then?"

Penn said, "The truth would have come out, of course."

"And everything would go to David," said Marcus.

"Naturally."

"How long have you known this, Penn?"

"Since you went off to war. Mother felt she had to tell me then, in case something happened to you. We decided not to tell Samantha or Tris. It was our secret."

A thought occurred to Marcus, and he smiled.

"What's so amusing?" asked Penn.

Marcus said, "All the time I was a soler, I felt cut off, thinking that my family didn't care what happened to me. But you did care, didn't you?"

Penn grinned. "I think I can assure you that no two people prayed more fervently for your safe return than

Mother and I." He rose. "You need to rest, Marcus. We should leave you now."

He took the cup with the solution of laudanum and offered it to Marcus. Marcus accepted it but did not drink from it yet. He wasn't quite finished.

He looked at his stepmother.

"What is it, Marcus?" she asked.

"I don't want you to worry about this, Helen. Things will go on as before, and there will be no scandal, I promise you. Penn and I have everything under control. Tristram and Samantha won't ever have to know anything."

She seemed dazed, but she nodded.

"Good. Now I need to speak to Penn. Why don't you go on downstairs and wait for him there."

When he and Penn were alone, Marcus came straight to the point. "This is an intolerable situation, Penn, this business about the succession. I could kill my father for what he has done to Helen, what he has done to you all. I meant what I said. You and I are going to take care of everything."

"I don't know what you mean."

"I mean that if anything happens to me, there will be no scandal. Good God! The marriage is recorded in the chapel register. All we need do is forge a marriage certificate. I don't know why you didn't think of it years ago, when I was away at war."

Penn looked dumbfounded, then he began to laugh. "I did think about it. But you're forgetting one thing. Our chaplain wasn't a priest then. How do you propose to get around that?"

"That's a mere detail. Let's add some other divine's name to all the records, someone who is dead and can't be questioned. And it will never come to that, now that you are all established in society. Why do you look like that?"

Penn shook his head. "I thought I knew you, but now I see I was wrong. We have more in common than I thought."

"Fine," said Marcus, and had to clear his throat before continuing. "Let's get onto it first thing tomorrow morning."

"Whatever you say, Marcus," said Penn, and they both smiled.

"Now," said Marcus, "let's get back to what happened tonight. You haven't told me yet how the militia came to be involved."

"Apparently, the militia were on their regular patrol, and *El Grande* passed them on his way to Heath House. When he found a trail of blood leading from a downstairs room on to the terrace, he turned around and called the militia in to help him find you."

"I wonder why he came back?"

"I don't know. But the major said he'll return tomorrow to go over things with you."

"So Carruthers wasn't with the militia when they found us? I didn't think he was, but I was pretty well out of it by that time, and couldn't make out who was there and who wasn't. I remember David smashing my face into the ground, then a terrible silence that was broken by *El Grande*'s unholy yell. I saw *El Grande* with the militia behind him, and that's all I remember."

"No, Carruthers didn't arrive until later after Catherine sent one of the soldiers to fetch him when they were bringing you home. He pretty well took charge of things here. By the way, he wants us only to say that you and David were attacked by highwaymen. That's what I told Samantha and what I shall tell Tris when he gets here."

Marcus nodded. "Obviously, we must keep this whole thing quiet. I don't want anyone asking questions about what David hoped to gain if he killed Catherine and me. Anything more on *El Grande*?"

"Not yet. But he's young and strong, and the major said he's been in worse fixes. Now drink down that laudanum."

"In a minute. If Catherine comes here, I don't care whether it's in the middle of the night, wake me up. Do you understand?"

"Yes, I understand, but you still have a lot of explaining to do, brother dear. However, let's leave that till you're on your feet."

Marcus drank down the laudanum and handed the glass to Penn.

"Now get some sleep," said Penn. He shut the door softly as he exited.

Halfway down the stairs, he stopped and thought about what Marcus had proposed to do about regularizing his mother's marriage. Though he was sure that Marcus and his wife would produce the next heir, still, Marcus's gesture touched him deeply. At the same time, his own behavior made him bitterly ashamed. He was thinking now of the previous night and his own sorry part in it.

If he had not been a drunken sot, he might have prevented what had taken place on Hampstead Heath. It had come to him during dinner that the murderer must be David, but he'd been incapable of acting on it. He'd been the butt of everyone's amusement, and whenever he opened his mouth, they had gone off in peals of laughter. And so, while Marcus and his wife were fighting for their lives, he had been sleeping in his bed in a drunken stupor. His head was still pounding and his throat felt as though he'd swallowed the Sahara Desert. But that was the least of it. Nothing could be worse than this unrelenting sense of guilt.

Never again! Never again!

As he said the words inside his head, he tasted the conviction in them, and he felt a glimmer of hope. One day, he would ask Marcus's forgiveness. There were a lot of people whose forgiveness he should be asking.

He went on down the stairs to look for his mother.

Upstairs, Marcus closed his eyes and willed himself to sleep, but he knew that in spite of the laudanum, sleep would not come easily. His thigh felt as if there were a fishhook embedded inside it. The last time he'd felt like this, Catherine had been there to nurse him.

He could not banish from his mind the picture of *El Grande,* unarmed, riding like a demon to save Catherine's life. He must have known that if he'd waited for the militia to catch up with him, it would have been too late for Catherine. And afterward, Catherine, weeping uncontrollably as she crouched over *El Grande*'s body. Until last night, he had never truly understood the bond that tied these two together. *El Grande* had come back for her. As for Catherine, she'd proved to him that *El Grande* was innocent by putting his own life in danger. She'd never doubted that young man. In all the time he'd known her, her loyalty to *El Grande* had never wavered. It was awesome, and it chilled him to his very soul.

Loyalty. Was that what it was?

He wasn't jealous. What he felt was too deep for jealousy. And he could not hate *El Grande*. His debt to him could never be repaid. But he pitied Catherine and he pitied himself. They were locked in a marriage that they couldn't get out of.

He let out a long sigh. Gritting his teeth, he carefully adjusted his position. The laudanum was beginning to take effect and he was glad. She would be with *El Grande* now. He wondered what her thoughts were. He'd made a botch of everything, even allowing his cousin David to take him by surprise. It was his fault that things had turned into a nightmare, and if it had not been for *El Grande*, he and Catherine would both be dead by now.

He wished he'd never become a soldier, never gone off to war, had never been rescued by *El Grande* and taken to his mountain hideout. And most of all, he wished he'd never fallen into the hands of Catalina.

As he slipped into sleep, another thought occurred to him. If he hadn't done any of those things, David would have succeeded in murdering him a long time ago.

Darkness had fallen, and in an upstairs bedchamber in Heath House, *El Grande* lay white and still in the big tester bed. There was a chair pulled close to the bed, and Amy was sitting in it. She had been there for hours while Catherine caught up on her sleep.

As she gazed upon the face she loved so well, more tears welled up. She'd given up on handkerchiefs and was using a towel to dry her face. She spoke in a soft undertone, addressing him as if he could hear her, pouring out her heart, pleading with him not to leave her. It wasn't working. He was going to die. She knew he was going to die.

On a teary sob, she rose and took a few paces

around the room, then stopped and looked at *El Grande*. "How can you do this to me, Robert?" she pleaded. "I wasn't looking for love. I didn't invite you into my life. You forced your way in. Now you're going to leave me, just like that? Oh, how like a man, and how right I was not to believe you!"

More tears fell. "I've told my sister that we're in love. She doesn't believe me, and now she'll never believe me because you won't be here to tell her."

There was no movement from the bed.

"Oh, I suppose you're happy because you're going to that God of yours. Well, you'll pardon me if I tell you that I don't think much of your God. He's never been a friend to me, and now he's my enemy." She looked up at the ceiling. "Are you listening, God? I'm never going to fall into your clutches, not after what you've done to Robert. Why did you have to let this happen to him? He's good through and through. If you'd wanted a victim, why didn't you take me?" This outburst was followed by a prolonged bout of weeping.

"Look at me!" she said. "I've turned into a watering pot, and it's all your fault, Robert. This is not me. This is not Amy Spencer. Oh, I know what you think." She moved to the end of the bed and gazed down at him. "You think you've reformed me. You're quite happy to go off to your God because you think you've saved my soul. Well, let me tell you, nothing could be further from the truth. If you leave me now, I'm going to go right back to being the old Amy Spencer."

Not a flicker of awareness showed in that pale face.

"I'm going to swear like a trooper. Bloody hell! Damnation! Sod off! What do you think of that? Yes, and I know a lot worse than those."

Silence.

"I'm going to give riotous parties. And I'll go to the theater, and sit in my box, and allow all those horrid, horrid lechers to paw me. Is that what you want?"

Seeing that this was leading nowhere, she knelt by the bed and took his cold hand between her warm ones. "Oh Robert, if only you would come back to me, I'll do whatever you wish. I'll change. I'll be a different woman.

We'll marry, and go off to Spain, and have babies, and I'll never try to hide my heart from you again."

She bowed her head. "I knew there would be no miracles for me. Oh God, just this once, give me a miracle and I swear I'll be the kind of woman you want me to be."

"Amy?" Cat stood in the doorway. "His eyelashes flickered."

Amy looked at *El Grande,* but could see nothing. "Oh God," she whispered. "Oh God. Please?"

El Grande opened his eyes. "Amy?"

She leaned closer to catch his words. "Yes?"

"Don't ever change. I love you just the way you are."

Amy sat back on her heels. "You were listening? All this time, you were listening!"

El Grande managed a weak smile. "God forgive me, but I wouldn't have missed it for the world."

Amy started to curse, thought better of it, and catching Catherine's eyes, began to laugh and cry at the same time.

Chapter 31

Catherine rearranged the decanter of sherry and glasses on the silver tray for the tenth time in as many minutes. Marcus was expected at any moment. Two weeks had passed since she had last seen him, two weeks of wondering and waiting and speculating on all the compelling reasons that had kept him away. She knew he was on the mend. Penn came every other day to keep them informed and to see how they were getting along. If it had not been for Penn, she would never have known how Marcus was.

She glanced up as *El Grande* and Amy entered the room, and her throat tightened. If any two people deserved their happiness it was these two. She couldn't believe now how naïve she'd been, thinking that *El Grande*'s only reason for seeing her sister was to reform her, and she'd thought Amy had been putting the wrong interpretation on his interest when she'd said that he loved her. Then, she'd seen them together and she'd felt as though she'd been struck by a thunderbolt.

They were so right for each other. Life had dealt harshly with them both, and as *El Grande* told it, they'd both been in search of their souls. He'd told her something else. He didn't want to turn the clock back. He loved Amy because she was who she was, and if she'd lived a different kind of life, she wouldn't be the woman he loved.

"We thought," said *El Grande,* "that we'd take a walk to the village."

"You're not going to stay and speak to Marcus?" She felt apprehensive at the thought of seeing Marcus alone for the first time since that night on the heath, and she couldn't help showing it.

El Grande said, "We won't be gone long. Ask him to wait for us. I'm sure you and he have things to say in private."

"Yes, of course," she said, trying not to sound as bleak as she felt.

Two weeks were a long time to wait for a sign from Marcus that he'd softened toward her. A word from him would have brought her running to his side, but that word never came. Instead, Penn had told her that Marcus wished her to remain at Heath House until things were settled between them. He would come to her when he was ready. She'd known a week ago that he was back on his feet. Then why had he waited so long to come and see her? She knew why, and she tried to brace herself for what was coming.

Amy kissed her on the cheek. "Just remember, my love, don't hide your heart, and I think Marcus may surprise you."

They went off arm in arm, and Catherine watched them from the parlor window till they were out of sight. *El Grande* walked with a cane and leaned on Amy's arm for support. Not Amy Spencer, but Amy who looked like a young girl and whose eyes glowed with the bloom of love. The odd things was, no one seemed to recognize her as London's foremost courtesan. That lady was known to be spending the winter months in Italy, and when Amy encountered people around the village, they saw what Catherine had told them to see, a friend who had brought her betrothed into the country to recuperate from a carriage accident. Even Emily, who had noticed the resemblance of Catherine's friend to Amy Spencer, accepted her story. It might have been different in London where Amy was well-known, but in this quiet backwater, where Catherine was well-known, her story was accepted without question.

Shaking her head, trying not to feel dispirited because Amy and *El Grande* would be leaving for Spain at the end of the week, she returned to her study. A few minutes later, the door opened and Mrs. McNally ushered in Marcus. He wasn't alone. Major Carruthers was with him, but Catherine had eyes only for Marcus.

He looked pale and thinner, with dark circles under his eyes. She wanted to fling herself into his arms, but sensed a reserve that made her polite rather than warm.

After the amenities were dealt with, and they were all sitting sipping sherry, they talked for some time about the night David tried to murder them. Of the three, Major Carruthers was the most animated and took up much of the slack in the conversation. He was elated that his theories had been so close to the mark. His error was in not realizing that everything tied together. When he saw that his companions weren't really interested in his theories, he, too, fell silent.

It was then that Marcus felt in his coat pocket and produced a packet of papers that were yellowing with age. "I came by these yesterday morning," he said. "After David's funeral, his solicitor approached me and gave me a key to a box that was held for David by Ransom's Bank in Pall Mall. Inside the box I found these, letters from my father to David's father that prove that David was my heir."

Penn had already told her his mother's story, but she was surprised that Marcus would say so much in front of Major Carruthers.

Noting the look she darted at Carruthers, Marcus said, "Major Carruthers is in my confidence."

Carruthers said dryly, "Only because he needs me to smooth things over at the War office. The official position is, David Lytton was murdered by highwaymen. As for the English soldiers at *El Grande*'s base, we are accepting that their deaths were accidental. The only thing that the Minister has been told, and the only thing he has an interest in, is that Lytton murdered Freddie Barnes in a lovers' tiff, and the Minister certainly doesn't want that to be made public. Barnes was his cousin, you see."

Catherine was smoothing out the letters Marcus had given her, but she wasn't really reading them. "What do you mean, 'they had a lovers' tiff'?"

Marcus gave her a level stare. "David and Freddie were lovers," he said.

"Lovers! But David seemed so . . . well, I never would have guessed."

"David made sure none of us guessed what he was really like."

"But how do you know all this?"

"In David's trunk, there were letters from Freddie also. Poor Freddie! He never knew that David was my cousin. He thought he was a deserter, and that's why he didn't want anyone to know he'd been at *El Grande*'s base. Freddie thought he was protecting him. I don't know why David didn't kill Freddie at once."

"For the money," Carruthers said. "David was in debt up to his ears. He had expensive tastes, and Freddie gave him whatever he asked. But when David decided to be himself in order to get closer to you, Marcus, it was time to do away with Freddie Barnes. At least, that's what I deduce."

"We found this in the box also," said Marcus.

Catherine held out her hand and he slipped a bracelet into her palm.

"The Wrotham bridal bracelet," said Marcus.

It was an exquisite piece, five cameos set in filigreed gold overlaid with vines and roses. One of those cameos was of Marcus's mother. Catherine found which one by looking at the inscription on the back.

"My father asked his brother to hold it for him," said Marcus. "I won't tell you what was in that letter, but nothing that is to my father's credit."

She returned the bracelet to Marcus. The thought crossed her mind that Marcus had not mentioned adding her likeness to the bracelet, and although she didn't much care for this particular tradition, she felt disappointed.

They talked at some length, clearing up various points. Finally, Major Carruthers rose to his feet.

"I came here to talk to Robert," he said. "Where may I find him?"

Catherine told him that *El Grande* and Amy had decided to walk to the village and she expected them back at any moment.

"Ah," said the major, looking from Catherine to

Marcus. "If you don't mind, I'll go after them. I could use the exercise."

There was a long silence after he left. Marcus looked at Catherine, looked away, and said in a curiously distant tone, "I've been to see my solicitors, Cat."

"Yes?" she said cautiously.

He looked up at her. "Actually, I saw them some time ago. I should have said something sooner, I suppose, but I got caught up in setting a trap for David. I've pursued every avenue open to us for a divorce and there isn't one. We have to live with this marriage, Cat."

He was very grave, and though her heart had given a leap at his words, it gradually returned to normal. "What did your solicitors say?"

He told her in as few words as possible, and at the end of it, a silence fell, not an empty silence, but a charged silence that eddied with strong undercurrents.

She understood at once where his difficulty lay. It was more than a question of their own personal wishes. If Marcus did not have an heir of his own body, Helen and her children would forever go in fear of discovery. Penn could not inherit, and neither could Tristram, or their children. If the truth ever came out, the scandal would crush Helen. She could not, would not allow that to happen. She, Catherine, had to give Marcus a son.

She said, "In that case, I suggest we make the best of it."

He said, "I promise I won't make undue demands on you. There might be long periods when we would choose to be apart. There is no shortage of Wrotham properties and houses. Perhaps you could choose one of them and make it your principal residence."

Every word he uttered seemed to hammer home a lance that was embedded in her heart. She didn't know why she was so surprised. He had never told her that he loved her, and even if he had, she supposed she had forfeited that love by what must seem to him one betrayal after another.

Rising slowly, she walked to the window. "I would never do anything to hurt your family," she said. When she was sure she had command of herself, she turned to face him. "What have you told them about me?"

"The truth, or as close to it as I thought advisable." He was watching her closely. "I told them that I fell in love with you in Spain and that we married. They know you were an English girl who was with British Intelligence. They believe that when you returned to England you kept your identity a secret because you were still working for British Intelligence."

"And when I became Catalina again? How did you explain that?"

"I told them that we were setting a trap for someone from those days whom we believed wished to kill us both."

"The Spanish vendetta?"

"I made use of it, yes. Only Penn and Helen know the truth about David. I've also told them that we now know the rumor about the Spanish vendetta was false, and that's why you can go back to being yourself."

"And what are we going to tell the world?"

"Exactly what I've told my family. Yes, I know it's going to cause a sensation, but there's no way around it. It will be a nine-day wonder, then something else will come along for people to talk about. In fact, I've taken the bull by the horns and talked to Melrose Gunn about publishing our story in *The Journal* once we leave London."

The thought of becoming an object of raging gossip should have made her writhe, but she couldn't seem to care one way or another. She felt numb, as though she had ingested a powerful narcotic that was slowly paralyzing all her faculties.

"I can't do anything for the moment," she said. "There's too much to do here." She knew that she was very close to tears, and she waited, for a moment, before continuing. "*El Grande* wants to see you before you go. Did you know he is going home to Spain to take up his life there?"

He had risen to his feet and his face, which was pale before, was now starkly white. "No, I didn't know," he said softly. "But I think it's for the best."

"Of course it's for the best! I'm happy for him, very happy for him." She pressed her fingers to her brow. "He should be back shortly. Would you excuse me? I have so much to do. Please," she looked around distractedly, "help yourself to the sherry while you wait."

"No need," he said, and started for the door. "I'll find my own way out," and he left her staring at a closed door.

His teeth were clenched so tightly together that his jaw ached. He wasn't aware that he was taking great strides until he felt a searing pain in his thigh and he began to limp. As he passed his carriage he saw a knot of people walking toward him. *El Grande* was out in front and he was walking with the aid of a cane. Marcus reminded himself that *El Grande* was using that cane because he had saved Catherine's life. He was also a man of God. He'd spent the last three years with the monks at Marston. In fact, *El Grande* hadn't done a single thing to deserve the hatred that burned in Marcus's breast, except force him into a marriage with a woman whose heart could never be his.

When the two men came abreast, *El Grande* was smiling. Marcus tried to do the same. Carruthers and Amy stopped a few feet away and tactfully admired a robin that was perched on the branch of a rowan tree.

Marcus said, "I never did have the chance to thank you for saving our lives." He came under a scrutiny that made him suddenly ashamed, and he went on in a more conciliatory tone, "I don't know what brought you back to Heath House that night, but whatever it was, I will always be grateful."

"What brought me back," said *El Grande,* "was that while I was waiting it occurred to me that you might have formed the wrong idea about Catherine and me. There was something in your face that night that troubled me. That's what brought me back. Or"—he paused—"you might say it was destiny."

Marcus reminded himself that he'd done his duty. He should shake the man's hand and go. "The wrong idea?" he said, baring his teeth. "Oh, there's nothing wrong with my ideas. I don't think I shall ever forget the sight of you, unarmed, riding hell-bent to Catherine's rescue."

El Grande cocked his head. Carruthers and Amy were forgetting to be tactful and had edged closer to eavesdrop on the conversation.

El Grande said, "And I shall never forget the sight of Catherine shielding you with her body while that murderous swine leveled his pistol at her heart."

"She shielded me with her body? That was a damn fool thing to do!"

"Wouldn't you have done the same in her position?"

"That's different."

"Why is it?"

Because he loved her.

Amy came up to them at that moment. "What are you saying to Robert?" she asked none too civilly.

El Grande put an arm around her shoulders and smiled down at her. "Lord Wrotham is thanking me for saving Catherine's life," he said.

The hostility in her eyes faded a little. "Well, I hope he thanked Catherine for all she did too. When I think of her out on that heath, with a murderer pursuing her—and Marcus no help to her—I could just die."

"Amy," chided *El Grande*.

Marcus was looking at them both as though they were invisible. Things that had hovered at the back of his mind were coming back to him. He remembered that chase on the heath and telling Catherine many times to leave him, but she refused. And in those last few moments when he'd been trying to hang on to consciousness, there was something else. He'd heard David's voice, and Catherine saying something in reply, but what had really registered was the bloodcurdling yell from *El Grande* as he'd ridden to their rescue.

What had David said, and what had Cat said in reply?

You first?

Better me than Marcus.

Carruthers clapped him on the shoulder, startling him back to the present. "Wrotham, where are your manners?" he said. "Aren't you going to wish the lucky couple long life and happiness? They're to be married in Spain."

The lucky couple? Amy and *El Grande*? He must have misunderstood. Then he saw the love shining in their eyes and, as with Catherine, the truth struck him like a thunderbolt.

"Oh, my God!" he said. "What have I done?"

He did an about-face and made for Heath House, uncaring of the pain in his thigh or the astonished questions that followed him. He burst into the house calling her name. In the study, he found the French doors ajar and he pushed through them and took the path to the heath.

He found her sitting on a bench that overlooked the pond near where that last scene with David had played itself out. Beyond calling her name, he didn't say anything, couldn't say anything. The swift walk back to her had taken its toll and he felt as weak as a kitten. As he came up to the bench and waited for his breathing to even, she stood up.

A glance told him that this was not the iceberg he'd left only a few minutes ago. Her cheeks were flushed and her eyes were vividly blue.

She said, "Do you know what my sister said to me just before you arrived?"

He shook his head.

"She told me not to hide my heart from you."

"Please don't," he wheezed. "That is, please don't hide your heart from me."

"Fine. Don't say you didn't ask for it."

It happened so quickly, he didn't see it coming. She gave him an almighty shove and, as he staggered back, he reached for her to steady himself, and they both went toppling into the pond.

He came up spitting.

She came up spitting fire. "You are the most uncouth, ungrateful, ungracious man I know," she yelled. "I was worried sick about you, and you waited two weeks before you came to call."

"That was because I thought you didn't want to see me. Why didn't you come to me?"

She ignored this moot question. "And another thing, I'm not ashamed of what I did. I was an agent. I was sworn to secrecy. I was good at my job until you came along. What did you think—that I would take one look at you and forget my duty to my friends and country?"

"You're right, that's exactly what I thought," he said.

There was only two feet of water in the pond and they'd done no more than come up on their knees. They were so intent on each other that they hardly knew where they were or that the temperature of the water was arctic. Marcus didn't even feel the habitual throb in his thigh.

She pounded him on his chest with her index finger. "Well, you were wrong. I take back every apology I ever made you. I never betrayed you. If I betrayed anyone, it was myself and my own principles."

"Did you apologize?" He put his hands on her shoulders. "I don't remember. None of that matters now."

"Oh no!" she said scathingly. "All that matters to you is the succession. All you care about is producing an heir to protect your family."

"The succession?" He looked at her blankly. "I don't give a damn about the succession! Besides, I've taken care of all that. I've made things right for Helen and Penn. The succession is quite secure."

"Really?"

"Really!"

She couldn't keep her temper at boiling point when he was so reasonable. He was more than reasonable. He was looking at her with an odd light in his eyes.

She sniffed. "The only thing I truly regret is that I forced you to marry me. Marcus, I'm sorry. I wish I could undo the wrong I did to you. To my dying day, I shall always regret it."

The hands on her shoulders tightened, and the look in his eyes had turned fierce. He gave her a shake. "Sorry? Sorry?" he roared. "Good God, woman, if you had not forced me to marry you, how would I have found you again? I'm not sorry. I would have searched the world for Catalina and would never have found my Cat of the glorious flame hair."

"Marcus." She gulped. "What are you saying?"

"I love you, you idiot. I've loved you from the moment I opened my eyes in that small priest's cell and saw your face hovering above me. I loved you when you were Catalina. I loved you when you were Catherine, and I loved you when I thought you were plotting against me. Now, do you think I might have the words from you?"

"Oh, Marcus," she said, leaning into him. "I don't know why I love you. You're utterly impossible."

"Call it destiny," he said. "From the very beginning I was your destiny and you were mine."

Tears welled in her eyes.

"What is it?"

"I was thinking of our very first kiss and how I went and spoiled it. Don't you remember? I bit your lip and pretended that you had tried to ravish me."

"Then let's do that kiss over," he said.

Their lips met gently, sweetly, then in the space of a single heartbeat, they clung together so that not even a shadow could separate them.

ABOUT THE AUTHOR

ELIZABETH THORNTON holds a diploma in education and a degree in Classics. Before writing women's fiction she was a school teacher and a lay minister in the Presbyterian Church. *Dangerous to Hold* is her eighth historical novel. Ms. Thornton has been nominated for and received numerous awards, among them the Romantic Times Trophy Award for Best New Historical Regency Author, and Best Historical Regency. She has been a finalist in the Romance Writers of America Rita Contest for Best Historical Romance of the year. Though she was born and educated in Scotland, she now lives in Canada with her husband. They have three sons and two granddaughters.

Ms. Thornton enjoys hearing from her readers. Her e-mail address is <thornton@pangea.ca> or visit her at her home page:

http://pangea.ca/ ˜ thornton

Don't miss the next breathtaking romantic tale
of thrilling adventure and fiery passion
from the bestselling, award-winning "genre
superstar"*

Elizabeth Thornton

Available Spring 1997 from Bantam Books

*Tessa Lorimer thinks she is the luckiest girl in
the world. After a bitter, harrowing childhood,
she had escaped her guardian's clutches and
fled to her wealthy, doting grandfather. For the
first time in her life, Tessa is spoiled—yet one
thing blights her happiness. Her grandfather's
new secretary, the mysterious and magnetic
Ross Trevenan, has too much influence with
the aging financier. And in Trevenan's eyes,
Tessa can do nothing right. But she suspects
there is more to the cool, gray-eyed American's
plans than replacing her in an old man's
affections. And when a tragedy from the past
returns to stalk the present, Tessa's time may
have run out. . . .*

---

* *Romantic Times*

After Marcel and another footman had carried Beaupré upstairs, Ross lit a cheroot from one of the candles and wandered out to the terrace. There were still plenty of servants about tidying up after the ball, but Ross hardly noticed them. Deep in thought, he stood at the balustrade, smoking his cheroot.

He hoped to God he knew what he was doing. He hoped to God that Alexandre's trust in him was not misplaced. He couldn't help admiring the old man's acuity. Alexandre had known his conscience was bothering him. Now that they'd become friends, it seemed wrong to hope that Tessa Lorimer was the target of a murderer. But he couldn't change what he was feeling. Without Tessa, he hadn't a hope of catching his man. And because he felt guilty, he was inflexible in his resolve to fulfill all his promises to Alexandre respecting the girl.

At the end of the terrace there was a flight of white marble steps descending to the gardens. Ross idled his way down the steps and stood at the entrance to a stone gazebo that had a view of the Seine. The lights of a few boats winked at him from the river, but there was little else to see at that time of night. He drew on his cheroot and let the smoke out slowly, his thoughts still engrossed on the interview just past.

Since he'd arrived in Paris three months before, when he'd approached Alexandre with what he knew, there had been a marked deterioration in his friend's health—and that's how he thought of Alexandre Beaupré, as a friend. From the very first, they'd measured each other and decided they liked what they saw. Now it was obvious Alexandre's time had run out. They had to act quickly. The old man was right. His choices were appalling. He, Ross, was his best bet. That's why he'd turned the responsibility for Tessa's welfare over to him.

Responsibility wasn't the word for it. Chore, task, labor, problem—those were the words that came to his mind when he thought of what was in store for him. Tessa Lorimer was a law unto herself. Alexandre did not know his granddaughter half as well as he thought he did, and Ross had not wanted to disillusion him, not when there was so little time left to his friend. But *he* knew, because he'd made it his business to find out.

Without his volition, a picture formed in his mind. Tessa as he'd seen her on the dance floor, floating down the set with her partner. There was a sparkle in her eyes, and a soft, inviting smile on her lips. He'd thought that she wasn't merely beautiful, she was breathtaking, all the more so because her beauty seemed to come from some inner light. Before he could prevent it, the thought had flashed into his mind that Tessa's beauty was far more interesting than Cassie's had been because there was fire beneath it, and he'd felt, in the next instant, as though he'd betrayed his wife's memory, and he'd been furious with himself.

Tessa's beauty might well be impossible to eclipse, but in other respects, she was dismally lacking. The aunt and uncle in England who'd had the raising of her had described a girl who bore little resemblance to the charmer who had, in so short a time, wrapped Alexandre Beaupré around her little finger. She'd attended a number of schools, first-class establishments, every one of them, but she'd soon overstayed her welcome. All the people he'd interviewed who'd ever had charge of her told the same story—Tessa Lorimer was rebellious, defiant, incorrigible, and they'd all heaved a great sigh of relief when they'd finally seen the back of her.

It was her last escapade that had made the uncle and aunt wash their hands of her, not that they'd confided in him. They were too ashamed. He'd had it from one of the servants that Miss Tessa had run off with a handsome young footman, and after that Mr. and Mrs. Beasley never wanted to see her again, which surprised no one since they had two innocent young daughters of their own whom they did not wish contaminated by Tessa's influence.

No one knew what had happened to the footman. What was certain was that, shortly after eloping, Tessa had arrived on her grandfather's doorstep and had lived like a veritable princess ever since. She'd been indulged, petted, and pampered until there was no restraining her.

She'd had the good sense not to say too much about her early years, and not one word about her handsome young footman. The story she had concocted was that the Beasleys were insisting she marry some odious cousin, and she'd fled to France to throw herself on her grandfather's mercy.

Alexandre had told him the rest of the story with unmitigated pride. Therese, he said, had disguised herself as a boy and had bribed a band of English smugglers to smuggle her into France. One part of Ross's mind applauded her audacity. Another part of his mind was appalled. At the time, England and France were at war. Anything could have happened to her. A French warship could have blown her smugglers, and her with them, to smithereens. If she'd been caught, she could have been strung up as an English spy. And if her smugglers had discovered that she was a female, it was highly unlikely that they would have spared her innocence.

If she was an innocent.

He thought of her handsome young footman and a wave of anger surged through him. How dared he leave a young girl to fend for herself? If he could have laid his hands on him, he would have torn him limb from limb. The thought startled him and he drew on his cheroot, then exhaled a stream of smoke as he inwardly debated why he was so angry.

A movement on the terrace alerted him to the presence of someone else. When he saw a shadow move, he took a cautious step back into the gazebo, then another.

"Paul?"

Tessa's voice. There was a rustle of skirts as she descended the steps. Ross threw his cheroot on the ground and crushed it under his heel.

"Paul?" Her voice was breathless, uncertain. "I saw you from my window. I wasn't sure it was you until I saw our signal." Her voice took on a teasing note. "Or perhaps I was mistaken. Perhaps you weren't signaling me but had simply slipped into the gazebo for a quiet smoke."

Ross said nothing, but he'd already calculated that he'd stumbled upon the trysting place of Tessa and her French lover and had inadvertently given their signal merely by smoking a cheroot.

Tessa entered the gazebo and halted, waiting for her eyes to become accustomed to the gloom. "I wanted to thank you for the spray of violets. They really are lovely. But I had to burn your note." She laughed. "You mustn't write such things to me, Paul. My cheeks burned so hot, my maid feared I was coming down with a fever." She paused, and her voice turned husky. "Paul, stop playing games with me. You know you want to kiss me."

It never crossed Ross's mind to enlighten her about his identity. He was too curious to see how far the brazen hussy would go. She had, quite literally, backed him into the darkest corner of the gazebo.

Her hands found his shoulders and curled around them. "Paul," she whispered, and she lifted her head for his kiss.

Tessa was no stranger to a man's kisses. In France, she had discovered, young gentlemen were not so circumspect as their English counterparts, nor were French girls the least bit prudish. Her female friends weren't wicked, far from it; but they saw nothing wrong with indulging in a little kissing. They reasoned, and Tessa agreed with them, that it was the stupidest kind of folly for a girl to keep herself in total ignorance of what awaited her in marriage. Now, after two years in France, Tessa considered herself quite knowledgeable about men and their passions.

She also knew that by trysting with Paul in the gazebo, she was overstepping the boundaries of what a French girl would allow. But Paul was different. He was courting her. Perhaps tonight he would ask her to marry him. Then their kisses would be sanctioned by his ring on her finger. And if that was not enough to tempt her, there were Paul's breathtaking kisses. When he molded those experienced lips to hers, something peculiar happened to her insides, and that had never happened to her with any other boy. He made her feel quite giddy.

It was exactly as she had anticipated. His mouth was firm and hot, and those pleasant sensations began to warm her blood. When he wrapped his arms around her and jerked her hard against his full length, she gave a little start of surprise, but that warm, mobile mouth on hers insisted she yield to him. She laughed softly when he kissed her throat, then she stopped breathing altogether when he bent her back and kissed her breasts, just above the lace on her bodice. He'd never gone that far before.

She should stop him, she knew she should stop him, but she felt as weak as a kitten. She said something—a protest? a plea?—and his mouth was on hers again, and everything Tessa knew about men and their passions was reduced to ashes in the scorching heat of that embrace. Her limbs were shaking, wild tremors shook her body, her blood seemed to ignite. She was clinging to him for support, kissing him back, allowing those bold hands of his to wander at will from her breast to her thigh, taking liberties she knew no decent girl should permit, not even a French girl.

When he left her mouth to kiss her ears, her eyebrows, her cheeks, she said in a shaken whisper, "I never knew it could be like this. You make me feel things I never knew existed, sensations I've never experienced before. You seem so different tonight."

And he did. His body was harder, his shoulders seemed broader, and she hadn't known he was so tall. As for his fragrance—

Then she knew, she *knew,* and she opened her eyes wide, trying to see his face. It was too dark, but she didn't need a light to know whose arms she was in. He didn't wear cologne, as Paul did. He smelled of fresh air and soap and freshly starched linen. Outrage rooted her to the spot, but only for a moment longer. Those clever hands of his had slipped and were beginning to massage her bottom.

"Trevenan!" she gasped, and fairly leapt out of his arms.

He made no move to stop her but said in a laconic tone that grated on her ears, "What a pity. And just when things were beginning to turn interesting."

She was so overcome with rage, she could hardly find her voice, and when she did find it, it was high-pitched and unnatural. "*Interesting?* What you did to me was not interesting. It was *depraved.*"

As he advanced, she retreated. Though she felt a leap of alarm, she was too proud to run away. When he halted beside the stone steps, so did she, but she was careful to preserve some space between them. The lights on the terrace had yet to be extinguished, and she had a clear view of his expression. He could hardly keep a straight face.

"Depraved?" he said. "That's not the impression you gave me. I could have sworn you were enjoying yourself. 'I never knew it could be like this,'" he mimicked. "'You make me feel things I never knew existed.'" He began to laugh.

"I thought you were Paul," she shouted. "How dared you impose yourself on me in that hateful way!"

He arched one brow. "My dear Miss Lorimer, as I recall, you were the one who imposed yourself on me. I was merely enjoying a quiet smoke when you barged into the gazebo and cornered me. I didn't kiss you. You kissed me." His white teeth gleamed. "Might I give you a word of advice? You're too bold by half. A man likes to be the hunter. Try, if you can, to give the impression that *he* has cornered *you*."

The thought that this depraved rake—and he had to be a rake if his kisses were anything to go by—had the gall to give her advice made her temper burn even hotter. She had to unclench her teeth to get the words out. "There is no excuse for your conduct. You knew I thought you were Paul."

"Come now, Miss Lorimer. That trick is as old as Eve."

Anger made her forget her fear, and she took a quick step toward him. "Do you think I'd want your kisses? You're nothing but my grandfather's lackey. You're a secretary, an employee. If I were to tell him what happened here tonight," she pointed to the gazebo, "he would dismiss you."

"Tell him, by all means. He won't think less of me for acting like any red-blooded male. It's your conduct that will be a disappointment to him." His voice took on a hard edge. "By God, if I had the schooling of you, I'd soon make you learn to obey me."

"Thank God," she cried out, "that will never come to pass!"

He laughed. "Stranger things have happened."

He had argued her to a standstill. The thing to do now was to leave him with as much dignity as was left to her. She wasn't going to leave him with the impression that she had followed him into the gazebo knowing who he was.

She breathed deeply, trying to find her calm. "If I'd known you were in the gazebo, I would never have entered it." His skeptical look revived her anger, and she raged, "I tell you, I thought you were Paul Marmont."

He shrugged. "In that case, all I can say is that little girls who play with fire deserve to get burned."

She said furiously, "You were teaching me a lesson?"

"In a word, yes."

Her head flung back and she regarded him with smoldering dislike. "And just how far were you prepared to go in this lesson of yours, Mr. Trevenan? Mmm?"

He extended a hand to her and without a trace of mockery or levity answered, "Come back to the gazebo with me and I'll show you."

He was serious, and the knowledge was like a slap in the face. This was the man who never tried to conceal his contempt from her, who never so much as asked her for a dance at her own ball. He disliked her intensely, but that wouldn't stop him from taking her like a common trollop in the gazebo. Then he would discard her. She'd never been so humiliated in her life. With an exclamation of hurt pride, she wheeled away from him and went racing up the stairs to the house.

Ross gave her a few minutes before he followed her in. He'd taught her a lesson he hoped she'd not soon forget. Her reckless disregard for the rules that were laid down for her own protection could lead her into danger. He didn't regret teaching her that lesson, for he'd learned something about Tessa Lorimer that pleased him enormously.

She was still an innocent.

His lips quirked when he remembered her words. *I never knew it could be like this. You make me feel things I never knew existed, sensations I've never experienced before.* So much for Paul Marmont and her handsome young footman, he thought, and snapped his fingers.

He'd learned something else, something about himself that did not please him half as well. If she had not put a stop to it, he did not know where it would have ended.

Scowling, he felt in his coat pocket and withdrew his watch. It wasn't too late to visit Solange. A few minutes later, he was in a cab and on his way to the Palais Royal.

DON'T MISS THESE FABULOUS
BANTAM WOMEN'S FICTION TITLES

On Sale in April

THE UGLY DUCKLING

by New York Times *bestselling author Iris Johansen*

A thrilling tale of romantic suspense in a spectacular hardcover debut.
"Crackling suspense and triumphant romance with a brilliant roller coaster of a plot." —Julie Garwood   ___09714-8 $19.95/$24.95 in Canada

Experience the enchanting wit of New York Times
bestselling author Betina Krahn in a delicious new love story

THE UNLIKELY ANGEL

From the author of *The Perfect Mistress*, a tale of romantic entanglement between a cynical rake and a selfless beauty whose good deeds lead to scandal, intrigue and passion.   ___56524-9 $5.99/$7.99

DANGEROUS TO HOLD

by nationally bestselling author Elizabeth Thornton

"A major, major talent . . . a genre superstar." —Rave Reviews

The passionate story of an unscrupulous man suffering from the wounds of betrayal, a beautiful imposter with secrets of her own, and a desperate plan that could spell disaster for them both.   ___57479-5 $5.50/$7.50

From the exciting new voice of Karyn Monk

THE REBEL AND THE REDCOAT

When a handsome stranger risked his life to save beautiful, patriotic Josephine Armstrong, he didn't know that they were on opposite sides of the war . . . or that one day she would be forced to betray him, leaving him to gamble everything on the chance that he can make her surrender—if only in his arms.   ___57421-3 $5.99/$7.99

"This is a new author to watch." —Romantic Times